The Silicon Lathe
A Novel

Steve Jackowski

ISBN: 978-0-9899729-1-8

DEDICATION

To Karen Noël

ACKNOWLEDGMENTS

I've dedicated this, my first novel, to Karen Noël, the love of my life, whose constant support helped me achieve success in the Silicon Valley. I'd like to thank Jo Minola who read the manuscript and convinced me it was important to publish. Finally, I can't say enough about Jill Warwick whose careful reading and insightful comments made this the book that it is today.

Steve Jackowski

PREFACE

Carson Ingles the third smiled as Jack walked out of the Catalyst. He owed so much to Jack.

Once one of Silicon Valley's early moguls, Carson had fallen prey to his own desire to be better than he was. Cocaine, which initially made him even more brilliant, had been his downfall. He'd lost the love of his life, his fortune, and so many brain cells that he now had only a fraction of his former mental capabilities. Still, with Jack's help, he was no longer a homeless junky. The pending ten million dollar settlement would reestablish his strategic consulting business and put him back among Silicon Valley's elite. He'd been clean for nearly two years and he knew that finally, he could stay that way. The money wouldn't be his ticket back to the street this time.

Carson reached into his pocket and pulled out a cylindrical metal container. He really didn't know how he'd managed to keep it through the years in the gutter. He'd sold, pawned or traded his homes, his cars, his artwork, and all of his high tech toys for coke. But somehow, he'd managed to hold onto the last of the box of Cuban cigars presented to him by the president of Sony in celebration of successful completion of a high tech consulting project. Funny, it was the shortest report he'd ever written. True, it had taken months of research and countless hours of competitive product evaluations and late nights working with the Sony engineers to solidify the gadget's reliability, but he had delivered his three-word recommendation: Go for it. They happily paid his two hundred thousand dollar fee.

Sony took the restructured product to market and within a year, sales climbed to over one hundred million dollars. Carson smiled at the memory of just one of his contributions to the high tech world. He took a sip of his brandy and removed the cigar from the tube. The aroma assaulted him and brought back memories of evenings with Nancy in front of the fire, sipping brandy and sharing a cigar, both in silk pajamas like a couple out of a thirties film.

Lost in reverie, Carson took out his lighter. He was brought back to reality by a gentle touch on his arm. The bartender nodded at the no smoking sign behind the bar, and then wordlessly lifted his chin, indicating the back door. Carson had forgotten about California's new no smoking policy in public places, which even included bars and restaurants.

He got to his feet a little unsteadily. The two scotches while talking to Jack and the subsequent brandy and a half cast a warm glow over the bar. They also seemed to be pressing on his bladder.

Carson put the cigar back into his pocket and made his way to the men's room with the gait of someone who's had a bit too much to drink, but isn't quite drunk. He stepped up to the urinal, set his brandy on the top, and felt the overwhelming satisfaction of release. It had been a good day.

His moment of solitary serenity was interrupted by a tall thin man in a leather jacket with slicked hair who stepped up to the adjoining urinal. He certainly wasn't a Santa Cruz local and didn't look like a tourist. He nodded at Carson, but Carson ignored him. They washed their hands and left the men's room. Carson turned left and opened the door marked exit with his shoulder. He reached into his pocket and pulled out his cigar. It was a crisp clear night, but a sudden gust of wind brought the stench of stale urine and rotting food from the dumpster from across the alley. Carson knew this wouldn't do. This was supposed to be a celebration and he wasn't about to light up in a dirty alley. Unfortunately, he couldn't think of anyone who would share this moment with him, but that time would come soon. Maybe he could even look up Nancy.

Carson turned to reenter the Catalyst. Suddenly he was slammed from the side and knocked to the ground. The brandy glass and cigar fell from his hand and Carson watched stunned as the glass shattered and its contents mixed with the oily water and disintegrating cigarette butts. He started to turn to look up but his head was seized in two vise-like hands and was slammed against the curb. Carson's last image was the delicate wrapped leaves of the Cuban cigar soaking up the filth of the alley.

CHAPTER 1

"What's behind you doesn't matter."
- Jean-Paul Belmondo, after throwing the rearview mirror out
the window of his stolen car in "Breathless".

1

The headstone was in place. The coffin had been lowered into the grave. Ignoring the shovel, I picked up a handful of dirt, dirt that would later cover the last remains of Carson Ingles. I looked around and was disappointed that I was the sole witness to Carson's interment. I'd hoped that at least a few of his coworkers would attend the meager funeral service. Carson had no immediate family and all the friends and colleagues Carson had known, all the people who owed their careers and success to Carson, and all those who once loved him had written Carson off as a drug addict and failure.

Once at the top of his field and world-renown, Carson certainly took a plunge. Yes, he had a fatal flaw that derailed his success, but he was back on track. He was under control and on the road to making a real difference. He would have been great again.

Carson deserved better than a violent death in a stinking damp alley among cigarette butts and discarded crushed bottle caps, his clothes soaking up the stale urine and vomit left behind by drunks and drug addicts.

Carson's rise, fall, rebirth and premature end touched the lives of so many people I've worked with in the Silicon Valley over the last fifteen years. Some of us made it, some didn't. Many worked hard; a few worked smart; some just stole what they wanted, slithering their way into the graces of those with vision and finding surreptitious means to skim monies or recognition from the truly deserving. And then there were those single-minded few, so convinced of their righteous missions that they would do whatever they had to, no matter how unethical, to succeed, to become legends in the Silicon Valley much like the Captains of Industry of the nineteenth century.

But Carson was different. Success came easily to him because people were drawn to his extraordinary intelligence and simple integrity. His soothing baritone voice and avuncular manner charmed even the most hardened executives while he pried open their minds to enable them to recognize their errors or to visualize new concepts. He had a gift for seeing simple solutions to complex problems and for being able to communicate those solutions with non-threatening credibility. The reputation of his honesty soon preceded him and he became one of the most famous and recognized technologists in the country.

Of course temptation can lead us all astray. What tempts you may mean nothing to me, but there's something out there that can seduce us all – money, power, success, notoriety, lust, love, even honesty and ethics. Too much of anything can become a trap from which you never escape.

After achieving so much from a life filled with early tragedies, who could have foreseen that Carson would fall victim to his own desire to prove himself worthy?

The police say Carson's death was an accidental homicide as the result of a mugging. I think I know better. No one is willing to pursue my theory that a major recognizable figure in our industry could have been behind the death of a simple computer consultant. It would be like saying Bill Gates did it.

I never imagined Carson's life would turn out this way. Of course, I never imagined my life would turn out this way either.

Like so many young people starting out in the Silicon Valley, I was confident. I knew I was smart, probably smarter than most, and I believed that I could not only achieve financial success, but that I could make a major contribution to improving the world around us by creating technology to make us more productive and to give everyone more flexibility and free time. I certainly relished my free time. I really thought I could have it all, working hard and playing even harder. Meeting Carson, I knew it was possible. I emulated him as best I could, but my own arrogance and blindness to the motivations of others less naïve than I certainly set me up for disappointments. I had a plan. It included success, reputation, and family. But ultimately, life got in the way.

I tossed the handful of dirt onto Carson's coffin. As I turned to leave the deserted cemetery, the impact of Carson's death sent me back. I couldn't help trying to understand the events that led me to Carson and both Carson and me to where we ended up.

2

It all started over thirty years ago. I was several years into my career and didn't know the meaning of failure. The future was a straight line to my success. Somehow, even when it started to change, I didn't recognize the signs.

"Got a minute?"

I looked up from the design document I was reviewing to see Ronn Regen standing at the door to my office.

Ronn's shaggy dark hair and overgrown mustache couldn't conceal a line of new stitches along his right cheekbone.

"What happened to you?" I asked, "Or can I guess?"

"I got tagged by a mallet. I was breaking in my new pony in a scrimmage with the team and she turned short as Bob and I were both going for the ball."

Ronn was the most unlikely-looking polo player I'd ever seen. He looked and dressed as if he had just come off a cattle drive: scuffed western boots, jeans, long sleeved shirts, hands like shoe leather, and a permanent 3-day beard – before it was fashionable.

It was hard to believe he was one of Silicon Valley's top independent software developers. He lived on Garnet Ranch in the hills overlooking Saratoga and Cupertino in one of the ranch hand's shacks. In fact, he was a ranch hand, working Garnet after hours and on weekends.

His polo team was equally unlikely. They were all ranch hands who shared a love of horses and horsemanship, but who eschewed the posh image of the polo set. It was worth going to the US National Polo Championships in Montecito, south of Santa Barbara, just to see the looks on the faces of the elite when Garnet's Raiders took the field.

"So how many stitches does this one make? You know that the insurance industry rates equestrian sports as having the most fatalities of any recreational activity. Statistics say you don't have long for this world if you keep playing polo," I told him for the umpteenth time.

"Like surfing, skiing, white water kayaking and HANG GLIDING weren't dangerous. Face it. You're an adrenaline junky just like I am," he retorted.

"It's not about adrenaline. It's about control. I like to take a challenge that nature provides and develop the skill to eliminate the risk. I don't do team sports. I compete with myself and with everything nature can throw at me."

He laughed, "It's not nice to fool with Mother Nature."

"Okay. Okay. We've been round and round on this. You may be right, but I think you have more scars and broken bones from polo than I have from all of my sports combined. Injuries tell the bottom line and you must admit you have me beat there. "So, what's on your mind?" I asked.

"Well Jack, you know I've enjoyed working with you and Skynet for the last year. You guys are always pushing the networking envelope – "

"Ronn, are you sure you don't want to do this over dinner in a nice restaurant where I can't make a scene?"

He grinned. I could almost see the teeth underneath the mustache. "No seriously, I've been contracting for the last ten years and I've decided to settle down."

"You mean you're getting married and retiring from the software business?" I asked, incredulous.

Ronn was the consummate cowboy bachelor. He met women in the local watering hole and regularly charmed them into coming back to his place on the ranch to listen to the rain on the roof as they sipped brandy by the fire. I often asked myself how the Marlboro Man could be alive and well in the Silicon Valley.

"No. I've been offered a fulltime position with a consulting firm. You should meet these guys. It's like going to work in a think tank. They're brilliant. Their business plan is to bring in the top talent from the Valley and let each person develop his business under their umbrella. It's sort of like a law firm. We bill hours at high rates, or develop a team to work with us. Then regularly through the year, the partners share the profits. They have a contract lined up for me and seem to think they can keep me busy and challenged. From the types of companies they're working with, I think I'll learn a lot.

"I know there's a standing offer for me to come here, but with the situation you're facing I could never do it."

Ronn was right. Skynet had problems. While we were growing by leaps and bounds, were considered to be the gurus of networking worldwide, and had developed the first email client for the nascent Internet, along with sophisticated software products for companies like IBM, Crown Zellerbach, Fairchild, Visa, and MasterCharge (now called MasterCard), we were ultimately a mom and pop shop.

8

Don and Madge Johnson had founded Skynet. Don had a PhD in Electrical Engineering from UC Berkeley and had started Skynet as an offshoot and technology transfer from the University. Consolidated Shipping, the world's largest international shipping company, approached Don to see if he could commercialize the email software he and his graduate students had created as part of an ARPANET (the university-driven precursor to the Internet) research project. Consolidated anteed up $250,000 and Don, with no previous business experience, asked his wife Madge, who had an MBA, to put the company together. A year later, they recruited me out of IBM to corral their out-of-control software development group.

They gave me a decent salary, 1% of the company in stock options, and complete control over all software products. After meeting the 'team,' I quickly implemented and enforced a streamlined version of the IBM software development processes at Skynet, built some structure around the ragtag group of ex-students that Don had brought with him, and in addition to bringing in developers and management professionals I had worked with before, I employed a few high-powered independent contractors like Ronn to fill voids in our expertise.

I also brought in one of the best salesmen IBM ever trained. He and I played the dynamic duo on our major accounts. His glad-handing and excellent golf game complemented my ability to find simple technical answers to complex networking problems.

Now, we were turning out previously unseen network products for major industry players every four months and our revenues had grown from just under three hundred thousand dollars in sales the year before I arrived, to a forecasted twenty million dollars this year – outstanding growth for any company in less than three years. And all of this was done with no outside funding.

With our reputation and credibility, we required our customers to pay for our Research and Development expenses, pay for each copy of the products they deployed, and pay monies on an annual basis for maintenance and support. Our customers didn't mind. They felt that our software gave them a competitive edge. For companies like Visa and MasterCharge, our network optimizations saved them tens of millions of dollars each day. Venture Capitalists were calling non-stop offering a mezzanine round of financing for an Initial Public Offering of Skynet stock.

And that was where the problems started.

"You know we're likely to IPO in the next year. I could offer you options that would be worth several hundred grand after the IPO." I countered.

"Jack, as long as Don is involved in the company no VC is going to invest and no investment banker is going to take a mom and pop shop like this public. Madge is as tough as she needs to be and pretty damn sharp on the business and financial side, but the pair would never fly even if Don didn't have his 'problem.'"

Don's 'problem' was pot. The former university professor now spent most of his time stoned. He came into work only once or twice a week and usually reeked of marijuana. Madge and I had always tried to get him cleaned up for the VC meetings, but invariably, he would 'do a doobie' before walking into the conference room. Embarrassment would ensue.

"I know you think you have a couple of mil coming with this IPO," he continued, "but it ain't gonna happen. You met guys like this in college – guys who just couldn't use it recreationally like the rest of us. They may have once been brilliant, but as we all know now, pot makes you stupid.

"You know, you should blow this hot dog stand and come join me at CIA. I'm sure they could use someone like you. With your track record, you could write your own ticket, maybe even build your own mini-empire within their company."

"CIA? You're going to work for the CIA? "I asked, incredulous.

"No, not THE CIA! CIA – Carson Ingles Associates, though I suspect Carson feels no shame in capitalizing on confusion from the name."

"I don't know, Ronn. I have it pretty good here. I've got complete control over all but the financial side of the company, a good salary, bonuses, and a great team. Maybe Don will get straight. Or, perhaps Madge can convince him to step out and let me take over that side of the business. After all, there are millions at stake here."

"Jack, Jack, Jack," Ronn said shaking his head. "It'll never happen. I won't push you now, but if you change your mind, you can always reach me at the ranch. I'm sure you can take on a CIA project and start bringing your team over as you grow your part of the business. Think about it."

Of course I didn't think about it then. I had it too good. It was 1983. The Internet was something only a few of us knew about. IBM had shipped the first Personal Computer two years before, but it hadn't taken off yet, and I had the perfect Silicon Valley lifestyle: creative control over my job with a work hard, play hard philosophy.

Although there were some all-nighters and work on Saturdays, Sundays and holidays when project deadlines loomed, for the most part, work consumed about 50 hours a week. I even had time to teach an occasional networking class at UC Santa Cruz, and to speak at industry conferences. In spite of my position in industry as a Vice President of Software Development, teaching was my first love. There's nothing so rewarding as seeing a student or employee suddenly grasp a concept that had eluded them and put it to practical use.

I had recently broken up with Susan Brown, my girlfriend of three years, who had been a graduate student in English at Mills College, the only West Coast Seven Sisters School, located on a secluded campus in the Oakland hills. She shared a love of hang gliding with me, so on weekends in the spring, summer and fall, we were usually off on hang gliding trips to mountains within a few hours' drive of the Valley. Unfortunately, she had taken a doctoral fellowship at Boston University after completing her Master's at Mills. We now wrote and called each other regularly, but had agreed that a long-distance romance wouldn't work. The BU opportunity was one she couldn't pass up, and having spent part of my life in the East, I knew I didn't want to give up my California lifestyle even though jobs were plentiful with the companies springing up along Route 128 in that area.

Although I had given up on hang gliding competitions after losing (read death!) some overly competitive friends, there was nothing better than challenging myself to a hundred mile out and back flight in the Owens Valley, a couple hours soaring at 11,000 feet over Lake Tahoe after launching from Slide Mountain, or soaking in the remote hot springs near Elk Mountain after a day of chasing thermals north of Clear Lake.

During the long summer days, I even managed after work flights at Waddell Creek, Westlake Cliffs, or Tunitis Creek, relaxing fifteen hundred feet over the ocean in smooth air, arms relaxed on the control bar as I watched the sun set over the Pacific, solitude complete as I absorbed the beauty of the California coast.

I surfed most mornings before work at Boulders, my 'secret spot' north of Santa Cruz, paddling out into the glassy seas enveloped in thick California fog, getting my requisite minimum of 10 waves before heading to the office.

During winter holidays or weekends, it was powder or mogul skiing at Kirkwood in the Sierra Nevada and big wave surfing on the North Coast.

I had a challenging job, professional recognition, decent income, and more fun than anyone deserved. This was the California lifestyle. What more could I ask? For a military brat whose father qualified for welfare in most states he was stationed in, I had come a long way. It was like banking my glider into a thermal. There's a sudden surge of power in the air, a quick adjustment to set a perfect circle and then you're spiraling up – there's nowhere to go but up and you think "take me!" as the ground and the earthly world gets smaller and smaller. You and Mother Nature are in perfect synchronization.

They say that a hawk or eagle circling in a thermal believes it is stationary and that it is making the world turn below it.

3

Most people don't know what a thermal is. They see hawks and eagles soaring in circles and don't connect this to the magic thermodynamics that enable those of us without engines to soar to tens of thousands of feet upwards or to fly hundreds of miles without an engine.

A thermal is a bubble of rising air generated by a relatively hot spot on the ground. It doesn't have to be really hot; some of the best thermals I've found have been on snowy days. It just requires a difference in temperature. Thermals are a lot like bubbles in a soda glass. The carbonation is less dense than the liquid so it rises. Warm air is less dense than colder air so it too rises until it either encounters warmer air or loses its heat.

The eagle, hang glider pilot, or sailplane pilot glides through the air searching for these bubbles. In practice, more time is spent searching and gliding downward than climbing, but sometimes a single thermal can take you up ten thousand feet or more, so you have a lot of time to glide to find the next one.

You're climbing smoothly upward at nearly two thousand feet per minute and you're relaxed. Trees, cars, and buildings that you once could see clearly are becoming too small to see. The thermal is getting bigger. It's merging with other bubbles rising off the valley floor and now the craggy treeless peaks of the White Mountains are below you. The bighorn sheep you passed on the way up are just specks of white below. You widen and flatten your circle. You relax. The air becomes thinner and colder and you look at your altimeter and see that you're passing 15,000 feet. You're enveloped in crispness, clarity, and purity. No smog. No noisy cars, no people to challenge your decisions. You realize that you're further from all other living things than you've ever been before. You're suspended miles above the earth by a bit of Dacron and aluminum and the only way you got here was by the skills you've practiced and mastered. Except for the sound of the air passing under your sail, the only thing you hear is the chirping of your variometer telling you you're still climbing at fifteen hundred feet per minute. You switch it to silent mode to enjoy more solitude than any earthbound person has ever experienced. You start to think about oxygen.

The other thing about thermals that most people don't realize is that while the thermal is going up, the air around it is going down to fill the space evacuated by the rising bubble. Traversing the boundary between the rising air and the falling air can be quite a shock.

Suddenly, you're pitched ass over teakettle. Like Icarus, you're falling out of the sky downward at more than 2000 feet per minute. You've made a mistake. You got lazy and flattened your circle so much that you hit the thermal's boundary and the nose of your glider was pitched down while the tail was still climbing. In the old days this meant an unrecoverable dive – certain death. With today's equipment, you just have to be patient, knowing (or hoping) that the downward moving air doesn't go all the way to the ground.

4

It was Monday morning at Skynet. While taking a shower after surfing, I had come up with the answer to a problem posed to us by Visa, one of our major financial services customers, which was headquartered nearby in San Mateo. They leased an expensive satellite connection to Asia which retailers and banks shared to get credit authorizations and funds transfers. Periodically, the connection would drop for a few minutes, then it would come back up. While the connection was down, credit card processing stopped across all of Asia, costing merchants, banks, and our client lots of money. The telephone companies in the various countries had assured them that their circuits were working correctly, so we had been called in to see if we could spot the problem. We quickly determined that the problem had to do with the combination of the delay caused by the satellite connection (even at the speed of light, a communication with a satellite incurs nearly a half of a second of delay on each transaction) and the polling protocols Visa's mainframe computers used. However, we didn't see a solution short of replacing the mainframes or rewriting their networking code, at costs of tens of millions of dollars.

Why is it that a task of mindless personal hygiene is the source for so much inspiration? I know it's not just me. Everyone I talk to says they get their best ideas in the shower. You're alone (it doesn't seem to work if you're not), hot water is pounding on your back as you soap your arms and wham! You have the answer to a problem you weren't even thinking about. Perhaps we should require several hours in the shower for everyone every day. In addition to cleaner people, maybe we could find answers to the Middle East crisis, world peace and global warming.

I stood at the whiteboard in front of part of my team explaining my design for a system that would use a non-delay sensitive protocol over the satellite link while spoofing the mainframe protocol on both ends of the network. We'd fool the mainframe into thinking it was talking to a local credit authorization device, and would use a better communications protocol over the satellite link. I had drawn a state diagram for the new system. At the time, the concept of using state diagrams was very new, so I explained to the team how they worked.

"You've all taken programming classes and I bet your first

assignment was to describe how to tell a robot to brush its teeth

"The purpose of the task is to show you that you must think of every detail sequentially and you have to prepare to handle conditions that you wouldn't expect in the normal course of events. For example, if the top is already off the toothpaste tube, you don't want to tell the robot to remove it.

"State diagrams go hand in hand with event-driven software. This is a significant level above the standard sequential if-then-else programming you learned in school. The basic idea is that rather than doing things sequentially, you think about the different states that a system can be in and all things that could conceivably happen in each state. Then, while in each state, if a certain event happens, you decide what to do.

"Life is not sequential. You can't write software thinking you know what will come next any more than you can live your life by a script. The way you react always depends on the situation you're in. If a gunshot goes off behind your head, you'll react very differently in a restaurant than you would on a rifle range. Our software needs to be more like real life – driven by events. Surprisingly, in addition to becoming more adaptable to unforeseen things happening, we actually end up with less code to write.

"In this case, we can use the events to – Oh, hi Don."

Don Johnson, our errant CEO had just walked into the conference room. He was dressed in soiled jeans, an untucked long sleeved plaid shirt and hiking boots. His eyes were red, the pupils almost filling the irises, and it was clear that he was stoned again.

"Is that a state diagram?" he asked. "State diagrams are really cool, man. We used a lot of event-driven code in designing ARPANET. Tell me what you dudes are up to. Maybe I can help."

Even after knowing him for the last few years, I found it hard to believe that this educated former University professor and CEO of a multimillion dollar company could talk like a high school stoner.

But he was the CEO. He had written some groundbreaking code for the ARPANET, and it was his software that got the company launched, so I continued to lay out my design for a new front-end processor that we could develop to solve our customer's problems. In fact, it was clear that this could be a product that would allow mainframe computer systems to communicate across the new packet switching networks that were appearing across the world and which would ultimately become part of the backbone for the Internet. My protocol team of three guys and two women were rapt. Don stared off into space and didn't seem to be paying attention. After explaining the entire design, I selected Cheryl as the project lead and asked her to gather the rest of the group to divide up the components. Don didn't seem to notice that the meeting had ended and I left the conference room to call the lead network architect at Visa to tell her that we had a great solution to their problem. As I hung up the phone, Don walked into my office. His eyes looked almost normal. He took a seat and smiled. And then the bottom dropped out.

"Jack, I've been out of the company too long. I really don't know what's going on any more. It wasn't that long ago that there were just a few of us here. Now there are almost a hundred people in the company and I don't know very many of them. I want back in. Madge says you've been doing an incredible job, so for now, I'd like to follow your lead and maybe take on a project. You know I'm a great designer and can even still write code if I have to."

I'm sure my face paled. I know my stomach did a flip. I felt a sudden need to run to the restroom, but I did my best to maintain. The old cliché is that your life passes before your eyes just before the end, but in this case, the future raced through my mind and I felt every gut-wrenching minute of the next six months in a matter of seconds.

Don would take on a project and because of his absences, we'd cover for him in front of the customer. When the project succeeded, Don would declare that he was back in full form and that he wanted to control the software development organization. My role would become babysitter, and clean up man. I'd work behind the scenes to put things on track while Don basked in the glory of his technical comeback.

"Have you spoken to Madge about this?" I asked.

"No, but she's my wife and I know she'll be glad to see me back at work."

I knew the answer but I asked "What project did you have in mind?"

Don replied smugly "Why the VISA project of course. No

one in this company knows state machines and event-driven code better than I do and the protocol mapping you designed is great. I don't know why I didn't think of it before. I'll go talk to Cheryl and will let her know that I'm taking the lead. God, it's good to be back!"

With that, he left. I walked into Madge's office.

Madge was of medium height and had long brown hair. Her stunning blue eyes revealed a quickness of intelligence that often left you startled. The extra hundred pounds she carried melted away as soon as she opened her mouth. There were countless times where I had come in to explain why we were delayed on a project, and with no software development experience, she had come up with suggestions that made a huge difference, helping us to deliver on time and under budget. She also taught me everything I know about project sizing, coercing engineers to estimate accurately, and how to bid customized development effectively from a financial point of view. Madge was the financial brains of Skynet and eminently practical. I knew she'd have an answer to this one, so I recounted the morning's events and expressed my concerns.

"Don's taking on a project?" She mused. "It's been a long time since he did anything like this."

Taking these to be words of concern, I jumped in. "Madge, why don't you talk to him? Visa is a critical customer and we can't afford Don's inconsistency on this project. I really don't want the team to see Don's problem."

Her blue eyes flared. "Jack, remember who you work for. Don started this company and while he's had his problems in the past, if he says he's coming back, if he says he'll work for you to act as a project lead, I know he can do it. He is the most brilliant person I've ever met and I knew it was only a matter of time till he'd wake up and decide to take control over the company he started, and drop his habit."

I could tell by looking at her that there was no use in arguing. How had Madge, a cut and dried businesswoman, almost drill instructor tough, turned into that love-struck puppy? She would never have let me put an untried project lead on a customer contract that was this important. Why couldn't she have talked Don into dipping his toe by taking on a small project, then taking on more when he proved himself? Why such blind faith?

I headed back to my office, closed the door and picked up the phone. "Hey Georgette," I said when she answered the phone. "Problems with Susan? Missing her more than you thought?" Georgette asked, hearing depression in my voice.

"No," I responded. "I just need to talk. How about El Burro at seven? I'll buy."

Georgette agreed to meet me at the Ms. PacMan table – our usual after-work hangout. A few margaritas, some friendly competition over Ms PacMan, and conversation would flow.

I had met Georgette in college. Through the course of our four years taking Computer Science courses, we traded off finishing first and second in most of our classes, anticipating that as the best of the best, we'd one day see success beyond that of mere mortals. Georgette was as much into individual sports as I was and we quickly discovered a common love for whitewater kayaking and skiing, risk sports where we excelled, again, thinking our practiced skills made us invulnerable.

Georgette was poetry in motion in the moguls, upper body completely quiet as her knees absorbed bump after bump. When we saw that the snow level was below four thousand feet, we knew that the cold air was going to create perfect powder, not the infamous world-renown Sierra Cement. At first light, we'd leave messages for classmates asking them to get notes for us and we'd head up to Kirkwood or Sugar Bowl to lay fresh tracks in virgin snow.

During the spring when the surf was usually flat, Georgette and I were river rats. In whitewater, she knew no fear and seemed to be able to spot a line and then demonstrate the skill to hit that line through the most treacherous rapids. She'd take the biggest drops into the nastiest holes and pull off exits where we'd be rescuing others who were endlessly recirculating. We worked our first few college summers as guides for Northern California Whitewater, taking drunken college students, corporate executives, and families down the many Class 3 and Class 4 rivers cascading with snowmelt from the highest peaks of the Sierra Nevada Mountains.

Like me, Georgette was a military brat. She too attended more than a dozen schools before graduating from high school, relocating at least every two to three years. And, like me, she had problems remaining in relationships. Our early upbringing had patterned us to need significant change every two to three years and it just seemed that after two or three years with the same person, we each needed to try someone else. We called this the military brat syndrome. While she and I had a brief fling during one of our summer whitewater trips, each of us recognized that we didn't want to ultimately become a victim to the military brat syndrome ourselves, so we'd settled on remaining best friends and this idyllic relationship had continued through the years.

We graduated together, worked our way through grad school in parallel, and she took a job at AT&T (still Ma Bell in those days), while I went to IBM (Big Blue). We had a long discussion about careers and futures when I left IBM to join Skynet. Our respective big companies offered guaranteed employment, great benefits, a surprising amount of individual recognition, lucrative stock purchase programs, and a clear ladder to climb should you have the inclination to do so. In retrospect, I now see that many of my friends who remained with IBM over the years saw as much or more financial success than most of the entrepreneurs I know. And they didn't have to suffer the constant stress, broken marriages, and crashing failures that most of us did. But I didn't know that at the time. If I had, perhaps my life would have turned out very differently. I know I would never have met Carson. From my perspective then, Skynet offered me the opportunity to build something from almost nothing, to take control of my future and escape what I thought of as the trap of a big company career. I quit my job at IBM, but Georgette remained at AT&T.

5

I left the office about 6:45 and drove over to El Burro, the local Mexican Restaurant and watering hole. Fortunately, the Ms PacMan table was free, so I snagged it, flagged down the waiter, and asked for a pitcher of margaritas on the rocks and two glasses. Georgette arrived at the same time as the margaritas, chips and salsa.

Georgette was small and trim with an athletic build. She kept her brown hair short because she didn't like the hassle of caring for longer hair, wore makeup sparingly, but dressed in suits as required by most of the large companies at that time. She wasn't what the average male would call stunningly beautiful, but her irrepressible energy level made her someone you just couldn't wait to meet and talk to. Once they got to know her, most men were intimidated by her quick wit, intellectual versatility and no-nonsense approach to male-female interaction. For me, these qualities made it easy for us to be best buddies.

"You look like your aunt just died." She said as she took the seat opposite me. "Got any quarters?"

I reached into my pocket, placed a stack of quarters on the table, put two in the machine, and pressed the two-player button. Immediately the machine jumped to life, and the standard electronic ditty started to play as the characters in the game did their dance around the screen. Georgette waited patiently as I finished off the first two mazes and as the game did its 'They Meet' show, she asked me what was up.

"Don's decided to take an active role in the company again. He wants to take over a key project with Visa, acting as project lead and implementing my design." I lamented.

The blue maze appeared and I went back to eating dots and avoiding the ghosts. I finished the three screens and when the next little show started, I continued. "I've built this company without him. We're on the verge of an IPO, have great technology, and I'm going to lose it all. I can see what's going to happen."

The peach colored mazes appeared and before I ate a row, I was caught by the red ghost.

"I've never seen you blow it so fast." She said. "You don't really think Don will hold it together long enough to have any real impact, do you? He'll probably flake out like he usually does and things will go back to normal in a week or two. Be patient and hang in there. I'm sure it's not as bad as you think."

She then started her game. On the first few screens, she looked relaxed and hardly paid attention. As she broke into the peach colored ones where I'd blown it, you could see the increase in her concentration and intensity, revealed in the almost child-like way she bit her lower lip.

I guzzled my first margarita and poured myself another as she knocked down screen after screen. What she said made perfect sense. It had happened before. Don would start showing up at work for a few days, then he'd disappear again. Why did this time feel different?

She finally lost, four screens past me, and as I took my turn, she said, "I wanted to talk to you too. You remember Marty, my boss? He's asked four of us to join him in a startup. He thinks we can build an inexpensive modem for the home market. He's convinced the Internet is going to take off and that everyone will want to dial in.

"Aside from your issues with Don, you know I've envied the freedom you have to create your products. As Chief Technical Officer of Modular Communications, I'll be in the same place. Of course we'll be going a few months without salaries, but Marty has lined up a corporate customer who will place an initial order with up front monies. You know that AT&T's divestiture is about to happen, so we see some opportunities there with the regional phone companies as well. What do you think?"

In years past, AT&T had been the only telephone company in the United States. Its predecessor, American Bell was founded by Alexander Graham Bell in the 1870s and the company, which started as a monopoly because of its patents, had become the world's largest government sanctioned monopoly as it grew throughout the 20th century. Now, with a number of smaller pretenders to the throne, the government had decided to break up AT&T, and eliminate the monopoly. The portions of the company that operated local telephone service would become independent while AT&T would focus on long distance, offering interconnection between the local providers. The idea was that competition would benefit consumers as they had more choices for service and potentially lower costs. It also opened the market to companies like MCI to compete with AT&T for long distance service. AT&T even had to give up the Bell name. Hence, Ma

Bell had truly met her demise. This divestiture signaled the beginning of the end for a variety of monopolistic industries as the government decided that capitalistic competition should extend its reach into regulated industries and utilities. The airline deregulation was not too far in the future, and the ill-fated power company deregulation wreaked its havoc on us, especially here in sunny California for many years to come.

"It's funny," I replied. "I always thought that you'd either climb the corporate ladder at AT&T and end up Chairman – er, Chairperson, or that we'd start a company together with your telephony experience complementing my data networking.

"Marty certainly understands business. Doesn't he have a Stanford MBA? If you have a customer to provide initial funding, and opportunities with the post divestiture AT&T, I'd say go for it!"

Georgette responded, "I believe it's still chairman. I thought I might try to become one of the few women executives in big business too, but with the divestiture, AT&T is being split up. It's hard to see a path upwards with the impending chaos. I think it's a good time to leave."

We engaged in some typical chit chat as we played a few more games. My game was definitely off that night as she trounced me in every one. As we polished off the margaritas, I asked, "Dinner?"

"Not tonight." She replied. "I have dinner reservations at Le Papillion with John.

John was her boyfriend of about a year and a half. He was a former Stanford fraternity president and football star who was working in his father's commercial real estate business. Georgette found him 'pretty to look at and fun in bed,' but lacking a bit in mental capacity.

"Sounds like a dear John dinner," I quipped.

"You're right," She said. "There's no future there and if I'm going to start a new company and maintain my current lifestyle, I don't have the time to babysit this relationship. John can be so needy and insecure."

"With you as a girlfriend, most men would be insecure," I commented. "I never really liked John anyway. He's too good looking."

We split the check as always. Georgette headed off to her dinner and I drove home hoping she was right about Don.

6

Since I always felt good after a morning surf session, I had called Mark Russell, my doctor and fellow surfer, and asked him to join me in the surf the next morning. I suspected it was going to be a challenging day with Don's return to active duty at Skynet. A few crisp, clean waves would prepare me for the day ahead. Mark was waiting in front of his Santa Cruz home, bundled in sweat pants and hooded sweatshirt. The steaming cup of coffee on the hood of his car had melted the frost from a foot-wide circle around it. His board was on the ground beside the backpack that held his wetsuit. John's house was completely dark and I knew that he had slipped out without waking his wife Janet or either of his 6-year old twin daughters, Lucy and Vanessa.

"How's it look?" he asked.

"According to the weather radio, the swell is from two hundred ninety degrees, eight feet every fourteen seconds and the wind is light offshore. It sounds like a perfect day at Boulders."

Boulders was my 'secret spot' north of Santa Cruz. While the waves in Santa Cruz were crowded, relatively few people ventured north, especially during the winter. Although none would admit it, the colder water, bigger surf, and perpetual possibility of an encounter with a Great White shark terrified most of them. Add in the fact that virtually no one knew the location of Boulders and of those who did, even fewer would brave the climb down the treacherous cliff, and I could count on waves to myself virtually every surfable day of the week. After years of surfing it alone, I had a bad fall from the cliff and Susan had convinced me that I should bring someone along in the future. In attempting to keep my promise, if I could find someone to join me, I would, but if not, I'd still go it alone.

"Want some coffee?" Mark asked as we headed north on Highway 1.

"You know I never touch the stuff. Caffeine is a nasty drug that brings people up, then they crash, then they have another cup, then they crash again. You're a doctor for God's sakes. You know what it does to people. Think of the headaches people go through when they try to quit. It's worse than many hard drugs. Plus, it makes you colder in the water."

"Yeah, but it makes me warm now, and I have no plans to quit drinking it, so I don't worry about withdrawal."

Doctors!

We talked about previous days at Boulders until we pulled over on the shoulder of Highway 1 ten minutes later. As we walked through the artichoke field in the light fog, we could hear the waves crashing. When we looked over the edge of the cliff, we saw that it was one of those classic days, six to eight foot surf with long right-breaking walls and a nice tube possibility on the inside. We quickly suited up and then carefully climbed down the hundred foot cliff. Waiting for a lull, we jumped into the fifty-four degree water and paddled out. A harbor seal with its doglike face swam up beside me as I crested the first wave, then he rolled over and looked at me upside down. As we slid down the back of the next wave, we were doused with the spray caused by the offshore winds blowing the tops back over the waves. Tiny droplets from the spray floated like glass beads on the surface tension of the water. What a great start!

Sure enough, it was as good as it looked, a perfect day with only two of us out and many waves going unridden. About an hour into our session, Mark took off on a great wave and I pulled into the one behind it. He was paddling out as I was coming towards the inside section where that perfect tube set up. I hit the lip of the wave and showered him with water careening off my board as I cut back and set up for the section. I pulled into the barrel and as water caressed my head, I dropped a bit lower and crouched tighter. I was completely enclosed in the wave looking at the light a few yards ahead.

It's funny. When you're inside a wave, it's quiet. Actually, it's not, but the sound of the crashing wave outside is muffled inside and you have this sense of silence. Even more strange, time seems to stop. A two or three second barrel seems to last forever. But when you pop out, it almost seems like it didn't happen.

Pleased with another perfect wave, I started paddling back into the lineup. Mark was fifty yards further out and was paddling over the top of an oncoming wave. As he disappeared behind it, I heard him scream.

It's funny how you remember moments like that. You've heard of shark attacks, but you never think they'll happen to you. But that scream. I'll never forget the sound of a grown man screaming.

I sped up my paddling and as I crested the wave Mark had

crossed, I saw two gigantic fins headed rapidly straight towards him. They extended nearly four feet in the air and seemed to dwarf Mark who was paddling prone on his board. As fear set in, my rational mind took hold.

"Sharks don't travel in pairs," I thought.

Sure enough, the next thing I saw was the black and white body of the first killer whale, which submerged and swam under Mark followed by the second one. The whales continued south. I paddled up to Mark.

"I'm getting too old for this," he said. "I think I need to go in and clean out my wetsuit. That was terrifying. Have you ever seen killer whales before?"

"No. I've been surfing here for more than fifteen years and I've never seen them. I don't think they attack humans unless provoked."

We surfed for another hour, then started the ascent back up the cliff. Mark went first and as he reached the top, he said, "Jack, you're not going to believe this. Look at the sun!"

It was somewhat overcast with fog, but you could just make out the golden disc of the sun through the clouds. Only it wasn't a disc. It was half a disc.

"I forgot about the partial eclipse today," I replied. "What a great way to view it!"

It was a perfect ending to a memorable session. I dropped Mark at home half an hour later and Janet stepped out and waved as Mark approached the front door. It was 8:30am and time for me to head into the office to see what havoc Don could wreak today.

7

I headed across the Santa Cruz Mountains on serpentine Highway 17, catching the tail end of the commute. More and more people chose to reside on the coast in the clean air beach town that would later be nicknamed Silicon Valley Beach, living in or around Santa Cruz and driving to and from the Silicon Valley each day. Tens of thousands faced the accident laden Highway 17 every morning and evening. By getting to work after 9 am, I generally managed to miss the chaos of the competitive, rage filled Santa Cruz to Silicon Valley commuters.

The two hours of surfing had left me relaxed and unstressed. I pulled into Skynet at 9:15 am, and much to my surprise, there, in the parking lot, was Don's BMW.

And so it begins.

Don's office was the first one, just past the receptionist's area. Facing Technology Drive near the San Jose Airport, Don's windows were floor to ceiling glass and he could watch the planes taking off and landing. As I walked by, he called out, "Hey Jack, come look at this. You're going to love it."

On Don's desk was a large state diagram that I recognized as a more detailed version of the one I had produced the day before. Next to it were pages and pages of pseudo code – English-like high level instructions that we used as part of our designs. I didn't realize that Don knew what pseudo code was.

On the far side of his desk was the document entitled Skynet Software Development Standards that I had written and made mandatory for the programmers when I had joined the company three years before. There were paper scrap bookmarks throughout and I could see that he had used a yellow highlighter on the pseudo code section.

Don continued, "I took your state diagram and refined it to the next level. That's what Cheryl said was the next step. Last night I read the development standards – they're good. I see why we've been so much more successful since we adopted them. This morning I created high-level pseudo code for all the sections and I think we're ready for a design review. What do you think?"

I carefully went through everything he produced. It was really quite good. I said so and we scheduled a design review for the afternoon.

As I walked by Madge's office on the way to my own, she

asked me to come in.

"How's it look?" she asked.

I knew she meant Don's work and I told her it was perfect - that he had accomplished more in one evening than any of our project leads could do.

"He accomplished more than that," she said, almost to herself. Then she blushed like a school girl when she realized she had said it out loud. Conservative, tight-lipped Madge was love struck with her own husband of fifteen years. I guess it was nice to see.

"It's good to see him focused again," I said, feigning ignorance of the meaning of her comment. "We're doing a design review this afternoon and will be dividing up the sections among the programmers."

Even as I said it, I knew that Don would want more to do.

Months went by and it was now 1984. California did not see a repeat of the devastating rains of the 1982-1983 winter when people lost their lives in floods, landslides, and avalanches. The term El Nino had just become popular to explain the weather anomaly and it had abated this winter. Orwell's vision of the future had not come to pass and we were all relieved that freedom was increasing in the world instead. Lotus 1-2-3 and VisiCalc shipped their first products for the IBM Personal Computer and suddenly everyone from households doing their budgets to large corporations had to have Personal Computers with these programs to do financial planning. A few flecks of gold had been spotted in Silicon Valley.

New companies started springing up, all trying to capitalize on the true computer revolution. Before, serious computing was done on multi-million dollar mainframe computers that could fill most houses. Individuals were relegated to toying with hobby machines and while Apple Computer was making strides, they had primarily focused on the education market. But now, the race was on. IBM's sudden domination was a surprise and ultimately short-lived as manufacturers like Compaq and countless Asian companies reverse-engineered IBM's machines and developed 'clones.'

Most of this was due to my former boss at IBM, Don Estridge. Shortly after I left the company, Don gathered about a dozen top engineers in Boca Raton, Florida and did a skunk works project – a project that wasn't sanctioned by IBM headquarters. This group produced the Personal Computer and Don was one of the first in IBM to forge outside partnerships with both small and larger companies. Previously, IBM customers were 'blue' shops; no non-IBM gear was allowed. Don changed that, and the PC took off. Unfortunately, Don's untimely death in a plane crash in Dallas in 1985 allowed IBM to reintroduce their standard management and business processes into the PC group and IBM lost its momentum.

Ironically, I flew into Dallas on business the day after the crash. Wreckage was still strewn on the sides of the runway and this loss of a visionary who I had known so well a few years before, became a personal tragedy. You're on your way to making a difference, creating a new form of light for the world, and someone pulls the plug.

Realizing the potential of the Personal Computer, after Don's death, IBM put an executive from headquarters in charge to replace him. Some say that IBM intentionally slowed the progress of the PC to prevent other companies from encroaching on their customers. Others say that the old-school IBMers just didn't know how to approach this exploding market. In either case, IBM quickly lost its dominance in the PC market. What a legacy!

Georgette's new company, Modular Communications started to sell their modems to corporate users who could now call in to their mainframe computers from home, and Georgette was actually collecting a salary. At Skynet, we too saw the burgeoning opportunity. As a networking company, we could anticipate a time when all these computers would have to talk to each other. We had countless ideas for new products and our customers were buying our software and were funding more and more R&D.

Don had proved me wrong. He did not return to his laid-back ways. I'm not sure what it was that inspired him, but he was back with a vengeance. He worked at least twelve hours a day and was there most weekends. More than once I'd come in early, late, or on weekends and heard giggling or moaning from behind Madge's closed door. While she was as shrewd as ever in her financial and business management, it was clear that she had changed too. She greeted everyone with a smile and almost pranced as she moved about the office. The three of us had met with several Venture Capitalists and we had multiple term sheets. We just had to decide which way we wanted to go. Everyone was happy except for me and my project leads.

While Don was clearly brilliant and working hard, he had returned to his old software development style. He started cutting corners, encouraging the leads and their programmers to bypass the development standards to save time. Documentation was suffering and I knew that many of our latest products would be difficult to maintain. When customers had problems, found bugs, or needed enhancements, it would be nearly impossible for someone who hadn't written the code to fix it. I tried to explain this to both Madge and Don, but money was rolling in and the projects were being completed in record time. To them, the shortcuts appeared to be working.

Worse for me, Don was doing my job. He wasn't acting as

President and CEO, he was leading software development. More than once, we'd had confrontations in front of the team in a design review. As part of my standards, I insisted that everything be built modularly to ease maintenance and to facilitate mixing and matching components when creating new products. Don didn't feel we needed to take the extra time to do this, in spite of my protestations that it would save time and money in the long run. Since he was the CEO, he could overrule me and he did, too frequently. My project leads saw the problem too, but what could we do?

I called Ronn and set up a lunch meeting in Los Gatos at the California Café in Old Town. I arrived a few minutes early as usual and was sipping iced tea when Ronn hobbled in on crutches, his right leg in a cast from the knee down.

"I don't even have to ask, do I?" I said, "Polo again, right?"

Ronn placed his crutches against the wall as the waiter helped him into his seat. "A margarita on the rocks, por favor," Ronn told the waiter. He turned to me and grinned. "Aw, it was just a stupid accident. In our Sunday scrimmage, Bessie stopped short of the ball as Mack was crossing ahead of her. I went head first over the pommel and landed okay, but Mack's horse stepped on my leg in the commotion. The cast will be off in a month, but I can still play like this."

"Maybe it's not the sport that's so dangerous. It's you," I replied. "You're nuts! Give it a rest already!"

"I love it when you get angry," Ronn joked, his grin even broader. "So did you call me to give me shit about polo or did you have something else on your mind? Ready to jump ship?"

"Well, tell me more about CIA. How's it going?" I asked.

"I love it. Carson lines up these great customers. He does high level consulting for them and at the end of his project the customers ask him if his company can implement his recommendations. That's where the rest of us come in. Steve, his second in command is currently leading a team at Hewlett Packard. They're all working full time there billing lots of hours at high rates. I'm working for ALM, that new telecommunications startup. After Carson helped them lay out their product plans, he asked me to build their management system. I've got a team of four subcontractors working with me on it, and again, we're billing machines. The bucks are rolling in.

"Even better, they're coming my way. Every quarter, Carson

and Pam, his Chief Financial Officer, sit down and divide up the profits among all of us. It's not an equal split, but I got twenty five grand last quarter, on top of my salary.

"Not only that, but do you know what we did between Christmas and New Year's? Carson took all of us and our significant others to Acapulco. We stayed in a huge hotel and partied late into the night every night.

"The last night we were there, Carson held an open bar in his suite which overlooked one of the pools. About 3am, everyone had gone back to their rooms, Carson's girlfriend Nancy, had gone to bed and Shelly, Steve's wife, had gone up to their room. Carson and Steve were sitting on the balcony sipping brandy and smoking cigars, when Steve, who's a crazy Aussie, dares Carson to jump from the balcony into the pool below.

"They're both quite drunk, but Carson is smart enough to tell Steve he'll do it if Steve goes first. Picture this – Steve is about 35, 6'3 and built like a runner, long, thin and wiry. Carson looks to be 40-ish, with a big dark beard, long hair pulled back in a ponytail, and a body like Santa Claus. Imagine a portly nineteenth century captain of industry and you've got Carson.

"Of course, being an Aussie, Steve can't refuse a challenge so he strips down stark naked and jumps. It's the deep end of the pool and only twenty feet up, so it wasn't a problem. Steve starts yelling at Carson to jump and because he can't let his second-in-command best him, Carson undresses and executes a perfect swan dive into the pool.

"As they got out of the water, they realized they didn't have a room key or any clothes. Using executive privilege, Carson tells Steve to find a security guard who's patrolling the grounds and to go in and get some clothes for him, or at least a towel.

"So there's Steve wandering around bare as the day he was born looking for a security guard in Mexico. I could die laughing just thinking about it. He finally finds one but the guy pulls out a gun. Steve doesn't speak Spanish and if the guard could understand any English, he certainly couldn't get anything out of Steve's Aussie accent, which becomes more pronounced when he's stressed. The guard decides to take him to his boss, so he marches the unclothed Steve to security office, which is across the grounds from the main hotel. Steve sits there shivering, even though it's eighty degrees, while he waits for the security boss to show up.

"Meanwhile, Carson is having a nice moonlit swim in the pool. Another security guard on patrol spots him and tells him in Spanish that it is forbidden to swim in the pool after midnight. Carson, who speaks a little Spanish, says something like 'No key, can you help?'

"The guard asks him his room number and his name, calls the front desk on a Walkie Talkie and opens the concession stand where he grabs a towel for Carson. He then opens the door to the hotel where the concierge is waiting with a spare key to his room. He goes up and crawls into bed with Nancy, never thinking about Steve.

"In the security office, Steve is getting pissed. Sorry, that's the wrong word for an Aussie – he was pissed before he jumped off the balcony. He's fuming. He tries to walk out but the security guard stops him. Steve takes a swing at the guard who quickly ducks. If Steve were sober, the guard would have been lying on the floor, and Steve might still be locked up in a Mexican jail, but as it was, the guard just handcuffed Steve to the desk and walked out. He gets on his Walkie Talkie and tells the other guards that he has a crazy naked gringo in the security office who just tried to hit him. He asks the front desk to call the police.

"Fortunately, the guy at the front desk had a good head on his shoulders. He put two and two together, realizing that he had just let a naked Carson Ingles into the hotel, and he goes out to the security office and saves the day.

"I don't know if CIA will ever be welcomed back into that hotel, but I do know that Shelly, Steve's wife, beats him up about his irresponsibility daily.

"What a great trip! I love this company! So what's the problem at Skynet, as if I couldn't guess?"

"If I were in a Western, I'd say 'This town just ain't big enough for the both of us.' You were wrong about Don. He's given up the dope and is back at full throttle in the company. Unfortunately, he's doing my job, and while he's good on a technical basis, he doesn't know how to manage a software development team. My team is confused. They don't know who to follow. They know my standards are critical, but Don is the boss and now that he's no longer listening to me, things are headed downhill fast and I have no control. Control. That was the original idea. Now it's gone and the friction between Don and me is building. It's time for me to move on before I do or say something I'll regret."

Ronn became more serious. "I know this is tough for you, but it's a good decision. You know that if you leave, the VCs will walk. The company becomes a mom and pop shop again and when they check on the impact of your departure, they'll get an earful from your team. Still, I see your problem. If Don is involved, there really isn't room for two VPs of Software Development, if he goes back to his old ways, you've got a stoner CEO. You're in a lose-lose situation. You've gotta leave."

Over lunch, Ronn told me more about CIA and how it operated, and described Carson and Steve in more detail. He promised to have Steve give me a call to set up a meeting. The next day Steve called my office and invited me to lunch.

9

At noon on the dot, I walked into L'Auberge du Soleil, a pricey French restaurant in Saratoga. The maitre d' said that Monsieur Caples had already arrived. He led me to the back of the restaurant.

Steve was exactly as Ronn had described him and as I imagined. It was clear that women would find his chiseled face and blue eyes quite stunning while men would recognize him as someone who took care of himself. His sun-streaked light brown hair fell onto his forehead. Add in the Aussie accent and friendly Aussie camaraderie and you have a man who could charm the pants off the ladies and be just one of the guys.

He stood as I approached, held out his hand and said, "Jack, I've heard a lot about you. Sit, let's have some lunch and chat."

Steve poured me a glass from a bottle of Mt. Eden Chardonnay, and began to tell me about myself. I was quite impressed. He had done his homework. He knew the situation at Skynet, knew of my background with IBM, my teaching at the University, conferences I'd spoken at, papers and articles I'd written, the kinds of sports I liked, and he listed a number of people we both knew, including executives at some of Skynet's customers.

Without letting me get a word in since our initial greeting, he proceeded to make me an offer, "Jack, we want to hire you. CIA is in a critical place. We need you to help us climb to the next level. Right now, Carson is our lead consultant. I'm stuck at HP with the rest of the team, but I want to move up. Unfortunately, I can't be looking for new customers and billing at HP at the same time.

"What we want you to do is become a lead consultant like Carson. You can approach your existing customers and line up some consulting contracts. In all likelihood, you'll find more than you can handle and you can leverage me out of HP. Then the three of us, you, me, and Carson, can build team after team and grow the company much faster than Carson can do by himself.

"I can offer you 50% more than you're making now and 15% of the quarterly profits, which would likely double your current salary. When can you start?"

This whole meeting had caught me completely off guard. Steve didn't ask for my resume, didn't pose any questions, didn't even talk with me to get an idea whether I could think on my feet. On the one hand, it seemed incredibly impetuous. On the other, I was, of course, quite flattered. Although I usually think about these things and discuss them with Susan and Georgette, I decided to go for it.

"I think Skynet would need at least a month to transition," I replied.

"Try to make it two weeks," he countered. "I'm glad to have you on board. I'll get a formal offer letter out to you this afternoon. Talk to Skynet and let us know when you're available to get started.

"By the way, do you run? Yeah? Well, how about a run tomorrow after work at 5pm with the rest of CIA? We usually put in 4 or 5 miles at a 7:30 pace, maybe a bit faster on a good day. We start out at our office, so why don't you come by? You can see the office, meet everyone, I can give you the offer letter in person and you can get to know everyone on the run."

"Sounds good," I replied. "It would be great to meet your team."

We ordered lunch and Steve began to tell me about himself. I finished my glass of Chardonnay and switched to iced tea as the waiter brought out gourmet entrees. The big surprise, at least to me, was the size of the portions. Apparently, here at Auberge du Soleil, you could get excellent French food without leaving hungry.

Steve had grown up in Brisbane, Australia. His father was a banker and his mother taught school. He lived in an upper middle class neighborhood and while he was active in sports, particularly rugby, he didn't get into surfing and water sports like most of the kids his age.

When he became a teenager, his parents sent him to a prep school in Sydney and he learned to love the culture of the big city. He applied to several universities in England and in the United States. He decided on University College of London because they were beginning research into Computer Science. Upon completion of his studies, he returned to work in his father's bank where he learned the practical application of computer technology in the banking industry and where he streamlined and helped automate manual processes, making the bank one of the most technologically advanced in Australia. He learned about electronic funds transfers, credit card issuance and processing. Realizing that Australia was far from the center of technology, he started looking for ways to get to the States to advance his career. Because he managed the implementation of online credit processing to support VISA in his father's bank, one of the executives at VISA offered him a freelance consulting job helping set up networks for new banks in the United States. Steve moved to California. For 'two years, he lived the classic bachelor lifestyle. He loved San Francisco, the parties, theater and culture. With his ready charm and unusual accent, he became a great womanizer with no ideas of settling down. At some point, immigration became an issue and Steve knew he had to make a change. At a VISA Christmas party, he met Shelly, a financial analyst with the company, and two months later they were married. Steve applied for and received his green card. Shortly thereafter, Steve met Carson at Bank of America where he had gone for a seminar that Carson was teaching about networking financial databases. He approached Carson and asked him to lunch, and Carson invited Steve to join him at CIA. Life was good for Steve.

When Carson handed over the HP consulting contact to Steve, Steve recruited three top programmers out of VISA to work on the resulting projects, and CIA had begun to grow. Carson was happy, but was a bit complacent. He enjoyed a wealthy lifestyle and felt he had everything he needed, money, toys, and prestige. Steve wanted to show Carson the next level. He believed that CIA could be a consulting empire like EDS, Electonic Data Systems, Ross Perot's company, which had just been acquired by GM for two and a half BILLION dollars.

I was needed to leverage Steve out of HP and then the two of us would take the world by storm. Carson's name and reputation would open doors, Steve and I would develop our respective empires in tandem. It sounded too good to be true, but somehow achievable. The industry was hot, I had contacts and a reputation, I could recruit plenty of programmers, so why not?

10

The next day, I left Skynet early and drove over to the CIA offices in Los Gatos. A pretty young receptionist who introduced herself as Donna rose from behind the high, curved reception counter and asked me if I wanted coffee, a soft drink, or a glass of wine, all of which I declined. She picked up the phone to call Steve and asked me to take a seat. He'd be with me shortly.

The reception area was a far cry from what I was used to at Skynet. It looked like the entrance to a high-end law office. The carpet was a low thick pile in a pattern of navy blue and maroon. Large tropical plants were well-placed around the area and were visible down the hall. The walls were covered in a soft lighter blue material and aside from the air bubbling in the wall-to-wall tropical aquarium on left side of the room, the area was remarkably quiet. The large silver CIA logo centered behind the reception area was sharply defined against the darker background. I felt as if I had stepped into an office of privilege, wealth, and cool sophistication. This was a far cry from the cubicle filled offices of most companies in the Silicon Valley. I settled into a plush couch and picked up a magazine from the rosewood coffee table.

Five minutes later, Steve appeared and apologized for the delay. He directed me to the restroom where I changed into running gear. I noted that the restroom had a shower, something I'd previously seen only in industrial offices with hazardous materials. I could get used to a place like this.

When I came out of the restroom, Steve introduced me to Rick, George, and Dan. Dan and George were almost twins. Both were 5'10, with lean runners' bodies and dark hair. Rick was blond and burly. Although taller than the rest by an inch or two, he looked to be forty pounds overweight. I wondered if he'd be able to keep up.

"Don't worry about me," Rick said reading my silent appraisal and look of concern. "This is just pregnancy weight. I mean my wife is pregnant and I eat with her. We're not as active as we normally are so I've put on quite a bit of weight. I've decided to join the guys on their afternoon runs to see if I can drop it."

We took off down side streets until we reached the railroad tracks that led into the hills above Cupertino. Steve and Dan took the lead, George followed them and I paired off with Rick. Rick told me about his wife Kathy and the pregnancy, their first. Rick had been an NCAA runner in college and he and his wife had run together up until the 6th month of her pregnancy when it got to be too much for her. Rick had stopped too, hence the weight gain.

Rick then talked about the work he had done at VISA over the years which focused on high speed transaction processing systems. He was doing similar work at HP. It was clear to me that he was one of the top software developers in this field and that CIA was lucky to have recruited him. Clearly, he would be in demand by major companies across the country.

I caught up to George just as we turned onto what one day would be Highway 85, the cross-valley freeway that had been tangled up in legal and funding wrangling for at least ten years. For now, it was an open space corridor with a few pieces of private property.

George too, was an expert in transaction processing and networking systems. He was single and loved the perks that came with working at CIA. He talked about the money, fine wine, and trips. Had I heard about the Mexico bash? I assured him I had and caught up to Steve and Dan as we turned up Prospect Road. We ran single file up to Highway 9 and then I doubled up with Dan as we turned onto the trail along the railroad tracks to begin the loop back towards the office.

"Hey, look at that! Dan said, "See the group of quail up ahead? Look about twenty feet in front of them. See the one on the sign next to the tracks? He's the lookout. Watch!"

Sure enough when the lookout spotted us, he let out a shrill whistle. The flock of quail ahead consisted of six or seven adults and a perhaps two dozen little ones. At the sound of the whistle, two of the adults turned towards us as the rest marshaled the young ones into the bushes.

"Check this out," Dan said.

As we approached, the two remaining quail began to run. They took off directly down the path in front of us and frantically ran a criss-cross pattern, looking harried and out of control as we followed. About ten yards beyond the spot where the flock had turned off, the two split off the trail, one to each side of us.

"Isn't that amazing?" Dan said. "Everywhere I encounter quail when running trails at this time of year, it's the same pattern.

Later in the year when they grow up, they pretty much all stick together, but when the little ones are around, there's a lookout, the herders, and two decoys. Just like we saw, the lookout spots danger and signals, the herders head the little ones to safety and the decoys try to convince you that they can be caught as they lead you away from the flock. Pretty amazing that birds can construct such a well-defined social defense plan when humans can't."

In talking to Dan on the way back, I quickly learned that he was the leader of the group. He had attended St. John's College in Santa Fe, and their cross-disciplinary program mixing philosophy, classics, mathematics, and technology had clearly given Dan a well-rounded perspective. While he appreciated Steve for hiring them, Dan didn't appear to be in awe of him, but Dan couldn't stop talking about Carson's genius.

"Did you know that Carson never finished High School?" he asked. "His father committed suicide when Carson was ten and his mother never recovered. She did the same a year later, leaving his thirteen-year old brother to fend for the two of them. An uncle took them in but they ran pretty unchecked; the uncle was never around.

"At eighteen, Carson walks into IBM headquarters in Armonk, New York and asks to take the DPAT – the Data Processing Aptitude Test that IBM administers to all prospective employees. They turned him away but he kept coming back – every day - in a cheap, used three-piece suit, white shirt, red tie and some kind of wingtips he found in a thrift store. Finally, after getting Carson to promise never to return if he failed the test, a manager in the employment office let him take the DPAT and he aced it. Apparently, it was one of the highest scores they had ever seen.

"In those days, IBM was hiring anyone who could do well on the DPAT. They gave it to thousands of people, then tracked their programming careers. They found that higher education had little to do with programming success and that musicians seemed to be the best qualified for programming careers.

"Carson was sent to programming school, then for special training in database technology. By the end of the class, he was challenging the trainers with new ideas. They had him write code for a while, but it wasn't long before he transferred to Santa Theresa Labs in South San Jose and became one of their lead database designers. Since all major companies use huge databases, Carson got to know lots of people and after he introduced IBM to the concept of relational databases, he left the company and formed CIA as a one-man consulting firm.

"It's been going really well for him and I think Steve's idea of expanding the firm into a high-end consulting group is a good one, but I'm a bit worried. Carson's brother committed suicide last month and lately I get the sense that Carson feels he's on an inexorable path to the same self-destruction. I sure hope he can hold it together. He is CIA.

"Want to pick it up a bit?" Dan asked, noticing that I wasn't working too hard to keep up.

We raced back to Winchester Boulevard where we began our cool down. We started walking back to the office as the others caught up one by one.

"You know Rick used to be a great runner in college." Dan said. "He'll get it back."

Rick caught the rest of us five minutes later as we neared the office. It was clear that Dan and Rick were best friends. They kidded each other ruthlessly as we finished our workout.

"So, what do you think?" Steve asked.

"You've got a very sharp group of guys there," I replied.

"Got time for dinner?" he asked.

I said that I did and after showering, I got into Steve's new BMW.

"We've got to get you one of these," he said.

"What's that?" I asked.

"A company car." He responded. "You'll need something better than your Subaru wagon when you wine and dine our clients."

I ignored the comment about my beloved Subaru. This car had carried six hang gliders and seven people up a treacherous four-wheel drive road in the Owens Valley in hundred degree heat. With its all-wheel drive and low center of gravity, it had safely avoided a jack-knifed truck that was blocking most of Highway 88 during a near-whiteout blizzard on the way to Kirkwood. In driving rain over Highway 17, I had escaped major accidents as cars turned 360s in front of me. This was the perfect car. Why would I want anything else?

Steve pulled up in front of, surprise, surprise, L'Auberge du Soleil and handed his keys to the Valet. We entered the restaurant and the maitre d' greeted Steve, "Bon Soir, Monsieur Caples! Comment allez-vous?"

"Tres bien, Richard," Steve replied with terrible Aussie French accent. "Your best table for two, please!"

Richard led us to a quiet table in a secluded corner nook. Steve ordered 'his usual,' which turned out to be a martini with two olives, while I asked for a Perrier. We started an extraordinary meal with the same Mt. Eden Chardonnay, and truffle and escargot appetizers. Steve then proceeded to order a very fine Ridge Zinfandel for the main course. We had small glasses of Port with our exquisite chocolate desserts, and Richard offered a selection of brandies and cigars after the meal. I accepted a Grand Marnier and turned down the cigar while Steve asked for a cognac and a cigar I'd never heard of. This was clearly one of the best, and most expensive meals, I'd ever had.

"You could get used to this, I'm sure," Steve said. "We have an open account here, so you never have to pay a bill. Feel free to come here for lunch or dinner any time, with or without clients.

"So, when can you start?"

"I'll give a month's notice to Skynet tomorrow, and after I hear what they have to say, I'll get back to you with a start date," I answered, completely enthralled with my prospects.

Steve drove me back to my car, reminding me to start thinking about a new car. I went for a long walk to clear my head of the alcohol before my drive home. Highway 17 was nearly empty and I arrived home thirty-five minutes later. I sat down at the desk in the second bedroom that served as a study, wrote my resignation letter and went to bed dreaming of infinite possibilities.

11

The next morning I felt a bit queasy from the rich food the night before. I skipped my morning surf session and headed directly into Skynet, arriving just after six. As the first one to arrive, I had the place to myself. I went to my office and started drafting a transition plan, describing how, over the next few weeks, I would help Don and Madge find a replacement for me and would then train and hand off each project to my replacement. I had a few candidates in mind, former colleagues who knew software development processes and had experience managing groups of this size. They would need to be strong enough to keep Don in check, while giving him enough room to keep working with a small subset of the projects and the associated teams. The rest of the projects would need more direct management by a seasoned professional. I laid out each project, where it stood, and what the issues were with the personnel in each. At eight, Don and Madge strolled in and I asked to speak with them both.

We went into Don's office and I closed the door. I handed Don my resignation and the transition plan as I told them I thought it was time for me to be thinking about moving on. I walked them through the transition plan and described two candidates who could replace me. I suggested that these people could help them close their venture round. They asked me to excuse them and I went back to my office. Five minutes later, Madge walked in.

"Jack, we were thinking along these lines ourselves, so the timing is good. However, we won't need a transition. We'd like you to leave right now before the rest of the staff gets in. I'll get you a couple of boxes from the storeroom. Please pack and be out of here in the next half hour. I'll prepare your final check."

I was almost too shocked to speak, but managed, "Madge, I don't think this is a good idea. We could have a smooth transition. If I just leave, a number of the projects will be in trouble. Also, most of the programmers will wonder what happened, and the VCs will have second thoughts. Don't you think my plan would be better?"

"No," Madge replied. "You've had a good ride here but as you said, it's time for you to move on. Don can pick up everything and I don't think we'll have any problems with the programmers or VCs. This is the way we want to do this."

With that, she turned and walked out. There really wasn't any rancor in her voice. She appeared to handle this as if she were just paying a bill, which I guess she was when she returned with my final check and two boxes.

She waited in my office while I packed my things. I tried to protest, but she just shut me down. I felt like a criminal as I watched her make sure I didn't take any company property. When I was done, she walked me to the front door, and wished me luck in my career. Don didn't even come out to say goodbye.

Three years of my life. I had built the company from five programmers to nearly one hundred. Revenues had grown from three hundred thousand dollars to over twenty million, and all I had to show for it was my final paycheck and options that I needed to exercise within thirty days. I really didn't have the fifty thousand dollars to exercise the options at a dollar per share. I was just stunned that they could let me go so easily. Hadn't I helped build the company, didn't that mean something to them? I thought of the team as my family. I certainly spent more of my life with them than I did anyone else. Didn't I at least merit a going-away party?

On the other hand, I'd been through this before. Every time my father received a new assignment, we moved. One day I was in sunny Hawaii with my friends, the next I was in the cold, snowy Northeast, knowing no one.

I could do this. The answer is as Jean Paul Belmondo said in the original version of Breathless as he tore the rear view mirror from the car and threw it out the window, "What's behind you doesn't matter!"

Of course, in the same film, when the brakes of the car failed, he said, 'Brakes, who needs brakes? Cars are meant to go, not stop!"

12

I drove home checking the surf on the way. It was a typical Santa Cruz summer day, no surf and building winds. It wasn't a day for surfing.

I put on running clothes and drove along Highway 9, stopping and parking just outside the entrance to Henry Cowell Redwood State Park. I stretched and started running along the River Trail. In the winter after a big storm, runoff from over one hundred square miles of the Santa Cruz Mountains fills the San Lorenzo River. It often runs in torrents, overrunning its banks, ripping out the roots of giant redwood trees and propelling them towards the ocean like matchsticks. In tamer conditions, it's a great Class Three to Five whitewater river with some challenging rapids. In the summer it's a trickle of water with a few well-concealed swimming holes where you'll find naked people frolicking after braving a long hike and difficult climb to reach the water.

The River Trail runs along the river for about a mile. Most of the trees are scrub oak, large Douglas fir, Ponderosa pine, and redwoods. Most people think of redwood trees as rare, beautiful things. Those who live in the San Lorenzo River Valley know them for what they are: weeds. Clear a sunny area in the midst of redwoods, and by the next spring, hundreds or thousands of seedlings will spring up around you. By the following year, small trees are three to six feet high, and within five years, you can't see the sun. Nonetheless, the trees are beautiful. Countless animals make their homes in them. They often have dramatic bases that are split among multiple trees that appear to have fused; sometimes as many as ten trees grow as one. Actually the secondary trees have sprouted from burls that form when the tree is damaged. These large bulbous growths that make spectacular carvings or furniture when cut will harbor sprouts that grow into additional trees from the same trunk. The bases also create damp, moss-filled hollows that you can use as a shelter, almost a cave. The trees can grow a hundred feet tall or more with a hollow trunk that you could park a car in. Large stands of trees create rainforests in the Santa Cruz Mountains that collect water by trapping the moisture from the fog and dripping it onto the forest floor, even during the dry summers.

About a mile up the trail, you're surrounded by redwoods. The oak, pine and firs have disappeared. Redwood fronds cover the ground, making a soft, silent surface to run on. The air and ground are damp and unlike the scent of bursting pine you had in the sunny flats, you now smell mildew and decay. After you pass the steelhead trout hatchery, you cross a narrow hand-hewn bridge and start climbing; the trail winds its way up the side of a canyon created by a seasonal creek. After two miles and six hundred vertical feet, you meet Pipeline Road, the service access used by the Rangers. Soon after crossing the road, the redwoods disappear. The ground turns to soft deep sand. The few trees are scrub oak and pine, and still the trail climbs. You've just gone from damp rainforest to arid desert. At this point, I start thinking about walking. I'm only four miles into the run, but trying to run in soft sand up a steep hill is murder. On the other hand, it's just what I need to wear myself out.

When I reach the Observation Deck at the top of the park, I'm exhausted. I'm sweaty, grimy, and overheated. Fortunately, it's downhill all the way back. I choose from one of many descending single-track trails and pick up my pace as I wind my way back to the car. When I finish, I check my watch. I've run a little over eight miles in an hour. Not a great pace, but with the climb and the sand, I don't feel too bad. I head back home and as I walk in the door, the phone is ringing. I pick it up to the voice of Cheryl, my former top project lead. She's angry. She attacks with no chance to interrupt her.

"Jack, what the hell do you think you're doing? How could you just walk out on us? Do you have any idea what this means to us, to the company, to me? I can't believe you didn't talk to me. How can you abandon us to that flake?"

And she went on. And on. Then she hung up.

I took a shower, slipped into shorts and a polo shirt and called her back. Fortunately, Skynet had a direct dial system. I didn't have to go through the receptionist.

"Cheryl, don't hang up. You don't have the whole story here."

She didn't hang up, so I continued.

"Yes. I did give my notice today, but I gave a month's notice and a transition plan with recommendations for my replacement. I didn't mean to abandon you. They walked me to the door with no chance to talk to anyone. You saw that things weren't working out with Don. I felt I needed a change, but I would never just walk out on all of you."

After a brief silence on the other end of the line, Cheryl decided to speak to me, "Jack, I had a feeling it wasn't like they said it was, but I was just so shocked. I can't imagine what you're going through. After building this company, they just throw you out? They didn't even try to keep you? I don't know. Maybe this is worse than I thought.

"Listen, everyone is upset. They want to know what's going on. Can you meet us tonight after work, say seven at Maxwell's? Call it a going away party. We'll buy."

I agreed to meet them and called Steve to set a start date. When I told him what had happened, he suggested I take two weeks off and start work then. After realizing that I hadn't taken more than a day or two off at a time over the past three years, I agreed.

At seven that evening, I walked into Maxwell's, the upscale bar in the Red Lion Hotel. The hostess led me to a private room that I didn't know existed. There, I found twelve of my fifteen team leads. Pitchers of margaritas and beer littered the table as did several platters of fried calamari, zucchini sticks, and jalapeno poppers. I took a seat as Cheryl poured me a margarita. She recounted the events of the day.

Don and Madge had called an all-hands meeting and told the company that I had left. They would not be hiring a replacement as Don would take over all of the projects. They expected everything to be as it was before. When Cheryl and others had asked questions about specific projects and customers, they were told that Don would be coming up to speed and not to worry. This was not the time for questions. Everything would be clear in a few days.

After dismissing everyone, Don and Madge called the project leads, one by one, into Don's office for a status meeting. Don took notes and assured each that aside from now reporting to him, everything would be the same. By the end of the day, panic had begun to set in among the leads. Only a few had worked with Don, and while they agreed he was very smart, they also recognized that he had no ability to manage a customer project to completion. Cheryl mentioned that the missing project leads were afraid that they would lose their jobs if it was discovered they met with me and that all the project leads had asked their programmers not to come for that very reason. She asked if there was room for any of them where I was going.

I described CIA and what my new job was. I told them that I could not solicit them or I'd be subject to a lawsuit. However, I was permitted to tell them where I was going and if anyone wanted to contact me at CIA, they certainly could. I also suggested that they wait and see how things went at Skynet. If Don could pull it off, or if he realized his error in time and hired a replacement for me, the IPO was going to generate a lot of money for each of them. I encouraged them to stay and try to make it work. If it all failed, they could always come to me. They knew how to reach me.

After that, it turned into a friendly going-away party. We joked around, had lots of food and drink, and around ten everyone headed home. They had to go to work the next day. I didn't.

I decided to take a great hang gliding trip. I could start at Slide Mountain where you launch from the ski area parking lot and moments later are at twelve to fifteen thousand feet over Lake Tahoe and the rugged Eastern Sierra. I could travel south on Highway 395 to Lee Vining, the small town on the banks of Mono lake. It had another eastern Sierra launch three thousand feet over the lake, and after a few thermals, you found yourself over Tuolumne Meadows in Yosemite National Park. Then, on to the Owens Valley again for the 'big city' flying. In the Owens you could fly as high and as far as you wanted. The record was over three hundred miles. I could fly both ends of the valley, starting in the north near White Mountain Peak, then trying out Mount Whitney on the south end. Finally, on my way home I could check out the newly opened Dunlop at the base of King's Canyon. I'd heard good things about it. All in all, this trip would be a good way to clear my head and get ready for a new phase of my career.

CHAPTER 2

"When once you have tasted flight, you will forever walk the
earth with your eyes turned skyward, for there you have been and
there you will forever long to return"
-     Leonardo DaVinci

1

I returned from my trip late on Friday night. I was to start work at CIA Monday morning. While I had some great flights, I had also camped in the desert for ten days. I managed to bathe every day, usually in one of the many hot springs that dotted the Eastern Sierra, or in a hot creek in the Owens Valley, but the constant exposure to the sun, even with my dark sunglasses, left me with a non-stop headache. I was ready for the cool summertime coastal fog and I rolled down my windows when the mist speckled my windshield as I entered Santa Cruz.

The next morning I arose to overcast skies and temperatures in the fifties, a welcome change from the hundred to hundred and ten degree heat of the desert. I put my board in the car and headed north to Waddell Creek, both a hang gliding and great summer surfing spot.

While Santa Cruz has world-famous waves throughout most of the fall and winter resulting from swells generated by storms moving across the North Pacific and Gulf of Alaska, in the summertime, the surf is inconsistent at best. During our summer, it is winter in the Southern Hemisphere. Hence, large swells generated from storms there have to travel significantly greater distances, losing much of their power encountering adverse winds and currents on an eight to ten thousand mile journey to the California coast. Worse, the Monterey Peninsula blocks many of the swells generated by storms directly to our south or southeast. Often, however, Waddell Creek, which is west of the Monterey Peninsula, picks up some southerly surf. When large south swells hit the reefs south of the creek, long left-breaking waves form perfect tubular barrels. In fact, one portion of the reef is named Banzai because of its remarkable Banzai Pipeline-like tubes – at least we locals would like to believe they're comparable.

I made a U-turn across Highway 1 into the dirt 'parking area' across from the Big Creek lumber mill. Several cars were already there, so I knew the surf was at least rideable. As I suited up, I noticed a plane had been rolled out onto the small dirt airstrip. Most people don't know that this two hundred yard dirt path perched on the edge of a seventy-five foot cliff is an airstrip, but I knew the owner. I grabbed my board, locked my car, and jogged over to the plane.

"Nice day to fly," I said to the lean, well-muscled middle-aged man who was conducting a pre-flight of the plane.

"Jack, it's been a while. Not flying today?" he replied.

"No Bud, the winds are forecast to be down all day and since there's a south swell running, I thought I'd grab a couple of hours in the surf."

As a hang gliding site, Waddell is a bit unusual. You launch from the seventy-five foot bluff directly over the ocean. With a good onshore wind, you rise smoothly a few hundred feet above the cliff. There are no thermals here, simply wind hitting a vertical face and being deflected upwards. Across Highway 1, behind the lumber mill, a ridge rises over a thousand feet. On a good day, you can cross the highway and ride the lift up over the top of the ridge. The ridge sits above a valley and below the larger Santa Cruz Mountains. In the summer, the air inland warms while the breeze coming off the ocean is quite cool. Because of the shape and position of the ridge, warm air often pushing from inland toward the sea meets the cooler air and, of course, rises above it. For a hang glider, this is a perfect condition. If you can make the transition from the cool air into the warmer air, you can climb thousands of feet and travel in smooth warm air above the thermal boundary. On this day, however, there was no coastal breeze and Waddell was not flyable, at least for a hang glider.

Bud offered to take me for a short flight, but the surf beckoned.

Bud McCrary is an amazing person. During the nineteenth century, his family purchased much of the Santa Cruz Mountains and began logging. Unlike the giant timber companies who lease national forest lands, the McCrary's own their land. They treated timber as a crop – one with a long maturation period. Instead of clear cutting, they rotated areas so that over the course of many lifetimes, they would continue to have trees to harvest. Today, over a hundred years later, Bud and his brother Lud have inherited the family business and not only continued in the conservationist tradition, they have expanded on it.

They had recently donated the coastal section of what is now Big Basin State Park to the State of California. This addition opened a beautiful valley along Waddell Creek to the public and enabled the Park to create the Big Basin and Skyline to the Sea trails. Bud's wife Emma is a consummate horsewoman, so the family created public riding trails throughout their property and in parkland and open space areas through Santa Cruz, Santa Clara, and San Mateo counties. When it was recognized that steelhead and salmon catches had declined, the McCrarys set up fish hatcheries on multiple creeks of their property and encouraged neighboring landowners to do the same. They opened their land to hikers and campers and are the most generous people I have ever met.

Bud even went so far as to permit the Monterey Bay Hang Gliding Association to use his property as a launch and landing. In addition to the launch on the bluff, Bud opened up a launch from the top of a ridge a thousand feet above Waddell Creek. Where most landowners feared lawsuits from injuries in risk sports like Hang Gliding, Bud was well aware of the new State laws that encouraged landowners to open their property for recreation and indemnified them as long as they were not negligent in their upkeep of the opened areas.

We had even convinced Bud to try Hang Gliding, but we couldn't get him to completely give up his engines. It was impressive to watch him take off from this short landing strip, but even more impressive to watch him land, skirting the trees at the south end of the runway, avoiding the rotor, the wind phenomenon created behind a sheer cliff edge that could slam a plane or glider into the dirt, and somehow coming to a stop just before the runway turned into ice plant and poison oak. I had flown with him a few times and it always seemed a miracle that we survived the landings. You may have heard the term 'postage stamp' landing area to describe a tiny airfield. Since Bud's runway was narrower than his plane, tear that postage stamp in half vertically, put half of it on a cliff edge with the other half hanging off, and you have a good idea of Bud's landing skills.

Waddell Creek itself starts in the mountainous area of Big Basin Redwoods State Park. Several waterfalls along the creek beckon photographers and overheated hikers. In dry years they dwindle to trickles in the summer, but become spectacular raging torrents again from late fall through early spring. The creek has carved out a beautiful canyon filled with wide open meadows and stands of pine and fir trees. As it nears the ocean, the area around the creek becomes marshy and is filled with birds. Ducks, egrets, great blue herons, and some ocean waterfowl make their nests among the reeds, brush and trees. Precipitous tree-covered ridges over a thousand feet high guard the south and north sides of the canyon so its only access is from the ocean, or through the trails from the Big Basin Park Headquarters some eleven miles to the east.

The creek passes under a low Highway 1 bridge and seeps into the sand during the summer. To the south of the creek is a wide expanse of beach that runs several miles along spectacular cliffs with waterfalls and sand dunes abutting it. There are some great places to sunbathe and even better places to jump off the cliff or the top of a hundred foot sand dune and fall tumbling into the soft sand below.

To the north of the creek, the highway passes under three hundred foot vertical cliffs that regularly close the highway when heavy rains cause cascading rocks to cover the roadway. The prime surfing area is a few hundred yards south of the creek below the lumber mill.

I walked down the small road that Bud had created to provide beach access. I passed the brown pelicans standing on the shoreline rocks and paddled out. Nearly endless lines of black cormorants flew south, so low they almost touched the water; the rapid beating of their wings sounded like frantic whispers. Pelicans circled and dived, plunging into the water only a few feet outside the surf lineup. The smelt were running and birds of all kinds knew about the feast. It was good to be back in the cool moist air. I didn't miss the desert.

After two hours of good surf, it got too crowded for me so I went home and showered. I checked the local paper and saw that my favorite alternative theatre, the Nickelodeon, was showing a Bertrand Blier film. With my minor in French, I had come to love French film. Worse, I was a sucker for French romantic comedies, and the idea of spending a few hours in the dark immersed in another language – pure escapism - seemed just the thing to help recover from the non-stop sun of the Owens Valley.

2

After a weekend of several films and the cool fogs of Santa Cruz, I was ready for work on Monday. I decided to go in early and face the Monday morning commute over Highway 17. I realized that I had not set a time to show up for work at CIA.

I walked into the office at 8:30 and Donna greeted me by name.

"There's no one here except me and Pam," she explained when I looked down the halls and saw only darkened offices. Ronn is at ALM, but should be back about lunchtime, Steve and the guys are at HP, Carson asked if you could come by his apartment at seven this evening for dinner – I'll give you directions - and Pam, our controller and head of admin is waiting for you. She will get you set up. Welcome!"

The CIA space was U-shaped with offices around the outside and the reception area, bathrooms and a kitchen in the middle. Carson's office was the first one on the right as you entered, and Steve and the others' offices were also on the right, down the hall. As Donna led me down the hall on the left, I realized that I hadn't seen this side of the space before. Where the windows in the offices on the right side looked out over Vasona Park, the opposite side revealed only the parking lot and street.

We reached the first office, which was out of site of the reception area, and Donna knocked on the door. Inside a tall, thin woman in her mid-thirties began to rise from her desk to greet me. Pam Mason was conservatively dressed in a dark blue suit with a small-collared white blouse that was closed at the neck. Even sitting at her desk, she had kept her suit jacket on. She appeared to be of Basque or Castilian heritage. Her dark hair was pulled back in a tight bun, and aside from the small posts in her ears, I couldn't spot any jewelry. Her makeup was applied sparingly. From my male perspective, I could only spot mascara which she had used to darken lashes above her already deep brown eyes. She narrowed her brow as she quickly appraised my appearance, and held out her hand as she said, somewhat skeptically, "You must be Jack, the great company builder. I'm Pam, the Carson Ingles Associates Controller."

Compared to the other offices I'd seen in CIA, Pam's was quite spare. Furnishings consisted of a black metal desk with a fake wood laminate top, three black metal four-drawer filing cabinets which blocked the view out the windows, a metal bookcase, a simple, 'non-executive' desk chair and two identical visitors' chairs in front of the desk. There were no plants, no artwork, no pictures on the desk, only papers, a mechanical pencil, a computer, an empty Inbox and an Outbox with several documents in it. This was in stark contrast with the rest of the offices I'd seen. All of them had rosewood desks, rosewood credenzas, sleek leather executive chairs, some piece of modern art, oriental carpets and lots of plants.

I noted the firm, confident handshake and took one of the proffered chairs. "I hope I'll prove to be an asset," I replied, immediately realizing what a stock, interview-like answer that was.

Pam got right down to business; no idle conversation to be had here. She gave me employment forms, explaining each one, including the Patent, Confidentiality, and Non-disclosure Agreement, then led me to the corner office next to hers. She pointed out the computer, mentioning that it was a CPM system and that it used WordStar software for word processing. She asked me to complete the forms and return them to her and told me that Steve had indicated that I'd be spending the next few days writing letters to my contacts indicating I'd changed companies and could now be reached at CIA. She explained that although I couldn't solicit clients from my previous employers, if my letters were just informative about my change and about my new company, but did not actually ask them for business, there could be no legal ramifications from Skynet. Donna would take care of mailing and could assist me with the system and printing if I had any questions. My business cards were in the box on the desk. I thanked her and she turned and left. All business.

Steve and I hadn't discussed titles so I opened the business cards and was quite surprised. My title was 'Master of the Universe!' I looked further into the box and discovered that only ten cards included that title. The rest described my position as 'Senior Consultant.' No doubt about it, Steve had a sense of humor.

I filled out the employment forms and dropped them in Pam's Inbox. Since I had never used WordStar before, I asked Donna to help me with basic commands. She also showed me a nice feature that let me create a 'form' letter with placeholders for the name, address, and greeting. I could key in all of my contacts into a separate file, then run a merge against a 'form' letter and it would produce customized letters for each of my contacts. She suggested that when I was done, or had a dozen or more done, I copy both files onto a floppy disk, and let her run the merge and print the letters on company stationery. She'd pass them back to me for signature and then mail them.

She handed me a box of floppy disks, but I noticed they were not so floppy. Over the years, I'd always worked with five and a quarter inch diskettes. They were thin and flexible, so the name floppy made sense. This system used the new three and a half inch square, hard-shelled disks. The actual data storage was protected in inflexible plastic. Little did I know that these would one day become the standard 'floppy' disks.

I was deep into data entry a few hours later and looked up when I heard a light tapping on the doorframe to my office. There stood Ronn with a brace on his leg, his right arm in a sling, and a big smile pushing out from under the mustache. "I'm glad you made it," he said. "And yes, I dislocated my shoulder going head first off Bessy again. I had no problems playing with my cast or this new leg brace that I have to wear for three more weeks, but I landed wrong when I tried to protect the leg and my arm went backwards. This time I'm out of the game for at least a month. Next week I start physical therapy. I know they're going to torture me, but with the Nationals coming up in three months, I need to get my shoulder back."

"What, you're not going to try to play left-handed?" I joked.

"Actually, I did try that over the weekend, but I still need my right arm for the reins and I couldn't even hit the ball when it was standing still with no competition," he said with all seriousness. "I'm just going to have to wait it out. Let's get some lunch and talk."

We headed over to the company cafeteria, L'Auberge du Soleil. Richard greeted both of us by name and showed us to a table. I thanked him in French and we engaged in a short conversation where I told him that I had spent six months surfing, reading and eating in the Basque region of France, and he told me that he had grown up in Sarlat, in the Pays D'Oc, attended a culinary academy in Paris, then moved to the States to try out his own variation of Country French cuisine. He appreciated the use of ingredients he had sampled in Provence, but loved the spiciness of the Basque meals, especially the seafood. That explained the large portions! Richard was not only maitre d', he was also head chef and owner. I was glad he had met with success and his food made me reminisce about the time I had spent in Southern France.

I had taken two quarters off from the University during my third year. I was having difficulty deciding on a career, as I seemed to love every class I took. Math, Computer Science, Comparative Literature, French, Philosophy, Political Science, Economics; it just didn't seem to matter. Of course in spite of this, I majored in surfing. An uncle suggested I take some time, get surfing out of my system and decide what I wanted to do, so I lived on pennies for several months while working full time and saved enough for six months in the south of France. I lived in a small town called Guethery, a few doors down from the sixteenth century church that dominated the village on the top of a hill overlooking some of the world's best surf. The Basque region, at the border of France and Spain on the Atlantic straddles the ten thousand foot peaks of the Pyrenees. It is bounded by the ocean to the west and there is a break in the continental shelf that focuses waves on this part of the coast. It was not unusual to see thirty-foot surf there. To the east of the coast, white stucco homes with red tiled roofs peppered the rolling green hills. Instead of street numbers, houses had names, strange names like Txamarka or Bostako Etxea, with lots of Xs and Ks, letters you don't often see in French or Spanish.

The Basque women were stunningly beautiful, raven-haired and dark-eyed. The food was nothing like anything I had eaten before. They seem to have taken French country dishes like white bean cassoulet and added unusual spices to create unique dishes. Since most of the locals were fishermen, seafood reigned supreme, topped with pungent red sauces.

My days were spent surfing; my nights reading, and the total immersion in the language and culture finally helped me know what I wanted to do with my life: I wanted to make enough money to be able to retire and live an ex-patriot life in the Basque region of France. I decided to settle on a major that would lead to wealth and my return to paradise. Computer Science seemed like the right way to go.

During my months in France, I studied the history of the region. To the east was the area Richard was from. The Pays D'Oc was the site of the Hundred Years War. Control of the area passed between the British and French countless times during the conflict.

It sits between the much-romanticized Provence and the Basque region. The hallmark of the region is the Dordogne River, which runs through a verdant, tree-covered valley dominated by troglodyte caves on the cliffs above. Countless ruined and restored castles dot the countryside with several spectacular battlements acting as sentinels over the river. Since it wasn't far away from Guethery, I was able to kayak the Dordogne River a few times. There wasn't a lot of whitewater, but every month at full or new moon, there was a strange phenomenon called a Tidal Bore. A Tidal Bore is a wave created by the radical changes in tides at the mouth of a large river. They only occur at high latitudes in places like France, England, Canada and Alaska. The waves can travel over a hundred miles up a river, and a few kayakers have ridden a Tidal Bore over twenty-five miles. I only managed three or four miles the few times I tried it, but what a way to experience the Dordogne Valley! Recently, I've heard that even longboard surfers have discovered these waves and if lucky, can now experience the longest rides of their lives.

I explained all this to Ronn as we started our appetizers. Instead of wine, which Steve seemed to drink at lunch, I asked for Perrier, and Ronn chose iced tea. I mentioned to Ronn that I was going to Carson's that evening for dinner.

"You're not going to believe his place," he said. "First, he lives with his girlfriend, Nancy. Actually, I think I'll hold off and let you discover what Carson's life is like. You might end up choosing what he has over a future in France. You guys have a lot in common and I suspect it wouldn't be hard for you to duplicate his success."

"Okay," I replied. "But what about Steve? He certainly comes across as a likeable type, but there's something I can't quite put my finger on. Some of his affectations seem a bit pretentious and I get the impression he's putting on a show every time we meet."

Ronn smiled. "You've already picked up on part of the dynamic here. I'm not sure it's a bad thing, but Carson and Steve are polar opposites. Carson is incredibly bright and has an easy-going integrity in everything he does. Success has come to him naturally as a result of his honest work. I don't want to color your impressions of him; you'll know more when you meet him.

"Steve, on the other hand, is ambitious. He's decided he's

going to be successful and I don't think he'll stop at anything to get there. Most people just see an Australian good ol' boy with a ready smile and charm up the wazoo. They don't realize that there's non-stop calculation going on behind the grin. He's always looking for the edge.

"Of course if you want to grow a company, you need that kind of attitude. Carson has personal success with his own consulting, but he wasn't building a company with futures for other people. Steve is doing that. But Steve sees people as stepping stones. That's why he chose you. He thinks you can give him a big leg up. I don't think he's particularly malicious – at least as long as you're on his side and don't cross him. If you team up with him, I think you'll find that you can gain a lot from his drive.

"Right now, I don't work with him much. He's locked in at HP. Carson set me up with my current gig and I've spent a lot of time with him. Still, he's not someone who'll ever be a multimillionaire entrepreneur – not unless he hires someone like Steve to lead the charge, which he did."

Well, every company had politics. I hoped that the relationship between Steve and Carson was synergistic. I really didn't want to end up in the middle of a power struggle. Right now Carson had control. I hadn't even met the guy, but everyone seemed in awe of him, even Steve. Steve was in a cage at HP, and I had the key to let him out. I hoped I wasn't about to open a Pandora's box.

3

After a great lunch, Ronn dropped me back at the office. I spent the afternoon getting dozens of addresses entered into the system. I handed Donna floppy after floppy. I entered names while she printed, packaged and stamped, and by the end of the afternoon, she had a large stack of envelopes ready to go out. I asked Donna what Carson's favorite bottle of wine was and she suggested that if I wanted to bring a gift to dinner I take flowers instead. Carson was a wine connoisseur and had quite a collection. I'd have a hard time picking, and perhaps being able to afford, anything interesting that he didn't already have. It seemed a bit strange to buy flowers for my new boss, but I decided to follow her advice. I stopped at a local florist and picked up a fall mix, then drove over to Carson's apartment.

I pulled up to the guard gate at the entrance to Vasona Terrace, a very private community that bordered Vasona Park. Although I'd driven by this entrance several times, I had never noticed it. I didn't even know that there was such an upscale complex in Los Gatos.

The guard called Carson for approval and after giving me directions and instructions on where to park, he opened the gate and let me through. I parked in a visitor's space and found my way up to Carson's apartment. A very attractive blond, who I took to be Carson's girlfriend Nancy, answered the door. We introduced ourselves as she invited me in. Nancy was of medium height and clothed in a white cashmere sweater with a tight fitting dark skirt. Her blond hair was pulled back into a ponytail and her blue eyes bespoke a solid intelligence and supreme self-confidence. Everything about her said old money, not that I'd had much experience with that sort of person.

If you remember my background, you may recall that I am the son of an enlisted man in the military. I grew up poor and considered my current lifestyle with sports toys, new car, a small house on the Westside of Santa Cruz, and three month's salary in the bank to be quite a step up. I was completely unprepared for Carson's lifestyle.

The floor to ceiling glass windows looked out on Vasona Lake. The apartment was done in primary colors with cherry wood furniture. One entire wall was taken up by a huge aquarium filled with exotic fishes. As I looked at the art on the walls, the sculptures and the antiquities that dotted tables around the living room, I realized that the plush office where I now worked was an extension of Carson's home, which I later learned was one of two. This one was his weekday home.

Nancy led me to the study, which was much more. Today, many homes have home theatres, but in 1984, I'd never seen one. Carson was about to insert a golden disc about the size of an LP record into a machine. He turned as he heard us approach, put the disc down and greeted me warmly in a sonorous baritone voice.

Ronn was right. Carson was a young version of Santa Claus. His full brown beard framed his face and seemed to intensify blue eyes that revealed a distinguished, yet relaxed, self-confident contentment. Curly dark brown hair was pulled back in a low revolutionary-war styled ponytail. His portly body was dressed in a dark slacks and a colorfully patterned light sweater, suede slippers covered his feet. His expansive energy and contagious enthusiasm seemed to fill the room. I had met a few charismatic individuals before, but Carson was beyond compare.

"Watch this," he said as he inserted the disc into a machine.

Instantly the large screen across the room jumped to life. An icebreaker was pushing its way through ice floes. A combination of snow and aquamarine water cascaded off the bow as it moved forward. Penguins and seals cavorted not far away. Classical music served as the background for a narrative describing this Antarctic expedition. But more interesting than the subject matter was the resolution of the picture. Most televisions and even movie screens are composed of small granular colored pixels that are plainly evident when you approach, and they only merge together to create a recognizable image from a distance. Even close up, this four-foot diagonal screen seemed to display a perfect image with remarkable clarity.

"Pretty amazing, huh?" Carson said proudly. "This is my new toy. I'm doing research on video storage formats and media for Sony."

Over the course of the coming months, I would learn that Carson often chose his clients so that he could get cutting-edge, experimental toys from them. He would do product and technology evaluations and the companies would happily donate some sample product, even when that product cost tens of thousands of dollars once it reached the market. Of course, many clever toys never received enough demand to actually be mass-produced by the companies, so Carson also ended up with many interesting museum pieces of failed technology.

Nancy took drink orders and tended bar while Carson began to interview me. We discussed companies we knew in common. Carson solicited opinions from me on specific new technologies, how I thought they could be positioned, and how some small companies might stack up and compete with the larger players in the industry. Nancy wasn't silent throughout this discussion. She would regularly jump in and confirm or question market numbers or financials that Carson and I put forth.

"She's an investment banker in high tech," Carson told me, smiling at Nancy. I again saw pride in his look.

At one point during the course of the conversation, he handed me a menu (that had no prices!) from Le Casque d'Or, a well-known posh Los Gatos restaurant. Nancy called in our orders and an hour later, not only did the meal show up, but so did a staff of caterers. They brought out appetizers, set up a table, and then served us dinner and dessert. As we moved back to the living room, they cleared the table, I heard some washing noises in the kitchen, and they disappeared.

"We really don't have room for a live-in staff, and I'm not here all the time anyway, so this is a nice compromise," Carson explained.

"But on to business. I can see from our discussions that you'll make a fine consultant. In your past positions, your primary job was to convince customers that you had the right answers to their problems, then to sell them a solution that your teams would implement. In our world, you get paid for the first part. The customers will pay for your opinion and then you can choose whether you take the relationship to the next step. In the past, I've always elected to do strategic level architecture of the solutions along with market positioning, but have left the implementations to their in-house staff or I've recommended contracting firms. Steve has convinced me that we can grow a larger business if you, he, and I get paid for finding these opportunities, then use our own hired staff to do the implementations. This is what we're doing at HP and what I have Ronn doing at ALM.

"While you're drumming up new opportunities over the next few weeks, I have a project I need some help with at ALM. As you know, they build private telephone systems for large companies. With the advent of the PC, they've expressed interest in adding a small PC to each phone. They'd like to combine voice over the telephone with data access to IBM and other mainframe computers in a single desktop box. I don't know much about IBM networking or how we'd mix data and voice. I'm not even sure it's a good idea. So, first you'll need to determine the feasibility of the idea, come up with a technical design, then do some preliminary market analysis to see if this would be viable. I can help you with the market sizing.

"The deliverable for this project will be a report describing your results, and you'll be presenting the report to the executive committee at ALM. Keep in mind that they're not paying by the page. They're paying for your expertise. In some of my projects, the final report after months of work contained just one word: either 'Yes' or 'No.' We often bid fixed price efforts, but in this case, I think we'll go hourly - $300 per hour, so please keep track of your time. That doesn't just mean hours you're on site, writing at the office, or doing field research, it also means any time you're thinking about the project, even in the shower."

We finished the evening with brandy. Carson offered me a cigar. "It's Cuban, you know." But I declined. We agreed to meet at ALM at nine the next morning to get started.

I reviewed the evening and realized that I was pleased and excited by my new opportunity. For the first time in my life, I had a mentor. I'd served as mentor many times in my young career, but never before had I met someone from whom I felt I could learn so much. I could see the brilliance in the man, his casual confidence, and his love of the finer things in life. It barely troubled me at all that he could cross the line a bit.

4

Surfing is not what most people think it is. Films and popular culture have presented it as either Beach Blanket Bingo-like parties on the beach with everyone sharing waves, surf odysseys where you meet friendly people around the world as you search for the perfect wave, or hard core life-threatening big wave surfing, where one mistake means certain death.

In reality, surfing is much less romantic. First and foremost, it is the hardest sport I've ever tried. You're skiing intermediate and advanced slopes after a week or two of trying. You can be soaring a hang glider within a couple of months of your first run down a sand dune. You can be paddling intermediate Class 3 whitewater after several days on a river. But with surfing, after two or three years of practicing every day, you might be an intermediate level surfer.

Part of this is strength, conditioning, teaching your body to do something unnatural, learning the timing the breaking waves and understanding the differences between waves on a beach break, reef, and point. You also need to know about tide changes, rip tides, wind forecasts, storm and swell prediction, and even water pollution levels which rise on the season's first big swell or first major rain, both of which wash decaying matter from the hillsides and beaches into the ocean. I've already mentioned sharks. But more than that, it's cutthroat competition. There are tens of thousands of surfers and they all expect to catch every wave that rolls in.

Most surf spots have locals. These are the surfers who surf there every day. Take a wave that 'belonged' to a local, and you will be physically attacked by his friends when you get out of the water. Your car will be vandalized; your girlfriend threatened.

Even when you're a local, there are often so many people in the water that you'll be lucky to get more than five waves in an hour. With fifty-degree water and wind, even with your wetsuit, you get out of the water so cold that you can't put your fingers together. You might even have to ask a stranger to open the door to your car because you can't grip and turn the key yourself. And then there are the bad days. You paddle out, almost reaching the lineup – the place just outside the breaking waves where you wait to catch the oncoming swells, and a much larger than normal set of waves approaches. You use all your strength to try to paddle over the wave, but it breaks on top of you. You think this is okay because you and your board have punched through the wall of the wave and you are in the sunlight beyond. Unfortunately, the force of the wave and the vacuum created as it tubes and barrels towards the beach grabs hold of your feet which are not all the way through. The wave sucks you back into the hollowed hole from the collapsing tube and you are rolled over and over for what seems like minutes, even though it is only twenty or thirty seconds. You finally get free of the wave's clutches and float to the surface. You quickly grab a breath as the next wave in the set breaks right in front of you. You attempt to duck dive, to force you and your buoyant board deep under the oncoming wave, but when it's big, you can't get down deep enough. The wave grabs you and your board and hurls you shoreward in a mass of churning whitewater. You're thrown upside down, sideways, in circles, sometimes bouncing off the bottom, stuffing your sinuses with water that will flow freely from your nose later in the day when you bend over to kiss someone. When you finally escape this wave, there are more. You may successfully duck dive, but with each successive wave, you lose more ground; you're almost back to the beach.

On a bad day, it's all about luck and timing. You try to paddle out again, and just as you reach the lineup, you repeat the experience. After several times, you're exhausted. Shoulders ache. Arms refuse to move. As you try to get speed to paddle over the next set, you're too weak and it just gets worse and worse. In spite of all the energy expended, you're now cold. You've spent more time below the water than above it and the wetsuit doesn't help much. Tired and cold, if you're a real surfer, you don't give up. Ultimately, you luck out, there's a longer lull than normal and you make it out to a chorus of, "Man, you really got worked in there!" And now you face the competition for waves.

Maybe you get lucky. Maybe your friends feel sorry for you and let you have one of the best waves of the day. You drop to the bottom of the overhead wave and look upwards. You aim your board at the feathering lip and feel the acceleration of you and your board as you rise upwards to meet it. With perfect timing, your board and the wave meet and the falling water forces you back to the bottom. You repeat this over and over. It's a dance. You're in perfect harmony. You look down the line of the wave and you see a concave section ahead. It's already starting to pitch over. You have a choice. You could turn down and safely end your ride as the rest of the wave closes out ahead. Instead, you go for it, crouching, then extending your body forward to add speed. As you reach the edge of the concavity, you squat low and sure enough, you're inside the wave with small window of light out ahead. You hold on and pop out a few seconds later to imagined cheers from the beach. Of course, no one saw it. The guys in the lineup can't see the front of the wave and are looking at the next ones in the set anyway. It's yours and only yours, and somehow even for just one perfect wave, the struggle and fatigue and stuffed sinuses were worth it.

5

A few days later, I was in the office working on the ALM project. Things were going very smoothly. The ALM executives trusted Carson's recommendations and had made their design teams available to me. I was making excellent progress and expected to have my preliminary presentation done within a week.

I looked up from my computer to find Steve at my door.

"Come on Jack, it's almost seven," he said. Let's go grab a beer!"

I told Steve that I really couldn't stay long since I had to drive back over the hill to Santa Cruz. We took separate cars and I followed him to a bar near Steven's Creek Reservoir called The Red Cockade. Once inside it looked to be some kind of cross between a western bar and a yuppie hangout. The CIA guys were seated around a table with two pitchers of dark beer before them. Rick got up as I approached and offered me his seat. He needed to get home to his wife.

Steve sat down and elbowed me in the ribs. "Jack, get a load of those Sheilas over there!" he said indicating a blonde and a brunette sipping glasses of white wine a few tables away.

I nodded, then started talking to Dan and Ronn who gave me updates on their projects. At some point, the conversation turned to politics and we all debated the intelligence of Ronald Reagan, the United States President. Through the course of our conversation, I realized that although Dan probably held the most liberal views among the group, he seemed to appreciate the Reagan presidency the most. Although he hadn't voted for him, he defended his intelligence and recounted several impromptu speeches where Reagan came up with obscure facts when questioned by reporters. And although Reagan had campaigned on an ultra-conservative platform, he had refrained from implementing anything seriously conservative. He also seemed to have surrounded himself with trustworthy staff and delegated responsibility well. Ronn liked him because he was a cowboy. We kidded him, as always, about his own name, Ronn Regan.

Meanwhile, Steve called the waiter over and ordered 'two more of the same for the pretty ladies at the table across the way.' When their drinks arrived, they looked his way and beckoned him over. "Duty calls," he said as he rose and crossed over to their table.

At my look of astonishment, Dan said, "Get used to it. This is Steve. Even though he's married, I guess he never got over being an Aussie playboy. The women love his accent."

When I left about an hour later, I looked over at Steve. The women were laughing at some comment he had made and his right hand was casually resting on the thigh of the blonde. Shaking my head and nodding at the guys, I left and drove home over Highway 17.

6

On my way to work the next morning, my reliable Subaru started to make a banging noise underneath. It wasn't too bad going downhill, but when I stepped on the accelerator, it felt like something was going to burst through the floor. I was pretty sure I knew what the problem was because this had happened once before. In fact, as I looked at the mileage, I realized that previously, the problem occurred at forty-four thousand miles, and I now had almost ninety thousand on the car.

I slowed down and we limped into the Subaru dealer. I told them I thought that the CV joint was going out. They crawled under the car, moved the driveshaft from side to side and confirmed that it looked like the constant-velocity joint was failing.

The Subaru was the first mass produced all-wheel drive car (not counting the Jeep). It is similar to a four-wheel drive vehicle except that it's always in four-wheel drive. You don't have to change from normal two-wheel drive to four when you go off road or when the weather turns bad. Even better, you don't have to lock the front wheel hubs as you did on four-wheel drive vehicles back then.

The CV joint sits on the driveshaft and the driveshaft is enclosed in a tubular metal sleeve. The joint is about three inches in diameter and looks like two large circular links in a chain. Its job is to maintain a constant rate of turning between the front and rear differentials. When the joint weakens, the driveshaft becomes loose in the middle and it bangs on the sleeve. If you don't replace it, the joint will break and your car will stop. It might also damage the differentials.

The dealer said that they should be able to have the car ready for me by the end of the day. I gratefully accepted a ride to the office and their offer to pick me up when the car was ready.

Once in the office, I spent the day working with Carson on the ALM project. We had scheduled three presentations, one for each stage of our progress on the contract and we were printing and copying our slides onto transparencies, then doing dry runs of the presentation.

A little after 4 o'clock, Donna interrupted us to say that the Subaru dealer was on the phone. The dealer apologized, but the truck that was supposed to deliver the part hadn't arrived. It had mechanical problems on its next-to-last stop. A new truck would be there in the morning with the part, so I couldn't pick up the car until late the next day. They'd send a car to pick me up and would give me a loaner car.

I went back to Carson's office and apologized, "Carson, my car's going to be in the shop until tomorrow so I need to go down there to get a loaner car. They close at five, so I have to cut our session short."

"Jack, believe me, I know car problems. My Jag is in the shop at least half the time. But when it's out, boy what a great car. It's not like driving anything else. The Brits know how to spoil you like the Germans never will. Speaking of the Jag, why don't we keep working and you can just take the Jag home."

I started to protest, but Carson just cut me off, insisting I borrow his car. I called the dealer and canceled the ride, and when I returned to his office, Carson had opened a bottle of wine.

"It's another one from my Ridge subscription. This time it's a Cab, but it's not York Creek, so I suspect it won't be fantastic."

We tasted the wine and agreed that while very good, it wasn't a classic Ridge. Of course, what did I know? I wasn't a wine connoisseur – yet! An hour later, we finished the first of the three presentations and Carson drove me to his apartment in his 8-series BMW.

The '84 Jaguar XJ-12 was much bigger than I expected. In fact, it was larger than any car I had ever driven. Carson handed me the keys. I opened the door and slid into the luxurious interior. Carson went around to the passenger side, got in and explained the seat adjustment, location of the lights and parking brake, the operation of the stereo system and the built-in car phone.

"It just came out of the shop, so I'm not anticipating any problems, but if you do have a problem, just dial 1 and send on the car phone and it will call the salesman who will arrange road service and a replacement car for you. Assuming it runs well, keep it as long as you need to."

"You have your Jaguar salesman's number programmed on your car phone?" I asked incredulously.

"He knows I'll continue to buy new model high end Jags from him and that I've already sent several people his way. Given the time this car has spent in the shop, it's the least he can do. I love this car in spite of its mechanical weakness," he said fondly, almost as if he were talking about a faithful aging dog. "Enjoy the drive. You might become a convert!" Carson stepped out of the car and closed the door. I was enveloped in silence. Even though the car was running, I couldn't hear the engine. Carson waved as I pulled away. I was touched by his generosity. He didn't know me well, but he had lent me one of his most prized possessions.

Over the years, I'd learn that this was the epitome of Carson. He had succeeded in business in spite of being scrupulously honest and truthful. He projected his comfortable self-assurance on everyone he met and he assumed that others were like him. Somehow, he felt that his material acquisitions should be shared and he found great pleasure in seeing his friends and acquaintances enjoy things that they likely couldn't afford on their own. It was benevolence without arrogance. Carson shared openly and I never saw him exhibit any type of possessiveness. As I think back, I realize that I never saw Carson angry either. He accepted people's mistakes and failings with understanding.

I stepped on the accelerator as I took the onramp to Highway 17. This wasn't a car, it was a rocket ship. With twelve cylinders, I was doing seventy miles per hour before I merged into traffic. I assumed that such a large car would be difficult to handle in the curves. I was wrong again. As I accelerated on the backside of each curve, the Jag lowered, hugging the road with no signs of slipping. The sheer power of the acceleration combined with the centrifugal force reminded me of the experience of catching a thermal. Driving a car like this could be addictive.

Part of the problem with not being able to hear the engine or wind noise is that you lose track of speed. As red lights flashed in my rearview mirror, I looked at the speedometer and discovered I was going seventy-two in a fifty zone. In California, you can be cited for reckless driving if you are caught traveling more than twenty miles over the speed limit. This could be bad news.

I pulled over in the next turnout and found Carson's registration in the glove compartment. When the CHP officer approached, I handed him my license and the registration.

"I've got you at sixty-nine in a fifty zone," he said. Then noticing the mismatch between the names on the registration and license, he asked, "Not your car?"

"My Subaru broke down today and my boss lent me his car.

I'm sorry. I drive 17 every day, but in this thing, I lost track of my speed."

"He lent you an XJ-12? How lucky can you get?" he asked incredulously. "Look, I don't usually do this, but I'm not going to ruin your day. I'll let you slide on this one. Just slow down and keep an eye on the speedometer. Okay?"

I thanked him profusely and continued my drive home, keeping my speed at fifty until the highway became freeway again. I don't think the car liked going so slowly.

7

Over the next couple of months, things went exactly as planned. I finished my first assignment with ALM and they loved the results. We proposed that we supply them a team to help them build the product we had designed. They not only agreed, they extended our consulting agreement by asking me to look at building additional products to help integrate their system into other corporate networking environments.

Many of my contacts were ecstatic to hear I was consulting with CIA and had offered us contracts. One of these was Paul Franklin, a friend of Georgette's who was now leading the data division of the post-divestiture efforts at Pacific Bell, the former Pacific Telephone portion of AT&T. Historically, Pacific Telephone as part of AT&T had only supplied telephone circuits to homes and businesses. Paul wanted to look at all sorts of value added services that the new Pacific Bell could provide. He hired us to come up with some ideas.

This was the contract that allowed Steve to leave HP. He quickly promoted Dan to account lead for HP and stepped out to join Carson and me on this large creative project. Carson and I were booked elsewhere so we could only work about half time on the PacBell contract while Steve was able to devote almost all of his time to it. What leftover time he had, he poured into looking for additional business.

In the three months since I'd started, we had managed to grow the company from the original six consultants to twenty-one. Many of them had left Skynet to join me. All were billing at least eighty percent of the time and revenues were soaring. Pam even started talking to me on a regular basis. She'd drop by my office to talk about the business, what new opportunities I saw and whether we could sustain this level of business. She started to discuss the financials and her concerns. Addition of employees was expensive. We usually had to pay the employees for six to eight weeks before we saw associated revenues from their clients. Surprisingly, our margins were high enough that we had sufficient cash to carry us through these growth times.

Much as Carson had become my mentor, turning me into a real consultant that could work with upper level management and boards of directors for some of the country's largest companies, so too had I become a mentor to Dan. I found a great consulting contract for Dan with one of my contacts and used this to leverage him out of HP. I passed on what I had learned from Carson, and I was pleased to be working with someone who would equal or surpass me someday, much as I hoped to equal Carson.

I mentioned that we had hired employees from Skynet. According to Cheryl, the first to leave Skynet, things were going downhill fast there. The VCs had backed out, stating that they might reconsider if Don and Madge would hire a replacement for me or one of them would step out of the company. Worse, several of the largest customers had asked for enhancements to custom products that were built for them and the programmers were struggling to update the software. The lack of documentation and modularity meant that things broke when even minor changes were made.

Skynet had sent us a cease and desist letter stating that we were raiding their employees. Our attorneys pointed out that there was no solicitation, no phone calls or mail from us to them, and that if people were bailing from a sinking ship, Skynet might want to try to make repairs to the damaged vessel rather than taking shots across our bow. I love attorneys with a sense of humor who can use metaphors effectively.

A few weeks after the end of the quarter, Pam called a company meeting. We were running out of space, which was obvious as we all tried to jam into the CIA conference room, so she told the team that Carson, Steve, and I would be helping her find a larger location. In addition, she announced that to celebrate our record results, she had rented The Catalyst, an upscale nightclub in Santa Cruz, for a company party, which would include dinner, dancing to live music, and formal attire. I suspect the Santa Cruz venue was a nod to my efforts.

8

The Catalyst of 1984 was not the same as it is today. Not only was it in a different location, it was a much more upscale club. I had heard of it, but I'd never been to one of the headliner concerts by groups like Crosby, Stills, Nash and Young, Jerry Garcia, or Neil Young with Crazy Horse just a few months before.

When I walked in, I couldn't have been more surprised. This wasn't a modern nightclub, I must have stepped back into the 1920s! There were Greco- Roman columns, sweeping marble staircases and Maxfield Parish originals on the walls. The whole place had an art-deco motif.

I was barely through the door when a stunning waitress in a strapless floor-length black cocktail dress handed me a champagne glass and poured me Dom Perignon. I'd had champagne before, usually moderately expensive local bottlings. I wasn't really fond of it, but I must admit, the Dom was something different. The bubbles were smaller and more intense, and the champagne itself had a very clean, refreshing taste, not cloyingly sweet or tongue bitingly dry as so many others I'd tried.

Seeing me enter, Steve waved me over. After exchanging pleasantries with the CIA gang, he ushered me towards a small dirty-blonde haired, mousy-looking woman sitting alone on the other side of the room.

"Jack, this is my wife, Shelly," he said. "Why don't you two get to know each other?"

With that, he turned and disappeared into the crowd.

Shelly looked up as I offered my hand. While her overall appearance from afar may have been mousey and retiring, I found myself almost overwhelmed by the huge green eyes that looked at me amusingly from a pixie face. I realized that I was staring, almost transfixed by the depth and beauty of her. I'm sure it had only been a second, but it seemed like days.

"Shelly, I've heard a lot about you," I stammered, trying not to blush.

"And I've heard you're the genius that has started CIA and Steve on the path to fame and glory," she replied laughingly, her eyes sparkling with good humor.

Another waitress, clad in the same black gown glided between us, precariously balancing a tray of canapés and a bottle of Dom.

As she refilled Shelly's glass, I took in a bit more.

Shelly's green and black satin dress emphasized her shapely thighs and hips and drew your attention away from her smallish breasts. While low cut, the dress had a flouncy thing that covered the chest making you think you saw more than there was. Her bare shoulders and arms were strong. I guessed she had been a swimmer, as deltoids, triceps and biceps were clearly defined. Her hair was cut in a Barbra Streisand-like bob, expensively styled, still somehow not radiant. But the eyes.

"So what does a Financial Analyst do?" I asked when the waitress had slipped away.

Thus began my first conversation with one of the most amazing women I have ever known.

Shelly explained that the title was quite generic and was used in a variety of businesses, but in VISA, she was one of many who were responsible for maximizing the revenue of the company by managing float. Although I had worked with companies like VISA, MasterCharge, and American Express, I really didn't know how they made their money. I mistakenly assumed that the interest paid on outstanding balances went into their coffers, but Shelly informed me that this was not the case. Most of the money went to the banks. In fact, originally VISA was a non-profit organization run by a consortium of banks. Although there were some transaction and initial signup fees that went to VISA, most of their money was made on float. Literally billions of dollars were in float – not in the bank or in the customers' or merchants' accounts at any given moment, and by properly managing this money, VISA made its profit. They were essentially a service network that managed not only credit card transactions, but that also tied into international money transfer systems like SWIFT. VISA had recently introduced the first ATM network and was expanding into debit transactions. Eventually VISA envisioned a cashless society. However, with the dramatic changes in the financial markets, a team of Financial Analysts did non-stop tracking, prediction, and rapid investment of funds.

One of the tuxedoed waiters announced that dinner was about to be served, so we moved towards the tables that had been set up for groups of eight, wedding reception style. Since there were no nametags, Shelly and I settled at a table with Dan and Roberta, his wife, Rick and his wife Linda, and Ronn and his date, Barb.

A few tables over, Steve was engaged in deep conversation with Pam, and Carson and Nancy were holding court with some of the newer employees and their spouses. Carson's baritone laugh resonated throughout the room and it was clear that his inexorable charisma had the table rapt – all except Steve and Pam.

Over dinner, Dan talked about St. John's and I must admit that I was envious of his Classics education in a school with no majors that focused on teaching all aspects of literature, history, mathematics and science as scholarly pursuits. He seemed to miss the clean air and great powder skiing found in New Mexico. While I'd driven through the state a few times with my parents as we moved from one military base to another, my recollections were of high desert. His descriptions were of a tree-covered temperate paradise, even in the summer.

His wife Roberta, who was a psychiatric nurse, regaled us with horror stories of seemingly normal people who just lost control, and well-meaning relatives who demanded their release when it was clear treatment was required. Rick and Linda talked about baby preparations, and late term pregnancy problems as the baby was due within a week. And Ronn told hilarious tales of his countless injuries and how they were just freak accidents. But we were all surprised when Barb began her own accounts of cracked ribs, broken bones and stitches. She was a rodeo rider and her stories put our polo–playing friend to shame. It was clear that if sports injuries were a measure of macho, he'd lost. Nonetheless, Ronn looked at Barb with true admiration.

When the wait-staff brought dessert, I excused myself and went in search of the restroom. As I made a wrong turn towards a back entrance to the kitchen, I almost ran into Pam and Steve. Pam had her back and one foot up against the wall, knee extended, possibly between Steve's legs but it was hard to tell from that angle in the dimly lit corridor. Steve's hand rested against the wall over her shoulder and he was leaning in close. Knowing I was in the wrong place and not wanting to create an embarrassing scene, I turned around before they spotted me. I asked a waitress for directions to the restroom.

By the time I got back to the table, the band had abandoned the sultry jazz they had played during cocktails and dinner, and had moved to a mix of rock and roll, blues, and swing. Before I could sit down, Shelly asked me to dance.

I like to think of myself as a good dancer. I grew up with music in the house. Before I could walk, my mother would polka around the house with me for what seemed to be hours at a time. When I did learn to walk, we waltzed and polkaed nearly every day. By the time I got to elementary school, I was a dancing fool. At home and on the radio, Nat King Cole and Frank Sinatra sang romantic ballads in swing time. My mom taught me to dance swing.

While most kids avoided dance classes during physical education, I loved the square dances and the archaic minuets. I was too young to know about the jitterbug era of the fifties, but by the early sixties, I was doing the Freddie, the twist, mashed potato, jerk, and every new thing the older kids were dancing. In high school, Motown consumed me and my friends, and we spent every Friday and Saturday night at the teen club on the military base dancing until we dropped.

In college, the only physical education classes I took were dance classes. I started with social dance, then full-on ballroom, then began to focus on swing and its predecessor, Lindy Hop. And, when disco came along, I had no problem keeping up with the craze, since it was an amalgam of so many dance forms. While the music was repetitious, hoards of well-dressed people began to do more complex dancing than the free-form rock and roll partner-less dances of the sixties. The style of music didn't matter to me. If there was music and I could move to it, I'd have a good time. In later years, I became a hip-hop fanatic.

Rock and roll is fine and I can always dance with abandon and unbridled self-expression, but there is something unique about partner dances where two people really do move as one. That's the other thing. When you find a good dance partner, there's only one thing that's more intimate than the perfect harmony of synchronized dance moves. And I guess that's the ultimate form of dance itself.

Since most women know a few swing moves, or can follow a lead through them, I took Shelly's hand, led her to the dance floor, rock-stepped and led her into an easy inside turn. Immediately I could tell she knew how to dance. Her turn was perfect and she finished right on the beat ready for the next one. The easiest way to tell a good dancer is by the tone in the arm. Most people don't realize that it is easy to lead and to follow if the pressure exerted by the leader is exactly complemented by the follower. A loose, limp arm means you have to drag your partner through any move. Tone allows you to lead with a light touch. It's a connection that enables you to sense what the other is doing instantaneously.

I led Shelly into an easy tuck turn and as she pulled off a double turn instead of a single, I could see she had also had ballet training. This was going to be fun. Swing is a six-count dance and is pretty easy for most people. I decided to try some Lindy. Lindy is an eight-count dance, which means you have a lot more to do within the same time. Today, people remember a Gap commercial where couples are dancing to a lively swing tune called Jump, Jive, and Wail. There are lifts, spins, and jumps. That's Lindy Hop.

I rock-stepped again, but this time triple stepped. Shelly knew exactly what to do. She came forward with hips and legs swiveling, one hand waving coquettishly in the air. On the fourth count, we came together, turned together and completed our first swingout as we spun out holding each other with one hand at arm's length. Then we picked up the pace. I threw every combination I knew at her, going from Lindy to swing and back, adding in some Charleston, tandem, countless turns, and several jumps. By this time, the other dancers had made room, forming a circle around us. The band picked up the tempo and extended the song, then blended in a fast Louis Jordan number. At one point, I closed up our position, her right hand in my left, her left on my shoulder and my right arm creating a frame as I held her just at the shoulder blade. We did a series of fast pivot turns, across the length of the floor, ala Fred Astaire and Ginger Rogers. As the song came to a close, I set up a triple inside turn, leaned her against my right side, and as I gently prodded her back with my left hand, she wrapped her right leg around my right calf. On the last beat, I pulled forward with my left hand and she dropped with a half turn as she finished, her head a foot or so above the floor, one leg poised demurely in the air, smiling up at me as I looked down at her, and the crowd cheered and applauded. The band took a break and nodded in our direction as they exited the stage.

Remember what I said about that connection - dance and intimacy? The French have a phrase: coup de foudre, a lightning strike. In English, we call it love at first sight. Our language can be so mundane sometimes. Maybe it should be love at first dance; that's much more poetic.

We were both breathless – from the dance. Shelly's face and chest were flushed and sweat was beginning to mark the satin of her dress. I knew I didn't look anything like a composed Fred Astaire. My Tux was soaked. Two waiters stood by our table with large carafes of ice water, which we gratefully guzzled. Steve, looking a bit drunk, came over with Pam.

"I didn't know you could dance like that," he said to Shelly, his accent the strongest I'd heard.

"Where'd you learn Lindy Hop?" I asked.

"You mean jitterbug," she replied. And turning to Steve she said, "It's been years since I danced at all, and I guess there's a lot you don't know about me." Turning briefly back to me and smiling, Shelly thanked me for the dance, then frowned as she took Steve's hand.

Trouble in paradise? In that moment, it certainly was a pleasant thought.

Pam announced that she had to leave early. Steve and Shelly moved on to Carson's table, and after the band break, I did some easy swing with Roberta, danced some standard rock and roll with a very pregnant Linda, and tried some West Coast Swing with Barb on a semi-country number.

I kept looking over at Steve and Shelly, but they were involved in a heated discussion. I stuck with Perrier for the rest of the evening, and when the band finally wrapped it up at 1am, I headed home alone.

9

I was working on yet another report for ALM the following Wednesday. I hadn't seen Steve or Carson since the party. I could have caught up with Steve at the Red Cockaide since I learned he spent almost every evening there. Because most of the rest of the staff were working on customer sites, Pam and I had lunch at the company cafeteria and she opened up a bit and told me about her background.

Her father was a larger-than-life real estate magnate in Texas and she had grown up as the only child in a wealthy household. Her mother spent all of her time pursuing Dallas society while her father was always out with the boys. In other words, she never saw her parents and was raised by a live-in nanny and a housekeeper. When she was six years old she gave a piano recital for her parents and several of their friends. One woman commented on the fact that Pam's ears stuck out and the next week, Pam was in surgery having her ears altered. Somehow, although they were almost always absent, Pam seemed to get in their way. Her father teased her constantly about her lack of intelligence until she reached puberty when he began to chide her incessantly about her looks. Her mother refused to let her participate in any sports. It was unladylike.

When she went to college, her father told her that he had set up a trust fund for her in the amount of four million dollars. If she was good, it would be hers when she turned twenty-one. At twenty-one, he told her she was too young for so much money, but once she graduated and had a career – say at twenty-five – it would be hers.

Pam was now thirty-three, unmarried, lived alone in an apartment in Los Gatos, and still hadn't seen any of her trust fund. She felt as if she had avoided life, 'being good,' waiting until the money was hers before her real life could start. Now that it looked like CIA had a future, perhaps she could make enough on her own to tell her father where he could shove her trust fund.

Like almost everyone in the company, she thought Carson was brilliant and she admired his integrity, but she believed that it was Steve's single-minded drive that would ultimately allow her to break away from her father.

After this sobering lunch, having learned more about Pam

than I really wanted to, I went back to work on the ALM report. When the phone rang, I was thrilled to hear Shelly on the line.

"Hi Jack, it's Shelly." She said.

"Hi Shelly, it's good to hear from you. I'm glad you made it home safely from the party. Steve seemed a bit out of it."

"Well, actually, we almost didn't make it home at all – at least together. Steve insisted on driving even though he was drunk. We got about two blocks and were pulled over by a Santa Cruz cop. I did some fast talking, trying to keep Steve calm while mollifying the cop, and after I traded places with Steve, the cop let us go. Steve certainly doesn't need a DUI. I think this scared him a bit. No, I hope it did. I'm sure if we'd made it on to Highway 17, the Highway Patrol would have thrown Steve in jail.

"Anyway, that's not why I called. First, I wanted to thank you for the other night. I haven't had so much fun in years. But the real purpose of the call is to invite you to dinner on Friday. Steve would like to have you, Dan, Rick, and George over for a chat about the company. He seems really excited. I'm not sure why he'd didn't want to invite Carson, or why he asked me to call everyone instead of doing it himself, but here we are. Can you make it?"

I replied that I could. She gave me the address, we set the time, and I didn't try to take the conversation any further. I was a bit surprised to discover that they lived in an apartment not far from downtown Los Altos. With Steve's sense of his image and style, and what I knew to be two solid incomes, I thought they would have lived in the Los Altos Hills, one of the more expensive areas in the Valley.

10

I was the last to arrive at dinner having been caught in some bad traffic crossing the Valley. Shelly answered the door and ushered me in to their modest two-story apartment or townhome. Everyone was sipping beers, but I asked for water. Shelly served us a nice dinner, Coq au Vin, wild rice, and broccoli. We went through three bottles of Steve's favorite Chardonnay as Dan, George, and Rick updated us on their projects. Steve, who usually tries to command the center of attention said very little and seemed quite agitated. While his interaction with Shelly was civil, you could almost feel the heat from the friction between them.

We all helped Shelly clear the table except Steve who waited impatiently. Shelley brought in a chocolate torte and excused herself. Clearly the meeting was about to begin.

"Guys, you have to try this." Steve said as he brought out a bottle of wine. "This is a late harvest Zinfandel from Page Mill Winery. It's great with chocolate."

I was skeptical. I loved Zinfandels and I was a true chocoholic, but putting the two together? The wine was thick and very sweet. With a small sip your head filled with the aroma of Zinfandel. In a regular bottle of Zin, you get a hint of its flavor as the alcohol and often other varietals dilute the unique taste. This was like a Port or liqueur. The almost cloying sweetness of the late harvest wine complemented the chocolate torte perfectly.

Steve continued. "The reason I wanted to get together with you is that something big has happened. You know I've been working on the PacBell contract with Paul Franklin. Jack's been looking at their international side and packet switching opportunities, Carson's been working up strategies for managing the huge databases handed off by AT&T, and I've been looking at the back office management, billing, interfaces to AT&T and the other Baby Bells, and ways to automate all of this. We've built up a lot of credibility with upper management at PacBell. Our recommendations so far have been right on the money, literally.

"Anyway, I gave Paul a preview of my report that describes a new system to bring all of the diverse back office functions together with a single management system. Knowing that

PacBell spends hundreds of millions a year on their current systems, I proposed fifty million dollars to rebuild and consolidate the systems. I also suggested that this could become the standard for all of the Baby Bells and new long distance companies, and that we could give PacBell a commission on future sales if they funded this. I've got a great name for it too, Project Hydra, a resilient centralized system tying multiple arms together. Paul will present this to the Board once I finalize the report. He's confident they'll go for it on his recommendation."

Dan, Rick, George, and I sat in stunned silence. Fifty million dollars? Suddenly Rick's pager went off.

"I've got to go," he said, jumping to his feet and rushing to the door. "Linda's going into labor!"

"Steve, this sounds fantastic," I said breaking the silence that loomed in Rick's wake after we all wished him and Linda good luck. "We've got a lot of work to do to scale CIA up to support a contract like this."

"Well, Jack, that's just it," Steve replied. "I'm thinking CIA shouldn't do this. We should start a new company that has a clearly defined focus: building back office products for phone companies. I was thinking that Dan, George and Rick would make great leads on different parts of the project. Of course, since Paul is your contact, you'll have to explain the transition of the contract from CIA to NewCo.

"You know, VCs always put the generic label of NewCo on a new company that hasn't been named yet. I think NewCo would be a great name for a real company. It emphasizes newness and innovation. What do you think?"

I responded cautiously. "Steve, it's an interesting idea, but I think there would be potential problems with Carson. We all signed Patent, Confidentiality, and Non-disclosure agreements and the work product from CIA's consulting efforts belong to CIA."

Dan jumped in without hesitation. "Steve, I'm surprised Carson isn't here. This is completely unethical. Carson started this company and his efforts ultimately resulted in this opportunity. Count me out if you try to slip this one away from CIA!"

At this point Steve was seething. He pushed back is chair and slammed the door to the apartment on his way out.

"That was uncomfortable," George stated matter-of-factly.

"I'm just a programmer. I really don't want to get into any of these politics. You guys work this out and let me know what we're going to do."

Dan stood up. "I think I'll be leaving," he said. "He'll have the weekend to cool off and we can talk about this on Monday. George, shall we?"

"I'll wait for him and see if I can get him to look at this rationally," I said. "If Steve wants to own a company based on CIA intellectual property, I suspect Carson will help him get it started, keeping a portion for CIA, but giving Steve a shot at a creating a big opportunity that would benefit both. Carson doesn't strike me as anyone who wants to build an empire, unlike our angry friend who just stormed out."

Dan and George called goodnight to Shelly as they walked towards the door. Shelly came out and hugged them both before they left. Then she turned to me.

"I didn't hear the words, but I got a sense of the tone. What happened?" she asked, returning to the table. She picked up a glass and poured herself some of the Late Harvest Zinfandel. She raised the bottle towards me and I nodded to indicate that I'd join her. I settled into an overstuffed chair as she took a seat opposite me on the sofa.

"Didn't Steve tell you about his grand scheme?" I responded.

"I knew he was excited, and it clearly had to do with work since he was almost bursting at the seams with child-like excitement before you guys arrived. But no, he didn't tell me any details. We don't really have that kind of relationship."

"So what kind of relationship do you have, if you don't mind my asking?"

Shelly looked at me for a moment, her brows and lips pursed slightly and I could see calculation going on. Was I someone she could talk to? She apparently decided I was and continued.

"Well, it started as one of convenience. Steve needed a Green Card, and I needed or wanted to get pregnant. I had turned thirty with no long-term romantic prospects in sight, and my biological clock was sounding loudly. Steve was attractive and charming and it seemed like a good fit. My parents love him. He's ambitious and in many ways a younger version of my father.

"Unfortunately, while Steve got what he wanted, my side of the bargain hasn't been satisfied. At first Steve didn't want kids. He didn't want to be slowed down in his career. But after three years, I realized I was running out of time and I stopped birth control. I'm still not pregnant. Steve is hard to pin down. I find him watching porno movies late at night when he could be upstairs getting me pregnant, and I know he's got interests elsewhere, but I want a home and a family and I intend to get it. I've got an appointment at Stanford next week for a fertility analysis. Steve refuses to go, the asshole.

"So that's my tale of woe, what's yours?"

I filled her in on Steve's proposal and the reaction he got from us. I also told her that Rick had run out before the rift because his pager had gone off. Linda was probably at or on her way to the hospital now.

"You know," I said, "Although his lifestyle would suggest differently, Carson isn't interested in making a lot of money. He loves his job. He loves giving advice to major players in the industry. He doesn't feel he has to actually build an economic dynasty. I don't think Carson is going to have a problem with creating a new company and letting Steve have a significant share."

"But Steve wants it all," she responded quietly.

"I certainly do," Steve half-shouted as he came through the front door. "Are you the only one left, Jack?"

"Look Steve, on Monday, why don't you and I sit down with Carson and propose that you start a new company under the CIA umbrella. I don't think Carson wants to run a fifty million dollar company, so he'll give you a big share and name you President and CEO. If you're successful, you should be able to build a substantial opportunity.

"This way, you avoid any taint on NewCo, and there's nothing to explain to Paul Franklin or the rest of PacBell. He gets it all: a company dedicated to building his products, and a parent consulting firm that can continue to help steer the direction of the company, maybe even help keep business flowing towards NewCo."

Although this last statement seemed to promise that NewCo would benefit from a conflict of interest, I knew Paul well enough to know that he'd never let that happen. It did seem to ring a bell with Steve though and he agreed that my proposal to speak with Carson on Monday made a lot of sense.

11

Months passed and it was 1985, the year that Gorbachev became Premier of the USSR and would start the process to eliminate the Cold War that all of us Baby Boomers had grown up with. Soon the inane lessons learned from the 'Duck and Cover' nuclear attack drills of our elementary school years would fade as the omnipresent immediate threat of nuclear war disappeared into obscurity. At CIA, it was the opposite. We were expanding without fear or reservations but an insidious threat was growing among the founders.

CIA and NewCo were going as planned. Carson had given Steve forty-nine percent of NewCo, the title of President and CEO, and complete operational and budgetary control. Steve had laid out specific milestone deliverables with PacBell that, if met, would ensure fifty million dollars paid to NewCo by the end of 1986, twenty-five million dollars a year on this project alone. The upfront monies had been received and we'd moved into much larger offices with a physical split between CIA and NewCo. Project Hydra was well underway and NewCo was ahead of schedule, a real surprise to the bureaucrats at PacBell.

NewCo and CIA shared a lobby and receptionist, but there were two logos on the wall behind the reception desk, and if you turned right, you went through a door to the NewCo offices while CIA occupied the smaller, left side of the building. We had begun staffing the project by making it known that we were hiring. We also put some of the Valley's best contract programmers to work with plans to turn them into fulltime employees.

Pam did the financials for both companies. Carson and I acted as advisors and recruiters, and we continued the consulting work for the other parts of PacBell's post-divestiture efforts.

We decided that CIA would continue to be the high-level consulting company while NewCo would be a product company. We had grandiose ideas that CIA, with our executive contacts in large corporations and visibility into the needs of these companies, would be the incubator for new ideas that could ultimately lead to many subsidiary product companies like NewCo. CIA would be the goose that laid the golden eggs. Carson might inadvertently end up owning an empire.

I had great hopes that Dan would remain with Carson and me

on the CIA side, but he saw significant opportunity for himself in NewCo, once he understood that Steve had done the honorable thing with Carson. Steve appointed Dan as Vice President of Development, and I watched with mixed feelings as my protégé went out on his own. When the HP projects were completed, Rick and George moved to NewCo, and as other projects finished, other consultants move to NewCo as well. Over the course of 1985, CIA, the consulting firm, would be reduced to Carson, Ronn, me, and seven other protégés that worked for us. Technically though, since 51% of the net profits of NewCo were supposed to end up back in CIA, Pam had created an arrangement where a large number of those working at NewCo were actually employed by CIA; NewCo was our customer. This allowed her to reduce the tax burden by more evenly distributing the expenses and revenues

But on this sunny February day, I was quite content with the state of the company. It was more like when I started. There was plenty of money, interesting projects, and good people to work with, especially Carson. And, speaking of the devil, he walked into my office.

"Hey, Jack, I just got off the phone with Alan LaMonte. He'd like us to join him at his place in the eastern Sierra the weekend after next. This is kind of a thank you and brainstorming session combined. Some big companies are courting him for possible acquisition and he'd like to pick our brains. He knows that if he does it as an expensive weekend of entertainment, not only can he write it off, he can also get 'free' consulting from us. I think it would be a good thing to do, so I'm inviting you and Ronn. It's a weekend retreat, so bring a date. We'll be on our own during the days and getting together for dinner, drinks and possible all-night discussions on Saturday evening."

Alan LaMonte was the founder and CEO of ALM, still one of our premier customers. He was a former AT&T engineer who had the idea of creating private telephone systems for companies. Knowing that the phone company makes its money through a statistical model that has many fewer circuits than actual subscribers, he had reasoned that instead of having one phone line per phone, a company could save a fortune if they purchased a system from him that managed large numbers of phone connections within a building, then used fewer lines to connect to the telephone company. Before he developed his switch, called a public branch exchange or PBX, if you had a hundred employees, you paid the phone company for a hundred phone lines and you paid them every month. With Alan's PBX, you could have a hundred phones in your company all connected to his switch, but only have ten or twenty lines to the phone company.

Some years later, in the aftermath of the 1989 Loma Prieta earthquake, I'd understand just how far the telephone companies went with their statistical use models. Right after the earthquake, I picked up the phone and didn't get a dial tone. I assumed that phone lines must have been down. As it turned out, the telephone infrastructure was fine. The phone company had a limited number of dial tones available. With everyone calling loved ones, they ran out. So, if you waited a few minutes, when someone hung up, you'd get a dial tone.

I had met Alan a few times during presentations of our business and technical recommendations. He was in his late thirties. His brown hair had a touch of gray around the ears and it was clear from the leanness of his face that he kept himself in excellent physical condition. I had heard that he spent two hours every morning in a scull on Lexington Reservoir, rowing and gliding across the glassy water for the length of the lake before returning to the oar house located on the dam.

Like Carson, he had charisma. You definitely knew he was in the room even if he never opened his mouth. I learned that he had started the company by luring a few other AT&T engineers to join him at ALM, and with the help of 'angel' – private party – investors, he had launched the company that now was doing hundreds of millions in sales each year with remarkable growth rates. Their IPO raised a substantial war chest for the company and made Alan and a few of his founders quite wealthy.

Carson informed me that he and Nancy, Ronn and Barb, and Alan and his wife would be flying up in Alan's private jet. Alan had a Suburban waiting at the Lake Tahoe Airport and his place was about thirty minutes away. He invited us to join them on the plane, but knowing that I'd prefer the freedom of my own car, I declined. Then I called Georgette who agreed to come both for the skiing, and for the business opportunity of meeting Alan.

12

I picked Georgette up Friday evening at seven and we loaded her skis onto the car. We decided to ignore the first part of Carson's directions, which instructed us to take Highway 50 across the Sierra to Highway 89. Highways 50 and 80 are the main winter routes across the mountains. Because of this, they are unforgivingly crowded with San Francisco Bay Area residents scrambling to the mountains for weekend skiing. When the weather is bad, it can take as long as eight hours to make it up or back on these roads as two-wheel drive vehicles and trucks have to stop and put on tire chains. Even in good weather, the traffic jams turn a four-hour drive into six.

We decided to take Highway 88, the only southern route open in winter. 88 is a largely unknown route and is actually a more direct route to Alan's place above the Carson Valley. Even better, while Highways 50 and 80 have chain control checkpoints, Highway 88 does not, and with my four-wheel drive Suburu, I can just breeze through.

I updated Georgette on the progress of CIA and NewCo, while she told me how Modular Communications was continuing to grow. They had just raised some additional funding and were now looking at new technologies.

"Have you heard of this company called Samcom Systems?" she asked.

"Yes. Aren't they the guys that left Stanford after working on ARPANET and the Internet?"

"Yeah. They're starting to build routers which they think they can sell to corporations to connect to the Internet. They want to turn the corporate world away from IBM's protocols towards IP – the Internet Protocol. Initially, I think their products are gateways. They support whatever protocol a company runs internally, then encapsulate it in IP so that the company can access and use the Internet for networking. It's a lot like X.25."

X.25 was a protocol used in packet switching networks. Rather than requiring each customer to pay the telephone companies for leased data communication lines between their sites, packet switching networks purchased high-speed leased lines, then shared the paths among multiple companies. They provided connectivity in most major cities, and although it didn't cost more to send data five thousand miles than it did to send it one mile, the networks did charge for the amount of data sent. Packet switching was extremely popular in Europe where corporations could easily connect to their branch offices in other countries, and we had recommended that PacBell implement a packet switching network to enhance their service offerings in the Western United States.

Georgette continued. "Marty and I are thinking about this market. You know that in Europe, and even in the US, many people use our modems to dial into packet switching networks. It wouldn't be a big deal for us to enhance our modems to act as IP routers. I know the Internet isn't much now, but we think the PC market will explode over the next few years and we suspect Samcom might miss the consumer and home market for Internet connections. What do you think?"

"If you have the R&D budget, I think it's a great place to explore. On the other hand, it will be years before people have multiple computers in their homes and the Internet is the prevalent networking technology. Even worse, what can you do on the Internet today? Limited email with Unix command-line interfaces?"

In those days, there were no browsers or user-friendly email programs. In fact, when you used a computer, everything was line-at-a-time. Meaning you could input one line at the bottom of the screen and the computer you were connected to could only send you one line of text. Graphics, as we know them today, didn't exist. While certain companies like IBM created full-screen displays for data entry and output, none of the systems on the Internet could do this.

I continued, "No average user is going to accept this. I think there's a missing piece here and it might be foolish to jump too soon. If you're right about Samcom, they'll help develop the Internet and the corporate market, that missing piece will fall into place, and when consumers become ready, Samcom will be so focused on the corporate environment, they'll leave the door wide open. So, in a nutshell, I'd say wait a couple of years before you invest too heavily unless you can get a customer or the government to fund it. Actually, I think BBN has lined up some interesting contracts from ARPA in this area recently. Why don't you talk to them?"

BBN is Bolt, Beranek and Newmann. Initially a consulting

firm, they became the primary technology supplier to ARPA (the government's Advanced Research Projects Administration). It was once said that any technology in networking found its roots in BBN research. That is certainly true for the Internet. Unfortunately, while imitators like Samcom ultimately became technology behemoths, BBN never grew to be terribly large.

"What do you mean by 'a missing piece'?" she asked.

"I don't know. I've used the Internet for years for email, but entering one line at a time and not being able to see what you've written before is a problem. It's hard to use. And think of all the information that's available. It, too, is only text-based line-at-a-time stuff. I think we need special programs to create and manage mail. We also need some way to present full screens of data, maybe even pictures to make it interesting and usable for the average home computer owner. That may someday be a business in itself, but it's not there now, and until it is, the Internet will be just for us computer geeks.

"But you know, even if someone developed all that, the 4800 bits per second that the fastest affordable dial up modems provide aren't going to cut it. Maybe you should be working on inexpensive faster modems."

"Don't worry about that," she replied. "We're always working on new modulation schemes and we'll be able to get a lot more speed out of regular dial up lines. That's one area where we'll be a player."

Shortly after we passed the two thousand foot elevation sign, the light rain, which had followed us for the entire trip, turned to snow. Even in the dim amber interior light of the Subaru, I could see Georgette grinning. We would be skiing the lightest, driest powder the next day. The all-wheel drive Subaru was happy in its element. Like a ski boat in the water, it carved twin wakes of snow behind us as we climbed towards the Carson Pass summit.

13

Carson's directions were excellent and we arrived at Alan's place about eleven. The gated driveway had been plowed, and there was about six inches of new powder on the ground. Since this was the east side of the Sierra and storms drop most of their moisture on the west side as they rise to cross the summits, Georgette and I knew that there would be at least eighteen inches of fresh powder in the morning at Kirkwood, thirty minutes back the way we came.

Alan's chalet was a grandiose structure of logs, volcanic rock, and glass. It sat perched on a south-facing hillside overlooking the Carson Valley with the lights of Carson City visible off the left side of the house and the snow-capped peaks of the Sierra to the south and west. The entire south side of the building seemed to be glass with barely enough wood to hold it together. Enormous decks extended out the front of the house and we could see steam rising from multiple hot tubs embedded in them.

The hand-carved front door opened before we reached it and a very tall redhead wearing a thick black robe greeted us. "Hi, you must be Jack and Georgette. I'm Jane. Come on in."

Jane appeared to be in her mid-thirties. She was about six feet tall and quite buxom. Her red hair was piled on her head and held in place by what appeared to be lacquered chopsticks. It became almost strawberry blonde as we moved under some brighter recessed lighting, but reddened again suddenly as we approached the blazing stone fireplace that resembled the old cooking fireplaces found in European castles – large enough to park a car in.

"Let me show you to your room so you can put your things down," she said, then she corrected herself as she saw us exchange an amused but uncomfortable look, "Rooms?"

"Rooms, if that's okay,' Georgette replied. "We're close friends and really don't have a problem sharing a room, but if you have an extra, it would be nice."

Jane suggested we leave our bags at the foot of a sweeping knotty pine staircase near the front door, and gave us a quick tour. As we ascended the stairs, we realized that the main room on the ground floor had what must have been a thirty-foot ceiling with floor to ceiling glass. On the far side of "the living room,' which contained four separate groupings of sofas and chairs, tables, and their own individual carpets, we could see the kitchen and dining areas, all part of the same wide-open space. The dining table was the largest redwood burl I had ever seen, at least fifteen feet in length.

The second floor was like a large loft. There was an open area with book-filled shelves around the sides and a pool table in the middle. It looked down onto the living room, kitchen and dining areas and we could see through the massive glass windows that several people were in two hot tubs outside. The rest of the second floor included 4 bedrooms with their own baths. Each was decorated in a rustic, western style. Jane explained that each room had a theme related to a personage of the Old West. Of course, Carson and Nancy were staying upstairs in the Kit Carson room.

It felt as if we had walked into one of the great lodges, like the Ahwanee in Yosemite Valley.

We descended another staircase on the opposite side of the house near the dining area and learned that the rest of the downstairs had four more bedrooms, each with its own bath, and there was a stand-alone dressing/powder room which included another bathroom. Our rooms were side by side on the ground floor. Mine was the Fremont Room, named after General Fremont, who blazed the first trail across the Sierra near where Highway 88 ran, and Georgette's was the Calamity Jane Room.

"Calamity Jane was one of my favorite characters. Jane said as she opened the door to Georgette's room. "Her real name was Martha Canary and she was orphaned at age ten. She lived on her own, learning to ride and shoot better than most men her age. Before she was twenty, she was working as a scout for the United States Cavalry. There's an interesting story about how she got her nickname. She was working as a scout in South Dakota for a Captain Egan.

"One day Captain Egan and his men were surrounded by Indians. They were fighting for their lives against a much larger Indian force. Captain Egan was wounded and was knocked to ground.

"Martha rode into the battle, lifted the captain in front of her on her saddle, and dashed out. They got through unscathed, but every other man was killed.

"After recovering from his wounds, Captain Egan, recalling the hell that she rode through, named her 'Calamity Jane.' But this was just one of countless incidents where Calamity saved soldiers, stagecoaches, and injured men.

"I've got at least one story for each room. Let me know if you want to hear some during your stay.

"Can I get you something to drink? Jack, I've heard you love chocolate. How about hot chocolate with Crème de Cacao?" I nodded and thanked her. "Georgette, what would you like?"

"Hot chocolate with Crème de Cacao sounds good to me!" Georgette replied.

"I'll be back in a jiffy with the drinks. Get settled and if you're not too tired, we can talk in the living room, or if you're feeling brave, you can join everyone in the hot tubs. Bathing suits are optional, but so far, no one has taken that option. There are robes in the closets of your rooms."

With that she turned and left us. Georgette and I decided that a hot tub sounded like a great way to relax after the long drive, and we agreed to meet ten minutes later. I unpacked, put my bag in the closet, undressed, and put on a sumptuous thick white Egyptian cotton robe. As I stepped out of the room to knock on Georgette's door, Jane appeared with two drinks.

"It looks like you've decided on a hot tub," she said. "Should I leave the drinks with you or meet you outside?"

"I'll take them and we'll see you out there shortly." I replied.

I knocked on Georgette's door and she appeared in an identical white bathrobe. We sipped the steaming dark chocolate and headed outside where we found Alan, Jane, Carson, and Nancy engaged in a raucous debate in one tub and Ronn and Barb about ten feet away in the other. We chatted briefly with the folks in Alan's tub, but they shooed us away after recognizing we were freezing.

"Get in here and get warm!" Ronn ordered from behind a cloud of rising steam.

As we doffed our robes and slipped into the soothing swirling water, Ronn continued, "Isn't this the life? Can you believe the house? I could get used to this."

We settled back and looked at the last quarter of the moon as it rose above the Sierra crest. Even with so little moon, the reflection off the snow created a surreal almost-twilight. We settled back into relaxing silence broken only by short stretches of quiet conversation. Within thirty minutes, we were all ready for bed.

14

Georgette and I slipped out of the house at 7:30am the next morning and raced over Carson Pass to Kirkwood Ski Resort. We jumped from the car, put on our boots, grabbed our gear and raced to the ticket window. By time we reached the line at the Cornice Chair, it was 8:30am. We were the fifth and sixth in line – not too bad! The lifts wouldn't be open for thirty minutes unless the operators took pity on us.

The problem is that the lift operators have to work, so they'll typically punish frantic powder hounds by delaying the lift openings on premier powder days, especially on the weekends. We were in luck, however. A few minutes after we got in line, two employees with the day off asked for cuts in line if they could get the lift open, and sure enough after witnessing some blackmail, we were on the chair at 8:45.

Kirkwood is a wonderful place to ski. As far as terrain difficulty, it's probably number three on the West Coast behind Squaw Valley and Alpine Meadows, but for quantity and quality of snow, Kirkwood is number one. It gets more snow than any resort in North America, and because of its elevation and location at the Sierra Crest away from Lake Tahoe, it gets the best powder in the area. Even better is the fact that Kirkwood doesn't go crazy grooming all the slopes. While they run SnowCats over some well-known runs, the majority of the terrain is untouched except by skiers (and in recent years, snowboarders). This philosophy creates opportunities for untracked powder and a day or two later, great moguls.

When you learn to ski, there are just a few fundamentals, the primary one being if you weight the edge of your left ski you will turn right and vice versa. If you want to stop, or slow down you use your edges to grip the snow and turn you until your skis are perpendicular to slope of the hill. This is all possible because the edges of the skis are curved and if you set a ski on edge, it will turn. As you advance, you become increasingly dependent on your edges. If you want to make quick maneuvers or sudden stops, you must move from the edge of one ski to the edge of another instantly. At some point, it becomes second nature. Then there's powder.

In powder, your edges don't work at all. If you weight an edge on a ski, it just sinks and pretty soon, one ski is diving lower and lower while the other, unweighted ski, is floating higher and higher. Of course, this means disaster and a fall into icy white oblivion. If you don't have powder straps and a ski comes off during a fall, you may not find it until the summer thaw. It can travel hundreds of yards in any direction hidden under the snow.

So, to learn to powder ski, you must forget everything you first learned about skiing. Instead of weighting one ski to turn, you weight both skis to sink, then unweight both skis simultaneously, point both together in the direction you want to go, then weight them again to sink and complete the turn. There are no sudden stops. Some people think they need to lean back to keep their skis from plowing downward into the snow, but this just tires you out. Once you learn the proper technique, powder skiing is effortless.

The biggest problem with skiing powder is that on main runs, it's gone within an hour. In some major resorts like Squaw Valley, even the most remote powder is gone within two hours of the resort's opening. But at Kirkwood, Georgette and I knew that we could ski untracked powder all day, and sometimes, the second day after a storm as well. We were ready!

As we rode up the lift, we looked down on the pristine untracked fields of white. It wouldn't last long. Before we got off the lift, the guys three chairs up started their descent on the run next to the chair, laying parallel non-stop serpentine S-turns down the face of the mountain. Georgette and I stopped briefly atop the cornice, then she jumped, grabbing the tails of her skis for an instant before landing in the deep light feathery snow. I followed and we too started painting our own canvas of S-turns down a little known run not far from the chair.

Like getting into a tube surfing, or locking into a thermal that takes you skyward, skiing powder is one of those moments of perfection, harmony, and perfect synchronization with nature. You're floating effortlessly. Unlike regular or mogul skiing, there's no impact, no force. It's an almost magical feeling of flying through feathers. Picture a massive sand dune, then change the sand to feathers and imagine jumping your way down the dune surrounded by feathers, never touching anything solid. That's almost as good as skiing powder.

We didn't stop. We skied right up to the lift and jumped on, impatient at its slowness as it took us up for the next run. I looked at Georgette and saw a reflection of my own ear-to-ear grin. I was too happy to talk. The back of her hat had a line of white across it. While the snow was only mid-thigh deep with a few deeper places, the steepness of the slope caused the plume of snow behind her to graze the back of her hat at each turn. I knew my hat had the same white line. Riding up the lift, shouts and hoots of sheer joy echoed off the volcanic rock cliff faces as other skiers found their own forms of paradise.

After an hour and four runs, the main trails were tracked up by us and other skiers. We headed off to more distant terrain. On the far north side of Kirkwood is an area called Lightning and we traversed the top of the mountain for five to ten minutes to get there on our next runs. In one large snowfield, instead of skiing beside Georgette, I skied behind her. I laid down my S-turns at exactly the opposite of hers, creating linked figure eights down the mountain. My left turns exactly crossed her right turns at the apex and my right turns crossed the tops of her left ones.

By noon, Lightning was also skied out. We knew that our next destination was Eagle Bowl. While other runs on the mountain were visible from the lift or the road in, Eagle Bowl was largely unknown. It was here that we could ski the rest of the day by ourselves. Unfortunately, when we got there we discovered a Closed sign. Although we were tempted, we decided that Eagle Bowl could wait for the next day.

"Trees?" I asked.

"Trees!" she answered, and we spend the rest of the day skiing powder in the treed sections of the resort.

At 3:30pm, the lifts closed. We had only eaten gorp and chocolate that I had brought in a small backpack, and we had finished the bota bag of water I carried along, so we were tired, hungry and thirsty. We grabbed a quick sandwich at the lodge and then headed back to Alan's.

Alan and Carson were engaged in a serious conversation while Nancy and Jane sat across from each other in overstuffed chairs reading.

"How was the skiing?" Alan asked.

"Excellent!" We replied in unison, unable to stop smiling.

Jane offered us a drink and we gladly accepted a repeat of the previous night's hot chocolate with crème de cacao. We filled them in on our skiing experience and the spectacular day on the slopes. Noting our glances at the hot tub, Alan suggested we take a soak. Georgette and I went to our rooms to get out of the ski clothes and then headed out to ease our aching muscles in the hot tub. We followed that by a quick nap before the scheduled 7:30 dinner.

15

Refreshed from our naps, Georgette and I accepted cocktails from Jane. Ronn and Barb had returned from a day of gambling at Stateline on the south shore of Lake Tahoe. We noticed that Barb's right ankle was wrapped and she had crutches beside her.

"How'd we miss that?" I asked her.

"We only saw you in the hot tub last night. My crutches were lying behind us. It's no big deal. I twisted it on bad landing when I jumped from my horse to rope a calf. I'll be as good as new in a week or two."

"You guys are really two of a kind," Georgette commented, smiling at them.

We talked for a few minutes about our respective days. Ronn's "don't pass, don't come" system had made him nearly a thousand dollars and Barb had broken even at Blackjack.

I was familiar with Ronn's system, as years before I had tried to learn everything I could about gambling. I favored Blackjack because I could make the odds even with some simple rules and a bit of card counting. I also enjoyed the experience of watching and talking to the people. Five or six people sit on stools at a green half-moon table, and most of them are tourists from around the country or the world. At a Blackjack table, you often meet the wives of men who are shooting craps, honeymooners hoping they'll win a bit to help launch their financial futures, and others like me who find Blackjack relaxing and the tables convivial environments to waste a few hours and forget the stresses of a normal life.

These days, to discourage card counting, the dealers use four or more decks of cards and deal from a shoe. Most of the dealers are friendly and they actually help inexperienced players with their hands. The Blackjack 'pits' are usually very calm places and in general, people don't win or lose too much money.

Occasionally, a table gets hot. Having studied mathematics in school, until I began gambling, I didn't believe in luck. Then I saw hot tables and cold dealers. While we know that the casinos make their money based on the odds, and they do win in the long run, if dealers have long losing streaks, the casino first rotates them to other tables, then if the dealers continue losing, they send them home, sometimes canceling future shifts. I finally realized that statistically, streaks, winning or losing, will happen. And, statistically, there will clearly be some people who are always lucky and some who will never win. Most of us sit in between. Like Blackjack, at Craps, you can turn the odds to near even with some more complex rules, but these systems require a lot of bets and you win big and lose big, usually breaking even in the long run. The best system is Ronn's, but it's hugely unpopular at the table. Basically, you bet against the dice. You bet that the shooter will lose.

At a typical lively table, fifteen to twenty people gather around a race-track shaped table, each competing for a space. People often stand sideways, lined up chest to back with just one arm free, dangling over the table, to place bets or to roll the dice when their turns come, and they are all cheering and calling out numbers, hoping the shooter will make a pass or hit their numbers. When a streak occurs at craps, the entire casino knows about it. Everyone at the table cheers, laughs, praises the dice and the shooter at the top of their lungs, and can't wait for their turn with the hot dice. Superstitious croupiers will swap out the dice to try to break the streaks, but the entire table becomes infected with a contagious positive energy that both captivates people and feeds on itself. For a few minutes, maybe even a half hour in unusual cases, everyone at the table finds a unique synergy in overcoming the odds together: Us against the normally inexorable forces of the universe, and we're winning!

If you're the shooter, you can be godlike in your actions and magnanimously bless everyone at the table with your luck, leading your sheep against impossible odds. As a kid in college, I experienced this once. I made fifteen straight passes and was pleased with my winnings of over a hundred dollars at the end of my roll. Suddenly a chip came flying my way as a player at the end of the table tipped me a hundred dollar chip. I later learned that he had made over twenty-five thousand dollars on my roll.

So, when you start betting against everyone there, you will find yourself on the receiving end of visual darts and arrows. You're clearly a non- believer, a pagan communist who wants to prevent everyone from experiencing the sublimity of a rollicking ride as they spit in fate's eye and rise above the norm.

Sometimes, even the most unassuming patrons will ask you to leave in no uncertain terms. You can appeal to the croupiers, but unless you want a scene, it's easier just to move on. I had tried the system a couple of times, but couldn't stand to be the most unpopular person in the club, and I understood the draw and excitement of the more illogical hope to finally be part of a lucky streak. More often though, playing it straight, you'll end up losing, sometimes a lot. I now prefer the safer, less volatile game of Blackjack.

And while we all like to think that the big gambling done at Craps, Blackjack, Roulette, and other tables are our chances to win big, the casinos make their money on slot machines. Even with their margins set to low single digit numbers, the rapid fire, non-stop money going through those machines generates far more revenue than all the table games combined.

Turning back to Ronn and Barb, I joked, "I bet you were real popular today."

"It wasn't that crowded, and I was only chased away from one table. I won, and that's what matters," Ronn replied. "I like the energy, excitement and pace of the Craps table, even if I'm not very popular. Besides, most people don't even notice how I'm betting."

We discussed the merits of Blackjack and Craps a bit more, then seeing that Jane and Alan were working on dinner, Georgette and I went to help. Alan was wearing rubber gloves and I followed him out onto the deck where coals in a stone-faced built-in grill were glowing red hot.

"Why the gloves?" I asked as he began to remove salmon filets from a green and orange mixture.

"This is one of my favorite dishes, but you don't want to get the marinade on your hands, especially if you wear contact lenses like I do. This is a mixture of orange juice, lime juice, garlic, olive oil and habanero peppers – the hottest peppers in the world. I only use a small amount for flavor more than hotness, but the oil from the peppers gets everywhere. I wear the gloves so I don't end up burning an eye out when I remove my contacts later.

"Jane is making coconut rice with habaneros as well. That is intended to be spicier, as is the habanero-lime butter that you'll use as a topping on both."

Less than ten minutes later, Alan pulled the fish off the grill just as Jane, Georgette, and Nancy brought in a spinach salad, the coconut rice, and broccoli. Simple in appearance, the flavors were unlike anything I'd experienced before. I had heard of habaneros peppers, but thought they were for masochists. Now I knew that in addition to the heat, in small quantity, they offered a rich, almost nutty taste with just a bit of a bite on the tongue. Dinner conversation began with each of us recounting our day. As usual, Ronn got the biggest laugh when Barb described in more detail how he'd been asked to leave – not just a table, but a casino.

As the food settled in, the physical fatigue enabled both me and Georgette to relax into the conversation, which slowly found its way to a technology discussion. Opinions flew in all directions as Georgette, Carson, Ronn, and I presented new ideas for data and voice products along with our opinions of the future of networking, while Jane and Nancy questioned how we would get any of these ideas to market. Alan sat back and listened with interest, a satisfied smile gracing his lips.

Seeing Barb's eyes glazing over, I tried to reengage her by asking about her last rodeo, but she just smiled and waved me off, knowing that there was no way to derail the escalating discussion that Alan had so cleverly started. The discussions continued through dessert – a delicately orange-flavored crème brulee - and spilled into the living room as brandies were served in front of a raging fire. Carson lit up a cigar, and when the conversation paused, Alan took the opportunity to excuse himself.

16

We were all settling down into a comfortable evening, Georgette and I were mellowed by the physical effort of the day, the fine dinner, and the wine and brandy. Seeing the fire fading a bit, I stood up, walked over, placed two madrone logs onto the glowing coals, and stirred them, encouraging the fire to reemerge. Everyone in the room seemed almost hypnotized by the dancing flames and a comfortable silence fell like a warm blanket over the room.

Alan returned a few minutes later carrying a small leather pouch cinched at the top. He placed a notebook-sized rectangular mirror onto the inlayed coffee table, opened the pouch and withdrew a small silver scoop, like a miniature flour scoop. He filled it with a crystalline white powder from the bag, and poured that onto the mirror. He then withdrew a single-edged razor blade from a slot inside the pouch and began chopping and arranging the powder into thin white three-inch lines. His practiced hands seemed almost balletic, like a Japanese steakhouse chef, as he finished the sixth line with a flourish. He then produced a small silver tube, placed one end in his right nostril, closed his left nostril with his left forefinger, bent over the mirror, placed the end of the silver tube at the base of a line and the line of powder disappeared up his nose as he slid the tube forward, sucking it up. With hardly a pause, he switched hands, placing the tube in his left hand, and proceeded to vacuum up another line into his left nostril. With that, he turned to us, faced flushed, smiled, and offered the tube.

As it probably was for almost everyone, college was a drug haven. Students were either getting high or experimenting. Pot use was rampant and for those who wanted mind-expanding experiences, there was acid, mescaline, and mushrooms. Among the engineers and pre-med students, we saw a lot of uppers. Many became speed freaks. But somehow, I had never run into cocaine or heroin, the 'hard drugs.' I guess my crowd wasn't rich enough for the first or desperate enough for the latter.

My attitude on drugs has always been one of you use yours, I'll use mine. Even today, I see no real difference between the caffeine-addicted yuppies whose moods rise and fall more often than coastal tides between cups of strong coffee, and cocaine users who need their next line to make it through their next high-powered meetings. Of course, the latter is illegal. Most of us seek some kind of chemical boost to make life a bit more bearable, so why is one 'better' than another? Why do we outlaw drugs and end up financing murderous drug cartels?

In other words, I've never been terribly judgmental about individual choices like this. I'll take chocolate injections along with my 'risk' sports. You can choose alcohol, pot, coke, whatever.

I don't know if it was our military upbringing, but neither Georgette nor I had become regular users of any illegal drug, even in college. We drank socially and tended to pass on the rest.

"No thanks," I replied to Alan's offer.

"I think we're soaking up the warm after burn of a day of heavy exercise, a fine meal and nice wine," Georgette completed.

"I haven't done this before, but I'm always open to new experiences," Carson said as he moved forward and Alan handed him the gleaming silver tube.

Carson looked around the room and seeing no one looking shocked, tried his first line.

"Wow, that's like having coke – I mean coca cola - come out your nose. It burns. I don't feel anything else, what's supposed to happen?

"Try another line and wait a few minutes," Alan responded.

Carson complied. He reversed hands and took the second line up his left nostril then handed the tube back to Alan who chopped and arranged several more white tracks on the mirror. Nancy, Barb, Ronn, and Jane each took their turns and the conversation started up again, nonchalantly, as Alan kept the mirror ready for its next visitor.

While we continued to brainstorm technological possibilities along with market and financial implications of each, I think Georgette and I also stepped back a bit. In addition to holding up our end of the discussions, we were now also observers. How would the drug affect these high powered individuals?

From what I could see, Alan became more animated, Ronn started talking faster, Barb seemed happier and more interested in the conversation, and Nancy and Jane seemed about to be overwhelmed by sheer joy, arguing confidently with the technological leaders and grinning ear-to-ear. I likened this to the feelings Georgette and I experienced earlier in the day with our own pristine white powder.

All my adult life I had heard horror stories about cocaine. From the amusing "It's God's way of saying you have too much money," to stories of paranoia, self-centeredness, and battles with murderous drug dealers, I was convinced that if it wasn't evil in itself, it was certainly the path to it. Now I was beginning to question that.

The ideas were coming fast and furiously now, and it seemed like the volume and intensity had been turned up a notch. Nonetheless, I found myself asking if we would have come up with so many clever concepts and their counterpoints if not for the drug. I also watched Carson. Carson's presence in a room was always charismatic. His innate self-confidence and avuncular attitude made you want to both listen, and open up to him. This didn't change with the cocaine, even after many more lines through the evening. If anything, Carson grew more expansive without any hint of becoming overbearing. His thought processes seemed clearer and more focused. He was able to more quickly understand technical nuances in areas he'd never been exposed to before, and his presence and good nature seemed to envelop us like the heat from the fire, warm, comforting, and somehow inexorable.

Sometime during the evening, Alan had found a notebook. By eleven o'clock, he had filled pages, and I think everyone felt we had exhausted the topics of Alan's future business directions. Georgette and I excused ourselves, telling the others that we'd be heading out early for the snow and thanking Alan and Jane for their hospitality. As we walked towards our rooms, we heard Carson's mellifluous voice beginning to weave an enchanting tale from the past. I fell asleep wondering whether the old sixties' motto about better living through chemistry might not have some truth in it.

Georgette and I took a little more time in the morning. We packed, and sat down to a light breakfast of bagels, cereal and orange juice. As I was finishing up a thank-you note, Jane came down the stairs dressed in a green chenille robe that set off her untamed red hair. She looked tired, almost stumbling as she walked.

"Are you guys always up so early, and so chipper in the morning?" she asked.

"Guilty!" I replied.

"That's disgusting!" she continued. "We ran out of aspirin upstairs so I'm only down here long enough to find and swallow a whole bottle."

"Do you guys always party like that?" Georgette asked, smiling broadly.

"No, but Alan thought this was a special occasion. He really appreciates all that Carson and CIA have done to get us to where we are today and he wanted to do it right."

"Well, we certainly had a good time!" I replied. "We're heading out to see if we can repeat yesterday's skiing and will be heading home from there. The house is amazing, the food was delicious, and your hospitality was the best. Thanks!"

We hugged her goodbye, asked her to thank Alan for us, and watched her trudge back up the stairs as we closed the door behind us.

Once in the car, I asked, "What did you think?"

"This has been a great weekend. I really appreciate meeting Alan and Carson. They really know what they're doing. Sometimes I think success is more a question of having and living a vision, than anything else, and both Carson and Alan know themselves and seem to have a clear direction. I hope I can get there someday soon. I was also pleased to see Jane and Nancy holding their own. I usually find I'm the lone woman in a room full of ambitious males. Sometimes the testosterone could kill you. But these two ladies, while not technologists, certainly understand business and markets, perhaps better that the men do. I'm envious of what looked like two perfect teams. Both Jane and Nancy complement their mates and clearly maintain their equal footings.

"I hope I contributed something. I know I got a lot out of

last night's debates. I'm going to steal variations on a number of the ideas we discussed. I don't think any will compete with where Alan wants to take his company, but I'm going to sit down with Marty and kick some around as possible future directions for Modular."

"But what about the cocaine?"

"What do you mean?" she asked.

"Don't you think it actually enhanced the discussions? Did you see Carson grow even larger than he normally is? Didn't the ideas and even the disagreements become sharper? I know I wasn't high, but as an objective observer, I thought I saw a wonder drug there."

"Jack, that's the kind of thinking that got Sherlock Holmes. Granted he was only a fictional character, but I've known quite a few coke heads. At first it's innocuous. Cocaine is a stimulant. It steps up your metabolism, speeds your thinking, and builds confidence. In small quantities, it may be beneficial from time to time, just as a doctor might prescribe an upper to a depressed person, though I personally think that the higher you get the further you fall. In the long-run though, people want more. I don't know if they build up a tolerance, I suspect they do, but where there's an up, there's a down. Think how Jane looked this morning. You know what an alcohol hangover is like. The down from cocaine can be a real crash. Then you want more to bring you up. Then you think that if you were brilliant with a quarter gram, a half would make you even better. Over time, clarity leads to paranoia.

"In our normal state we all have fears but we discount most of them. You might be lying in bed and briefly think that the ceiling could fall on you, but you quickly realize that the building is sound and the chances are too small to worry about. With coke, particularly in the down times, you begin to think about the termites, dry rot, the impending earthquake or a million other ways that the ceiling might fail and as you start to discount one, you come up with arguments to counter that, and on and on.

"After withdrawing from the world, you want to feel all-powerful and omniscient again, so you do more coke and you're on top of the world. Pretty soon, coke is all that matters. You discard your friends and family. You spend every cent you have for your next high. Your work suffers because you're more focused on where your next buy is coming from than you are on the things that should matter. Add in the paranoia, and your life is trashed."

As I pulled into Kirkwood, I glanced over. Georgette's eyes were filled and tears spilled over, running down her cheeks onto her turtleneck where they rested, unabsorbed.

In a thicker voice, Georgette turned to me, angry. "Don't ever think drugs are going to make people better than they are!"

We bought our tickets in silence. I felt ashamed for having brought Georgette to this state. Thinking back, I couldn't ever remember seeing her cry. At the same time, I was confused and half way up the Wall, I asked if she was okay.

"I never told you what happened to my kid brother, Mike. He graduated from USC film school three years ago. I think he was one of the most gifted writers I've ever known. He was also very aggressive and put himself in front of major studio players from the time he started at USC. Less than a year after graduation, he wrote a screenplay and was paid $250,000 for it. He quickly got caught up in the Hollywood crowd and the parties, living the lifestyle. But, some people can do coke casually, and others can't.

"Mike and I had stayed in touch over the years and I saw the cycle I described, but it was his life. When he hit bottom the first time after burning through all his money and his 'friends' quit giving him freebies, he called me. I paid for a drug rehab program in Arizona, away from his friends, and I really thought he was back on track. He was writing again and had sold another screenplay. Then he vanished. I haven't heard from him since."

"I'm sorry. I didn't know."

We got off the lift, took the first drop off the cornice, and then traversed over to Eagle Bowl. Without even stopping at the top, Georgette raced downward in the deep untracked powder, sinking and rising. From my vantage point, she disappeared into the white blanket, then reemerged, floating above it all. I chased behind her, but didn't catch up until we reached the lift. She was more relaxed on our next run and we playfully crossed eights on several more untracked runs until the warming sun made the snow too heavy.

In the afternoon, we moved back to the main part of the mountain. Soft, fluffy mounds had formed as the result of other skier's paths down the mountain. These moguls were more challenging than powder, but as much fun in their own way. Standing at the top of a mogul field, the slope looks like thousands of white eggs haphazardly arrayed below you. Intermediate skiers see them as obstacles, mounds of snow that must be avoided. Unfortunately, the distances between the moguls are small and if you go between two, there's usually another in your path directly below. If you try to avoid a mogul, you often keep your weight back. Not only does that make it difficult to turn your skis, it also means that if you hit an irregularity, like the front or side of a bump, you'll be thrown backwards and will fall.

When I first started skiing them, I always tried to envision every turn from the top of the run to the bottom. But as my technique got better, I realized that I only needed to look two or three moguls down the hill. Keeping weight and hands forward, when you hit a bump, even head on, your weight ends up centered over your skis. Skiing on top of the bump, your edges are freed. You can easily turn in any direction as you just point your skis down the mogul and you can make very quick turns on each bump. This is as much a mental game of confidence as it is physical skill, but once you have it down, each run is a surprise as your body finds a rhythm to turn the chaos of erratic piles of snow into a hop and slide playground. I like to think I'm pretty good in moguls, certainly not competition quality, but I'm always humbled when I ski with Georgette.

We rode the Cornice chair up to Look Out Janek, one of the most challenging mogul runs at Kirkwood, and while I tried to keep up with Georgette, she was more intense, skiing top to bottom without stopping, then waiting patiently for me at the lift. We skied until the sun dropped behind the mountain and the light became flat. When the lifts closed at 4 pm, we packed up and headed back to the Bay Area, three hours away.

Georgette slept all the way home, and when I finished helping her unload her gear, she gave me a prolonged hug and said, "Be careful, Jack. I wouldn't want to lose you."

CHAPTER 3

"All or nothing at all!"
- Anonymous

1

I arrived at the office Monday morning and was surprised to see Pam filling a legal-sized brown leather brief bag with transparencies, reviewing each one before placing it into a manila folder in the bag.

"Going somewhere?" I asked.

"Steve has lined up a meeting with Bell South in Atlanta to discuss Project Hydra. I'll be presenting the expected financial returns and pricing. We have two days of meetings scheduled with a possible follow up day, and will be back on Thursday or Friday. Sorry I don't have time to talk; our flight leaves at 11am from San Francisco."

Working in my office an hour later, the phone rang.

"Jack, I need a favor," an exasperated Shelly demanded when I picked up the receiver.

"Uh. Hi Shelly. Sure. What do you need?" I replied, shaken by her tone.

"My bastard husband decided to take a week-long trip this morning. He knew I had an examination scheduled at the fertility clinic and I needed him there. I haven't told my family or any of my friends about the fertility problems, so I'm stuck. I'm not about to tell them now. The clinic is doing a procedure that will leave me unable to drive. Can you take me there and give me a ride home tomorrow at ten am? Actually, the appointment is at 10 am, can you pick me up at 9:30?"

I agreed to pick her up and had just hung up the phone when Carson walked into my office.

"How was the skiing yesterday?" he asked.

"The skiing was great, almost as good as Saturday," I replied, but felt a sense of foreboding as I remembered Georgette's admonition about drugs and the story about her brother. "Thanks for inviting us. We had a great time and Georgette was really impressed by Alan and got a lot out of the discussions."

"Alan was impressed by her, too. Do you think she'd be open to a job offer?"

"I'll pass it on, but she's CTO at a startup that's seems to be growing steadily, so I doubt she'll change ships now. I think she's ambitious enough to want to build a company the size of Alan's on her own."

"Well, let me know if she'll consider it. Actually, I'd love to have her on our team. She'd make a great consultant.

"Alan really felt he got his money's worth. I thought it was a very successful weekend. It's rare to combine fun and business like that, usually if you add fun to the mix, no work gets done. I especially liked the synergy that developed with the 'outside parties.' Jane, Nancy, and Georgette all made major contributions. We should think about doing more things like that. By the way, have you seen Steve around?"

"He and Pam are flying to Atlanta for a meeting with Bell South. I think he's out all week. Is there anything you need that I could help with?"

"No. I'm just losing track of what's going on at NewCo and wanted to catch up. If you're free for dinner, come by my office about 6. A new shipment of Ridge wines came in today on my subscription and I can't wait to try one."

I spent the rest of my day checking up on projects, talking to customers, and writing reports. At 6 o'clock, I walked into Carson's office. On his desk sat an open bottle of a new York Creek Zinfandel and two claret glasses. Seeing me at his door, he invited me in and poured the wine.

"It's a bit young," he said, "but I bet this '84 is going to be a classic. I think I'll order a couple of cases."

We enjoyed a lavish dinner at the company cafeteria. Richard plied us with his latest specialty, a spicy Basque seafood dish and Carson and I discussed ALM's plans, the growth of NewCo, and how comfortable we both were with CIA at its current size.

As I drove back over Highway 17 to Santa Cruz, I couldn't help wondering about the future. Could we really control Steve and his unbridled ambition? Would Georgette succeed? Could Carson and I maintain the comfort and integrity of CIA? And almost unbidden, came thoughts of Shelly. Did we have a future together?

2

I rang Shelly's bell at 9:30 and she stepped out without inviting me in - all business.

Brushing past me, she said only, "I really appreciate this, Jack."

I walked her to the car and opened the door for her. She slid in, uptight and clearly angry, arms crossed and a sour look on her face. I closed the door and walked around to the driver's side.

"Bastard! Bastard! Bastard!" she shouted as I stepped in and started the ignition.

Seeing my wide-eyed look of alarm she continued, "I'm sorry. I'm just so embarrassed and pissed off. He knew. He knew I'd waited months for this appointment. Instead, he schedules this trip so he can shack up with Pam. Bastard! Bastard!"

We drove in silence for the several minutes it took me to screw up my courage to talk to her.

"So, I don't mean to pry, but what's happening today? Is there anything you need me to do other than drive?"

"No, no. Again, I'm sorry. You remember I mentioned that I was going in for fertility testing a few months ago?"

I nodded.

"Well, they didn't find anything conclusive. Apparently, I have a minor amount of endometriosis, but it shouldn't be enough to cause fertility problems. Stanford has a new technique call video laparoscopy. They make an incision at the navel and insert this flexible tube with a small camera attached. They can look at ovaries, fallopian tubes, pretty much anything. I get a local anesthetic at the navel and some relaxation drug, and that's all there is to it. It's amazing what they can do with technology today!" Turning towards me she asked, "Are you okay?"

I don't know what it is. With my sports, I've seen and been involved in countless bloody injuries and never felt queasy or went into shock. I can get through the most critical situations, focused on the goal - survival. But seeing someone I care about go bravely through elective surgery makes me ill. I guess I have too much time to think about it. I break out into a cold sweat and begin to shake. My stomach flips and flops and I'm sure I'm going to throw up. I was once told this is a rush of adrenaline as part of a protective instinct, but I think I'm probably just a wimp.

I was touched, concerned, and impressed by how cavalier

Shelly could be about someone penetrating her abdomen and rooting around with a camera. I'm sure I would have worried myself sick, or avoided it completely had the roles been reversed. And this without the support of her husband or family!

"Sure. I'm fine," I finally responded. "I'm impressed that you can do this so confidently and that you have the drive to pursue it without Steve's support."

"It's not about Steve. It's about what I want, and I want a baby."

We arrived at Stanford in plenty of time. I was surprised when Shelly directed me to what looked like a typical office building some distance from the main hospital. Given that she had waited several months for the appointment, I was even more amazed to see the circular waiting room deserted. The lights were dim and recessed, the carpet and furniture was plush, and the walls were padded with a soft gray, probably sound absorbing material from the floor half way to the ceiling. The only real direct light emanated from the reception window where Shelly checked in. We waited in silence, thumbing through magazines until Shelly's name was called. A shaft of light spilled through a sudden opening in the wall – a door, now revealed, that was almost imperceptible in the darkened room. A silhouetted figure stepped into the room.

"Mr. Caples, you can join us if you like," the nurse said to me as Shelly walked towards her.

"No, no. Jack is just my ride." Shelly replied, and with that, she disappeared, the door vanishing seamlessly like the entrance to the spaceship in The Day the Earth Stood Still.

An hour passed and my stomach roiled as I became increasingly worried. My imagination took me through perforated organs, internal bleeding, and excruciating pain. Was that moaning and crying I heard, or just my fears coming to life?

While I flipped through the pages in National Geographic, I couldn't read. What if she died in there? Continuing in my science fiction paranoia, I felt like the man in the To Serve Man episode of the Twilight Zone: alone in a spaceship on my way to becoming dinner for the benevolent-looking aliens.

Finally, feeling almost like I'd lost track of day and night, the nurse reappeared, transported from the other world behind the door into my solitary chamber.

"Mrs. Caples is doing fine. She'll need thirty to forty-five minutes to fully recover from the sedative. You can wait or come back then."

I decided I needed some fresh air so I left and went over to Stanford Shopping Center where I found Mrs. Fields selling her cookies. Although they were the rage in the San Francisco Bay Area, no one imagined then that Debbi Fields would build a world-wide cookie empire from these humble beginnings. I guess this is a lesson to us that high-tech is not the only Silicon Valley path to success.

I quickly scarfed down two of her gooey, slightly underdone chocolate chip cookies, savoring the buttery flavor which complemented the large, melting semi-sweet chocolate, and took a bag of six more with me. Perhaps Shelly would be hungry.

Five minutes after my return, Shelly emerged on the nurse's arm. She looked pale, weak and frail. I went over to her and she seized my arm. After confirming there was no paperwork to finish, we walked to my car.

"That was pleasant," Shelly lamented sarcastically as she carefully slid into my Subaru. "I really appreciate the ride and your patience, but I can't believe Steve let me go through this alone.

"It was okay at first. The shot they gave me relaxed me and the local and initial incision didn't hurt at all. But when they inserted the camera and began rooting around inside me, I thought I was going to die. You have no idea what it's like to have a foreign object crawling throughout your insides, poking organs, distending your abdomen. And the doctor is climbing all over everywhere to get the best angles, and while he's looking at what he's doing, he's also looking at the monitor to see what the camera sees. Then if he suspects something, he forces the tube in closer. Imagine the worse intestinal cramps you've ever had and you're not even close. Think of the movie Alien!"

I pulled away slowly and the greater the detail Shelly went into, the more my lower abdomen clutched as I imagined the procedure.

"So, did they tell you anything?" I ventured cautiously.

"Just that there's nothing wrong with me. It's probably Steve, the bastard. I got a great bargain with him. At least now, he'll have to go in for fertility testing.

"I don't get it. What's the big deal? He's embarrassed to give a semen sample. It's not like you guys don't do that all the time, right?"

Seeing me blush, she apologized, "Sorry. I'm just so angry. That was the worst experience of my life and I went through it because Steve is afraid to beat off into a cup. I really shouldn't be taking it out on you."

Release of the pent-up anger in these outbursts seemed to drain her and before we reached her apartment, she fell asleep. I parked and gazed at the beautiful woman sleeping in the seat beside me, her face and body finally relaxed.

Ten minutes later, I roused her gently and helped her up the stairs to her apartment.

"Can you stay?" she asked sleepily.

"Of course," I replied.

I helped her to her bedroom. She sat on the queen-sized canopied bed, kicked off her shoes, pulled off her socks, and without even a glance at me slipped out of her slacks and blouse, then picked up and pulled a large t-shirt over her head. The t-shirt read 'BABY' with an arrow pointed down below it. Under the shirt, she reached behind her and removed her bra, which she threw on the floor. She slipped her arms through the sleeves, pulled back the covers, and climbed into the bed.

"Wake me in an hour or so, will you?"

"No problem. I'll be here," I indicated a chair across the room.

With that, she turned away, curled up on her side and fell asleep very quickly, her rhythmic breathing causing the blankets to rise and fall gently.

I stepped out of the room and called the office to let them know I'd be out most of the day. I examined the books in the study and found one of my favorites, John Irving's The World According to Garp, then returned to the bedroom and read Irving's wonderful mix of irony, poignancy, and comedy until she awoke a little over an hour later.

"I'm starving," she said. "I didn't eat before the procedure. What time is it anyway?"

"It's a little past two. Can I fix you something? Do you have eggs? What would you like something to drink?

She nodded enthusiastically. "Eggs sound great! You'll find a container with English Breakfast Tea on the counter. I like it with milk and a teaspoon of sugar. Are you really going to fix me breakfast?" She asked grinning sheepishly.

I smiled and nodded, then went out to explore the kitchen. In the refrigerator, I found butter, eggs, tortillas, Monterey Jack cheese, fresh basil, and a jar of raspberry jam. The breadbox contained, surprise, surprise, bread. In a cupboard under the tiled kitchen counter, I found a well-seasoned cast-iron skillet.

I fired up the teapot on the stove, then, turning on another gas burner, I heated the skillet, and added butter and torn-up pieces of tortilla. I sautéed the tortillas, then tossed in several leaves of fresh basil. When the tortillas became slightly crispy, I poured in six beaten eggs. I popped two slices of bread in the toaster, and poured boiling water from the teapot over a teabag in a mug I'd found.

When the eggs were almost done, I turned off the burner, grated cheese over the top, then cut it into the eggs and tortillas with the spatula. I buttered the now-done toast and smothered it in raspberry jam. Removing the teabag from the mug, I added a splash of milk and a teaspoon of sugar. I put half the eggs on a plate along with the toast and a fork, then grabbed the tea and headed back to the bedroom.

"Smells great!" Shelly said.

"I tried to find a tray, but couldn't. I hope you like it. It's my breakfast specialty, huevos tortillas."

I placed the tea on the nightstand beside her and handed her the plate. She took a sip of tea, then a bite of eggs.

"Yum!" she said. "We don't have any trays. The last thing that would happen in this house is breakfast in bed. I haven't had anyone serve me since I left home for college."

"What a shame. You certainly deserve better."

I went back to the kitchen and put the rest of the eggs on a plate for myself. When I returned, we ate quietly and I could see that Shelly was lost in thought. When she finished, I cleared the plates, leaving her with tea, and then cleaned up the kitchen.

Shelly emerged in sweatpants and the same t-shirt. I looked at the 'BABY' and arrow, and noticing my glance, she smiled.

"Maybe someday, now that we know my plumbing is mostly okay. Thanks for taking care of me, Jack. I really appreciate this. I think I'm back to normal now. The breakfast really perked me up!"

With that, she threw her arms around me and hugged me tight, then pulled away suddenly.

"Did I hurt you," I asked.

"I am a little tender around the middle. Let's try that again."

She pressed herself against me and I felt the swell of her small firm breasts. I slid my hands down her sides, stopping at her small waist, then pulled away.

"Call me any time." I said, turning for the door.

"Jack?" Shelly called, following me.

I turned at the door and Shelly kissed me on the mouth. The kiss was gentle and sweet, her lips warm and relaxed against mine.

"You're a very special person, Jack. I'll call you in a couple days."

She squeezed my hand and I left, completely confused.

3

The next morning, I awoke before first light and turned on the weather radio. The surf was huge and the winds were light. I had spoken with my surfing buddy, Mark, the night before, but he had an early morning appointment, so I grabbed my 'semi-gun,' a longer, faster board meant for bigger waves. This was a very special board that I'd had made for me by David Mel, uncle to the now-famous big wave rider Peter Mel. David was one of a few people experimenting with non-fiberglass boards and mine was beautiful. He took a foam blank, shaped it to my specifications, and covered it in a mahogany veneer, then sealed the board with epoxy. Epoxy boards are becoming quite popular now, but in 1985, this was a real innovation.

The board was a bit heavier than a fiberglass board, but I found that helpful in dropping down big waves. The last thing you want on a huge wave is to be held at the top by the air rushing up the face. If the wave breaks before you drop down it, you could be seriously hurt as the top of the wave pitches forward, taking you with it, pummeling you into shallow water below.

Driving up Highway 1 as dawn broke, I could see clean long lines of swells breaking in places that rarely have waves. I knew the swell was far too big for Boulders – at over ten feet, the waves at Boulders became crashing closed-out walls with nowhere to ride - so I continued up the coast to Scott Creek, the best big wave break in California (we didn't know about Maverick's back then).

Scott Creek looked perfect. Long right-breaking walls started breaking about a quarter of a mile out and raced for hundreds of yards before ending in the strong rip tide at the mouth of the creek. I couldn't tell how big it was since no one was out, but because I was supremely confident in my big wave surfing abilities, I didn't even hesitate. After all, I had surfed Guethary in France at over twenty feet and California waves didn't have the power of French or Hawaiian waves.

I suited up and jumped into the riptide. Once of the nice features about Scott Creek is the riptide. While most people have been taught to avoid riptides, surfers know that these are the best way to get out past the breaking waves. At Scott's, the creek has carved out a deep channel in the reef, so all the water rolling in from the breaking waves to the north rushes out again through that channel. I jumped into the fast moving river of water and in no time was well beyond the breaking waves.

I paddled into the lineup and took off on my first wave. I'm what's called a goofy foot: I stand with my right foot forward. On right-breaking waves, I ride backside. My back is to the wave. I've always loved this extra challenge and after making the drop and hearing the lip crash behind me, I drew out a long bottom turn and aimed for the top of the wave, some fifteen feet above me. Over and over I carved large turns into the face. The ride ended abruptly as I turned out into the riptide for my paddle back out. My second ride was similar to the first and I thought it was the beginning of a great session. I waited in the lineup for the next set, reminiscing about other big days. This was one of the biggest I'd surfed in California. As I gazed to the west, I saw mountains approaching. I started paddling as fast as I could to try to make it over the oncoming waves. The first wave was feathering across the top as I barely made it over the top. The wave behind it was even bigger and I didn't think I had a chance. Adrenaline was now firing in my system and I gave it everything I had, again paddling at least twenty vertical feet upwards. I just barely made it over, hoping that the next wave wouldn't be any bigger. But it was. My shoulders were burning, my heart pounding and I began hyperventilating to try to store as much oxygen in my lungs as possible for what was likely to be a long time underwater.

I reached the crest of the wave just as the lip pitched outward. I grabbed my board and held on as I fell twenty to twenty-five feet backwards, landing on my back. The force of the fall knocked the wind out of me. I saw stars, little flashes of light racing around the inside of my head, and just when I thought things couldn't get worse, the wave crashed down on top of my board, driving it into my face. I felt my nose separate and then all hell broke loose.

I held on to my board fiercely believing that it was buoyant and would eventually make it to the surface, but we were bounced off the reef over and over and I lost all sense of direction as I was tossed and flipped uncontrollably. I had been through situations like this before, so I wasn't worried until my lungs started burning. I released the board thinking that its added flotation was keeping me inside the whitewater rushing to shore, then immediately regretted this action as I realized that my leg was attached to the board and I'd be dragged if I couldn't get it off. Fortunately, the power in the wave snapped my surf leash and I was free. I thought I could make my way to the surface, but I swam into the bottom hitting my head. I tried to grab the reef, hoping I could hold on until the wave passed, but I was ripped away and thrown up and down, end-over-end, my arms and legs whipped around like a rag doll's.

I didn't know how long I'd been under, but with lungs demanding me to breathe, I began to realize that I had gone too far this time. This was the end. My life didn't pass before my eyes, but I did accept my fate. I worried about the people I was leaving behind. I began to sink into unconsciousness. The pain in my lungs became a part of me, but it was somehow less insistent as I started to fade away. I felt my mouth opening and broke the surface as I inhaled water. Coughing and spitting water, I looked to see a wave about to break on my head. I sucked in air, stifling the coughs my body demanded, and pushed myself under, hoping to escape the oncoming wave.

It didn't work. I couldn't get to the bottom and the wave grabbed me and once again I was captured by chaos. This felt more like a normal thrashing, and I knew I'd survive and would rise to the surface, which I did, less than thirty seconds later. Unfortunately, the wave had deposited me in the riptide, friend to surfer, enemy to swimmer. I was now a swimmer.

I swam perpendicular to the riptide as it pulled me outward and eventually I made it into the surf break. Thinking I could body surf a ten-foot wall of whitewater, I swam hard to catch the wave, but went through another cycle of the Scott Creek washing machine as the chaotic whitewater had too much power for me to maintain any direction. Again, I ended up in the riptide and I paused, exhausted, and tried to think my way out of the situation.

The water was fifty-two degrees. Yes, I was wearing a wetsuit and booties, but how long could I survive before hypothermia set in? I did a body inventory. My broken nose had stopped bleeding. My muscles were beginning to stiffen and I was cold and very tired. I was also light-headed. I guessed I hadn't had a normal amount of oxygen for several minutes. I coughed and coughed, spewing water from my lungs, then vomited my breakfast into the raging current. Then I came up with a plan.

I let the riptide carry me out past the break, swam south about a quarter mile from Scott Creek, then shoreward into the breakers. The waves were big, but there were no well-defined rip tides, and forty minutes and countless thrashings later, I washed up on the beach where I vomited salt water onto the coarse sand. I lay there shaking from the cold, my arms quivering from the exertion. I think I may have dozed off for a few minutes when a woman nudged me with her foot.

"Are you okay?" she asked. Seeing me open my eyes and nod, she continued. "I saw that wave crush you and you didn't come up. Then a second wave broke over the spot you went down and you still didn't come up. I saw your board wash into the rocks on the other side of the creek and then you were up and in the rip tide. I thought about getting help, but didn't want to lose sight of you. You didn't seem panicked so I waited, hoping someone else would come down to the beach so I could send them for help."

I struggled to my feet and staggered back up the beach. The tide was dropping so I was able to make my way north along the beach to retrieve my board. I found it lodged in the rocks. At least a foot of the board was missing; the nose had been broken off. How ironic! The fin boxes were ripped out leaving three gaping holes in the bottom, dirty white patches ruining the grain of the mahogany. The bottom and rails (sides) were covered in dings and scratches, but the top was largely unscathed, probably protected somewhat by the thick coating of wax.

The nose and fins were nowhere to be found so I picked up the remaining piece and walked up to my car and drove to Doctors-on-Duty, affectionately known as doc-in-the-box. After verifying I didn't have a concussion, they straightened and butterflied my nose, then sent me on my way with a prescription for painkillers that I threw away.

I never have been able to get over my fear of big waves. I relive that experience in both sleeping and waking nightmares. Was it the two-wave hold-down? Or, could it have been the time in the water and my near inability to get back in? Maybe if it had been one without the other, or if someone had been there to help me.

Now, if I do go out on a big day, I'm too conservative. I think I see a large set coming and I paddle out too far to catch the waves, then paddle back into the lineup. Other surfers wonder why I over-paddle the waves. Years ago, if I started paddling out, others followed quickly in my wake. They knew I could see waves they didn't. Now, they look embarrassed for me. Since that fateful day, I almost never go out where the waves are larger than ten feet. You'd think that over time, you could get it back, I don't know why I can't. I now have a lot more non-threatening fun on the smaller days. Other surfers still respect my skill, as I shred the medium sized waves, but I know that on big days, I'll be watching instead of riding, or I'll look for a smaller perfect wave at another spot rather than face the power.

I have newfound respect for the big wave riders who get through incidents like mine. Of course, maybe they're smart enough not to surf alone. I still do.

4

Of course, Ronn was in the office when I got in at almost noon. I'd spent almost two hours at doc-in-the-box and now, in addition to my swollen nose, the areas below my eyes were puffy and darkening. By the next day, I'd have two beautiful shiners. "So what was it? Rocks in the river, a tree skiing, a crash hang gliding, or did you just pick on the wrong guy?" Ronn asked.

"Surfing." I replied, then turned away.

"Surfing?! Isn't that the sport that Frankie Avalon and Gidget did? How can you get hurt surfing? I thought that was the safest of the things you do. And you give me shit about polo. Okay, tell me the gory details. I love gory details."

"I don't want to talk about it. "

When I glanced back at him, his face revealed a mix of surprise and concern. I think he could see the residual fear there. My self-confidence was gone. I was shaken. I had been surfing for over twenty years and considered myself one of the best in the water. Now I'd taken a big step down. I wasn't invincible. I couldn't accomplish everything I set my mind to. I was assailing myself with self-doubt, and Ronn could see it. His look softened.

"You know Jack, a few years ago I tried to break a new stallion that Garnet brought to the ranch. I'd always found the process of taming a horse a fascinating one.

I'd spend days with this horse, getting him used to me, leading him around the corral, even getting him to accept a saddle. A big part of the process is building trust and I'd done this many times before. I was sure he was ready. On my first ride, he threw me. This shouldn't have been a big deal, but I hit the ground hard and saw stars, the wind knocked out of me. You know that fear when you think you'll never breathe again? That's where I was. The next thing I knew, I saw a massive body and two hooves coming down right at my head. I froze in terror, gasping for air, and it's a good thing I did, because the horse only wanted to show me that he was boss. He stomped the ground on either side of my head, but for a moment, I was sure I was dead. It's funny, I wasn't frightened at that moment. Afterwards, I was afraid of horses for months. If I had moved or tried to get up... But as they say, you have to get back on the horse."

"I might get back on the horse, but it'll be a tame one," I replied. "I know you play polo, but do you still break horses?"

"Actually, no, I don't."

"Well, I suspect there are some people who are lucky and don't lose their confidence in something they love. Maybe they make it through life without any loss of self-esteem and direction. But for me, I know I'm going to second-guess myself in everything I do, not just surfing and sports, but everything."

"It'll fade with time, Jack. Trust me."

"I'm sure this particular event will. But I was too cocky. I don't think I'll ever feel invincible again."

"We're all mortal, Jack. Some of us just take longer to figure that out. A few unlucky ones never do."

5

The next day, most of the swelling had gone down. I'd spent the night applying icepacks and taking Advil and now I could at least breathe through my nose and speak without sounding like I had a bad cold. But I definitely had two black eyes.

When I got to the office, Donna remarked that I looked much better. "I have some cover-up that you could put under your eyes," she offered. "You'll look perfectly normal."

I thanked her for the offer, but refused, and secluded myself in my office for the day. A few minutes after five, my phone rang.

"How are you feeling?" Shelly asked.

"How did you know I was hurt?"

"Donna told me all about it when I called in. Are you okay?"

"Well, I have two black eyes and a broken nose, but I'm feeling much better today. How are you recovering from the procedure?"

"I'm still a bit tender around the navel, but the rest of me seems fine. I've been stretching and doing yoga without any pain and the stitches are supposed to come out in a few days."

"Steve is still in Atlanta. He didn't even call to find out how it went. I bet he thinks I didn't go.

"Anyway, I'm going stir crazy sitting alone in the apartment. Dogtown here in Mountain View, has a live blues band every Thursday night. How about some dancing? I really enjoyed our one dance at the Catalyst. Want to see if we pull it off in our crippled states tomorrow night? I'm sure we'll make a pretty pair."

I hesitated. What was I doing? Was I really going to pursue this relationship with Steve's wife? They were married no matter how weird their relationship seemed. On the other hand, she was clearly not happy with Steve. He had affairs and didn't want a family. Maybe it made sense. If it worked out, she'd make a great partner for me in more than just dancing. Recalling the synchronized connection during our one dance, I realized I couldn't say no. How often in your life did you find something like this?

"Okay!" I replied enthusiastically. "When should I pick you up?"

"Why don't you meet me at Café Napoli on Castro Street at

seven for dinner and we'll walk over to Dogtown afterwards?"

I agreed, then called to make dinner reservations for two at seven the next evening.

6

Before leaving the office the next evening, I was tempted to take Donna up on her makeup offer, but the color under my eyes was fading. Now it was a mix of yellow, dull green and gray.

I arrived at the restaurant a few minutes early and was led to a booth with a table covered in the standard red and white checkered tablecloth. Empty straw-covered Chianti bottles filled small shelves bordering the top of the booth, a small votive candle flickered on the table next to bottles of olive oil and balsamic vinegar, and a small bowl of freshly-grated parmesan cheese. I had just glanced at the wine list when the maitre d' escorted Shelly to our table. I rose and carefully kissed her on the cheek.

"Your nose looks painful, but I can hardly see the bruising under your eyes."

"I'll try to keep my nose away from your navel," I quipped in a lame attempt at humor.

"Too bad. That would have been a good place to start," she replied suggestively.

The busboy placed a basket of warm breadsticks and a small bowl of spiced cream cheese on the table and asked if we wanted water, which we accepted.

"I'm really looking forward to dancing," she continued. "I think I told you at the Catalyst that I hadn't danced since college."

"And where was that?" I asked.

"Oh, life history time? I guess it's only fair. Steve has filled me in on you."

"I graduated from Stanford, then stayed on for my MBA. I grew up here. My parents have lived in the same house in the Los Altos Hills for over thirty years. My father is retired now. He was a senior engineer at Lockheed. My mom was the typical upper middle class housewife, bridge clubs, Tupperware parties, you know the drill. I have an older brother who really hasn't amounted to much, but my parents think he walks on water. Me, I've been trying to convince them I can be more than wife and mother. Funny, isn't it? Here I am trying so hard for a baby."

The waiter approached and asked if we were ready to order.

"Any specials?" I asked, quickly looking through the menu.

"We have a special appetizer: Dungeness crab cakes topped in a sun-dried tomato cream sauce and served with baby greens. Our dinner special is shellfish linguine: mussels, clams, and scallops tossed with olive oil, garlic, red peppers and linguine. It's excellent. All our dinners include soup or salad. The soup of the day is vegetable minestrone."

"Give us a couple of moments," I requested.

"Can I get you an aperitif while you decide?" he queried.

Shelly shook her head so I told him we'd order wine with dinner.

"Want to share the crab cakes?" I asked Shelly. Seeing her nod, I continued, "I haven't been here before. Do you have any recommendations?"

"That shellfish special sounds good, but my favorite on the menu is Spinach Capellini. It's chicken, spinach, garlic, and red peppers with Capellini pasta."

I glanced over to the waiter, who, seeing my raised eyes, came over. We ordered the crab cakes and a bottle of Chianti Classico Riserva. Shelly stuck with the Capellini and I asked for the shellfish special. I offered the breadsticks to Shelly, then took one myself. If these were an indication of quality of the food, we weren't going to be disappointed. More homemade bread than breadsticks, they were soft and warm, brushed in olive oil and sprinkled with oregano and dill. I tore off a piece and dipped it in the spicy cheese. What a great start! The crab cakes arrived. The tangy sauce was a perfect complement to the crispy cakes and their steaming crab-filled interiors.

"So Shelly, you know I like you, but I'm not really sure what's going on here. You're married to Steve, but you seem interested in more than friendship with me."

"Can't friends be lovers too?" she responded with a smile, then turning more serious, she said, "Look, Jack, my relationship with Steve is a marriage only in the legal sense. There's no intimacy there; we hardly tolerate each other. Right now, I need more. I know you felt the connection when we danced. It was like we'd known each other for years. We moved so well together. I want more of that. I don't know where it's going, but I guarantee that Steve doesn't care. Can we take it one day at a time?"

I agreed that we needed to explore 'us,' but I was afraid to ask her if she'd leave Steve for me, or why she hadn't left already. Perhaps I didn't want to know the answers.

Our dinners were excellent. For dessert, we split the house bread pudding, cinnamon and raisins embedded in warm yeasty bread, all smothered with a sauce of Jack Daniels, butter, and sugar. The vanilla bean gelato on the side provided a cool palate cleansing contrast to the richness of the rest of the dessert.

After dinner, we walked the block and a half to Dogtown. The band had already started and a few couples were dancing. Shelly and I found a table close to the dance floor then ordered Calistoga's from the waitress. I paid for the drinks and gave her a sizeable tip. We might be running a small tab since we wouldn't be drinking, but the waitress wouldn't suffer.

The band started playing a slow blues number with a lyrical sax. I led Shelly to the dance floor, took her in my arms and began to dance. Swing is fast, high-energy music and the dance moves are almost frenetic. Timing needs to be perfect or someone falls. Blues, on the other hand, is sensual. Surprisingly, you can use the same moves as swing, but you have to slow way down, and you have to add something to fill the time.

I led Shelly from our closed position through two sensual dips. In each, she slowly extended one leg upward as I lowered her towards the floor, her head tilting back as far as it would go. She shook it from side to side as she came up, and after a pause where her huge green eyes locked onto mine, I turned her out into a double turn and a standard two-handed bridge. In a swing bridge, holding both hands, you raise them over each other's heads and pull back quickly catching each other with one hand. Our variation had us move to one hand, but we didn't pull back. Instead, I held her hand on my shoulder as she slowly moved around me grazing my body, first from behind, then my left side, then the front of me where I led her through an outside turn and caught her as she came around, slipping my arm around her waist and lowering her again.

With each dance, we grew bolder. Time was filled with touching. I'd hold her right hand with my right, then lead her towards me turning her so her back was against the front of me. I'd slide my hand down the length of her arm, across her shoulder and down to her waist, and then I'd slide around her, now face to face and I'd turn her from the waist and catch her. The variations were endless. Even the faster songs invited more sensual, if not downright sexual, moves.

It was an evening of touching unlike any I'd experienced

before. After nearly two hours of dancing, we were both exhausted and excited. Still, I knew I wasn't going home with her. I couldn't see us in Steve's bed.

We stepped out into the chilly night air, our ears ringing from the music. The silence was almost palpable. Radiation fog created a shallow moist blanket that obscured cars parked on the street, but it was crystal clear just above them. Shelly took my arm as we walked to her car.

"You know, Jack, you're so different from Steve. He's always calculating the advantage, always looking for the edge. There's a part of that I admire, but it comes with a price. He'll never be the open, caring, trusting individual you are - and he can't dance. You remind me of a younger version of Carson. You succeed at your level without having to stab anyone in the back. You're a very special person."

With that said, she turned her face up to me. I kissed her goodnight, a long open-mouthed kiss, and allowed myself to fantasize that we could have evenings together like this for the rest of our lives.

7

Steve and Pam returned from Atlanta on Friday looking happy. Since I didn't work with NewCo on a daily basis, I wasn't privy to their progress other than what I heard from Dan and Pam in one-on-one discussions, usually over lunch. In a week or so, I'd know what had happened with Bell South.

One of my favorite customers from Skynet was Carrier Packaging. Although their business was delivering freight nationwide, their CEO, Craig Partage fancied himself a technologist. He wanted his computer and networking systems to be more than state-of-the-art. They had to be something his competitors didn't have. He had funded several key product developments at Skynet, and he had recently contacted me to see if CIA could help him with his 'Star Wars' strategy.

Star Wars was a popular term at the time. Not only was there the movie, President Reagan had created the Strategic Defense Initiative, commonly known as the Star Wars program, a military gambit ostensibly intended to provide a space-based anti-ballistic missile shield. Although it was never really developed and deployed, it may well have caused the Soviet Union to spend itself into oblivion.

Craig's Star Wars plan was a bit different. Most trucking and shipping companies have the same basic problem: How do they track the shipments? For truckers, their delivery challenges also include items delivered to the wrong locations or lost, theft, and even hijacking. Craig envisioned a system where all trucks and contents could be tracked in almost real time using a combination of satellites for tracking, and computers on board each truck to enable each trucker to update his or her position as well as the current inventory in the truck as deliveries are made.

Carson and I had rented a five-bedroom house at Pajaro Dunes, a gated community on the beach about ten minutes south of Santa Cruz, for a brainstorming and planning session with Craig and his Administrative Assistant. They were flying in on Saturday and then out again on Monday morning.

A regular site for executive retreats, Pajaro supplied everything, flip charts, easels, overhead projectors, tape, notepads, coffee service, snacks, and catered meals. The homes are nestled among high sand dunes with wooden walkways connecting them to the community hall and to the almost endless beach.

I had left reminder messages with both of Carson's answering services – Carson didn't believe in answering machines, he wanted you to reach a real person - and he was ready to go when I stopped by his Los Gatos apartment Saturday afternoon. Carson and I went to the San Jose Airport in Carson's BMW to pick up Craig and Bill, his Management of Information Systems (MIS) director.

We only waited a few minutes before their plane arrived. At that time San Jose had no jet ways, and I spotted Craig coming down the steps from the jet, shielding his eyes from the blinding California sun. Craig was in his early forties, about five foot ten with thinning dark hair and quick brown eyes. He was fit, and like his companion, quite pale. I forgot about winters in the Midwest. You didn't see the ground for at least three months and you were lucky to see the sun for more than a few hours a week.

Craig and an extremely tall, gaunt looking man, who I took to be Bill, approached us.

"What happened to you?" Craig asked upon seeing my face.

Other than a little swelling and bruising on my nose, I thought I was back to normal. Apparently, I was wrong. "I'll tell you the harrowing tale over dinner tonight, Craig."

We exchanged introductions, picked up their baggage, and loaded up the car.

"Have either of you been to Pajaro Dunes before?" Carson asked as we left the airport.

"I've been to Monterey and Carmel many times, but never to Pajaro. Craig responded. "Bill?"

"No. This is my first trip to California. I'm a Minnesota farm boy, born and bred."

"Bill, don't bullshit these folks. The closest you've ever been to a farm is a Christmas tree farm."

"Well, I think you'll like the beach," Carson offered. "I thought we'd get settled in this afternoon, then head to a great Mexican restaurant in Watsonville for dinner. We can start our planning session tomorrow morning."

Everyone agreed that this sounded like a good plan.

"I can't believe we're going to the beach in March. It was below zero when we left Minneapolis this morning," Bill said.

We spent the hour-long drive to Pajaro describing the wonders of California to Bill, taking Highway 101 south through the Silicon Valley to the town of Gilroy, garlic capital of the world, and up and over the winding Highway 152 towards Watsonville and Pajaro.

"So these are the famous California mountains," Bill said as we crested the summit at Mt Madonna.

"No, Bill," I replied. "These are just the coastal hills. While they do rise to a few thousand feet, like the Appalachians, the real mountains are a couple of hours to the east. I know this trip is a short one, but if you get the chance to come back, you should allocate some time to at least see Yosemite. "

Fifteen minutes later we pulled into Pajaro Dunes. The security guard at the gate handed Carson the keys and a map, and gave him directions to number 142, our home for the next two days.

I think Craig and Bill were wondering what they'd gotten into when they saw bleak grey exteriors of the homes with only a few small windows. Constructed of an indeterminate wood, the buildings conformed to community standards that minimized damage to the dunes while requiring them to blend in with the environment.

We parked in a small lot and made our way to number 142 across a path of wooden boards tied together with rope. Whatever fears Bill and Craig might have had about their weekend were assuaged when Carson opened the door and we all stepped in.

A staircase let to a loft from the tiled foyer and we could see that it overlooked the living room, formal dining room, and kitchen. The southwest corner of the living room contained a woodstove stuffed with wood and paper, ready to be lit. That part of the room was done in floor to ceiling river rock with a stack of wood not far from the woodstove.

Large glass windows and two sets of French doors opened onto a deck on the ocean side of the house. While the east side where we entered had no windows, the west side looked out over the dunes to the beach below. We could see a few people walking on the wide flat beach. Waves broke far out with no discernible pattern, the ocean chaotic and wild.

"Too bad you didn't bring your surfboard, Jack." Carson commented. "Maybe you could have taught these guys to surf."

"It's not really surfable here unless it's really small. The bottom is sand, no rocks or reefs to give the waves any shape, and we have to rely on shifting sandbars on small days to make it worth going out here. As you can see, it's quite big today and the waves come up and crash with nowhere to ride."

"I've surfed at Waikiki in Hawaii a couple of times," Craig said. "It looked nothing like this."

"And the water is in the low fifties. Hypothermia can set-in in twenty minutes without a wetsuit, and even with one, you don't want to be caught in conditions like these without your board," I continued, reliving my recent nearly fatal experience. "No surfing lessons this weekend."

We continued our tour of the house.

In addition to the kitchen, living room and dining area that were visible from the entrance, the downstairs included a large library with a small conference table that was set up with the presentation materials. It also sported a bathroom, and two bedrooms, each with its own full bath. The upstairs loft had a small sitting area, which overlooked the downstairs and there were three bedrooms, each with its own bathroom.

We chose our rooms. Carson and I took the two downstairs, and we all agreed to meet in thirty minutes to leave for dinner.

After unpacking and changing our clothes, we headed over to El Toro Negro in downtown Watsonville, about five minutes away. Carson's mood was expansive as he told Craig and Bill about the area.

"While the Midwest is the breadbasket of America, California produces most of the fruits and vegetables for the country. This area is almost all farmland and Watsonville is a farm town. The area is famous for its artichokes and Castroville, a few miles down the coast is designated 'The Artichoke Capital of the World.' They also grow lots of strawberries, Brussels sprouts, lettuces, along with most other cool-weather vegetables. Because we don't get snow and only see frost a few times a year, the growing season is year-round on the coast.

"One of the problems in the area is the farm workers. Surprisingly, most of them are legal aliens. We don't have as many issues as Southern California does on that front. But see those ramshackle buildings over there? Those are typical living quarters for migrant workers. Most don't have heat, the roofs leak, and sanitation facilities are sorely lacking.

"The workers themselves are primarily single young men or fathers who have left their homes behind, hoping to get permanent visas, and to save enough money to bring their families here. If they don't have children, they often bring their wives, who work side-by-side with them in the fields. The work is back breaking and it's not unusual to see them out in the sun for twelve hours a day. While they're paid hourly, it's usually minimum wage or less. Often they're paid by the job and end up making only a dollar or two an hour. The conditions are terrible, and while the United Farm Workers union has helped over the last few years, no one really polices the farms. It reminds me of descriptions of slavery I've read from the last century.

"Amazingly, quite a few succeed. They find permanent jobs, rent inexpensive homes or apartments, some even start businesses. These people work harder than anyone I've seen in my life, but there's still a strong racial bias in California and you don't see many Mexican Americans moving into the upper middle class. Even our industry, which probably has the best track record of including women and minorities, tends to shun Mexican Americans. Of course there's another problem that keeps them down - their kids."

We drove down Main Street and pulled into the parking lot behind the restaurant.

El Toro Negro was one of the finest Mexican restaurants in Northern California. Situated in the city's main hotel that was built in the 1920s, it featured a huge domed ceiling and walls painted with frescos of early California Mission life and some of the best margaritas on the West Coast. The dining room was filled with tropical plants. A mariachi band made its rounds and the servers wore brightly colored print shirts with dark trousers or skirts.

A dark-haired brown-eyed beauty in her early twenties led us to our table and handed us each two menus.

"We have three specials tonight," she began. "The first is Snapper Veracruz. This is Red Snapper sautéed in a spicy sauce of fresh tomatoes and red and green bell peppers. Our second special is Chicken or Pork Tamales. The tamales were made here today and are topped in a tomatillo salsa. And last and not least, we have Chicken Mole. Our mole sauce is made from unsweetened chocolate and dozens of spices. It simmers almost a week before we serve it.

"Ruben will be your waiter today. Enjoy your evening."

A busboy quickly put two baskets of hot tortilla chips on the table along with three small bowls of different kinds of salsa. "Can you believe this menu?" Bill asked, incredulously. "This is the drink menu and it's bigger than the dinner menu. There are two pages of margaritas alone, peach margaritas, mango margaritas, strawberry margaritas, margaritas with Cointreau, margaritas with Grand Marnier, blended, frozen, all different types of tequila to choose from and there's a page of daiquiris and another of drinks I've never heard of."

Ruben appeared and took our drink orders. We also asked him for two appetizers, Prawns Diablo and Taquitos. When he returned, Carson asked, "So Ruben, what do you do when you're not waiting tables?"

"I'm a Junior at UCSC."

"And what are you studying?"

"Computer Engineering."

"Well, we're computer geeks, so tell us what interests you."

"The curriculum at UCSC is primarily hardware, but I'm interested in software and ways to accelerate certain software operations in hardware and to move some hardware functionality into software. I'm really excited about graphics. I think graphics are going to be the next big thing in computers. Today everything is text–based. When that changes, computers will be for everyone."

"And have you interned anywhere?"

"No, I applied to a lot of companies last spring, but no one even called me back for an interview. Hopefully, I'll be luckier this summer."

Carson handed Ruben his card and said, "Call us in May. We'll probably have something for you if you don't mind driving to Los Gatos."

"Thanks! This is amazing. I've got to catch up on a couple of other tables, but I'll be back with your appetizers shortly. Thanks again! You won't regret giving me a chance. I'll work my – I'll earn my place."

Turning to us, Carson said, "See what I mean? A bright kid like that, and he can't even get an interview. They probably see the Hispanic surname on his resume and put it in the circular file.

"Let's look at the menus and decide what we're going to order."

Ruben returned with the appetizers and took our orders. The prawns were spiced with cayenne pepper and broiled. The taquitos were tiny tacos filled with chicken and deep-fat fried, served with a sweet and hot salsa. Carson excused himself and went to the restroom. When he returned, we polished off the appetizers and ordered another round of drinks. Dinner arrived shortly thereafter and we all raved about the meals. Carson kicked off a new topic for dinner conversation.

"Look at these frescos," Carson began almost angrily. "They depict the halcyon days of Mission life. But what they don't show is how the priests abused the indigenous Indian population. In other parts of the country, we killed off the Indian tribes in battles and put them on reservations. In California, the Spanish fathers conscripted them for hard labor, introduced disease, and destroyed their peaceful agricultural lifestyles. They were either assimilated or they died. There are reservations all over the country, but do you see any in California?"

Carson was holding court. I don't think I'd ever seen him so expansive. While everyone participated and put in their two cents on the subject, Carson frequently interrupted and pressed his points. Still, it was an interesting and lively conversation.

After dinner, Carson and Craig ordered coffee, while Bill ordered a Mexican coffee drink. We all predicted a big hangover for Bill.

We left the restaurant and got into Carson's car. We tried to pull out on Main Street, but it was filled with colorfully painted classic cars slung low to the ground, moving only at only a mile or two per hour, in parade-like fashion. Ear-splitting stereo systems each playing their own Mexican polkas battled with each other. Cars with air shocks bounced along, each trying to get higher than its neighbor.

"Should I be worried?" Bill asked.

"Only about all the different kinds of drinks you had," Carson quipped. Then, becoming a bit more serious said, "This is cruising. It happens every Saturday night. Many of them are in gangs, but if you let them do their thing, don't get in their way or confront them, there's no problem.

"This is that other problem I mentioned. The kids of these hard-working immigrant parents join gangs. Very few are like Ruben. Far too many end up on the street without an education."

When a clear spot opened up, Carson pulled out and we headed back to the isolation of Pajaro Dunes. It was late, and a couple hours later for Craig and Bill, who were operating on Central Time, so we all turned in.

I awoke at six the next morning and quickly put on my running shorts and a long sleeved t-shirt. While I considered trail running in the mountains to be the ultimate running experience, running barefoot on the beach comes a close second. I stepped quietly into the living room and was surprised to see both Craig and Bill stretching and dressed to run.

"We don't get to run much at this time of year back home," Craig said.

"How are you feeling, Bill?" I asked.

"I'm a bit shaky, but a run should help me sweat this out of my system. I've already had about a gallon of water this morning. So, where can we run?"

"If we go south, we'll hit the mouth of the Pajaro River after about a quarter mile, but if we go north, we can go almost fifteen miles without turning around."

"I think we can do two or three miles out, and then return," Craig predicted.

The tide was low and the beach was flat, so it was no problem running three abreast. On our way towards Sunset State Beach, we passed countless fishermen, other joggers, and even a few surfers. The dunes became cliffs, and soon the cliffs were dotted with huge homes.

"Oh my God! Look at that!" Bill cried.

Sure enough, a giant home teetered precariously, about halfway down the cliff.

"This happens every few years. Further north, the cliffs are made of rock, and when they start to erode, people bring in boulders to shore them up and to protect them from the waves, especially at high tide. In Capitola, some of the cliffs are faced with concrete. But here, the cliffs are mostly sand. Eventually, the wind, heavy rain, high tides, and waves will bring them all down. They'll become sand dunes like we have further south. Still, people continue to build their multi-million dollar homes as close to the cliff edges as possible. They want the best whitewater views. Sometimes it's a bad bet and the cliff and house can't be saved." I explained.

"Gee, that sure could ruin your whole day," Craig joked.

We got back a little after seven and went to shower and change. By time we emerged, a breakfast buffet of coffee, orange juice, muffins, scones, bagels, scrambled eggs and cereal awaited us in the dining room. Carson was sipping coffee, reading the New York Times.

Carson greeted us enthusiastically, "Morning guys! Ready for breakfast?"

We all filled our plates and poured orange juice and coffee.

After taking a bite of a bagel with cream cheese and a big swallow of orange juice, Craig moved into work mode, "So Jack, I've been in your planning sessions before, but this is new to Bill. Can you give us a quick description of what we'll be doing today?"

"When I moved to System Engineering for large customer accounts, IBM put me through training on how to conduct planning sessions. I've optimized it a bit, but it's worked well for the last ten years.

"One of the problems with brainstorming is that to get the level of creativity you need, you usually forego structure. Ideas are thrown around and some may get written down, but they usually end up being incomplete and later, without the group there to finish them, most of these ideas end up being either impractical to implement, or forgotten.

"What we're going to do is brainstorm freely at the highest level called Goals. Once we've established a number of Goals, we'll evaluate them, and if there are too many we'll eliminate some. When we have a workable list, we'll take each one and look at specific Objectives to reach those goals, but we'll brainstorm those Objectives. This is the next level of detail. Once we have a list of objectives, we pare down again by prioritizing them, and when we have a list of acceptable objectives, we identify specific Tasks to accomplish the objectives, then order them, cut the excess, and assign responsibilities. Tasks are the third level of brainstorming. We then look at exactly what it's going to take to accomplish each task, then each objective, then each goal, and we assess whether it's worth the effort and expense. In other words, we go top down, then bottom up, and at the end, we have a workable plan.

'As crazy as it sounds, we'll be filling up flip charts, taping them to walls, then consolidating and creating new ones. We'll go through a lot of paper and tape today. It may sound complicated, but once we start, I think you'll find it a great way to generate, record, and evaluate ideas.

"We can take turns being the scribe and I'll start. So, ready to create a plan for Star Wars?"

"Can we finish breakfast first?" Carson asked.

We did finish breakfast, though I noticed Carson didn't eat much. Of course he hadn't done a five mile run on the beach either. We adjourned to the conference room and went to work. Occasionally, you end up with dead wood in a session like this: people who don't understand the process, or whose ideas are ludicrous. Or, they can't listen to other people and won't moderate their positions even when it's clear their arguments are weak. Fortunately, the process eventually eliminates these ideas; it just takes more time.

Our session was one of the best I'd had. Take four aggressive, intelligent people who have the same goals, and you can accomplish a lot. Ideas came fast and furiously, and most were shot down. There were heated exchanges before anything was allowed to be written on the chart. No individual dominated. One minute, Bill would run up to the whiteboard and explain an idea. The next, Craig or Carson would run up and modify it, or come up with their own. The only odd thing I noticed was that Carson seemed to go on and off. He'd be really involved, then a while later, be looking out the window or getting up and walking around. Then he'd be on top of it again with brilliant insights. This isn't unusual, often participants need to clear their heads, but no one else in the group slowed for a minute. It was exhilarating, but exhausting. By noon, we needed a break.

Lunch consisted of plates of cold cuts, salads, and breads to enable us to make our own sandwiches. After wolfing down the food, Craig and Bill went out for a walk on the beach, Carson went to his room, and I took a glass of lemonade and sat on the deck watching the surf.

By two o'clock, we were back at it, and we kept working through the catered dinner, bringing our plates into the conference room. We finalized the plan shortly after midnight and although we knew we'd accomplished a lot, I don't think anyone would have been sad never to see each other again. These sessions can be intense and you really get to see sides of people you don't see elsewhere. Sometimes it isn't pretty. More often, people just need some space to recover.

But the plan was solid. Craig and Bill knew what was technically feasible, and Craig understood the costs of what we decided to implement. It wasn't his full Star Wars idea, but it was a solid start in that direction. I explained that I'd write up the plan on Tuesday and would send a copy to everyone.

The next morning, Bill, Craig, and I took a short run before heading to the airport for their 11:30am flight. At the airport, when their flight was called, Craig pulled me aside.

"Jack, I hate to tell you this, but I don't think you picked up on it. I'm pretty sure your boss over there has a drug problem."

"What do you mean?" I asked, shocked.

"I've known a few people like this, so maybe it's easier for me to spot the problem. Think back to dinner at that great restaurant. Remember how Carson went on and on about the Mexican Americans? "

"Yeah, but that's just Carson on a soapbox," I replied defensively.

"Maybe, but he left and came back fired up about another topic. I think the pattern was clearer during the planning session. He'd be involved, then fade, then he'd disappear, and when he returned, he'd be up and back in the thick of it."

Seeing disbelief on my face, Craig continued.

"I know it can be hard to believe, and I might be wrong, but keep your eyes open. If he really does have a problem, he could ruin his life and drag the company and you down with him. Be careful!"

With that, we walked back to Bill and Carson, shook hands all around, and Craig and Bill got on the plane and flew back to freezing Minneapolis.

9

Tuesday evening I was at home just about to settle down with a book. B. B. King played some lazy blues on the stereo, and the flames in the fireplace danced comfortingly and warmed the room. The doorbell rang and I expected to have to deal with a solicitor or Jehovah's Witness. I was startled to find Shelly at the door, clearly agitated.

She pushed past me into the living room. "That son-of-a-bitch still refuses to get tested. I showed him my results and he just smiled. 'Maybe this is the way it's supposed to be,' he said to me. He hardly paid attention when I reminded him of our deal and told him he'd better get down to the fertility clinic. I'm sure he was happy to know he's shooting blanks. He's probably having condom-less sex right now."

She continued almost ranting for several minutes, then burst into tears. I led her to the couch and put my arms around her. She was as tensely wound as a clock spring. I gently massaged her shoulders and pressed downward along her shoulder blades.

"Don't stop. I'm so wound up I could explode, and that feels so good."

She lay face down on the couch. I straddled her and began to massage her back. After a moment or two fighting the bunching of her sweatshirt, she said, "I think it would be easier without this in the way."

She pulled the sweatshirt over her head, then reached behind and unfastened her bra, rising a few inches as she pulled it off. I caught a brief glimpse of the curve of her left breast as she modestly lay back down and turned her head to the side. The well-defined muscles of the swimmer's shoulders I'd seen in her strapless gown at the Catalyst continued the length of her back but they were tight and knotted with tension.

I placed my thumbs at the base of her spine, my hands almost encircling her tiny waist and I began working upward and outward, thumbs leading the heel of my hand as I spread the muscles and helped her to relax. I moved upwards, until I reached her shoulder blades, downward along them, then moved back up to her neck. Reaching the base of her head, I moved her short hair out of the way and massaged her shoulders, arms, hands and fingertips. After kneading my way up her arms, I maintained a light pressure as I moved my hands down her sides back to her trim waist. A few inches below her waist, just below her hip bone and above the hip socket, I could feel the core of her tension. I increased pressure there.

Sensing I was struggling trying to work through her jeans, Shelly placed her hands beneath her and unbuttoned them, then pulled them loose so I could move my hands directly on her hips. She wore white thong panties, which covered very little, and I was able to massage the hip flexors and the top of her firm round bottom before working my way back up and down again.

Time passed and I could feel Shelly let go. Her back and hips were relaxed and heat rose from her pliant skin, perhaps from the warmth of the fire, or maybe from the easy friction of the massage.

I slipped off her shoes and socks and pulled her jeans off. She lifted her hips briefly to help. Then I began to rub her right foot, massaging her calf and the back of her thigh before working her back again, all the way up, then letting my hands glide along her sides down the left leg and left foot. I repeated this over and over again.

The air around us became filled with a sweet musky scent and at the top of the back of her thighs, I felt an intense heat and dampness. This time, when I reached her shoulders, I kissed the back of her neck, then with excruciating slowness, brushed my lips down her spine, pausing, kissing, then moving on. When I reached rise below her waist, I lifted the back of her panties, and continued peeling them downward. Shelly moved her thighs further apart making room for me. As my lips found their way to the source of the musky scent, I removed her panties and rolled her over, my mouth never losing contact with her, my nose slipping upward through warm wetness.

Shelly's hips rose as my tongue gently probed upwards and downwards alternating sides, brushing her clitoris lightly at the top. The rhythm and intensity of her movements increased and soon she was rubbing her pelvic bone against my upper lip as I moved my tongue faster and faster over her clitoris. Then, I teased her by raising it and moving feather-like above her. Her hips raced up to catch me, and as I licked the length of her, and drew all of her into my mouth, she did explode.

I stopped moving, my mouth in place until her breathing eased and her body went slack. I kissed her stomach and each breast gently, then rolled her on her side and faced her. Looking into those endless green eyes, now so open and content, I knew I was lost.

"That was – It's been so long!" she sighed, closing her eyes. When she opened them again, I saw a playful naughtiness as she rolled on top of me. Although she looked almost flat-chested in clothes, her breasts were incredibly full underneath and to the sides. Her light brown erect nipples topped the most perfectly shaped breasts I'd ever seen.

"You have the most beautiful body," I replied, my desire clearly evident beneath her.

"You know Jack, I've never seen you upset. You don't get angry, and even dancing, you're always in control. I want to see you lose it."

A little while later I did.

Shelly got up to pee then returned with a blanket she'd taken from my bed. We snuggled in front of the fire.

"You know Shelly, if you left Steve, you'd get half of his share of NewCo."

"Why Jack, that's brilliant. I didn't think you had a devious bone in your body. It's perfect. I'll tell him if he doesn't get me pregnant, I'll take NewCo. He'll be down at the clinic before I even finish my threat."

I asked her if she could stay the night, but she told me Steve would be home later. When she left, I realized that I hadn't told her that I meant she could afford to leave Steve so that she and I could ultimately be together.

10

Late in the afternoon on Friday, Carson dropped by my office.

"Hey Jack, Nancy's at her folks' for the weekend, so I'm heading down to my house in Aptos. Want to get together Saturday night? I've got some new wines you might like to try."

I had no plans, so I agreed. Perhaps I could find the courage to bring up the drug issue and the fact that a client had noticed. This would be a delicate subject and I knew that Carson would be embarrassed that Craig thought he was a drug addict.

Then again, perhaps the pattern that Craig saw was just coincidence. People look at the stars and connect points of lights into figures. They may see a bear or a lion, but the stars in the constellation are thousands of light-years apart. They look like they're part of a pattern, but in reality, they are completely unrelated. We humans are pattern-matching creatures. We often see them where they don't exist, hence the proliferation of conspiracy theories. I certainly hoped that was the case here.

Carson gave me directions to his home, which was about fifteen minutes from mine, and we agreed to meet at seven.

After a morning of fun-sized surf and an afternoon working around my place, I headed over to Carson's house. I traveled up Trout Gulch Road and then wound my way up Valencia School Road into the Aptos hills through a light mist that turned the redwood-lined road into fairyland.

Aptos is a small community a few miles south of Santa Cruz. The town center sits north of Highway One, and most of the homes dominate the hills above. Carson's house was further away than I thought. I drove at least ten minutes out of Aptos until I found it. I turned through the open gates and pulled over in the parking area. I got out of the car, and even at night, could appreciate the spectacular view from Santa Cruz to the Monterey Peninsula. The lights of Santa Cruz shone brightly below to the northwest, while those of Monterey lit the clouds like a lightning flash frozen in time.

Carson's home was newly built, but in the Victorian style. He invited me in, then took me on a tour. Although I prefer open, airy homes, I couldn't help but admire the ornate wainscoting, subtly patterned wallpapers, lush dark woods and plush oriental carpets. Most of the walls featured framed paintings, each illuminated with its own light source.

Carson led me to his library/study and my mouth dropped open. Consistent in its use of dark wood, floor to ceiling bookshelves covered every available inch of the walls. He even had a moveable ladder on tracks to access the upper shelves. A large antique desk sat centered about two-thirds of the way from the entrance and Carson had set up a cozy area in front of it with over-stuffed chairs, small end-tables, and a stand-alone bar. Three open bottles of wine and six glasses awaited our tasting. Carson poured a small amount of wine from one bottle into two of the glasses. We tasted and he moved on to the next bottle, pouring just a bit into the next two glasses.

When we had tried all three, Carson asked, "Which one do you like?"

"I'd pick the second one," I replied.

"I agree. It's an '81 Mondavi. Let's take it to dinner."

We got in Carson's Jag and drove down into Capitola Village. The mist had turned to rain and the wind drove sheets of water in vertical waves across the streets. We found parking surprisingly easily and went into The Ark. The Ark was an intimate restaurant with four tables downstairs and six upstairs. A roaring fire in a stone fireplace warmed the upstairs as large drops pounded the ocean-facing windows. The hostess seated us next to the windows in front of the fire. Carson handed her the Mondavi and asked her to have the waiter serve it with dinner.

"Great choice, Carson," I said. "This is one of my favorite restaurants. I often come here on stormy nights or after surfing."

"I guess it's just one more thing we have in common," Carson replied. "You know I'm really pleased with the way things have worked out since we hired you. Not only did you enable Steve to start NewCo, you've take CIA to its next level. Our reach and influence have now extended far beyond the few accounts I had. I think we'll find several more NewCos in the not-too-distant future."

The waiter came and I ordered the Coquilles St. Jacques with a cup of seafood chowder while Carson asked for the Beef Medallions in Cabernet Sauce with a spinach salad.

Carson continued, "Anyway Jack, I'd like to give you a piece of CIA. Today, Steve has twenty percent. I'd like to give you thirty-nine percent of the company in options. We need a Board meeting to approve this, but that's just a formality."

"Carson, that's very generous. I really appreciate this," I replied, touched by this unexpected development.

The waiter interrupted us with Carson's salad and my chowder. He poured us each a glass of wine.

"To my new partner," Carson said, raising his glass.

"To MY new partner," I responded, clinking his glass.

"This also gives you a piece of NewCo, indirectly. CIA owns fifty-one percent of NewCo. I think it's doing quite well, but Steve and Pam have been pretty tight-lipped about what's going on there lately."

"Yeah, I've noticed the same thing," I agreed. "Steve is ambitious and very aggressive. Aside from his extra-curricular activities, he certainly seems to know what he's doing. I think you need his take-no-prisoners approach to build a company like NewCo will someday be. I wouldn't worry about it. Just give Steve his head and sit back and enjoy the ride."

Our entrees arrived and we spent the rest of the dinner discussing the differences in business ethics between a consulting firm and a product company. We each had a piece of New York style cheesecake for dessert, then headed back to Carson's home.

I took a seat in his library as Carson opened the bar.

"Grand Marnier, right?" he asked raising the bottle.

"Sounds good"

Carson poured himself a Courvoisier, then took a seat behind his desk. He opened a drawer and removed a mirror, and a small bag. He poured white powder onto the mirror, and used a razor blade to create several lines of the drug.

"Want to join me to celebrate?" He queried confidently.

"No thanks." Then screwing up my courage I said, "You know Carson, when Craig pulled me aside at the airport, he told me he thought you might have a drug problem."

Carson looked at me for a moment, then looked to the side, lost in thought. Then he responded, "Drug problem. You're having a glass of liqueur, after splitting a bottle of wine with me. Do you have a drug problem?

"I've given this a lot of thought since that night at Alan's. Whether it's alcohol, nicotine, caffeine, or cocaine, it's a drug. You might even say that your love for chocolate or your sports are drugs and that you're an addict. The fact that cocaine is illegal is problematic. From a moral point of view, I have issues with the route it takes from its source to me. On the other hand, what makes it any worse than alcohol?

"Alcohol brings you down. It makes you slow and you lose your judgment. Most people want to legalize marijuana, which does similar things. Why not cocaine? At least for me, it sharpens things. I believe it enhances my ability to think and argue clearly. If this is true, where's the problem?

"So, while I'm a cocaine user, I don't think I have a problem. It doesn't adversely affect me, and I can afford it."

"Okay," I replied. "I must admit that I don't know much about the drug. It does appear to enhance rather than diminish you. So I guess it's not my place to say anything. On the other hand, if Craig noticed, others may too. Even if you believe this isn't a problem, the fact is the drug is illegal, and you could go to jail for simple possession. It's a felony. I think that's worth thinking about. After all, I wouldn't want to lose my new partner."

Carson didn't partake while I was there. Instead, we continued to discuss the topic and I must admit that when I left, although Georgette's warning echoed faintly in my head, I was convinced that Carson could handle this.

11

Monday evening I met Georgette at El Burro for Ms. PacMan, margaritas, and conversation.

"How are things?" I asked.

"Business is good. We've got a solid, growing customer base and are comfortably profitable. As I mentioned a few weeks ago, if we can come up with the next great thing, Marty has lined up significant funding for us.

"On the personal side, I've got nothing special going on. I've been putting in a lot of hours and really don't have the time for anything serious. I am going out once in a while. But I have a feeling you've got a lot to talk about, so jump in."

"Well, what do you want first, the good news or the bad news?" I asked.

"Let's see, how about the good news? I have a feeling that if we start with the bad news we'll never get to the good stuff."

I told her about my dinner with Carson and how he'd offered me a significant part of the company. I left out the cocaine discussion.

"Jack, congratulations! This is great. Be sure to get it in writing."

"Of course. After the Board meets, I should have my options. Carson is trustworthy."

"Trust is nice, but trust and a contract are even better."

Next, I told her about Shelly, how we met, the dancing, the evening out, her problems with Steve, and how she'd come over for comfort when Steve was giving her problems.

"Jack, I know you're starry-eyed about her so you probably won't be able to hear me, but you've got to be careful. You're a catch. You're active, considerate, fun to be with, and successful. What more could a girl want?

"It sounds like Shelly may be attracted to you, but if she wants to get serious, why wouldn't she leave Steve for you? He sounds like a real asshole, so there's got to be more to the story."

Seeing me about to interrupt, she put out her hand to stop me, then continued, "Yes, you've told me they have an arrangement that ensures his Visa status, and I know he's charming, ambitious, and on his way to building an empire, but the kind of woman that's attracted to that is not someone you want to be with. She must be getting something out of it or she wouldn't stay. She's got a good job and if she left, she'd get half of the burgeoning empire. It wouldn't be a problem for her to leave him, especially with you standing by."

"Maybe she just needs to be sure about what we have before jumping ship," I said, a bit too defensively.

"It's possible; not likely, but possible. I have a better theory. You know how we talk about the military brat syndrome? Well, I suspect she's got the First Lady Syndrome. Like a woman married to a Presidential hopeful, I bet she is attracted to power and will do anything to protect him and help him in his career.

"Yeah, I know, she's sleeping with you. It must be tough for her, waiting in the wings for the big show to begin. She probably needs something on the side to shore up her self-confidence.

"If you want to have a fling, go for it and keep it at that. If you really believe she's the woman of your dreams, you might want to back out now, before she becomes the woman of your nightmares and breaks your heart. Sorry for the pun."

I swallowed hard, looked down almost ashamed, and told her I'd try to keep it under control.

We were both hungry so we told the cocktail waitress we wanted to have dinner. She left, then came back a few minutes later and picked up our pitcher of margaritas and glasses.

"Follow me," she said. "We have your table all set up."

We left the cantina and entered the restaurant. El Burro had none of the elegance of El Toro Negro in Watsonville. The room was decorated in wild colors, yellows, deep reds, browns and greens. Travel posters of the Mexican Riviera hung over each booth. Mexican music filled the room, and the wait staff moved from table to table singing and dancing.

The cocktail waitress seated us in a raised booth that overlooked the spectacle of the singing and dancing waiters below. She refilled our glasses and wished us a great dinner. After a few minutes, our waiter broke away to come over and read us the specials. Without looking at the menus, Georgette ordered their gigantic Chicken Tostada and I asked for their Enchilada Suizas.

Then I began my story about Carson. Our meals came before I finished the Pajaro story, but Georgette's eyes had already begun to darken. I could see her hold herself back when I told her about Craig's comments, and she had no problem jumping in before I finished telling her about my conclusions after the dinner at the Ark.

"Lately I've been thinking my life was getting boring. Aside from the sports, I have virtually no love life and I'm working all the time.

"But I wouldn't trade with you for a second. Not only are you about to get yourself screwed in romance, your career is going to take some big bumps before crashing. Whether it's Carson, or maybe even Steve deciding that even if he doesn't want his wife, you shouldn't have her either, you've got trouble with a capital T and that rhymes with P and that means Pool which rhymes with FOOL, my friend.

"Carson may be brilliant and may think he can handle this, but that's what everyone thinks. I know my brother Mike thought that, and everyone I met in his rehab program was the same way.

"For God's sake, Jack, these aren't some loser heroin addicts on the street. They're all successful people who think this drug will give them an edge. Sometimes I think the saying is right: 'Cocaine is God's way of saying you have too much money.'

"Yeah, I know there are people like Alan who can use it casually. But I think if an achiever believes the drug gives him or her an edge, disaster will follow.

"I don't know what to tell you. You're not going to be able to convince him to stop. I predict the problems will start to appear in the next couple of months. The best thing would be to get that option agreement signed pronto. Then if he disappears like Mike did, you'll have control over the company.

After dinner, I walked Georgette to her car. Just before getting in, she turned to me, took both of my hands in hers, and after gazing at me for a moment with a motherly look of concern, she quickly kissed me on the lips, then got in her car and drove away.

Up until this point in my life, my romantic relationships had always been clearly defined. I'd meet someone, we'd hit it off, and we'd decide to start seeing each other. I could call her, she could call me, and we'd get together whenever we could. Once things got more serious, we'd stay in touch every day and wouldn't make social plans without including, or at least inviting, the other.

Even as a teenager, I never got into that 'will she call, will she go out with me' insecurity. But now, in my early thirties, I found myself waiting by the phone, hoping Shelly would call. I couldn't call her at home. Steve might answer. I couldn't call her regularly at work because that would set up trail. So, I waited and hoped.

At times, I was afraid to go out, for fear I'd miss her call. It didn't help that I had an answering machine. If she left a message, I still couldn't call back.

Worse, I started worrying that she wouldn't call again, that she and Steve had found common ground and I was now out of the picture. This was hell.

By Thursday afternoon, I was frantic. It had been over a week since our evening together. Not only that, I hadn't heard from Carson. Of course, we often went several days or even a couple of weeks without working together, but after the discussion with Georgette, I was a bit nervous.

Shelly finally called towards the end of the day.

"Want to meet for dinner?" she asked. "I have good news."

We agreed to meet at a seafood restaurant in Sunnyvale and when I arrived, Shelly was already seated, sipping a glass of Chardonnay. She kissed me on the cheek, then sat and looked at me. Excitement filled those gorgeous green eyes.

"Steve got tested," she said, breaking the silence. "His sperm count is low, but motility is good."

"Sorry," I replied, "I don't know what that means. Why is it good news?"

"Well, the first part of the good news is that he got tested at all. Your suggestion really worked.

"But even better, they can fix it. He just needs to supply three or four 'donations.' Then they mix them together, centrifuge them to increase the concentration, and I get pregnant by Steve through artificial insemination.

"Steve is actually happy. I think he's glad he won't have to have sex with me."

I couldn't imagine anyone being happy to not have sex with her, but I didn't say that.

"I should be ovulating in about ten days. I'll be taking my temperature and when it's time, I go in and have a date with the turkey baster. It's five thousand dollars per try, but hopefully it won't take us more than two or three tries."

We had a nice dinner. Shelly did most of the talking. She raved about the success rate of the fertility clinic and then moved on to work, which was going well for her. Visa was growing by leaps and bounds and with some initial success on debit cards was looking forward to a cashless society in the not-too-distant future.

I walked Shelly to her car and turned to kiss her goodnight. To my complete astonishment, she leapt upon me, throwing her arms about my neck and wrapping both legs around my waist. As she lowered herself and rubbed up and down against me, she said, "I want you Jack. It may take me a couple of weeks, but don't worry. We'll be together. I'm working on a big surprise for you."

She kissed me urgently, freeing one hand and rubbing my chest, then sliding it downward.

"I'll call you soon," she whispered as she let go of me and got into her car.

Somewhat shaken and more than a little aroused, I took a walk around the block. Was Georgette right? I suspected she was. Shelly wanted me, but I think she wanted me as someone to talk to, someone she could rely on, and someone to have sex with. Didn't friendship and sex make the right formula for a marriage or at least a relationship? Perhaps this wasn't the case for Shelly. If her relationship with Steve was indicative, she found marriage to be something of convenience, not passion. And if Georgette was right, Shelly saw marriage as a path to recognition and power. Somehow, it didn't fit. But then again, I wasn't thinking straight.

13

A week later, Carson and I had a meeting scheduled with American Semiconductor, another former client of mine from Skynet. Like Intel and Advanced Micro Devices, American Semiconductor manufactured microprocessor chips. The primary ingredient in the manufacturing process was silicon. Hence, much of the Santa Clara Valley was now known as Silicon Valley. Most successful semiconductor companies build and sell chips in high volumes at low margins. Because the manufacturing process is quite fickle, American Semiconductor wanted to provide real time quality control information to floor managers. This would enable them to stop a run of chips if the yield on a particular batch was below a certain quality threshold, potentially saving millions of dollars a year in chips, which had to be discarded. They hired CIA to help them design the system. I would provide the expertise in gathering the sensor-based real information from the devices and creating the network to deliver that information to floor managers, while Carson would design the database and reports that stored and formatted the information itself.

Our first meeting was set for ten o'clock, but by 9:30, Carson had yet to show up at the office. Donna told me she had not heard from Carson, so I walked into Pam's office.

"Carson and I have a meeting in thirty minutes with American Semiconductor, but he's not here yet. Have you heard from him?"

"No," she replied, "Give me a few minutes. I can usually track him down. Maybe he's stuck in traffic."

I waited nervously in my office and at 9:40, Pam came in.

"I found him at his house in Aptos. I think I woke him. He sounded terrible. He asked me to have you reschedule for next Monday or Tuesday. He's hoping to feel better by then."

'Okay. I'll call and cancel."

Monday at 9:15, Carson came into my office. "Jack, sorry about Thursday. I must have had a twenty-four hour bug. It really knocked me for a loop. Thanks for rescheduling for today."

We drove over to American Semiconductor and had an excellent meeting. Carson astutely identified several key issues with their approach and by the end of the day, we had designed a new system for them. Even better, they wanted us to provide three engineers for the next six months to help their team develop the system, along with design oversight by the two of us. Carson and I had dinner at L'Auberge du Soleil to celebrate our new half million dollar contract.

Friday of that week, it happened again. The two of us had a meeting scheduled with Alan at ALM. Carson didn't show, and Pam found him at his house in Aptos, sick. It appeared to be a relapse. Once again I rescheduled, and the following Monday, aside from a bad case of the sniffles which caused him to leave the room with handkerchief in hand, Carson was better and at the top of his game when we did our presentation to ALM.

Although I, too, am one of these pattern-matching humans, I didn't see a pattern yet. It was quite logical that Carson could get sick and have a relapse. Runny nose and red eyes certainly lent credibility to that theory. What I didn't know was that this would happen weekly for the next several months, and that Carson's runny nose was not a recurring cold, nor was it allergies as he later claimed.

Shelly's promise about us being together helped me relax. I didn't sit by the phone afraid to leave the house or my office. I assumed it would happen when the time was right. Of course, I felt that way for two weeks. As the third week passed, I asked myself if I'd misunderstood. Hadn't she said 'a couple of weeks'? Once again, I began to fret.

Somehow, almost as if she knew I was going out of my mind, Shelly called.

"Can you meet me tomorrow evening at seven o'clock at 6708 Juniper Way in Los Altos? It's time for your surprise!"

The next evening, I drove up to Los Altos. I parked in front of a large, but older house on a tree-lined street. A gated driveway led past the right side of the house. I started to walk down the driveway to reach the walkway to the front door when I saw a blue heart-shaped piece of paper taped to the gate. It read:

'Where would Steve have slept if he'd failed to get tested?'

I looked around for an outhouse, but spotted a doghouse and walked over to it cautiously. Fortunately, the owner was absent, but there was another blue heart taped to the front. It said:

'What was it that Eve purportedly tempted Adam with?'

This was an easy one. On the far side of the yard was an apple tree. Taped to the tree was yet another note posing the question:

'Who is the most feared person in a marriage?'

I pondered this. In some marriages the husband dominated, in others wives ruled the roost. A lover? That might fit our situation, but as I looked around, I couldn't see anything that fit. Then I spotted it.

Fifty yards past the apple tree and out of site of the main house was a small cottage. Smoke rose lazily from a stovepipe chimney.

Who was the most feared person in a marriage? The mother-in-law. And here was a mother-in-law cottage. On the door was another heart:

'Enter and find out what you've been waiting for!'

I opened the door and Shelly threw herself against me with an intensity I'd never felt from a woman before. As both my hands found her bottom, she again wrapped her legs around me and I lifted her. My breathing was heavy with excitement. She pulled back and said, "What do you think?"

Knowing she meant the cottage, I started to look around. To my right, an open door revealed a tiny bathroom with sink, toilet and shower, all nearly touching each other. Ahead, over her left shoulder I could see a kitchen area with a small wooden table set with bread, cheese, a bottle of wine and two glasses. A wood stove dominated the room.

"Let's go to the right," she commanded. I started into the bathroom with no idea how the two of us would fit. "No! My right!" she giggled.

As I turned to the left, I discovered an elevated bed built into a nook below the sloping ceiling. It reminded me of sleepers on trains I'd ridden in Europe, but instead of curtains surrounding the bed, they hung below it, concealing a storage area.

I lifted her onto the bed and climbed up, laying on top of her, my lips finding hers, my right hand seeking her breast. Shelly opened her eyes. Her face grew serious for an instant, then she grinned mischievously and playfully rolled me off.

"Come on, let's eat and I'll tell you all about it!"

She hopped down, then looking up at my swelling discomfort said, "Don't worry, we'll have plenty time to take care of that – more than once."

I took a seat at the table and Shelly poured the wine. Without looking at me, she used a small cheese knife to spread a thick layer of Brie on a slice of freshly cut French bread. Then she took a spoon and added a dollop of green pepper jelly to it. She repeated this with another slice, handed me the first, then raised her glass,

"To us!"

"To us," I replied, almost overcome with a mix of emotions, surprise, love, lust, excitement, and a bit of fear.

Shelly sipped the wine, took a bite of bread and cheese and gazed at me lovingly. I could have sat looking at her for hours. Then she started to explain.

"I've rented this place from a divorced friend of mine who owns the house. She needed some supplemental income. I jumped at the chance. She knows I have a bad marriage with Steve, and found the idea of a tryst in her backyard very romantic. It's four hundred dollars a month, and I was hoping you and I could split the cost."

Seeing me nod with wonderment, she continued.

"I'm taking a night class at CSM on Tuesdays and Thursdays."
It was Thursday. Did she have to leave? Noting my look of
confusion, she backed up.

"Sorry. I told Steve I'm taking a class at the College of San
Mateo on Tuesdays and Thursdays – not that he particularly
cared or really paid attention. The class runs from seven to ten,
so we can have three or four hours together twice a week. We
might even be able to do a Saturday or Sunday once in a while,
and if Steve is traveling, we could spend the night here. I have a
key for you"

I took the key, but for a moment was too stunned to speak.
What was I getting into here? I wanted Shelly and it was clear she
wanted me, but was I really ready to jump into such heavy
deception? Was I going to have an affair and cuckold Steve?

Our previous time together seemed almost an accident. I was
caught up in Shelly's neediness and I had hoped that it was the
first step towards a long-term relationship. Could I fool myself
into thinking this was a stepping-stone to something more
permanent? Would our time together convince her that I was the
one she couldn't live without? Or was Georgette right? Would I
dive into this looking for true love only to be devastated to
discover I was just an amusing pastime?

"Shelly, this is amazing and you know I want you, but where is
it going? Is this just a fling for you?"

Shelly rose, took my hand and led me over to the bed. She
unbuttoned my shirt and ran her hands over my chest. Then she
unbuckled my belt and unzipped my slacks.

"Jack, I don't know where it's going, but this feels right. Let's
just take it one step at a time, okay?"

How could I refuse?

15

I hadn't seen Carson in several days and realized that he hadn't given me an update on my stock options. I went over to Pam's office. As Secretary to the Boards of both CIA and NewCo, she should be able to tell me what the status was.

"Pam, have you got a few minutes?"

Pam closed a file she was working on and said, "Sure, Jack, come in on."

I closed the door and took a seat.

"A few weeks ago, Carson and I had dinner," I began. "He said he wanted to recognize my contribution to CIA and to the creation of NewCo by giving me thirty-nine percent of CIA in stock options. He expected these would be approved at the next Board meeting, but I haven't heard anything."

Pam's dark eyebrows rose and her eyes narrowed. "I haven't heard anything about this. Of course the Board meeting is in two weeks, so maybe he's planning to bring it up then."

"Can you tell me more about the Board and how it works?"

"Well, officially, there are two Boards, one for each company. I'm Secretary for both, Carson is Chairman of both, Steve is a member and we have one outside member, a friend of Carson's named Art Johnston.

"Art founded a company and sold it for several million dollars a few years ago. Now he travels a lot, sits on Boards like ours, and does private investments in small startups. Sometimes he comes in as temporary CEO and helps the founders raise venture investments, then steps out when they get funded. He's a very sharp man.

"The Boards have scheduled meetings twice a year, one in July and one in December. Occasionally, we have additional meetings, sometimes telephonic ones, but Art is often hard to reach, and you know how often you've seen Steve and Carson lately."

"Pam, this may be prying, and I don't need exact numbers, but can you tell me about CIA's arrangement with Carson?"

"Since you're going to be a partner, and a significant one, I really don't have a problem telling you how things are set up, especially since they'll have to change dramatically in the next few months. The IRS is really cracking down.

"Right now, I pay everything directly out of the CIA account.

This includes mortgages, car leases, even day-to-day expenses. Carson lives on credit cards and has ATM access to an account where I pay a 'salary' so that he can get cash when he needs it. Up until now, the IRS hasn't had a problem with this as long as I declare all of it as compensation to Carson, but the new rules will require me to separate everything. We can't be mixing personal and business accounts.

"I won't give you an exact number, but I can tell you that last year, his total compensation was several hundred thousand, and so far this year, he's spending at a much higher rate. We'll be discussing the whole restructuring at the Board meeting and I suspect we'll have to implement some expense controls."

I was surprised at Pam's openness. Hearing about the increased spending, I began to think about Georgette's description of her brother's downfall. Carson said he could afford his habit, but would that be true when the Board instituted 'expense controls'?

I considered telling Pam about my suspicions. I also thought about taking her to dinner to see if she'd open up about her relationship with Steve. Maybe I could find out if Steve was thinking about leaving Shelly. Or perhaps Pam and I were more alike than I thought. We were each caught up in opposite sides of a very strange relationship. After considering this carefully, I knew I'd hold my tongue. I'd be crossing a boundary to talk about her relationship with Steve, and I might just reveal too much about my feelings for Shelly.

16

The Board meeting took place as scheduled and I waited anxiously the next day to hear from Carson and Pam about my options. When Pam walked into my office at ten, I visibly brightened, but Pam wasn't smiling.

"Jack, I hate to have to have to tell you this, but Carson didn't show up for the Board meeting. I told the Board about your stock options, but the resolution needs to be made by Carson. I tried to track him down, but couldn't find him.

"About all I can say is now that the Board knows about it, I can work with Carson to draw up a resolution the next time I see him. I can then try to schedule a telephonic board meeting to vote on it. Sorry!"

"Pam, has this ever happened before? Has Carson missed a scheduled Board meeting?"

"No. He loves getting together with Art, so he never misses an opportunity. He knew about the meeting and I left messages with his services reminding him."

I now realize I should have thought about it more before opening my mouth, or perhaps I should have had a long talk with Ronn or Georgette, but I was too upset.

"I think Carson has a drug problem," I blurted.

Once out of the bag, you can't take it back. I'd do this again before I finally learned my lesson.

"What?!!" Pam asked, shocked.

"I think Carson has an uncontrollable cocaine habit," I said clearly.

"Have you seen him using it? Are you sure?"

I told her about the weekend at Alan LaMonte's, about the comments made by Craig at our weekend retreat, and about my discussion with Carson where he convinced me he could be user without being an addict. Now, adding in the missing meetings, and her comments about the large amounts of cash he was spending, I didn't think there was another conclusion.

"The weird thing about it, though, is that other than these disappearances, he seems to be able to control it. It really does enhance his thinking, which was pretty good to begin with. But now, I don't know. It's beginning to look like a real problem."

"Jack, I really respect Carson. He is the most honest, real person I've ever met. He gave me this job when I was a mess. If this is true, we really need to find a way to help him. I'm going to call Nancy. If the three of us can get together, maybe we can come up with a plan."

Pam also told Steve about Carson's problem.

17

A few days later Pam and I met Nancy at Carson's Los Gatos apartment. I hadn't seen Nancy since Alan LaMonte's weekend in the Sierra. Vibrant and brimming with self-confidence then, she now looked haggard and drawn. Weariness and sadness had taken hold.

"I've been going out of my mind," she began. "After Alan's, it just seemed like a fun thing to do, a way to recapture that weekend. Then, for a couple of months, I had no idea that he was using as much as he was. I guess he figured that if he could fool me, he could fool everyone.

"Even when I found out, I didn't think it was a real problem. It didn't seem to affect him badly. He was just more of himself. I didn't see any downs; he didn't get paranoid; there were none of the classic symptoms.

"One morning he didn't get up. He's always an early riser. At first, I thought he was sick. Then he asked me to go into his desk and bring him a leather bag. When I handed it to him, it was like a repeat of Alan's. He pulled out a mirror, razor blade, and cocaine. I realized the reason he hadn't crashed before is that he just stayed high.

"Even then it was okay. I wanted to believe he could handle it. But lately, he's been disappearing. I have no idea where he goes. I've found him in Aptos a few times, then he's gone again. And just when I think I'll never see him again, he shows up and appears normal.

"I haven't had anyone to talk to about this. He really doesn't have any family. I can't tell mine or any friends. His reputation would be ruined.

"He's a very bright man. I think if we could just get him to recognize that he has a problem, he'll get past it and become the Carson we know and love again. I've got almost five years in this relationship and I'm not ready to give him up to a drug."

I thought about this. In addition to the stock options, Carson was my mentor. He taught me everything I knew about being a high-level consultant with the big players. It was really the two of us at CIA. Sure Ronn was a good friend, but he operated at a different business level. He wasn't so much a consultant as a contract programmer and project manager. Would CIA be worth it without Carson? Would I really want to try to run the business myself if he disappeared?

I concluded that I didn't. After all, this was a drug problem. People kicked drug and alcohol problems all the time. We could certainly get him back. And if we couldn't? I realized that being under Steve's thumb with CIA and NewCo was not appealing. If we couldn't get Carson back, I'd leave and start my own company.

Pam interrupted my thoughts. "We need a plan. You both seem convinced that Carson doesn't think he has a problem. Even you two didn't think so until recently. I don't think we can get him to change until he realizes his life is a mess.

"Jack, next time he shows up, can you try to show him what's happening to CIA and its customers without him?"

I nodded.

"Nancy, can you tell him what will happen to your relationship if he keeps this up?"

"Of course," she replied, but she looked very uncomfortable.

"I can't cut him off financially, but I can certainly put some limits on the amount of cash available to him. When I see him, I'll try to explain how loss of his billing hours and new leads is hurting the company. Can you think of anything else?"

"Knowing the strength of Carson's character, he may be able to kick this himself if we all apply some pressure. But I think it would be a good idea if we did some research on rehab facilities. My friend Georgette knows of some. Her brother had a problem. I'll get some names from her. Maybe you two could try to find some others.

"What happened to your friend's brother? Did rehab help?" Nancy asked hopefully.

"Mike was in the movie business. Georgette sent him to a facility in Arizona, and he came back clean and jumped right back into work. Unfortunately, after his next success, he fell off the wagon and he disappeared. Georgette hasn't heard from him since."

We all pondered this for a moment.

"Of course, cocaine is all over the movie business. Mike was exposed to it at every turn. I'd like to think our industry is different. Carson should have a better chance," I said, attempting to sound optimistic.

We agreed to start our rehab research and to call the others if Carson showed up.

18

I didn't have to wait long. The following Monday morning, Carson walked into my office.

"Carson, I didn't expect to see you," I said.

"We have a meeting at ALM I didn't want to miss. Could you come into my office for a few minutes? I'll grab Pam and see you there."

With that he turned and left. Was I about to be fired?

I walked over to Carson's office and took a seat. I noticed that several packages from Ridge Winery sat unopened beside his desk. After a moment or two, Carson and Pam came in. Pam sat next to me and instead taking a seat behind his desk, Carson pulled up a chair and created a small circle with us.

"Nancy told me about your meeting with her," Carson said.

"Ah, Carson –" I said, but stopped when Carson pressed his right hand palm forward, a sign to stop.

"No Jack. I need to say this. You guys are right. I do have a problem. I thought I could handle it, but the stuff is too seductive. I know it makes me better, so how can I not be the best I can?

"Nancy told me her issues and described yours. You're right. We have a company to run, responsibilities to our clients, and new companies to start in the future. It would be irresponsible of me to continue to behave the way I have. I need to be more consistent, stop spending so much money, and break this illegal habit that could put me in jail.

"I see that while it may bring me up for short periods, the rest of my behavior has been abysmal. As our President's wife is so fond of saying, I'm going to just say no."

"Have you thought about rehab," I ventured?

"Nancy and I talked about this too. I think that with your help, I can do this myself. I got myself into it. I can get myself out.

"Pam, I think it's a good idea for you to limit my access to ready cash. Jack, I want you to manage me as you would a new employee. Please stay on top of me and my calendar. Nancy is going to try to keep me away from the stuff in our social life. Hopefully, in a few months, we'll have forgotten the whole thing.

"Pam, I know I missed the Board meeting, and I think you're aware that I want to get Jack stock options. Is there any way we can do that before the next scheduled meeting?"

Pam replied, "Of course. Give me the details and I'll draw up a resolution. Assuming I can track down Art, I can fax him the resolution and a consent and waiver form for a telephonic meeting. You guys can vote on it then."

"Make it so, Lieutenant," Carson joked, attempting to insert a bit of levity. "Jack, let's head over to ALM. I'm ready to get back to work!"

Our meeting at ALM went extremely well. Carson was back!

At one point, Alan dropped in to see how things were going. He seemed quite pleasantly surprised to discover Carson in the meeting. The three of us went to lunch and only discussed ALM business.

19

I had always found almost meditative solitude in surfing. Often at Waddell Creek or Boulders, I'd stop chasing waves for a few minutes and would soak in my surroundings. The glassy water teems with life. Adolescent sea lions leap from the sea in pairs or threes looking like a synchronized ballet from Sea World. The elder males look on, then give warning barks, baring their teeth, as if to say "Don't mess with our kids!"

Just beneath the surface small smelt migrate, rustling the surface or even leaping from the water if you get too close. Dozens of tiny jellyfish that look like tiny incandescent light bulbs, complete with filaments, dance along the currents while periodically their much larger umbrella-shaped cousins drift by, looking like colorful Tiffany lamps.

Looking landward, waterfalls tumble down the precipitous cliffs, while the tree covered Santa Cruz Mountains create spectacular hillsides and canyons that rise up from the coast. At moments like these, how can you not see the world as a beautiful place? Somehow though, these ephemeral moments of tranquility and wonder just didn't compare to my evenings in the cottage with Shelly.

When there, I felt as if I'd stepped into heaven. One of us would arrive and prepare a meal, usually something light. We'd catch each other up on our days, then we'd spend the next two or three hours in bed. When Shelly's 'class' was over, we'd leave together, kissing each other goodbye before heading home in our respective vehicles. It was all the good of domestic bliss without the reality.

The Thursday after meeting with Carson, I arrived early. I poured two glasses of a decent Chianti I'd picked up on the way, then prepared two small hearts of Romaine salads. I put some water on to boil, and began to sauté portabella mushrooms with olive oil, garlic, fresh basil, and a few dashes of crushed red pepper. When I heard Shelly's car pulling into the driveway, I put pasta in the water.

Shelly walked through the door, dropped into a chair and gulped down a glass of Chianti.

"Another if you please, kind sir!" she said.

I poured another glass, then stepped behind her and began to rub her shoulders. She let her head fall back and rest on my stomach.

"What's wrong?" I asked.

"It's been a rough day with me fighting to meet ridiculous deadlines at work. Just before I was about to leave, the doctor called and said it didn't take."

While she had told me that she and Steve were going to do artificial insemination, I didn't know that they had already tried. It felt strange to think that she'd done this a week or two ago without my knowing and that we'd continued to meet. I didn't say so.

"I'm sorry to hear that. Does it reduce your chances?"

"The doctor said that statistically, ignoring physical problems we don't have, about fifty percent have success the first time, eighty percent are successful within two tries and ninety percent within three. I'm just hoping we're not in the final ten percent who don't conceive.

"It's discouraging, but I'm not heartbroken over it. We'll try again in a month or two."

Halfway through her second glass of wine, Shelly began to relax. We shared a comfortable dinner and Shelly gave me the details of her rough day.

After cleaning up the dishes, we moved to the bed where Shelly was even more passionate than usual.

20

My relationship with Shelly was getting better every day. I believed that she truly loved me (she had said so on numerous occasions), but she was very happy with our current arrangement. Months had passed, and Pam finally tracked down Art in Greece and faxed him the paperwork for the telephonic Board meeting, which was scheduled to take place in less than a week. Carson seemed to be his old self, and from what I could see and hear, NewCo was growing at a comfortable rate.

I was back in the groove. I was effectively my own boss; my love life was fantastic; I had plenty of time for my sports; recognition in the industry; and I was making good money. In a week, I'd own a piece of both companies. How could it get any better?

"He's gone!"

I looked up to find Pam at my door. She stepped in, closed the door and continued, "Nancy just called. Carson was supposed to meet her parents for dinner last night and he didn't show; no call. His services have no idea how to reach him and he's not at either house."

"Any ideas?" I asked.

"When he did this before, no one could find him until he surfaced. When he came clean with us, we should have asked him who his suppliers were and where he goes when he vanishes. At this point, I think all we can do is wait.

"Jack, if I don't hear from him soon, I need to cancel the Board meeting. It would be embarrassing if he doesn't show again. The semi-annual meeting is only a month away, so in the worst case, your options will get voted on then, with or without Carson."

Carson didn't return that week, or the next week. As the December Board meeting approached, I decided I needed to meet Art Johnston. I called and reached him on the first try. We agreed to meet for lunch at L'Auberge du Soleil.

We arrived at the same time and Richard greeted me in French. I responded in kind, then introduced Richard to Art, which I discovered was completely unnecessary as they knew each other well. In French, Art asked Richard how business was and after we were seated and had placed our drink orders, I turned to Art and said, "Your French is quite good!"

"One of the nice things about being semi-retired is I get to travel. Every year, I set aside three or four months and I visit some part of the world I want to see. I immerse myself in the local culture and do my best to become fluent in the language. I did France two years ago, but I've been back several times. People claim the French are rude, but outside Paris, I've never found that to be true."

"I lived in the Basque region for six months some years back," I told him. The people were incredibly friendly and I was struck by the level of education, even among blue-collar workers. They could certainly hold their own in any international political debate."

We carried on with our pleasant lunch conversation. Art regaled me with harrowing travel tales and I shared a few of my own. As we were finishing lunch, I changed the subject.

"Art, you probably know that the main reason I asked you to lunch was to discuss my options resolution that's coming before the Board. I'm hoping you'll back me on it."

Art thought for a moment, then smiled warmly. "Jack, I saw CIA before you arrived and I see what has happened since. No one deserves a piece of the company more than you do.

"You know, when I'm not traveling, I spend my time helping young entrepreneurs get started. I've learned to recognize who's going to make it and who's not. There's no doubt in my mind that you're going to go far in this business.

"As far as the Board meeting is concerned, unless Steve presents an amazing argument against it, and I can't see why he would, I'll vote for your options."

We finished our lunch, which was one of the most enjoyable I'd had in years and I walked him to his car.

"Thanks again," I said, extending my hand.

He shook my hand warmly and said, "We should stay in touch, even after the Board meeting. You're almost as much fun to talk with as Carson. See you!"

With that, he drove away.

21

The morning after the Board meeting, I went straight to Pam's office when I arrived. Steve and Pam were in a heated conversation. Seeing me, Steve came forward and slapped me on the back.

"Good to see you Jack!" he said. "Let's go to my office and talk."

I looked past Steve at Pam. She mouthed silently, "I'm sorry!" and I began to worry.

Strangely, I realized that although we'd moved into these new offices at the beginning of the year, I had never actually been in Steve's. In direct contrast to Carson's use of rich woods, thick oriental carpets, and antiques, Steve had chosen a very modern décor. Abstract paintings dominated the walls while the desk, credenza, and even the bookshelves were made of metal and glass. Several pseudo-perpetual motion machines whirled, bounced, and rocked on the credenza.

I took a seat in one of the ultra-modern guest chairs and waited for the bad news. Steve moved behind his huge, almost empty tabletop desk, his legs and feet clearly visible beneath it.

He drew breath through his teeth and said, "Jack, I wanted you to hear it from me. I voted down your option resolution."

I almost screamed at him that if it hadn't been for me, he'd still be writing code at HP instead of sitting behind his fancy desk, but I decided to hold my tongue for once. Seeing that I wasn't going to lose it, Steve continued.

"Art fought hard for you, but with only two of us at the meeting, it was a deadlock and the resolution didn't pass."

Seeing my eyes flash and my jaw set hard, Steve went on.

"Look. Carson has vanished. We don't know when he'll be back, or what state his brain will be in when he returns. If I had voted for the options, you'd own more of CIA than I do.

"I don't give a rat's ass for CIA. I'd be happy to turn the whole thing over to you. The problem for me is that CIA owns fifty-one percent of NewCo. That means that with Carson gone, you, being the dominant shareholder in CIA could run NewCo. I can't let that happen. I'm building something special here. One day, NewCo is going to be a huge company with thousands of employees. I'm putting everything I have into it and I've got to stay the course.

"I've talked with Pam and Art about coming up with some way to restructure the two companies, but that requires a majority of the shares to approve, and Carson controls those. So, if we can get Carson back, we might be able to reduce CIA's ownership of NewCo, and you and Carson, if he's got any brain cells left, can take CIA and do whatever you want with it, leaving me with control of NewCo."

I thought about what he said. I had no desire to run NewCo. Steve appeared to be doing everything right there. His concerns were rational and his reasons for voting down my options made sense.

Interrupting my thoughts, Steve said, "Jack, I know I wouldn't be here if not for you. You can see my hands are tied. About all I can suggest is that if you can come up with a NewCo-2, I'll support you taking control of it. Sorry. I really don't know what else I can offer."

I stood up to leave and Steve came around the desk and offered his hand.

"You're a good guy, Jack. We'll figure something out."

I walked back to Pam's office.

"I'm so sorry, Jack," Pam said . "You know Art really pushed hard for you. He wouldn't change his vote, even with Steve's arguments. It's going down in the minutes that way, if that's any consolation."

"I guess we just need to get Carson back," I said.

Pam just shook her head.

"I don't know, Jack. This is a real mess. I can't help thinking there's something else we could do."

22

Over the course of the past year, Steve and Shelly had built a custom home in the Los Altos hills, overlooking the San Francisco Bay and Silicon Valley. I got my first chance to visit when Steve invited everyone at CIA and NewCo to Christmas dinner.

NewCo had held a lavish Christmas party for its employees a few weeks before at the St. Francis Hotel in San Francisco. Apparently, several key employees were upset that those of us at CIA weren't invited, so Steve decided to make a gesture by sharing his Christmas with us.

I pulled through the huge open gates and wound my way up the driveway to one of the largest homes I'd ever seen. I was directed to pull up to the front door. A valet gave me a claim check and took my car around the circular upper part of the driveway, parking it somewhere behind the house.

I walked up the flagstone steps and much to my surprise, a doorman greeted and wished me a Merry Christmas as I entered the house. I was immediately assaulted with its sterility. Everything was white, black, or chrome. The carpets were white; the walls were expanses of white broken only by an occasional piece of abstract painting, and the furniture was largely glass and metal. The white marble encased fireplace was lit and the metal fireplace insert was adding heat to the room. It certainly was formal.

Looking around, I realized that while I'd dressed nicely in woolen slacks and a button-down raw silk shirt, many of the men in the room were wearing coats and ties. Shelly spotted me and made her way over. She wore a floor-length green satin gown set off with ribbons of red.

I handed her a gift, a new pseudo-perpetual motion machine for Steve, which she placed under the tree. She kissed me chastely on the cheek then whispered seductively in my ear, "You'll get your present later."

"Actually, I have a present for you at our place. That one's really for Steve."

She took my hand and led me over to Dan, Rick, and George, who were engaged in a debate on President Reagan's Star Wars initiative.

"Merry Christmas guys!" I said happily. I hadn't spent any

time with them over the last few months and I certainly missed working with Dan, my former protégé.

"Merry Christmas, Jack," they chimed in almost unison.

A young woman carrying a tray came by with Champagne, followed by another with a plate of assorted appetizers. I took a glass and wolfed down a stuffed mushroom.

"So, how's Project Hydra coming?" I asked.

"Surprisingly, we're way ahead of schedule. We have several pieces already running in PacBell's system and a few others in Beta. We'll certainly beat the schedule. In fact, I think Steve has closed or will be closing some big deals with other telcos." Dan said. Then he turned a bit somber and continued, "I'm really sorry to hear about Carson. I never would have expected it of him."

"Well, we hope we can get him back," I replied.

We continued talking business for a few minutes and were then summoned to dinner. The dining room was right out of a movie set with a table set for forty people and seating cards designating our places. I sat between Dan on my left, and Linda, Rick's wife on the right.

When we were all seated and our glasses had been refilled by the waiters and waitresses, Steve stood to propose a toast.

"Merry Christmas everyone! A toast to an incredible 1986. We're going to take off like no one will believe!"

I spoke briefly on and off with Linda about the new baby and learned that she and Rick were finally sleeping through most of the night. At one point during dinner, I turned to Dan.

"So are you enjoying it at NewCo?"

Dan looked pensive for a moment, then replied, "Yes and no. I feel like I'm one of the crew working on a rocket ship that's going to launch. You try to focus on the job at hand, but you know the goal is the launch and the ride that follows.

"I know that NewCo is going to be big, and I'm one of the founders, so it's certainly a path to success. I have some reservations about Steve. He's so single-minded. I don't see any compassion or intellectual curiosity there. He's all business and I get the feeling that he believes that all is fair in business and war, or maybe worse, that business IS war.

"I kind of miss the consulting work at CIA. I got to meet a lot of people, help them solve their problems, and I was always learning something new. Plus, working with you and Carson felt like I was one of an elite troubleshooting team. We had some great no-holds-barred discussions.

"Now, I'm mostly a manager. I have a lot of people working for me and my time is spent on schedules and personnel conflicts. I sit in on design reviews. But I'm not architecting solutions anymore."

"Well, your future seems assured," I said, "In making that transition from consulting to project management, I guess you have to start looking at schedules and personnel issues as puzzles and problems to be solved."

"Yeah, but somehow in consulting, you're able to mix the business and technical. I feel like I'm all business now.

"On the other hand, looking at CIA, I guess it's not the same anymore. You're pretty much on your own at the high level now. That's got to be a bit lonely."

"It is," I said. "I'm sure hoping we can get Carson through this. He has a good heart and a great mind, and I don't see a lot of that out there today."

After dinner, I wandered the room and watched Shelly from afar. This wasn't the retiring woman I'd met and danced with at the Catalyst. She was definitely in her element as hostess.

At one point, she caught my eye, then came over and led me down a hall, ostensibly pointing and describing the artwork and taking me on a tour of the house. As we turned a corner, she opened a door and pushed me into a small utility room with shelves, one bare wall, and a single folding chair. After locking the door, she unzipped my slacks, and raised the skirt of her dress, revealing no panties.

"Here?" I said, excited but nervous.

"No, here!" she commanded putting one leg on the chair and gently pushing my head downward.

We made love hurriedly, standing up against the wall, a radical and exciting change from the cottage. We were careful to protect her satin dress and Shelly even had a towel waiting.

When we finished, she reached up and removed a package from a shelf. "Merry Christmas!" she said, her eyes filled with laughter.

I opened the box and found a beautiful hand-knit, corded white sweater. I slipped it on.

"How's it look?"

"Perfect!" she replied.

She listened at the door, then led me out. When we reached the end of the hall, she squeezed my hand, and without saying a word, turned back into the perfect hostess. I suspect our entire encounter lasted only five minutes.

I watched her for a while, then found Steve and thanked him for the party.

I went home to an empty house.

CHAPTER 4

"Are you warm? Are you real, Mona Lisa? Or just a cold and
lonely, lovely work of art?"
- Nat King Cole

1

1986 arrived, but there was no sign of Carson. This was a year of disasters and scandal. Just a few short weeks into the year, the Challenger Space Shuttle exploded, killing the first teacher in space and shaking America's faith in the infallibility of modern technology. Not long after, there was a core meltdown at the Chernobyl nuclear power plant. On April 15th, the US bombed Libya in an attempt to assassinate Mohamar Kadhafi, but killed his two-year old step-daughter and dozens of civilians instead.

But what caught the attention of American public were the Iran-Contra hearings where it was revealed that the government had illegally sold arms to Iran to raise money to illegally fund the Contras' revolution in Nicaragua. Everyone wanted to hear the confessions and patriotic defiance of Colonel Oliver North, whose boyish good looks and unapologetic self-confidence riveted people to their radios and televisions, much as they had been over a decade before with the Watergate hearings.

Just before lunch on the first day back after New Year's, Ronn came into my office.

"Happy New Year, Jack!" he said. "Remember when I came into your office at Skynet and you said 'perhaps we should do this over dinner'? I think we should go to lunch and talk."

"Okay, let's go."

I rose from my desk and followed Ronn out. It certainly looked like the year was off to a great start. No Carson, no stock options, and now the best of my staff was bailing out. What next?

We took Ronn's car over to L'Auberge du Soleil and Richard seated us immediately. After we both ordered iced teas, Ronn began.

"Jack, first, you can congratulate me. Barb and I are getting married."

"Ronn, that's great. Congratulations. You two seem like a great fit."

"Well, don't be too happy yet. You know I've lived on nickels and dimes over the last several years in spite of making great money at Skynet and here. I've been saving and investing my money, and living cheap in Garnet's shack. As strange as it sounds, I've got enough saved up to retire, so Barb and I have purchased a horse ranch outside Bozeman, Montana. We'll be moving out there in about a month.

"I can stay that long if you need me, but I'd like to transition out of ALM as soon as I can. You know, now that Carson is out of the picture and Steve's running NewCo, CIA just isn't the same. I don't mean you're not doing a great job. It's just that it's all work and no fun anymore. Steve has taken all the good people, us excluded of course. It's definitely time for me to leave. I've had a great ride, but as you know, writing code is not my first love."

Richard took our orders. I turned my attention back to Ronn and said, "Ronn, I'm going to miss you. You've not only been great to work with all these years, you've also been a good sounding board for me and have given some great advice. Plus, who am I going to compare injuries with now?"

"You can always come visit. It's only a two hour plane flight. There's some good skiing not too far away, and it really is God's country. Plus, I'm sure you'd love the whitewater."

We continued to talk about Montana over lunch, then Ronn drove me back to the office. He pulled into the parking lot, and before I got out of the car said, "Jack, you said I give good advice, so here's the last career comment I'll make. Leave CIA as soon as you can. You're as stuck here as you were at Skynet. With Steve taking everything for himself, and Carson absent, you need to just walk away.

"Hell, you grew Skynet from almost nothing to a sizeable company, and look what you've done here at CIA. NewCo wouldn't exist but for your efforts. You should really just bail and go out on your own. You can build your own CIA."

"Not CIA," I replied, "Turnkey."

"What's 'Turnkey'?

"Turnkey Communications is the company I'm planning to start someday to build networking solutions.

"So believe me. I've thought about it. But Carson has made me a very nice offer. If we can get him back, I end up with a big piece of CIA and NewCo. I have to ride this one to the finish to see if it's going to fly, if you'll excuse the mixed metaphors. If I can get Carson back and clean, I've got a great opportunity. If not, I can leave and start Turnkey then."

"I've seen cokeheads before," Ronn responded, a note of sympathy in his voice. "The ones who can't give it up are like

Carson. They think it makes them better than they are and they strive to be the best. I don't think Carson will give it up until it kills him. I strongly recommend you get out sooner rather than later."

"I'll think about it. In the meantime, I'll see what I can do about recruiting a replacement for you at ALM. I expect it'll take a week or two and we'll need a week of transition."

"I'll do whatever I can not to leave you in the lurch, Jack. We have plenty of time to talk. I'll check in a few days from now."

I got out of the car and Ronn drove off. I was now the sole senior technical person at CIA. It was starting to feel really lonely.

2

More news awaited me the next day when I arrived at the cottage to meet Shelly. I opened the door to find Shelly pouring two glasses of Champagne.

"What are we celebrating?" I asked.

"I'll give you a hint," she replied, almost too happy to contain herself. "This is the last glass of Champagne I'll be having for quite a while."

Sucker punch! They say when it comes to trouble, it doesn't just rain. Well, it certainly seemed to be pouring. What did this mean? Was it over between us?

I put on a smile and said, "You must be pleased. After all this hassle, you're finally pregnant!"

'Pleased doesn't begin to describe it. Finally, I'm going to have a baby. I think you're the only person who knows how much this means to me. Thanks for keeping me sane on the way."

"So, how does this change us?" I asked tentatively.

"Why, not at all," She responded, a puzzled look on her face. "I'm only a couple weeks gone now. I can't wait to have you share the changes my body is going to go through over the coming months. I know you'll love exploring the differences.

"It may get more difficult to make love the last few months, but I'm sure we can work something out," she said, her look becoming mischievous as she reached for and began unfastening my belt.

"To a healthy baby and safe pregnancy," I toasted, raising my glass.

"To a healthy baby," she answered, raising a glass with her free hand.

Sometime later, Shelly lay in my arms. I thought about these stolen hours. What was it that kept me coming back? The sex was great, but there was more. I realized that what I appreciated most was the intimacy. Shelly was so open with me. She was unashamed of her body and her desires and she let me look at her and touch her. Dressing, undressing, or just walking around naked, she'd see me glancing her way. Rather than covering up, turning away, or even putting on a show, Shelly would just slow down. Whatever she did then took longer. She wanted me to enjoy seeing her move, and I did. Her movements might be ordinary, but for me they became exotic. I wished I could paint so I could capture the tautness of her thighs, the strength of her arms, the turn of her head, and the roundness of her small bottom.

Together like this after making love, with one hand I'd often lift one of her arms over her head and begin stroking downward with the other, starting with her palm, then the inside of her elbow, under her arm, brushing the side of her breast, then down to her waist, hip, and thigh. When she lay back smiling with her eyes closed and luxuriated in the sensuality of my touch, I felt more appreciated than I ever had in my life.

As her beauty consumed me and I began to fall into an almost meditative trance, Shelly spoke softly, "Jack, there is something I have to ask you. Are you seeing anyone else?"

I sighed and looked deep into her large green eyes.

"Shelly, you're everything I need. I don't have or want anyone else. Why?"

"If you were, or if you decide to in the future, I need you to wear a condom when we're together. I can't risk the baby with a possible infection. I've even told Steve he will always wear a condom."

"I thought you weren't sleeping with Steve," I said, stunned.

"Ah, well, I don't, really. I mean it's not a regular thing, but it does happen sometimes."

Wanting details, but afraid to ask, or maybe just feeling I was in no position to ask, I held my tongue. I realized that if I'd known she was having sex with Steve, it wouldn't have made any difference, except I probably would have worn protection. Who knew where Steve had been?

"It doesn't matter," I said. "I want you and will be here as long as you want me."

We held each other a while longer, then got up, got dressed and left. I kissed her before she went home to her husband, soon-to-be father.

3

On Valentine's Day, Carson returned. He just walked into his Los Gatos apartment. Nancy tried to call Pam, who was out, then called me. Carson had shown up, exhausted, depressed, unkempt, dirty, and smelling foul. I said I'd be right over.

Nancy opened the door almost as soon as I rang the bell.

"Jack, come in. I'm glad to see you. I'm not really sure what to do."

"Have you guys talked? I asked.

"No. Not really. He walked in and I almost didn't recognize him. It wasn't just his clothes, it was his eyes. I'm, not sure he's the same person. I ran a bath, and as we waited for the tub to fill, he just wasn't there. He looked off into space as if I didn't exist.

'He's been in the bath about five minutes. What do you think we should do next?"

"Let's see how he is when he comes out. At least he's home. I was getting worried that something more serious had happened to him. It's been almost six weeks since Pam stopped putting money into his account and put a hold on his company credit cards. We thought that would force him back home sooner, and when he didn't show up, I imagined the worst."

"Me too. Who knows what can happen when you owe money to drug dealers?"

Nancy asked if I wanted something to drink and I accepted an iced tea. We had just started talking about the rehab research we'd done when the doorbell rang. Nancy welcomed Pam, who had come as soon as she picked up Nancy's message, and the three of us waited for Carson.

Half an hour later, Carson emerged. He was clean, but his dark hair and beard were filled with small dreadlocks. Had I just not noticed the streaks of gray in both? Surprisingly, he wasn't much thinner, but he looked diminished, with sunken, hollow eyes that almost pleaded for help. Looking at him, it was hard to believe that I'd ever used the word 'distinguished' to describe him.

"I screwed up," he said, his eyes seeking each of us in turn, glancing upwards, then lowering ashamedly.

"I'm sorry I let all of you down," he continued. "What's happing with the company?"

"We've been trying to cover up your disappearance, but after this long, most of our customers and both NewCo and CIA employees know something is wrong," I began. "Inside the company, the story is out. They all know you have a drug problem. I don't know whether it's made the rounds of the customers yet. And Ronn is leaving."

"The Board met and Steve voted down Jack's options," Pam said. "We held a special meeting this week and unanimously approved a measure to put you on leave from the Board. So, you're out and Steve is officially running both companies, though so far, he's left the day-to-day operations of CIA to Jack."

"Ronn is leaving and Steve controls everything?" he cried, sinking further into his chair, his shoulders sagging. "What a mess. I don't know what to do. Is there any way I can get my life back?"

Nancy moved beside him. She put her arms around him and he collapsed into her. After a few moments, she pulled back, lifted his face and looked deeply into his eyes.

"If you really want it back, there's probably a way," she said sympathetically. The three of us have been working on a plan since you left and if you trust us completely, we can probably do it."

"But first," I interrupted, "we'd like to hear what happened the last few months. How'd you get into it and what brought you back."

We all looked at him expectantly. He sighed and began.

"I was going along fine. We were working together and I was staying clean. My life was back on track, you were all happy with me, and I felt as if I could live without the coke. I must admit, it was there in the back of my mind, but I was sure I could control the impulse, just like you avoid looking at a pretty woman when you're with your lover.

"One evening, I went back to Alan's place after a working dinner and he offered me a few lines. I didn't think one time would be a problem, and it didn't seem to be. I only did the few and later went home feeling fine.

"The next morning, I woke up and was really down. I needed a hit to bring myself up. I called my supplier in Santa Cruz and met him. That was it. I went to my house in Aptos, then after using the gram he sold me, I called him back. I bought a key, emptying my bank account. Then it was non-stop party. I invited people over, including lots of strangers. I stayed in other people's places. As long as I was bringing drugs, I was welcome to the best room in the house. People took me out to eat, and it just went on and on.

"A while back – I don't really know when it was – my account balance was zero and my credit cards stopped working. For a while, my 'friends' hosted me, supplied me, or lent me money. When they got tired of my mooching, I went back to the dealer who agreed to float me. After all, I was a good customer who always paid. A week ago, he cut me off and I crashed at the Aptos house. If I heard a car coming, I went out the back and hid in the guest house. No one would give me a hit. My friends let me down. They wouldn't lend me money, and I got really depressed.

"I woke up this morning, turned on the TV, saw the date. Valentine's Day has always been a really special holiday for us," he said, looking lovingly at Nancy and squeezing her hand, tears welling up in his eyes. "I didn't know if any of you would still talk to me, but I felt I had hit bottom and that maybe you could help.

"Looking at you, I see what true friendship is."

With this last statement, he started crying, huge tears spilling down his cheeks into his beard. Nancy just held him.

I stood to leave and Pam followed my lead.

"Carson, we'll let you and Nancy have your Valentine's Day together. Tomorrow," I began, looking at Pam, who nodded, "Tomorrow, we'll be back. Nancy can give you the outline of the plan and we can all discuss it together. If you're game, we can get started."

Nancy held Carson as we made our way out.

I walked Pam to her car and asked, "What do you think?"

"Well, I'd like to believe he's hit bottom and truly understands it, but we've been through this once before. He was going along so well. I just don't understand how an intelligent – no, brilliant – man like Carson can fall back into something so destructive.

"I don't get it either," I replied. "From my conversations with him about it, I think he believes it makes him better. He has spent his whole life trying to prove himself good enough.

"You know he never went to college. In fact, I don't think he even graduated from high school. I've met a few other brilliant people like this and they all have an underlying insecurity. Even though they hold their own with their more educated counterparts, I think they always fear that they'll be found out; that the lack of formal education reveals a fundamental weakness. "In my experience, they often try harder. I think there's a desire to prove that they are as intellectually capable as someone with multiple degrees. They often continue to read and study long after the rest of us have quit.

"My guess is that Carson sees cocaine as one more way to catch up. Perhaps this oversimplifies the problem, but I think that's part of it."

Pam nodded, then just shook her head.

We agreed to meet at Carson's at noon the next day. I went back to the office wondering what I'd just committed myself to.

4

The next day, I found Pam waiting in her car when I pulled into the visitor parking area at Carson's. We greeted each other and walked to the door. Nancy answered our ring.

"Hi. Come in. I've made a light lunch for us all.

"Carson's ready. I've given him a basic outline and he knows what he has to do. I think he's really embarrassed, so if we can keep the conversation on specific tasks and avoid any recrimination or even discussion of how he got here, I think it will go smoothly."

Nancy raised crossed fingers and led us to the dining room where Carson sat. His beard and hair were now neatly trimmed and while he still had a haunted look, I could at least begin to recognize the Carson of old.

After selecting sandwiches from the tray Nancy offered and helping ourselves to homemade coleslaw with peanuts and cayenne, I sat down at the table to Carson's left and Pam took the chair directly across from him. Nancy passed out glasses of iced tea then pulled a chair up right next to Carson. A fleeting picture of Nancy spoon feeding him crossed my mind, but Carson just smiled gratefully and began to eat.

"So Carson," I said confidently. "I guess Nancy has explained the outline of our plan. I'll fill you in on the rehab program we've found and Pam can pick up with what happens when you get out."

At his look of fear I changed direction a bit and softened my tone. "Don't worry. It's not a prison. We've done quite a bit of research and have talked to people who have made it out clean. Unfortunately, for almost all of the places we've found, the recidivism rates are pretty high – over ninety percent. "

I looked at Carson and could see near panic setting in. This wasn't going well at all.

"Sorry. Maybe I should have started with what we have found instead of the problems with the others.

"It turns out that Stanford has been doing major research on cocaine addiction. They've discovered that for long-term users like you, the chemical structure of the brain actually changes. The cocaine addict can't get a sense of satisfaction or reward from anything but cocaine."

Carson's eyes brightened a bit and he nodded encouragingly.

I continued. "I obviously don't understand all the nuances of this new research, but it has to do with a substance called dopamine that is produced in the brain and gives a sense of pleasure. From what I gather, this normally occurs when you're having fun, or sometimes when you need to ignore pain or escape a bad situation without panic.

"Apparently, cocaine causes the brain to increase the dopamine production, but after prolonged use, the circuits of the brain change. They become more sensitive and don't produce as much dopamine on their own since they're getting dopamine from an outside source. When you try to quit, you have problems enjoying anything because your brain isn't stimulated normally, it has become reliant on the drug.

"Stanford has put a rehabilitation facility in place that combines therapy with a new drug called naloxone to encourage the brain to reconnect its normal circuits, along with behavioral training, sort of like the twelve step programs, to help eliminate dependency. They also do psychological counseling to try to find out what got you started in the first place. They want you to learn to recognize the patterns and to seek help if you feel you're going to slip.

'It's certainly something new, but their success rates seem to be pretty high, at least for the first year. They've only been doing this for about a year, so they don't know if it really works longer.

"The core program lasts six weeks. This is six weeks of living at their facility. After a few weeks, they give you passes to leave and they begin to phase you back into normal life, while checking to make sure you don't fall back into your old patterns. For another six months, they hold weekly meetings where they do blood tests and counseling sessions. The blood tests aren't so much to see if you're using again as to let them track the progress of the chemical changes in the brain. They want to see that you're getting back to normal dopamine function.

"Note that since it's Stanford, the facilities are pretty nice. It's more like a hotel than a clinic."

Carson looked hopeful, but didn't say anything. Pam picked up where I left off.

"Carson, Jack made it sound easy. I've talked to graduates of the program and believe me, it wasn't easy. A large part of this is that you'll have to learn to accept that you have a fundamental problem. Part of it may be psychological, but there are new theories out that some people have 'addictive personalities', that their brains are more susceptible to addiction that the average person's.

"In the program, they'll also be removing all legal drugs including tobacco, alcohol, and caffeine. I know you enjoy your cigars, brandies, and coffee. You may feel life isn't worth living without them, but Stanford says this denial is temporary. They want to work with a clean system at the beginning so they can judge the dopamine levels. Towards the end of the program, they'll let you reintroduce coffee.

"The thing we want you to know is that we'll support you through this. We all want the old Carson back. You may think that cocaine makes you better, but it has ruined you and almost taken this wonderful company you've built down with you. You were a rising star before…"

Carson looked down, appearing to withdraw. We finished our meals in silence and waited. Palpable tension filled the room. Nancy, Pam, and I exchanged looks of despair.

"So what happens after I get out?" Carson finally asked. All of us relaxed hearing the decision in his voice.

Pam continued. "One of the things that Stanford emphasized is that stress is a major factor in recidivism. We're hoping to ease you back into your old lifestyle without adding too much pressure.

"But you should know that it will be a while before you get control of CIA again. I've spoken with the Board, and they want to see you clean for a year before they surrender control again. You could force this, but I think that would be a bad idea. In order for the Board to agree to this rehab program, which isn't cheap, you have to sign a proxy giving Steve control of your share for one year.

"When you get out, we'll be removing temptations. I'll be controlling your money. I'll pay all your bills, and you won't have any real spending money. Nancy will take care of that. At CIA, you'll be working for Jack until he feels you're reliable and back to your old self and he'll be phasing in increasing responsibility.

"Nancy will be with you at all social functions and will intervene if drugs appear. It may sound like we're the police, watching your every move, but we hope you'll see us as a support structure, the people you can rely on to get your life back. It will be a long road, but we're all ready to walk it with you."

Carson teared up. "It's a lot. I mean, I'm not sure I can do this and it's a lot to ask of you to do this for a year. It sounds like prison, but I guess I deserve that."

"Carson," Nancy said, lifting his chin and looking deeply into his eyes. "It won't be prison. You have a big problem and from the research we did, the chances of solving it any other way are almost zero. We wouldn't be committing to this if we didn't love you and believe that you are a powerful person who can take control of his life again. This isn't a punishment. It's a way home."

Carson looked at us each in turn. We could see a mix of emotions: gratitude, embarrassment, a bit of anger, and somewhere in there, hope.

"When do I start?" he asked.

5

Nancy took Carson to Stanford the following Monday. I dropped by Pam's office that morning.

"So, what do you think?" I asked.

"Who knows? I was always in awe of Carson. Now I don't know what to think. I find it hard to believe that wreck we saw will ever become the man I admired. I doubt I can find it in me to see him without this flaw.

"Even if he comes out clean, I'll always be waiting for fall. Before, I trusted him completely. His integrity was an inspiration. How can I ever feel that way again?"

I thought about this and asked myself if I felt the same way. "I have faith in him," I replied. "I honestly believe that if he understands the source of his problem and the negative effects on his life and those who care about him, he's smart enough to quit for good.

"If the clinic can fix the physical part of his brain, the intellectual part should keep him from making the same mistake."

Pam just shook her head. She turned her dark eyes on me with a startling intensity. "It would be nice," she began, her mouth and eyebrows turned down, "But I think you're being naïve. People don't change, and as they say, 'Once a junkie, always a junkie'."

"Who says that?"

"Well, Steve for one. He thinks we're wasting time and money on Carson."

I thought about arguing, but knowing her relationship with Steve, realized it was a lost cause. I shook my head, gave her a slightly disgusted look, and left her office.

I hadn't spoken to Steve in quite a while. Whenever I saw him, I felt guilty about Shelly. On the other hand, he was out of the office most of the time, and the two companies' business really didn't intersect at all. With his single-mindedness about NewCo, I could certainly understand his perspective about Carson. Steve was driven to succeed and Carson was just something that would slow him down.

When I returned to my office, I called Georgette and filled her in on the events of the weekend. I described Pam's reaction, expecting a vote of confidence and hope, especially after I told her about Stanford and the chemical basis of addiction, but

Georgette was trenchant.

"Jack, wake up and smell the coffee!" she said. "This is life, not a fairy tale. There are no happy endings. We all end up dying in the end and there are countless tragedies along the way. I learned not to have hope after Mike. I believe there's nothing I could have done. Once he started down a path of self-destruction, there was no going back and no one could save him. "You should cut your losses and leave CIA. Carson isn't coming back, and if he does, you're just going to go through this again. Don't waste your career on such a long shot. You have the contacts; you know the business; go do it on your own."

If a part of me knew she was right, it was a very small part. I loved CIA. It was the perfect job. I had major influence over decisions made in some of the biggest companies in the country, dictated my working hours, and when Carson was around, had an incredible partner to brainstorm with. I had to give it a shot. Carson had taught me so much. This was the least I could do.

The next evening with Shelly, I found out she felt the same way. She went so far as to use Steve's quote. To her, Carson was a junkie and I was acting stupidly. I left early, angry and feeling more alone than I ever had.

6

Six weeks later, it was spring in California. The ugly brown rugs that topped the hills surrounding the Silicon Valley had turned into endless expanses of lush green. Wildflowers had sprung up on every unoccupied piece of ground and the orange-gold California poppies startled drivers and hikers with their striking contrast to the verdant landscape. Carson emerged from rehab as a person reborn.

Nancy drove him to work, walked him to my office and after wishing us luck, left us to get started.

"Jack, I feel better than I ever have," Carson said, his unbridled enthusiasm remarkably contagious. "I see it so clearly now. I know why I fell into addiction and I know how to avoid that trap. I'm also having the best time of my life. Maybe it's the drugs-"

Seeing me raise my eyebrows, he stopped, laughed, then continued. No, I mean the brain fixing drugs, naloxone and the other stuff they gave me. I can certainly enjoy things other than coke. I'm experiencing a clarity I never felt before.

"Of course, on coke, I thought I saw things more clearly, but it was sort of like looking through a microscope. I could see things I'd never seen and perceive details I'd never have experienced, but I couldn't see the bigger picture. Part of what I've learned is that the big picture is more important than the microscopic view. After all, that's the job I chose: consultant, providing the bigger view to our clients.

"So speaking of clients, where do we start?"

I told him about a new client, the May Company, one of the largest retailers in the country. They had thousands of retail clothing stores under several store names, but wanted to keep consistent pricing among all the stores across every chain. Each night, they'd take price changes and sale prices for their huge inventories and send them to the stores electronically. However as their head of data processing said, they were running out of night. During the day, their computer networks had to handle credit and sales transactions. They couldn't be downloading files once the stores opened. Everything had to be received before the stores opened. We needed to come up with some recommendations to help expedite the delivery of all these files. May was opening several new stores every day. They didn't want this data networking problem to limit their expansion. I asked Carson to research how other chain stores addressed this problem. I would look at the networking protocols that May used and the structure of their nationwide computer network, then we'd get together and start brainstorming a solution.

Carson was overjoyed. He thanked me and headed to his office to get started. It was good to have a partner again!

7

By June, the beautiful hills had turned brown again. California's nickname is 'The Golden State'. Most people believe that this is derived from California's history with gold during the mid-nineteenth century and the forty-niners who panned for gold in the Sierra Nevada foothills. From what I've been told, the word 'golden' actually refers to the color of the hills from late spring through fall, a golden brown. Whatever the etymology of the term, the lushness of spring had already been desiccated by the beginning of our rainless season. Although it's said that it never rains in California, it does. Our rainy season runs from November through April and it is extremely rare to see any rain at all from June through most of October.

The past few months had been good. Carson was without a doubt back in stride. Even skeptical Pam was warming up to his easy-going charm and wit. We were doing the best work of our lives and our clients were demanding more. We started recruiting additional people to help us with the work load.

NewCo had completed the initial work on project Hydra for PacBell and was now deploying the system in test offices. Steve was increasingly absent as he traveled extensively to promote the technology to telephone companies all across the country and around the world.

This allowed Shelly to spend several nights with me at the bungalow. I marveled at the changes in her body. The swelling of her breasts, the darkening of her nipples, her protruding stomach and a strange vertical blue line that ran from her navel down into her pubic hair.

Somehow I expected that as her pregnancy advanced, Shelly's libido would decline. I was wrong. She seemed to make love with increasing intensity as the months progressed and loved to try out varied new positions. Never had I felt so desired.

One evening, lying beside her, both of us covered in sweat after a particularly vigorous session, I looked over at her and was once again struck by her beauty. The pregnancy had brought on a combination of vulnerability, sereneness, and comfort with herself that made her infinitely attractive.

As I gazed into her endless green eyes, I said, "You know, it's true. Pregnant women do glow. Your face is always slightly flushed and your eyes are brighter than they've ever been, almost like there's a light behind them."

"Well, I may have a rosy glow now, but a few months ago I was glowing green. I felt like I had radiation poisoning. I'm glad the morning sickness went away.'

This was Shelly. As romantic as I tried to be, she always turned it around to something practical. That's not to say she didn't do romantic things. It's just that she didn't ever express it verbally.

I had always tried to believe that men and women were essentially the same. I theorized that the apparent differences, aside from the physical ones, were imposed upon us by society. Girls were raised with Barbie dolls and encouraged into domesticity. I can remember being struck with seeing two children playing with dolls. They were acting out their parents' relationship from going to work, to arguments. Boys of the same age were outside playing games of conquest and exploration. It became clear to me that with these additional years of play-acting and social role modeling, it was no wonder that young women were better at relationships than young men. They'd been preparing for their whole lives. I thought that if the roles were reversed, society might be very different.

But after sharing her pregnancy experience as much as I could, not being a physical part of her, I was starting to think that women were inherently more practical, that the nurturing impulses made them work at understanding relationships and that we males could never catch up after their head start.

As I looked at the women and men I knew, I realized that while women loved and appreciated romance, it was the men who lived through their own romantic notions. When push came to shove, men often made futile romantic gestures while women buckled down and got the job done.

I was clearly one of these romantic fools, in my job, my relationships, and even in sports as I quested after an unachievable perfection and harmony with the inexorable forces of nature.

After the breakup of AT&T, Pacific Telephone became the Pacific Telesis Group. The telephone portion of the company, Pacific Bell, was regulated by the Public Utilities Commission, which determined an acceptable level of profit for the company. However, Pacific Telesis operated other companies that could run unregulated. One of these was Pacific Telesis International whose mission was to develop new business opportunities all around the world.

I had been consulting for PacTel International since shortly after the AT&T breakup. Periodically, I'd be called in to review designs of networks in countries around the world and I had accumulated hundreds of thousands of frequent flyer miles enabling me to upgrade to first class on most of my flights. At this point in 1986, I was working on a contract with Telefonica, the Spanish telephone company. Telefonica had decided they wanted to add services to their nascent packet switching networks. They had developed a manufacturing facility to build state-of-the-art packet switches and were interested in selling these switches worldwide. They asked PacTel International to help them with the deployment of new services and to review the features of the new switches. If all went well, PacTel would resell the Telefonica products throughout the world.

Over the years, I had developed my own jet lag regimen. A few days before the flight I would eliminate all alcohol, then I'd begin shifting my hours to try to start sleeping and eating on the destination time. On the day of the flight, I'd eat only on the destination time. This usually meant fasting for most of the flight. For a trip to Spain, I'd sleep the Atlantic leg, then eat the breakfast they supplied on the plane. This way, I could fly on a Sunday, and after an arrival at 8am on Monday morning, check into the Grand Hotel in Madrid to shower and change clothes, and still make a 10am meeting with Jose Aguillera Entebbe, the CEO of Telefonica, alert and ready to work.

At one o'clock on this first day of meetings with Telefonica, Jose said it was time for lunch. He took me and three of the executives from the meeting to an ornately decorated restaurant called El Mar. Telling me to trust his choices, he conversed in rapid Castilian Spanish with the waiter and ordered for the entire table. While my French was fluent, my Spanish was much weaker. I could read the language, but had a hard time picking up more than a few words of the lisp-filled speech. When I tried to speak to them in Spanish, Jose suggested we stay with English. Although he said it was so they could practice their English, I could see in their faces that my few words had in some way irritated them. I later learned that like Parisians, Spaniards who spoke Castilian were not terribly tolerant of the bastardized Spanish of Latin America. I also learned that the lisp in the language (gracias is pronounced 'grathias') was not the original pronunciation, but was dictated by a king with a speech impediment centuries before.

The waiters brought out a veritable feast of seafood and handed each of us wooden utensils. While I recognized the mussels, prawns and a number of the other dishes, most were quite unfamiliar to me. One plate contained what looked like dark pasta with chunks of garlic. I helped myself to a small portion only to then notice the small eyes and mouths. This was a plate of tiny black eels.

As we ate, I watched the others and tried to imitate their use of the utensils, noting that for most dishes we used the wooden ones. Since I'd grown up poor with a very limited menu, I was always intrigued, and a little intimidated by unfamiliar food. Surprisingly, the eels were one of the best dishes. When we finished one platter, another with a different variety of seafood would appear in its place. This truly was a banquet beyond any I'd had before.

I also discovered quickly that business was not discussed over lunch. This seemed a most civilized practice. As it appeared the meal was drawing to a close, Jose spoke in his almost accent-less English, "Jack, I have saved the best for last. This next dish is considered to be the finest shellfish delicacy in Spain. It is in high demand, but very rare."

He motioned to the head waiter and two others came out carrying twin platters of vaguely familiar shellfish. Jose placed a few on his plate and then demonstrated how to eat them. The shell portion looked like the closed position of a child's hand making a bird-like shadow puppet. Below this white and gray-speckled shell dangled the 'foot', which resembled a miniature, two to three inch long elephant's leg. It was grayish-brown and wrinkled.

Jose split open the foot and proceeded to devour the delicate pink flesh inside. I did the same and found them to be delicious, almost a combination of a clam and a mussel in flavor, but unlike either, very tender. When three or four of the shells without their feet lay together in my plate, I realized what they were.

"Senor Entebbe, I know these. They are called gooseneck barnacles and grow all over the rocks at home. I've harvested mussels which grow in beds of these, but I've never heard of anyone eating the gooseneck barnacles."

"If this is true," he said almost conspiratorially and winking, "We should go into business together. These fetch nearly twenty thousand pesetas a kilo here!"

A quick calculation at the current exchange rate revealed that these common shellfish were worth over a hundred dollars a pound! I vowed to try them at home in October when it was again okay to eat California shellfish.

Our lunch lasted over three hours and I was surprised to find the headquarters of Telefonica deserted when we returned. Jose explained that they had a flexible working schedule in Telefonica. People started any time between 7am and 9am, worked four or five hours, took a four hour siesta, then returned to complete their work in the evening, finishing between 7pm and 9pm. We had returned during the siesta.

For the rest of the day, we worked out a schedule for me to meet with the key development people in Madrid as well as with the director of the manufacturing plant in Malaga, a resort town on the Gold Coast. Jose then asked me about CIA and what else we did. Although I worked under contract with PacTel, they asked me to use my own business cards. I told him about our consulting process and about NewCo. He was fascinated by Project Hydra and I promised to have Steve contact him.

Two days later I flew to Malaga and met with Esteban Castilla, the manufacturing plant director. The modern blue glass and steel plant was located among Southern California-like arid brown hills a few miles outside the seaside resort of Malaga. At lunch/siesta time, we visited a seafood restaurant on the boardwalk which ran for miles along the white sand beaches of the Mediterranean. What amazed me though was that the waves were six to eight feet. I hadn't seen the Med before, but given its size, I thought it was always flat. I turned to Esteban and asked him if this was rare.

"We get waves like this maybe twice a year," he said in heavily accented English, with his Castilian lisp. "When the Sirocco blows in the deserts of North Africa it creates these waves."

That evening, I took a walk on the beach. Although the winds were calm, there were two windsurfers on the beach. They had removed the sails from their boards and were trying to paddle out into the surf. It was clear they weren't wave surfers because they couldn't get out. The waves kept driving them back because they weren't able to find the channels. I watched for a while, and when they were exhausted, they gave up and sat panting on the beach. I walked over and in passable Latin American Spanish asked if I could borrow one of their boards. They replied in German that they didn't speak Spanish and I told them in my broken German that my German wasn't very good. I asked if they spoke French, and we finally settled on English.

They were a bit reluctant to lend me a board until I told them I lived in Santa Cruz. When they realized this was California, they enthusiastically encouraged me to take either board. I stripped down to my underwear and paddled out on a nine-foot windsurfer, trying to figure out what I was going to do with the straps that were irritating my stomach and legs as I paddled.

The waves were just wind swell. The Med wasn't large enough to generate the long lines we see in California. Instead these were short peaks and the rides were equally short. On my third wave, I manage to pull under the lip for a very brief tuck into a short-lived barrel. It collapsed on me and I popped out to cheers and shouts from the German guys on the beach. I caught a few more before the setting sun drove me shoreward. To think, I had surfed the Mediterranean!

They lent me a towel and I slipped back into my clothes. Over dinner, we exchanged surfing and windsurfing stories. When I went for a run on the beach the next morning, the Mediterranean looked like a lake.

9

NewCo continued to grow and prosper. They had installed evaluation systems in several telephone companies and if these succeeded, money would begin to pour in and the growth would accelerate.

Shelly called me on the eighteenth of August to say her water had broken and her parents were taking her to the hospital. Steve was on a trip in Atlanta. I found this strange, not so much because he wasn't going to be there for the birth of his son (confirmed months earlier), but because he had told the office he was on his way to Telefonica. Perhaps he had a connecting flight out of Atlanta.

I raced to the hospital. Shelly explained to her parents that I was her backup labor coach. In fact, I had attended all the birthing classes with her. Steve wasn't interested. He had told her that this baby thing was all hers.

Shelly looked fine when I arrived, amazingly composed for someone about to go through a life altering experience of intense pain. She insisted she was going to do a natural birth; she didn't want any chemicals affecting her baby.

After a series of minor contractions about ten minutes apart, the first major contraction hit and Shelly screamed. We had mentally prepared for this, but I think the reality finally struck with the pain. We waited in complete silence for the next one.

I've heard that the Chinese water torture is based on the idea that anticipation can drive you crazy. Time expands as you wait for the next drop to fall, and just when you think it's over, you get hit again. I think waiting on contractions is just as bad; you know another one is coming, but not when or how intense it will be.

Worse, for me, I wasn't sure I was going to make it. Every time a contraction came, my stomach roiled. I felt light-headed, much as I did at the fertility clinic almost a year before. Although I could stand pain affecting me, it tore me up to see someone I loved literally racked from head to toe with agony. Somehow, I had to find a way to withdraw. I needed to coach, not be part of the game. After all, I really couldn't be, could I?

When a contraction hit, Shelly would look to me with pleading eyes as if I could somehow make the pain go away. I wanted to fix it, but I couldn't. At some point, I found a way to step back from the moment and remembered the exercises from the class. We focused on her breathing, and mine.

After twelve hours Shelly was exhausted and so was I. The bad news was that she was only three centimeters dilated, not the requisite ten centimeters. At this point, over Shelly's vocal protestations, they began to administer drugs to speed the cervical dilation. Twelve hours later, she was only six centimeters dilated and they decided to do a Caesarean Section. Shelly was so physically and emotionally exhausted that she really didn't care. She just wanted to get this over with.

Since I wasn't family, I was banished to the waiting room with Shelly's father, Marcus. Her mother, Ruth, accompanied Shelly to the operating room. I made some small talk with Marcus, but the time passed very slowly. I understood that C-sections were now routine, but there was the chance we could lose Shelly. Marcus and I, both control personalities, were at our worst, feeling completely impotent as we waited.

A little over an hour later, we were allowed in to visit for a few minutes. Shelly was holding Lucas Walker Caples, and though exhausted, looked more radiant than I'd ever seen her. After years of wishing, hoping, and trying anything to reach her goal, Shelly finally had a baby.

Three days after the birth, Steve walked into my office.

"Jack, I want to thank you for being there with Shelly. I hear she had a rough go."

"No problem, Steve. How was Telefonica?" I parried, quickly changing the subject before I lost my temper with him.

"Jose has agreed to put in a trial system. Thanks for the lead and introduction. How's it going with Carson?"

"Steve, I know you're going to find it hard to believe, but it certainly looks like he's back to his old self. I think he's close to a hundred percent. He's doing great on the projects I've assigned and has started bringing in his own. As you know, we've been growing again.

"Of course, Pam is still keeping a tight hold on his spending money. I think Stanford is about done with him. He appears to be another success story."

"Don't be fooled, Jack," Steve replied, his face turned up in disgust at my unbridled optimism. "He'll slip again. They all do."

During each of the three days Shelly spent in the hospital, I stopped by at least twice and visited for an hour or two. When she left the hospital for home, her mother moved in with her and also hired a nurse-assistant to help with her care for the first week. I went to work as usual and visited Shelly and Lucas each day. Steve was largely absent, but Shelly didn't seem to care. Her dream had come true.

10

1987 arrived to a lot of optimism. Shelly had a new baby and she and Steve had hired a nanny. This allowed her to resume our meetings at the cottage. Carson was back in form, and from what we could see, NewCo was about to launch in a big way. In a few short months, Carson would be readmitted to the Boards of both CIA and NewCo, and I'd be on my way to financial independence.

Looking back at events of that year, the tensions with the Soviet Union eased even more as Gorbechav and Reagan met to sign the INF disarmament treaty. Gorbechav also implemented his policies of Glasnost and Perestroika which opened up the Soviet Union and its satellite countries to western visitors and to free elections.

Of course, after an accidental Iraqi attack on the USS Stark which killed more than thirty sailors, a missile exchange with Iran, inflated stock and bond prices, and corporate and broker scandals, the Stock Market 'collapsed' on October 19th, Black Monday, the single largest drop in the Market's history to that date. But early in the year, it looked like clear sailing for our businesses.

A few weeks into January, the normally measured, calm Carson Ingles stormed into my office. His face was flushed and his hands clenching and opening like he was warming up to start throwing punches.

"That son-of-a-bitch Steve has gone too far this time. I know I've got a few months before I regain control of the companies, but something has to be done. I gave up my Board seats voluntarily, but I'm going to have to force the issue through my stock ownership."

"Carson, didn't you sign a proxy giving Steve voting power over your shares for twelve months?" I asked cautiously.

"Yeah, but I'm prepared to sue to get them back. I can't accept unethical behavior in my companies."

"Slow down, Carson. Tell me what happened."

Carson took a few deep breaths, closed my office door and sat down in a chair facing me. He composed himself for a moment as if ordering his thoughts and suppressing his rage, and began, "I just got off the phone with Mike Cintelli of Cintelli Systems. Mike and I go back a ways. We worked together at IBM and he left to start a company that produced usage-based billing systems for data networks. He was well-funded and well-respected, and has made excellent progress with many of the telephone companies supplying his software systems to them. His employees are a tight-knit team. Most of them followed Mike from IBM and invested their own monies to help start the company.

Like NewCo's, most of the Cintelli systems are in trials, but the trials are going extremely well and he was expecting a significant upswing in revenues this year as the systems went live.

"During the middle of last year, Steve approached him and asked him to create an interface to Hydra. Seeing the value in the product and the apparent success that NewCo was having, Mike invested quite a bit of engineering time and resource to make this happen. As of the fourth quarter, his systems were running well and managed by Hydra. Steve was happy, the customers were happy, and Mike was pleased with the affiliation.

"In December, Steve approached Mike with a buyout offer. Steve offered four percent of NewCo shares in exchange for all of Cintelli Systems' shares. Since neither company is publicly traded, and revenues from product sales are not yet significant, valuation is difficult, but Mike wanted some cash and ten percent. During negotiations, he was willing to come down to five percent; he wanted to be in at least a voting minority position that the five percent level would afford him. He held tight at five percent and some cash.

"Over the holidays, Steve strung him along telling him that he was having problems rounding up the Board members for final approval of the deal. Thinking he had a deal, Mike spent even more money on the integration of the two products, and changed his formal presentations to include the two products as one. He actually closed some sales for NewCo.

"Behind the scenes, Steve went to Marco Software, a startup that's been pretty unsuccessful in competing with Cintelli. They readily agreed to be purchased for a nominal stake in NewCo. I guess they were about to fail anyway. Steve then went to every NewCo customer and told them that Hydra no longer worked with Cintelli's products. Every customer dropped Cintelli's product and in hearing this, Cintelli's investors pulled the plug. They're closing Mike down. He's out of a job. A promising company with superb products bit the dust because of Steve's sleazy approach to business."

I sat there stunned. I wasn't surprised that Steve would do something like this; I thought I knew his ethics, or lack of them, but I hadn't realized that Steve could wield this kind of power. Granted the company had some cash as a result of the large contract with PacBell, but to be buying companies, forcing others out of business?

"So what exactly do you want to do?" I asked tentatively.

"I don't know. I was too pissed off after the phone call to really lay out a plan. I just know that I can't be affiliated with someone who's so unethical and cutthroat."

"Carson, this is Steve. He has a single-mindedness about NewCo. This is his baby and he'll move mountains to ensure its success whether he has to be ethical or not. To Steve, Business is War, and all is fair in Love and War."

"That's not acceptable!" Carson exploded. "One way or the other, I'm going to stop him. If I can't get the control now, I can certainly stop him once I have my seat back on the Board and my proxy expires. In the meantime, I'm going to talk to him. Want to sit in?"

We walked over to Steve's office. I was surprised to find him in. Without any of the usual pleasantries, Carson launched into an assault on Steve's ethics. He paced across the room and back like a professor in a lecture hall, his hands folded behind his back. When he made an accusation, he would extend one arm and point at Steve like a lawyer showing a jury the guilty defendant in a summation.

For his part, Steve just sat quietly and listened. He seemed distracted, almost as if Carson weren't there. I had expected to act as moderator, but it was clear that Steve was going to hear him out and wasn't going to argue or interrupt.

When Carson had finished, he looked at Steve with an implied challenge. Steve responded quietly. We had to lean towards him to hear what he had to say. This was a technique I sometimes used when I needed to get the attention of a group of unruly people and it was working here.

"Carson," he began, almost whispering. "I really can't argue with anything you've said about the facts. You've got it right. I made Mike an offer he should have accepted, but he didn't and suffered the consequences."

Seeing Carson start to rise, Steve put up his hand to stop him.

"I listened to you, so please do me the courtesy of hearing me out.

"Ethics are fine in a law firm or a consulting firm. Your clients expect the highest standards of objectivity. But in the product world, it's dog-eat-dog. The best products don't necessarily win or even make it to market. You need to use every marketing and business advantage you have to be successful.

"You hired me to build a product company and make us all rich, and that's exactly what I'm doing. I'm giving a hundred percent to this effort and I'm not going to let anything or anyone prevent our success. Along the way I'm going to need help to grow the company. People will either join me on my terms or they won't. If they don't, they've declared themselves enemies. If they're not allies, they're enemies or potential enemies, and I have to defend against them, even eliminating them if necessary.

"This company already employs a lot of people whose families are dependent on the income we generate. It will employ many more and we'll make a positive difference to people in this Valley. They deserve the best I can do and I will protect them from competitors and from people whose ethical compunctions might jeopardize their futures and our chances.

"If you're worried about your reputation, let's make the division between the two companies clearer. I believe the missions of CIA and NewCo are completely different and thus must be governed by different standards. It's a cutthroat world in the product business and you have to be prepared to let some blood to succeed."

Carson had calmed a bit and was listening. However, it was clear he didn't agree.

"Steve," he began, "I've consulted at the highest levels of some large, successful companies, and while it's true that many were ruthless on their way up, others were not. I foresee a time when the public will reward businesses for their ethics and I'd like to see that happen with NewCo. We can set the standard of a benevolent powerhouse as we grow.

"Let's look at the case of Mike Cintelli. You know he's good. The best path to success is to partner with the best. If you're a '10', then you should partner with and hire '10s'. If you team up with '9s', as your organization grows, they'll hire '8s', who will hire '7s' with every level afraid to be challenged. If you don't set the standards of hiring the best, you'll end up with a mediocre

210

organization. Cintelli had the best product. You chose a third-rate competitor and I don't see this strengthening NewCo as much as Mike would have. You've made a big mistake."

"Carson, it really comes down to your definition of what a '10' is. From my point of view, if I'm fighting a war, I need someone who's aggressive and not afraid to be tough. Nice guys do finish last. I value toughness over niceness so I will team up with '10s', where '10' is defined by their toughness, but it will be on my terms and they will follow my lead."

"Steve, in several weeks, I'll have my Board seat back. I still own controlling interests in both companies, and I won't let this happen again. NewCo is run by the Board. It's not a one-man show."

With that, Carson got up and walked out. As I followed, it was clear to me that trouble was brewing. What was Steve going to come up with to stop Carson? I suspected it wouldn't be good, but on the other hand, it wouldn't help NewCo if Steve really crossed Carson. CIA still had credibility with a number of Steve's customers, and Carson could certainly do to Steve what Steve did to Mike Cintelli.

11

I lost two close friends to Hang Gliding-related accidents in 1987. The first, early in the year was Marty Freitas. I met Marty in 1978 in the back of a pickup truck riding up the mountain to the launch above Anderson Reservoir in the hills south of San Jose. It was winter and a storm had just passed. Looking across the valley as we wound up the hill, we could see scattered showers – gray streaks falling from towering cumulus clouds, and the valley floor was a patchwork quilt of dark spots, green squares of fallow fields, and golden sunlight where it broke through the clouds. Usually the air left in the wake of a cold front is unstable. The air close to the ground is relatively warm compared to the cold air aloft, so it rises. If it's moist, it forms clouds and sometime rains, so the cumulus clouds were good indicators that we'd be finding thermals.

I had been flying less than a year and had never flown this site before. In fact, this was to be one of my first attempts at thermal flying. Huddled against the rain in the back of the pickup, Marty opened up his backpack and pulled out several gadgets, most I'd never seen. He had windsocks and flags, unusual wind gauges, variometers, airspeed indicators, altimeters, oxygen devices, strobe lights for night flying, and much more, all for sale on the spot. I didn't buy anything from him then. I didn't really know how or when I'd use this stuff, but I kept running into him at different sites and at competitions. Ultimately, I bought most of my gear from him, and we often teamed up to take flying trips together. I always admired his industry and salesmanship.

As I mentioned, I was a neophyte pilot when we met. That first day at Anderson, I had visions of thermals taking me up higher than I'd ever been, but ended up with less than a ten minute 'sled ride', a gentle glide from the launch to the landing area.

While no one found much lift that day, Marty got the longest flight, over forty minutes. He had a knack for finding the smallest pockets of rising air and using them to extend his flight. His ability to 'scratch' was something everyone admired and I decided to emulate.

I met him at Marina Beach north of Monterey shortly after the Anderson flight and Marty invited me to follow him over the seven mile (each way) course from Marina to Sand City and back.

I've described thermals as bubbles of rising air. On the coast, you need wind. The wind hits the cliffs or sand dunes and is deflected vertically and you fly in the band of lift created by this deflection. At Marina, the sand dunes range from zero to over a hundred feet in height. To make the trip to Sand City and back, you have to learn to scratch through the low spots and regain altitude as you reach the high ones. Like a baby bird following its mother, I imitated Marty's every move and soon, after a few outings, became quite proficient at scratching for lift, sometimes mere inches from the ground with my wingtips just a foot or so away from the dune or cliff faces. I also followed Marty in light thermal conditions at Lexington Reservoir and Elk Mountain. The skills he demonstrated allowed me to become a ranked pilot in the years before I gave up competition.

Not long after I met him, Marty opened a shop and in addition to the gadgets, started selling hang gliders. In another year, he had started a manufacturing facility and by 1986 was the third largest manufacturer of Hang Gliders in the world. He test flew each glider he designed and made sure they were certified to the US Hang Glider Manufacturing Association's rigorous safety standards.

During 1986, Hamachi International, a multinational conglomerate offered to buy his company. Marty signed a three-year employment agreement, but gave up creative control of the company. Almost immediately, Hamachi demanded that Marty start building motorized gliders. They seemed to believe that this was a market that consumers would be interested in. The daredevil hang gliding market was too small.

I met with Marty after this decree and we both commiserated over the results of his acquisition. Sure, he now had enough money to retire on, but he was a prisoner for three years and had to do work that was contrary to his convictions.

Neither of us liked motorized hang gliders or ultralights. We believed they were dangerous, not only because hang gliders weren't built for motors, but because flying of any kind required substantial education. We had known too many power pilots who became dependent on their engines and died or killed others as a result. We fervently believed that all pilots needed to learn to fly without engines before they got their licenses. We also believed that they should be trained in spin recovery and should learn all aspects of micrometeorology. This idea of having the average consumer buy an ultralight and take off from his or her backyard seemed insane.

On Sunday, March 15th, 1987, I got an early morning call from Sharon, Marty's wife. He had been killed in his latest motorized glider. He was doing a test flight before the beginning of an Experimental Aircraft show, and the crossbar broke. The glider folded up like a shroud and the gasoline burst into flames on impact.

After mustering a few words of consolation, I threw my glider on the car and went down to Marina. The elements had decided to cooperate and I launched at just before 10am. I explored each nook and cranny of every dune from Marina to Sand City many times, remembering the flights with Marty and all I learned from him, and I remained in the air until the sun set, after eight hours of non-stop flying.

As if Marty's death weren't enough, I lost another friend. I met Jean-Michel Gascogne shortly after meeting Marty. Jean Michel had relocated to California from France and loved to fly. He was also a recently graduated aeronautical engineer and had decided to design hang gliders. After apprenticing with Marty for a few years, he went out on his own. I loved his gliders and while I was competing, I used his latest models. We didn't fly together recreationally. He was always working on or testing his new designs. At competitions, we'd usually hang out afterwards and talk about the events of the day, discussing optimizations for his gliders or plans for upcoming competitions. We weren't really close, but I still considered him a good friend.

In April, Jean-Michel approached me with his newest glider. Although he knew I'd retired from competition, he called and asked if I'd fly in an upcoming meet. It wasn't supposed to be terribly competitive, but he wanted to show off a few good finishes before the real competition season got underway in the late spring and summer. I reluctantly agreed to participate in this meet at Dunlap, near King's Canyon, in the south-central Sierra foothills just west of the Continental United States' highest peak, Mount Whitney.

The Dunlap hang gliding launch is from a long nearly barren ridge covered in low brush with a few pine and scrub oak trees. It's about twenty-five hundred feet over the landing area which borders turkey farms. Since the farms are largely dirt with no vegetation, they are an excellent source for thermals. Unfortunately, if you catch one of these thermals, you will spend the next several minutes climbing upward, enveloped in the smell of turkey droppings. Many people have prematurely exited rapidly climbing thermals just to escape the stench.

While all of us have fantasized about crossing the Sierra, soaring Mount Whitney, then continuing up the Owens Valley, no one has done it. Although we have flown well over a hundred miles from Dunlap and been as high as Mount Whitney, King's Canyon itself is treacherous and there are no landing areas if you should lose lift on your way across the Sierra.

I must admit, when I signed in for the contest, I liked the format of the meet. It was laid out like a tennis tournament. Two pilots would launch simultaneously and fly a twenty to forty mile course for time, with distance set by the meet director, depending on the conditions. The winning pilots from each heat would advance and compete against each other and losers would compete against losers, basically a round-robin tournament format.

On the first day, I was to be one of the sixth pair to launch. Jean-Michel was in the fourth pair. Those of us waiting watched carefully, as the first pilots were always the 'wind dummies'. We could see where areas of lift were working and benefit from their experiences. Unfortunately, the conditions weren't terribly strong and the first three pairs were scratching their ways north along the course, well below the launch. It looked doubtful they would complete the course.

I watched nervously as Jean-Michel and an unknown pilot launched together. Both searched for lift to no avail. The unknown pilot went south and seemed to be maintaining his altitude, but wasn't climbing. Jean-Michel went north and dropped lower and lower. Then, we could see Jean-Michel circling and climbing fast. He had found a great thermal that would certainly take him thousands of feet over the launch. Immediately, the unknown pilot raced over to join Jean-Michel in the thermal.

The rules in hang gliding are the same as the rules in flying sailplane gliders. The lower glider has the right of way. If a glider below you is climbing faster than you are, you must widen your circles and let it pass you. Part of this is etiquette; part of it is just basic safety. The lower glider pilot can't see what's above.

As Jean-Michel circled upward, he reached the level of the launch. The wind was blowing lightly towards the mountain so on his next circle, he drifted over us. The unknown pilot grabbed his parachute and shouted, "Just try to pass me up!"

All of us on the ground heard him clearly but I don't think Jean-Michel even knew he was there. As he completed his next circle about fifty feet above us, the two gliders collided. The unknown pilot tossed his parachute and floated safely down, landing a bit disheveled in some brush about thirty yards away. Jean-Michel tried to throw his chute, but it didn't open in time. While a fall from fifty feet in a hang glider normally wouldn't cause serious injury because the sail slows the fall, Jean-Michel went head first into a rock outcropping. I was the second or third person to reach him.

It was clear from the angle of his head and his open eyes that Jean-Michel was dead.

I ran towards the unknown pilot with fists clenched, ready to kill him. A few of my friends intercepted me before I got there, but they couldn't shut me up when the guy whined about his bent control bar.

They held up the meet for two hours. The unknown pilot was arrested after all of us told the police what had happened, but he ultimately escaped a manslaughter charge. People shunned him when he showed up at any hang gliding site and eventually he quit flying.

When they restarted the competition, I seriously considered flying – doing it for Jean-Michel, but I really couldn't do anything for Jean-Michel. I'd had it with competitive assholes who didn't give a thought to the effects of their actions or the harm they could cause others. I became discouraged with the sport and the people in it and although I continued to fly occasionally for many years, I seemed to spend less and less time doing it.

Nonetheless, as DaVinci said, "When once you have tasted flight, you will forever walk the earth with your eyes turned skyward, for there you have been, and there you will forever long to return."

12

Because of the competition, I had taken the Monday off as a travel day. I worked on Tuesday, but was quite subdued. I loved flying, but was really questioning whether it was worth the risk. I realized that it wasn't the sport itself that was so inherently dangerous, but the people in it. I thought more about competition and my reasons for avoiding these meets. I remembered that in college, I competed on the school's surf team and though I did well, I hated going out in the worst, sometimes unsafe conditions. I thought back to another hang gliding disaster.

Every summer, there's a competition in the Owen's Valley called the Cross Country Classic. Pilots from around the world converge on Bishop California to see who can fly the farthest. The Owen's Valley is located east of the Sierra Nevada and west of the White Mountains. It's a narrow valley created by the Owens River which runs through high desert. Hot springs, hot creeks, and artesian spring-fed ponds can be found in remote areas of the desert among sage and cactus if you know where to look. As you drive the dirt four wheel drive tracks, you have to avoid jack rabbits, huge creatures with ears as long as their bodies as they jump over the sage brush.

Most years, I took a trip to the Owen's during the Classic. While I didn't compete anymore, it was always fun to listen to a dozen different languages on the CB radio, and to exchange flying stories with people from around the world after the day's competition. I usually launched a mile north of the competition launch.

On the third day of the contest, we drove up to the launch and immediately decided not to fly. The winds were blowing more than twenty-five miles per hour and the forecast was for increasing winds. We decided to head over to the competition launch to see what was going in there.

Shockingly, two pilots were about to launch. We ran up to the meet director to protest this insanity, but he informed us of the rules. That year, the pilots had decided that the meet director should not decide which days were flyable. Instead, it should be up to the pilots themselves, who ostensibly had more experience flying and judging conditions than the non-competing organizers. Worse, the rules were such that if one person completed the course for the day and everyone else decided not to fly, that pilot would receive full points while the others received zero. On this particular day, the top ten pilots had already driven down the hill having determined that the conditions were not safe. The two pilots about to launch were way down in the standings and had decided to take a chance. If they could complete the course, they would move into the top rankings. I watched in disgust as the two pilots launched.

The air was bumpy. With the Sierra Nevada range several miles up wind, the flow of air across the Sierra, down into the Owen's Valley, and back up the White Mountains was disrupted and turbulent. The two pilots shot upwards as if rockets were attached to their gliders and in minutes, were several thousand feet above the eight thousand foot launch. A third pilot took off and we could see him tossed about like a piece of paper in a windstorm, but he too climbed. All three started north hoping to begin the course. I watched until they were out of sight. All around us pilots debated. If these guys were successful, everyone else would lose ground in the competition. Still, the more experienced pilots prevailed and convinced the others, especially the non-locals, that the conditions were unsafe. We headed down the mountain, had some lunch, and caught an afternoon matinee in Bishop.

That evening at one of many unofficial camping spots in the desert north of Bishop on Highway 6, we heard what had happened that day. The three pilots followed each other closely. They did make it to White Mountain Peak, which, at over fourteen thousand feet, is the second highest peak in the continental United States. They worked their way up the face of the massively precipitous stone face, but the wind speed continued to increase. At sixteen thousand feet, they couldn't make any forward progress against the wind and were blown back over the top of the mountain. One just turned downwind and flew as fast as he could. The other two tried to fight their way back to no avail. They were slammed into the ground in the rotor behind the mountain and killed instantly, a mile behind the peak. The other pilot traveled downwind nearly four miles and turned into the wind to land. Unfortunately, the wind speeds were nearing fifty miles per hour and he was blown backwards over and over, breaking his glider and almost every bone in his body.

Air doesn't usually slam into the ground. If it does, it bounces and creates a cushion at the surface. The exception to this is rotors. A rotor sets up behind the edge of a steep cliff or mountain. If you've ever walked to the edge of a cliff on a windy day, you may have been surprised to be hit in the back by wind as you approached the edge.

Wind blowing directly into an object like a cliff face is deflected upwards. At some altitude, the wind is moving parallel to the ground and at some distance behind the cliff, air above drops back down and resumes its normal course. This means that the vertical moving air creates a vacuum immediately behind the cliff face. The air behind the cliff fills the vacuum, hence the wind in the back. Now imagine you have a fourteen thousand foot mountain. With the wind blowing forty to fifty miles per hour directly into the face, the violence of the rotor behind the mountain must have been unimaginable.

When I first started hang gliding, it was a somewhat dangerous sport. Dozens of people were killed every year because of equipment failure or pilot error. In recent years, because of revolutionary improvements in glider design, parachutes, and pilot education and certification, the numbers of fatalities had dropped to the point where hang gliding is statistically safer than General Aviation, Scuba diving, car racing, equestrian and many other sports. But that was recreational flying. Competition was killing people.

13

I showed up at the bungalow early and fixed a light dinner of cracked crab, sour dough bread, drawn butter and a small salad, looking forward to sharing an evening with the most important person in my life.

While Marty's death a few weeks before had shaken me up, and I really missed him, somehow, witnessing Jean-Michel's crash and seeing his lifeless body had left me worried about my own mortality. We all know, or should know, that sometimes things happen that are out of our control. Death could come from a suddenly failing organ, as the result of competitive stupidity, or from that semi-truck driver that falls asleep at the wheel and hits you head-on. It can all be gone in an instant.

Some fortunate individuals go through life successfully ignoring this omnipresent danger; a few unlucky ones can't get it out of their minds and become fearful of any risk; but most of us encounter death from time to time and use it as a wake-up call. We rethink our priorities and usually live better, richer lives because at least for some time, we choose the important things over the mundane. It was time for me to tell Shelly about my feelings for her.

Shelly arrived cheery and talking. While she undoubtedly noticed my somber mood, she was clearly hoping for a light evening. I tried to oblige over dinner, but as she nuzzled her head against my bare shoulder and her hand rested on my chest after we made love, I began to talk about competition and its deleterious effects. I told her that I clearly understood the capitalistic model and that by competing we could make ourselves and our work better. On the other hand, with recent experiences in sports and at CIA and NewCo, it seemed that if the competition went beyond the collegial, like a footrace between two friends, it often turned ugly and the ultimate results benefited only the stronger or more cutthroat. In sport, people ceased to improve and some got hurt. In business, the best ideas or products were often lost.

"Shelly, I'm not just thinking about this in generic terms. I'm thinking about Steve and Carson and the differences between them. I admire Carson and believe he's right about Steve's approach to business.

"I don't know how you can stand to be married to someone

like him. I know it's been difficult. Or, at least it was when we first got together. He treated you terribly and even now, his focus is NewCo. You're definitely number two on his list – if that.

"I've been hoping that over time, I could win you over. I want you to leave Steve and marry me. We're such a good fit. We dance perfectly and we certainly are physically compatible. I can provide an excellent life, financial security, and a lot of fun. We wouldn't have to sneak around anymore."

Shelly looked up at me, then moved to raise herself onto one elbow. She appeared to be thinking about my proposition, but it turned out she was just trying to come up with the right thing to say.

"Jack, you know I care about you – no, love you. But there's a part of me you have ignored. I think you've consciously tried to avoid seeing this darker, more mercenary side of me. I know it's there and think it's perfectly fine.

"What you don't get is that I admire Steve. He is the husband I want in spite of some missing pieces to our relationship. You've been able to fill in those holes (she winked and reached out to stroke me).

"He's smart and incredibly ambitious. I love the fact that with Steve, you're either an ally or enemy. He'll defend his allies and will kill his enemies. It makes me feel secure. Someday he'll be incredibly rich and powerful and I'll be his partner. He'll need me to take off the rough edges in our social and political interactions.

"Just the fact that you don't like Steve shows that we're fundamentally incompatible. Our marriage wouldn't work. I want too much, much more than you'll ever be willing to give me. You're not able to do the nasty things required to really make it in this world.

"Jack, you're very much like Carson. I admire your great hearts, belief in ethics, and faith in people. I appreciate the romance and the way you treat me. Maybe someday when Steve achieves the success he wants, he'll come around and give me some of the things you do. Until then, I want to keep things as they are. We have a good thing here. Please try to accept that we're friends and lovers, but can't be anything more."

Remember I mentioned that there are times in your life where you say things you wish you hadn't? That once said, you can't take them back no matter what you say or do? That's what I did next as I asked, "What about Lucas?"

"What do you mean 'What about Lucas'? she asked, a confused look on her face.

"Well, I always thought Lucas was mine..."

I know I've mentioned Shelly's eyes many times. To me they were like looking into a lush green forest on a warm summer day, comfortable, deep and quiet. They changed now. The warmth vanished and instead, all I saw was cruel stone like the jadeite on the beaches of Big Sur, rough, swirled shades of deep green, cold and hard.

She leapt from the bed, dressed quickly, grabbed her purse and keys, then looked back at me with hate in her eyes. "Goodbye, Jack," she said.

14

Was it really over? Did it come down to my one stupid question? Worse, was I right? Was Shelly's son really my offspring? If not, wouldn't she have just said 'no'?

As I drove away, I was overwhelmed with emotion and burst into tears. What started as a few drops sliding down my cheek quickly turned into gut-wrenching sobs. My chest was heaving and I had a hard time catching my breath. Nausea overwhelmed me and I thought I was going to vomit. I had to pull over. I tried to think rationally about the situation, but all I could feel was loss. Shelly was a part of me. We danced together perfectly. Wasn't love supposed to conquer all? If she loved me, there had to be a chance.

I picked up my mobile phone and called her. "I'm sorry, Shelly," I pleaded, ashamed as myself for being so weak, but unable to shake the need to be held by her again.

"Jack, I'm sorry too. We had a good thing and although I could see your feelings for me, I thought we had clear boundaries. I was wrong. It was stupid of me to think we could go on like we were without you becoming too involved. I know this is painful, but we have to end it. You can't step back and all that will happen is that you'll become more resentful, and I'll be increasingly paranoid that you'll do something stupid. It's better this ends now, a bit painfully rather than very badly later on. Jack, don't try to call or write me. It's over. I'm sorry, but this is best for both of us. "

The phone went dead and I almost called her back. I could see the logic of her reasoning, but I wasn't feeling logical. All of a sudden I couldn't stop thinking about Shelly being with someone else. Somehow I'd accepted the fact that she still slept with Steve. I guess this was possible because I believed I was the superior lover. Now, I suspected that I'd be replaced. When I thought about someone else holding her naked body, caressing her breasts, burying his face – I had to stop thinking like this. It was going to drive me nuts.

A wave of sickness took a hold of me again and this time I opened the door and vomited bits of crab and bread onto the street. When my stomach was empty, I kept spitting bile and saliva for several minutes. I was drained.

I sat up and looked in the rearview mirror. What a disgusting pathetic creature I was. My face was covered in tears, snot and drool. Who was this guy and how could Shelly do this to me? Wasn't I the most honest, caring, loving person she would ever meet? How could she not see this? What kind of person was she?

My despair turned to anger. She and Steve deserved each other. They just used people for their own personal gain. Certainly, the powers-that-be would someday make sure both of them paid the price for their self-serving arrogance.

I started driving, but my mind wouldn't calm. One minute I'd picture Shelly and her cold aloofness. She could certainly step back from any situation. The next instant, I picture her after lovemaking, head against my chest, her body pressed up against me like our physical attachment could never end, her face relaxed in peaceful bliss. Then I'd see her like this with someone else and the despair would strike again, followed by anger, a never-ending cycle.

I found myself at Georgette's. I sensed the change in light from the peephole and she opened the door. Clad in a thin bathrobe, Georgette took one look at me and led me to the bathroom. She handed me a spare toothbrush, washcloth and towel, then she stepped out and closed the door. I could hear her footsteps as she walked away, then muffled voices. Oh God, what had I interrupted?

I blew my nose, washed my face, and brushed my teeth. I tried to compose myself and then stepped into the living room. Georgette was making hot chocolate.

"Georgette, I'm so sorry. I didn't mean to interrupt," I apologized, embarrassed at both the interruption and at my disheveled state.

"It's not a problem. I told him I had a friend in crisis and he had to go. He wasn't spending the night anyway.

"Here, take this," she said, offering me a steaming mug.

I gratefully took a sip and tasted a strong alcoholic orange flavor with the chocolate. She took my hand and we sat together on the sofa. After another sip, I put the mug on the coffee table then placed my head on her shoulder. She put her arms around me and held me close. She was redolent of sex, musky and warm and I felt my desire rising as I sensed her nakedness under the silk. I wanted her to take me, comfort me, consume me and make me forget. What was wrong with me?!

Georgette pulled my head to her breasts and then took my right hand and placed it inside her robe on her left breast. She opened the robe wider and I gently nuzzled my face inside, placing my lips gently on her right breast. Then I let out a sigh from the depths of my abdomen and just absorbed the warmth of her body. My momentary sexual arousal was gone. I felt more comforted and loved than I ever had in my life.

I don't know how much time passed. Georgette stroked my head and I might have dozed. When I became aware of us still sitting on the sofa, one eye pressed against her breast, I looked up at her. She enveloped me in a secure hug and then eased me away. It was almost like the closeness after making love, but somehow better, loftier, almost spiritual.

Then I talked. Georgette just listened, nodding encouragement from time to time. When I finished spilling all of my emotions and sat back exhausted, she let me to her bed and I held on to her through the night.

We shared a light breakfast in the morning and as she was about to walk out the door, she said sympathetically, "I hate to say that Shelly is right, but this is for the best. You need to look for a relationship with a future. Shelly is with Steve. She's like Steve. I know it's hard, but you'll get through it if you can just see the futility of what you've been chasing these past years. "

I walked over to the door and took her in my arms. "Thanks for last night."

"Don't turn this into a rebound thing," she replied. "Go surfing or flying and start clearing your head. Get a mission other than Shelly!"

She kissed me chastely on the lips and asked me to lock up on my way out.

15

On Wednesday, I returned to work even more discouraged than I was the day before. I'd lost two good friends and the love of my life. What was wrong with people? At least there was Carson. Shelly was right. I wanted to live with integrity, even if I didn't make it quite as big as Steve probably would. What was wrong with that?

I realized I hadn't seen Carson in almost a week. This wasn't unusual, but the Board meeting was coming up, Carson would be readmitted, and I'd get my piece of CIA. I wanted to talk to Carson to be reassured that our principles were valid, that I was making the right choices. Perhaps Carson would even be able to rein in Steve and NewCo, though I suspected some concessions were likely to be made on that front.

I walked over to Pam's office and asked if she'd seen Carson. She told me to close the door. She shuffled paper and looked around nervously as I took a seat. I had a feeling she had been hiding something and was about to come clean. I wondered if there was something about the Board Meeting, some extension on Carson's probation or some complication with my options.

"Jack, I don't know where to begin," she said, chewing on the end of a pen, her eyes never staying fixed on mine. "You know that Carson and Steve have different ideas about how to run NewCo. Steve and the Board saw this as a potential major issue and last week began to wrestle with how to resolve this amicably. It was decided that Steve should have complete control over NewCo. This meant that NewCo would have to buy out CIA's interest. Of course, with that proposal, Carson wanted Steve out of CIA, so he'd have to buy Steve out of CIA and the negotiations on price and restructuring started to get complex with Steve and Carson arguing. So, Steve decided to cut through it all with a simple solution. He proposed that NewCo buy CIA from Carson.

"The Board approved the purchase last week, and on Monday, the money was transferred into Carson's account. Steve now owns both companies."

Pam glanced briefly at my accusing eyes, then looked down at papers on her desk. I was stunned. This made no sense at all. The idea of NewCo buying out CIA's interest was a good solution. CIA would have had extra cash. We could have moved and expanded the business. There was no good reason for Steve to buy CIA from Carson. This just gave Carson cash.

"Dare I ask what the purchase price was?" I asked as it dawned on me what Steve was really trying to do.

"I can't tell you officially. This was a private transaction. However, it was in the low seven figures, so Carson won't go hungry. It's enough for him to retire if he wants or to restart a consulting company.

"Steve is in his office waiting for you. You should go over and talk to him. This isn't the end, it's a new beginning."

"Pam," I replied. "I can't believe you did this. You know Carson was clean and back in full form. With this much money, you've probably killed him."

I stormed out as tears spilled from Pam's eyes. She knew what she'd done.

I could see that Steve was on the phone as I approached the windows to his office. He waved me in and I waited, fuming until he finished his call.

"Jack, I can see you're upset, but please hear me out," he said pleasantly, trying to turn on all of his boyish charm. "Carson was a weak link in the companies. He's now got more money than he would ever had made just consulting and I'm free to build a company like no one has seen before.

"I'd really like to have you on the team, either as part of NewCo, or, if you like, running CIA for a while. Right now I think it's a distraction. We need to focus on NewCo's market penetration and new technology development. But, we do have an obligation to the existing CIA customers, so I'd like to phase CIA out as projects complete.

"I don't need an answer right now. Please cool down and think about it. I'm prepared to offer you one percent of NewCo as options. Believe me, this will be worth millions in no time.

"You look like you're about to burst or get violent, but don't do or say anything that will jeopardize your promising future."

My hands gripped the arms of the chair. My jaw clenched. My eyes were narrowed and if I were Superman, he would have been incinerated by my angry stare. He was right, I wasn't rational. I was ready to knock him out of his chair and pummel him until he bled and begged for mercy. He was so smug and confident, and he had probably just murdered Carson.

I took several deep breaths and tried to calm down. I should act out of calculation, not anger. I closed my eyes for a moment and pictured a pristine day in untracked powder. Then I looked up at him and said. "Okay. I'm going to take the day off and I'll be back tomorrow with my answer. Still, I don't know how you can live with yourself. Giving that kind of money to a coke addict is like giving a hand grenade to a small child. You've probably killed Carson."

"Jack, you know better than that. I haven't hurt Carson in any way. I've made him a rich man."

I got up to leave and looked back at him. The friendly look had vanished. The easy going, ah shucks good ole boy was a dangerous man on a mission. He'd just won a major battle and clearly saw his path to success. We both knew what he'd done. Steve just didn't have a conscience.

I tried to locate Carson, leaving messages at both of his services, but got no response. Late in the day, I finally reached Nancy who confirmed that Carson had vanished without a word. She sounded strangely calm, and I realized that she had found it within herself to move on. She took a few minutes to explain it to me.

"Over the last year, while things had looked good and Carson was living a clean life, I knew that he could slip at any time. Carson's addiction was just an axe waiting to fall. Living with this every day, I've been preparing myself.

"Part of me hoped that the threat would vanish, but another part hardened and prepared for the inevitable black day. I vacillated between getting close to him and withdrawing. Over time, I really became two Nancys, and it was as easy as flipping a switch to either be passionate about Carson or just a casual observer of our time together.

"Now he's gone and I know which Nancy I'm going to be from this day forward. I've closed the Carson chapter of my life. I'm not shedding any tears. I have no real regrets, or any desire to try to save him. Carson can only save himself. I've given all I can and I have enough self-respect to recognize intrinsic value within myself and know that someday I'll find someone else who will be a better mate for me".

I admired her practicality and I thought about this in terms of my own feelings. I wasn't so sure I could just give it up. I called Georgette and she beat me up until I saw what she meant about my future. I needed to take control of my own life rather than just riding along with others.

16

The next day I sat down with Steve to explain my decision. "Steve, I agree that CIA needs a transition period. I'll head up CIA and as we complete the contracts, we can move the programmers and consultants working on them into NewCo. From what I can see, if we don't take on anything new, we should be able to finish everything in two to three months. Please take this as my notice. I'll be leaving as soon as everything is wrapped up."

"Jack, I'm disappointed to hear that you won't be joining NewCo. I don't think you realize the opportunity for you here. You will be wealthy if you stay."

"Steve, you cautioned me not to say too much, so I won't. I'll help wrap up CIA and then I'll be on to something else. You and I have very different sets of ethics. Think of me as a sober Carson and you'll know you don't want me in your company."

"Okay Jack. So what are you going to do next?"

"Obviously it's not firm since I've still got a couple of months here, but most likely I'll start my own consulting firm."

"Jack, I don't mean to be a thorn in your side, but I do have to remind you about the confidentiality and non-compete agreements you signed when you started here. Since CIA will cease to exist as a consulting organization and NewCo won't be in that business, I can let the non-compete slide in terms of consulting. However, I can't afford to let you take our customers. You're prohibited from even contacting them for a year. And don't even think about approaching any of my employees. If you do, you'll be in court faster than Stefan Edberg's serve."

"Steve, I understand. I helped get this place going from almost nothing. I don't need your employees or existing CIA customers to launch my new company," I said, wondering if it were true.

I left his office, pleased with my decision and encouraged by the vote of confidence from Georgette the previous evening. For the next several weeks, things went smoothly, exactly as promised. Not surprisingly, Bell South's trial of the Hydra software resulted in multimillion dollar contract for NewCo and it was clear that several other telephone companies were going to follow suit. NewCo was certainly on a roll. The mercenary side of me began to wonder whether I could afford my principles.

I was working on finalizing a report for CIA's last customer, the May Company, when Dan, my former protégé and now head of engineering for NewCo, walked into my office.

"Jack, I hear you're leaving," Dan said, taking a chair opposite me.

"Yeah. Only a week or so left. I have to deliver this report to May and I'm out of here."

"Will you keep May as a customer?"

"Sort of. Peter Swartz, the head of Information Services for May knows that CIA won't be working for him again. However, Turnkey probably will. As he explained to me, if May approached my new company, there was nothing Steve could do about it. So there may be some additional work coming my way, but I'm not planning to solicit any CIA customers or employees."

"You know, I've been thinking about leaving NewCo. Maybe we should think about teaming up. I really miss the consulting side of the business."

"Dan, I don't think that would be a good idea. Steve would come after me even if I didn't solicit you. Also, how can you walk away from the millions you're likely to see when NewCo does its IPO?"

"Money isn't everything, Jack. I have some real problems with Steve's business ethics. Ever since he gave Carson all that money, I've been having real second thoughts. I don't think I can live with the company's 'take no prisoners' way of doing business and kicking any obstacle out of the way."

"'Money isn't everything?' I think that's only been said by people who have money," I replied.

"It true. I grew up comfortable. Not rich, but well-off. I've always believed I'd have enough money and an easy retirement no matter what job I chose. I picked NewCo because it looked like a great technological opportunity. I thought it would be fun to try out a ride on a rocket. But ethics are more important to me than money. I'd rather just get by with my ethics than be rich without them.

"I've got too many other things in my life that have value and they're measured in terms of who I am. I want the respect of my wife, children, friends and myself. I can't keep doing the things Steve is asking me to do, and I can't support him in some of his sleazy dealings."

"Dan, let me get out of here and underway with Turnkey, and then let's talk again. Say a month?"

"Jack, I don't know if I can wait that long. I've been talking to Rick and George about starting a new company ourselves, but they're afraid. They don't think they can go a couple of months without a paycheck when we first start out. Actually it's a bit more than that. Even if we have a contract when we walk out the door, we work thirty days before we bill and the customers won't pay for at least thirty days after that, so this isn't trivial for them."

"Okay. Let's talk as soon as I leave."

"Done!" he said, grinning and getting up to leave. "I think we'll make a great team!"

CHAPTER 5

"Life moves on, whether we act as cowards or heroes. Life has no other discipline to impose, if we would but realize it, than to accept life unquestioningly. Everything we shut our eyes to, everything we run away from, everything we deny, denigrate or despise, serves to defeat us in the end. What seems nasty, painful, evil, can become a source of beauty, joy and strength, if faced with an open mind. Every moment is a golden one for him who has the vision to recognize it as such."
- Henry Miller

1

I incorporated Turnkey myself by using Nolo Press' guide. I had a business license, a computer of my own, and my first contract. Lloyd Hirschberg, a long-time consultant friend of mine needed some help on a project with Hitachi. Hitachi was trying to understand the U.S. software industry and wanted a report on how software development was done. Lloyd had agreed to give me Turnkey's first contract as soon as I was out of CIA. I'd be writing what I hoped would be a definitive book on how to develop software, and would be paid twenty-five thousand dollars to do it. He even agreed to five thousand dollars up front to kick off the agreement. Turnkey would be cash flow positive from day one!

Georgette suggested we do a whitewater trip before I dove into the endless hours of my own startup. We decided to paddle the wilderness area of the Salmon River in Idaho – the River of No Return – an appropriate parallel to my upcoming venture. We'd spend five days on the river and would cover nearly a hundred miles in the second deepest canyon and largest contiguous wilderness area in the Continental United States.

Since neither of us had ever paddled the Salmon, we signed up with Wild Salmon Tours, a river guide and rafting company. Part of the challenge of a multi-day kayaking trip is transporting gear and food. Our smaller kayaks just didn't have a lot of room. The tour company used large oar-boat rafts to carry all the gear. In fact, this company provided sleeping bags, tents, and gourmet meals at specific stopping points along the river. The rafters and gear boats would head down ahead of us, we could paddle by ourselves and play to our heart's content, and a sweep boat would follow an hour or two behind us and any other kayakers to pick up stragglers. We just needed to reach their lunch and camping spots by specific times in the day if we wanted to eat. Each day, the guides would describe the rapids we'd face as well as landmarks for side trips off the river.

In the nineteenth century, miners and trappers had populated the Salmon. In fact, Lewis and Clark had, at one point, hoped to use the canyon on their way west but were stopped by formidable rapids and sheer canyon walls.

Since the beginning of the twentieth century, the campsites and homesteads had languished, abandoned to the harsh extremes of winter and summer. Most of the area had recently been declared part of the Frank Church River of No Return wilderness area and now there was no vehicle access for over sixty miles of river.

Georgette and I decided to power through the sixteen-hour drive to Salmon, Idaho. We shared a room with two beds in the Rustic Inn, a small motel not far from the Wild Salmon meeting place. We suffered through a jarring hour and a half ride across a washboard dirt forest service road to the put-in spot on the river in one of the company trucks. After visits to the outhouse, we sat patiently through the orientation they did for the rafters and spent a few minutes with one of the guides who, in addition to providing us with a printed description of rapids and landmarks for the day, assured us that this section was mostly Class 2 with some easy Class 3 waves and Devils' Teeth, a large, challenging boulder garden just a mile or so before our first campsite. The legend of Devil's Teeth is that a famous boatman named Johnny McKay, who was one of the first to run the river, encountered Satan at this point. The boulders are Satan's teeth which Johnny knocked out in his battle with the devil. We'd hear many such tales and legends on this trip.

Rivers are rated in degrees of difficulty from 1 to 5. Class 1 is flat water. Class 2 has easy rapids that are non-threatening and safe even for the most inexperienced boaters. Class 3 requires solid maneuvering capabilities and can be a bit dangerous if you make a mistake, but usually just results in a cold swim. Class 4 rapids are advanced rapids and you can expect significant injuries if you make a mistake. Class 5 water is for experts only. Death is possible if you make a mistake. Class 6 is all unrunnable water.

If you're unfamiliar with a stretch of water, it's a good idea to scout the rapids from the bank, identifying any obstacles in advance, and picking the best routes through the difficult sections. Georgette and I had agreed that although we usually only scouted Class 4 rapids from the bank, because of the remoteness and associated problems with any potential injuries or equipment damage, we'd bank scout all the Class 3 rapids. We decided to wait an hour before heading down the river after the rafters so that we could experience the solitude of the wilderness alone. In the meantime, we played around in the relatively calm water, stretching, getting wet, and loosening up with braces and a few Eskimo rolls.

The Main Fork of the Salmon starts out pretty tame, but the scenery is immediately spectacular. Aspens border the river and huge pine and fir trees perch perilously on the cliffs and hillsides above. I suspect the Aspens are stunning in the fall when they show off their brilliant yellow, sublime orange, and flaming red foliage.

What most people don't know about running rivers is that you see more wildlife on the river than any other way. Most animals expect predators from the land and are wary of humans who are hiking, driving, or even on horseback. But they all need water and can frequently be found drinking or bathing in the river, especially in remote wilderness areas. They don't expect to see you floating down the river, and they seem to stare unafraid, but in disbelief as you drift by. We were hoping to see big horn sheep, river otters, elk, deer, bald and golden eagles, and possibly bear and mountain lions, though the latter were not something I was looking forward to.

California has what are called pool and drop rivers. The water is generally seasonal, running only in spring when the snow in the Sierra melts or during heavy rains in the winter. The rivers themselves are strewn with large granite boulders and you tend to see long stretches of smooth flat water followed by short steep drops through shallow rapids into deep pools. A high flow for a California river is two to four thousand cubic feet per second. This is the amount of water passing a single point in the river. The Salmon, by contrast is a big water river with normal flows over twenty-five thousand cubic feet per second.

As we started, we were a bit nervous. Granted the worst rapid on the river was rated an easy Class 4 and this section was rated Class 2, but there was a lot of water. The river was deep and slow at the beginning and we couldn't help but picture this volume of water hitting one of our narrow California chutes. They'd be unrunnable Class 6. Of course, this river had been running at these volumes for thousands, if not millions of years, so the nature of the riverbed and associated rapids was quite different. Still...

We came around a bend and the river widened and grew fairly shallow. Ahead we could hear our first rapids. Below us we could see the bedrock and gravel bottom. As we got near the rapid, the placid, slow moving water began to accelerate. Suddenly the bottom was racing by and we were caught up in that point of no return where you have to take the rapid. Even after years of running rivers, it's a rush the first time you encounter a new rapid on a river you've never run before. That sudden surge in the power of the water demands you focus on what's up ahead. Georgette went first and I could see her disappear over a drop. When I followed, I got a quick shot of icy water in the face then pulled into the eddy where Georgette sat waiting for me.

Eddies are your resting and set up spots in a river. They're formed behind rocks or in places where the river bends and the turn of the bank creates a brief shadow to the flow. The water in an eddy along a bank actually runs in the opposite direction to that of the river itself. You can usually find eddies even in the midst of raging Class 5 rapids.

Georgette paddled out of the eddy and slipped into the small hydraulic reversal called a hole. She began surfing, first at the top, facing directly upstream, then turning perpendicular to the flow and side-surfing. At one point, she reversed the kayak and surfed the wave backwards. As she turned a 360, she caught an edge and flipped over, popping back up on the downriver side of the wave. She pulled back into our eddy and it was my turn.

In the late eighties, we didn't have the rodeo boats we have today. You couldn't do linked cartwheels with your boat in a hole, but surfing waves and holes was still a lot of fun and Georgette was one of the best play-boaters I'd ever seen.

After fifteen minutes of playing, we continued down the river, encountering a few wave trains, series of troughs and peaks that feel like rollercoasters, and more small rapids and holes. After paddling for about an hour, we spotted a large needle-shaped boulder on the bank. There were supposed to be petroglyphs a few hundred yards from the bank.

We got out of our boats and pulled hiking boots out of our dry bags. I threw Georgette an apple and we headed down the trail. Sure enough, after about a ten minute hike following an ill-defined trail through a rock outcropping, we could see that the sides of this mini-canyon had painted figures on horseback. While exciting, this was a bit disappointing. We had hoped for ancient petroglyphs, and clearly these were relatively recent since it was Europeans who brought horses to North America.

After exploring the canyon a bit more, we headed back to the boats. Lunch was waiting a bit further down the river and I was definitely hungry. I slid into my boat and was about to fasten my spray skirt when Georgette yelled, "Oh shit! Jack, help!"

I looked over and she was just standing there. At first I thought she was joking. Seeing my questioning look she said, "There's a snake in my boat!"

"So," I replied, "Just flip your boat over and dump it out."

"Get over here and look at this!" she ordered.

I reluctantly got out of my boat shaking my head. I should have known better. Georgette was tougher than I was. If she was nervous, there had to be a reason. There, in the bottom of her boat, was the biggest rattlesnake I'd ever seen. Its body was at least as thick as my forearm, and it was coiled up, probably asleep in the shade of her cockpit, its back covered in alternating patterns of black and tan diamond shapes.

"I don't think waking it up and dumping it on the ground in front of us would be such a great idea," she stated flatly. "We could drag the boat into the water, then flip it, but these things can swim and we'd both be in the water with our feet under the kayak. We couldn't run out of the water very fast. What do you think?"

I thought about it for a minute, then suggested, "Why don't we carefully and quietly carry the boat close to the water. I'll take my paddle, scoop the snake out of the boat and try to fling it into the water. We can use our paddles for defense if it comes after us. The blades are sharp and we could decapitate it if necessary."

Georgette nodded, but I could see she didn't think this was a good idea. "We could just wait for it to wake up and leave, couldn't we?"

"Georgette, I'm hungry. It could be hours before that thing wakes up and decides to move. Then again, who knows, your boat may be its new permanent home. After all, possession is nine-tenths of the law and I suspect the threat of death covers the rest."

We lifted the boat. Although it was only about six feet to the water's edge, we moved very slowly and it took and eternity to get there. Our plan was that if the snake woke up, we'd drop the kayak and run. Fortunately, or maybe unfortunately, the serpent slept through its relocation. We set the boat down and still it dozed.

My paddle is about six and a half feet long. I grabbed it and Georgette asked if I still wanted to go through with this plan. I suggested she step back. She asked me to wait, walked away, and returned a few minutes later holding a six-foot branch with a fork at the end of it.

"If it comes after you, I'll try to pin it with this branch and you can hit it with the blade of your paddle."

I moved to the river side of the boat and set the blade of the paddle in the middle of the snake's coil. The snake slept on. I then quickly jammed it under the snake and lifted. I was surprised at the weight of the thing. Of course my leverage wasn't good, but I muscled it and surprisingly, the snake unconsciously wrapped tighter around the paddle. As I lifted the paddle higher, the snake started to uncoil and I realized that it must be six or seven feet long, maybe longer. It was also sliding towards me down the paddle. I decided to throw snake and paddle into the river, launching it away violently with both hands like a Scottish sportsman doing the Caber Toss. Then I turned and ran.

Paddle and snake landed in the river a few yards from shore and the now angry snake swam away, its head above water and its massive body flagellating luxuriously behind it. We watched in amazement as the reptile made its way across the entire fast moving river and slithered up the opposite bank.

"I told you Class 2 water could be exciting," I quipped as we started down the river side by side after collecting my paddle.

Suddenly, Georgette pointed at the opposite bank and screamed, "It's back in the water and headed this way!"

I looked over and as I stroked on my right side, she rammed me on the left and flipped my boat. There I was, upside down with an eight foot rattlesnake coming after me. Had Georgette panicked and bumped into me trying to escape? I executed the fastest roll of my life and popped up to find Georgette laughing hysterically.

"When you least expect it, I'll have my revenge for that," I promised, but I must admit, I thought it was pretty funny too.

We picked through the leftover salad, fresh fruit and sandwich fixings the guides had set out for lunch. The rafters had been there before us and had eaten most everything. Still, since we had another three hours of paddling ahead of us, we didn't need a heavy meal to slow us down.

The whitewater wasn't terribly exciting. There was only one significant rapid that had bigger waves than we were used to paddling, but the scenery more than made up for it as we got deeper into the canyon. Plus, we'd had plenty of adrenaline in our systems for one day.

As we rounded one bend in calm slow moving water, Georgette exclaimed, "Jack, look over there!"

"You're not planning to flip me again, are you?"

"No, stupid! Look in that tree above the big boulder on river right."

"It's not – It is! It's a bald eagle!"

I had never seen one before. This one didn't look stately and elegant like the pictures. If anything, it looked rather gangly with a head that was much too big for its body and certainly far too white.

"I thought nature chose colors to help critters hide. Pure white is obvious and completely incongruous with the surroundings," I said.

"Yeah, but out here, the bald eagle is the top of the food chain. I suspect he doesn't have to hide."

Just then, the eagle lifted off from the tree, glided down to the river and snagged a large fish, which it dropped onto some boulders just across the river. The bird then landed behind the rocks. The movement was swift, elegant and, for the fish, quite deadly. I no longer thought of this bird as awkward.

After picking our way through Devil's Teeth, we caught up with the group at the first night's campsite. The guides gave us sleeping bags and tarps and pointed to a makeshift solar shower they had set up. They offered tents, but since it was a clear night, we decided to sleep out under the stars. We changed out of our wet things and headed down to our first dinner on the River of No Return.

They had promised a gourmet repast and except for the lack of wine, this was certainly the best camping dinner I'd ever had. The fresh salmon was perfectly grilled and topped in a huckleberry sauce. New potatoes and a ratatouille complemented this perfectly and their deadly dark chocolate brownies and huckleberry pie left both of us fully sated.

Over the campfire, our story of the rattlesnake took the prize for the day, but Georgette's tale of my panic got the most laughs.

With no city lights within two hundred miles, the stars were almost bright enough to keep us awake. But the excitement of the day combined with physical exhaustion sent us quickly off to sleep.

The next morning, we had a quick, light breakfast of fresh fruit, yogurt, and cereal. The main guide gave us more instructions. Today we'd encounter one of the most difficult rapids of this section of the Salmon. Of particular interest was Salmon Falls, which we would scout before running. We played in the river for half an hour after the rafts left and started on our way. Almost immediately, the river felt different. The canyon narrowed and the river rose. It exhibited real power it didn't have before and even the smallest rapids were challenging. The eddy lines, boundaries between the main river channel and the upstream-moving eddies, were intense. If you dug a paddle too deep on entering, the eddy just sucked you down and over. Georgette and I each did this once before realizing that we needed to pay attention to what looked to be calmer water, but which had a subtle, hidden menace to it.

The sky clouded over and it started to rain. Other than obscuring the scenery a bit, rain doesn't bother kayakers. We're wet anyway. It also didn't seem to affect the herd of big horn sheep that awaited us around a bend. One with spiraled horns larger than the rest stood regally on a rock above the herd, probably a lookout. As we approached, he turned and chased the others away from us. Whenever we heard rapids ahead or noticed a drop in the horizon, a sure indication that the river was about to take a sudden drop, we pulled our boats over to the bank or rocks on the side of the river, and got out and hiked or climbed down to where we could see the entire rapid so that we could run it safely.

At Salmon Falls, we explored the route carefully. At this water level, the falls was classified as an easy Class 4 rapid. However, there was a lot of water going over the falls. This created a cushion of safety against the sides of the narrow chute that we had to pass through, but could also result in a significant hydraulic just below. We decided on a route and with our hearts in our throats, I led with Georgette right behind me.

After being buried and surrounded in white twice, I emerged in a large pool below. I turned and watched as Georgette disappeared completely at the bottom of the falls, then popped up like a cork into the placid water near me. We heard a cheer and looked over to see the rafters watching. The guides had set up tarpaulin tent-like structures with lunch laid out under them to protect the food from the driving rain. We paddled to the shore, then hiked back up the falls to run it again, trying different routes and approaches. On one, Georgette, buried the bow of her boat at the bottom of the falls. As the kayak popped upwards, and seemed to stand on its nose, she spun the boat around in the air like a ballerina. She had just executed a perfect pirouette. We each ran the falls four times before stopping for lunch.

Since this was reputed to be the worst rapid on the river, we weren't too worried and had a playful afternoon paddling the rest of this stage of the trip. The rain intensified and we saw thunder and lightning as we pulled into camp for dinner. The guide handed us a tent and sleeping bags and we set up in a quiet place with a gentle downslope. He also pointed out the water spilling off discolored rocks just upstream. This was Barth Hot Springs and after setting up our tents, we spent an hour soaking in one of the makeshift rock tubs below, dangling our feet into the bone-chilling river when we got too warm.

After changing into dry clothes, we joined the group under the canopies which covered the food. If possible, dinner was even better than the night before, rain and all.

Georgette and I crawled into the tent after hearing and recounting many tall tales of the days' paddling experience. Of course, the guides could top any story we had to tell with harrowing accounts of things gone wrong on the River of No Return.

We were still wet and it was raining, so Georgette and I zipped our sleeping bags together and shivered together until the shared warmth of our bodies took the chill away. It always amazed me that we could do this. We'd known each other for years and now could hold each other like lovers, but remain as chaste as an elderly couple sleeping together in their infirm years. I turned my back to her and we fell asleep as she pressed herself up against me with one arm draped across my waist.

The weather cleared for the rest of the trip and the days were hot and dry, a stark contrast to the cold waters of the Salmon River. Day three was a lot of fun with several challenging rapids. Sunburn was our biggest threat. By the end of the fourth day, both of us had had about enough of the outdoors. We were ready for hot showers, real beds, and maybe a cool dark theatre to escape the unrelenting sun.

We survived the last day and took out several miles above Riggins, Idaho. The guides drove us to the quaint mountain town of McCall. Our car was waiting in the dirt lot behind the Hotel McCall where we had reservations for the night. We treated the guides to dinner and then did a fast trip back to the Bay Area the next morning. On the way, Georgette described the latest at Modular where things were going extremely well. They were up to forty people and comfortably profitable, looking at an IPO sometime in the future once they saw a new direction that needed funding.

We talked about my new company and Georgette recommended that I find a finance and administrative person so I could focus on the core business. As she pointed out, Carson had Pam when he started and she carried the business side while he focused on consulting and developing new customers. I agreed that as my company started to grow, I would do the same. I really didn't know much about keeping books, but since I'd always been able to learn anything I tried, I suspected I'd be able to step up to that too.

2

Upon my return, I started work. Just as I'd done at CIA, I prepared a letter about my new position and company and sent it to all of my contacts. Again, I was careful to make this an informational letter, not one of solicitation. I wanted to be really circumspect to avoid any confrontations with Steve, though I suspected he was far too busy with NewCo to worry about me picking up some consulting business from former CIA customers. I also called Dan and we agreed to meet for drinks at Jose's Cantina in Santa Cruz on his way home from NewCo.

Preparing the mailings was tedious and took all day. Fortunately, computing had come a long way and Word for Windows had an easy mechanism for mass-producing mailings.

Driving over to meet Dan, I couldn't wait to experience the tartness of the fresh lime juice in Jose's margaritas. That, plus their spicy salsa and hot chips, was a great way to top off the workday. Too bad they didn't have a Ms. PacMan machine.

Jose's was located not far from the Santa Cruz Wharf in the old train station. The main bar was wildly popular and they had live bands with room to dance four nights a week. Their sister restaurant, El Palomar, located downtown near my office was world-renown for its authentic gourmet Mexican food. Jose's had the same menu, but had a much more lively, less formal atmosphere.

Dan arrived before I even had a chance to place a drink order and we began to discuss our respective ideas for the company. Not surprisingly, we both had the same thoughts: strategic level consulting leading to custom development work, a hierarchical but egalitarian structure similar to most law firms, and the highest ethical standards for business. While I wanted to focus on networking software, Dan wanted to build real end-user applications. We decided we could do both; that, in fact, the two approaches were complimentary. Dan's side of the firm would build applications, while mine would build systems.

We also agreed to an initial fifty-five forty-five split of the company's equity, with me getting the larger share and then laid out a plan for distribution of equity and profit sharing to partners and associates as we hired them.

I thought Turnkey was off to a great start!

I spent most of the next day working on my report for Lloyd

and Hitachi. I realized I had a lot to write. I had written twenty pages and was well into a comparison of the classic top-down waterfall method with the relatively new concept of rapid prototyping, when, around five in the afternoon, Dan called.

"How's it going," I asked. "Did you break the news to Steve?"

"Well Jack, not exactly. I told Rick and George about my plans and they panicked. I think they didn't really believe that I would bail without them. Now, they want me to hold on and figure out a way to start our own company together. So, I hate to say it, but I think we're going to do our own company. Assuming they don't flake out in the next few days, we'll be giving notice next week and starting the Sailsoft Group. I won't be joining you at Turnkey. Sorry about that. I think we could have been a dynamic team.

"I'm hoping that we'll still be able to work together. Since we're not competing, I suspect there will be plenty of opportunities for you to pass on systems work to us and for us to use you guys to build complementary applications to our stuff."

"Dan, of course I'm disappointed, but this isn't a problem," I replied pensively. "I think we'll have ample opportunities to work together."

"Jack, I'm glad you're taking this so well. I was afraid you'd be upset. Let's get together for lunch in the next couple of weeks once I have a company started. I think this is going to be fun!"

Surprisingly, although Dan was going to be a great addition to Turnkey, and while I was looking forward to working with him as a partner, I wasn't upset at all. Turnkey was off on the right foot and all I could see for myself and for Dan, George, and Rick, were the infinite possibilities that come with running your own businesses.

Over the next weeks I set up meetings with Managers of Information Services (MIS) and Vice Presidents of Software Development as part of my research for the Hitachi report. I quickly wrote up different methodologies taught in software development classes, but I needed to find out who actually used them and how well they worked. I was pleased to find that most of the larger organizations kept excellent statistics on the numbers of problems reported in their products and on the amount of time required to develop them. Smaller companies didn't have much in the way of statistics, but I was able to meet with the programmers and the quality assurance people to see how the products were evolving. Unfortunately, it appeared my conclusions were going to be disappointing.

Most of the development teams rushed their designs. The programmers seemed to think they could just start writing code. Very few held design or code reviews and the results were that while many of these companies were quickly getting products or new services to market, I discovered that after the products shipped, programmers were spending eighty percent of their time on maintenance, fixing bugs. This meant that companies didn't have the resources available to build new products once their earlier ones shipped, and MIS departments couldn't keep up with their companies' demands for new offerings. Their developers were tied up supporting old products instead of developing new ones.

I realized that the software development industry was in a near crisis. Of course this was good news for me. A hit team that could build complex software efficiently would be in high demand.

One of my meetings was with my old boss, Evan Silvers at IBM. IBM continued to be the exception in building products. They still used rigorous development procedures, but had streamlined them significantly since I'd left the company. They also were using a combination of building prototypes as part of their designs, then using them to accelerate implementation, particularly of user interfaces.

I had taken Evan to lunch at a well-known seafood restaurant in Palo Alto. Over bowls of steaming clam chowder, Evan asked me why I wanted to know about their development processes.

"I'm writing a report for Hitachi on software development procedures used in the United States."

"Hmm, Hitachi, huh? They're now one of IBM's biggest competitors. I guess I really don't have a problem giving you the information since I don't really think their culture will let them develop software efficiently, but don't you think we should be cautious where the Japanese are concerned? "

"Why?" I asked, somewhat surprised.

"Jack, look around. The Japanese are buying up everything in this country. We've been flooded with Japanese cars, electronic products, toys, you name it.

"Countless skyscrapers in major cities are now owned by

Japanese conglomerates, hotels, ski resorts golf courses – I believe they're about to buy Pebble Beach.

"They may have lost in WWII, but it certainly looks like they're going to take over the world economically. Have you seen the number of Japanese visitors? Not only do we have tourists, but almost every meeting I go to has four to five Japanese businessmen there. No women! Not only that, their business dealings are unusual, to say the least. There's always one guy who's silent in the meetings. He's the boss. There are silent signals given, but he never speaks except on entering and leaving. "Be careful when dealing with them!"

Towards the end of my lunch with Evan, he let me know that he had several projects coming up that needed consultants. He asked if I could help out, and a week later, I brought in my first subcontractor to help out at IBM.

At both Skynet and CIA, the demands of the business sometimes required that we hire outside consultants. If the contracts were of significant durations, I'd try to convince these independent developers to join the company as full time employees. If not, I'd just mark up the cost of their services by thirty to forty percent and would bring them to the customer. Since we handled the project management and guaranteed replacements if a consultant got sick or dropped out, this worked out well for everyone. It provided a ready, low risk source of income, as we didn't have to offer benefits to consultants or pay them when no work was being done.

I dipped into my pool of consultants and found the right person for this initial job at IBM. Evan was so impressed with the combination of the consultant's expertise and my attention to detail in project management, that he asked for another consultant a few weeks later. Within six months, I had ten consultants working on projects for Evan and was making an average of three thousand dollars a month on each one. IBM projects typically last for at least a year, with two being average, so this contract, along with several high level consulting contracts I was working on, and a couple other accounts with independent contractors, meant that Turnkey was on its way.

3

By early 1988, the year that the U.S. shot down an Iranian Jetliner killing three hundred passengers and that the Soviet Union held its first democratic elections, I was still operating the company out of my house, had no employees, and no real overhead. We were comfortably profitable with very positive cash flow. I began to wonder what I should be doing with all the money that Turnkey was taking in.

The answer to that came in the form of a phone call from Stan Rathbone. I had met Stan at Skynet. At that time, he was running the MIS group for U.S. Paper Industries and had funded development of one of our products which was ultimately deployed to streamline the interactions of their many offices.

After leaving U.S. Paper, he had joined a small distributor of networking equipment as Chief Operating Officer. The founder was a crazy Italian named Robert Manzetti, who was a charismatic salesman but who had no sense for business. I had stayed in touch with Stan and had met Robert several times, usually at Stan's sports parties.

I periodically played basketball or flag football with Stan and his buddies. He was the classic fraternity type with lots of friends and an easy, glad-handing, slap them on the back style that both men and women found attractive. Tall and burly with thick blond hair and striking blue eyes, he loved sports and could discuss players in football, baseball, basketball, and his favorite, soccer, with incredible detail: statistics, performance, and even their personal lives. He loved Irish pubs and could be found drinking pints of Guinness most nights of the week.

In the first days of Turnkey, Robert called me because he had a need to sell a complex network in conjunction to a large corporation. I went on a sales call with him to provide technical support for the networking portions of the deal. Robert was incredible. He had the customer eating out of his hand within minutes. Unfortunately, in closing the sale, Robert promised to deliver things which I knew were impossible. I recounted this to Stan after the meeting and was told this was not unusual. Even worse, Robert frequently forgot the promises he had made, as once he was onto the scent of another victory, he would let previous commitments slide. The thrill of the chase motivated him. Staying around to help the customer actually get the system running was of no interest.

After years of trying to keep Robert under control, Stan had decided that he just needed to fold up the company. Robert had made promises that couldn't be kept and suppliers who had offered discounts and lines of credit were now threatening lawsuits for failed commitments and lack of payment. Customers were threatening suits for non-performance.

Stan worked hard to convince the suppliers to accept pennies on the dollar, then quickly sold the remnants of the company, saving Robert from bankruptcy and satisfying the irate customers that this larger acquiring entity could provide better support. Stan had called me to ask if I needed any help on the business side of Turnkey.

Looking at our growth and remembering Georgette's advice, I set up a meeting with Stan at my house in Santa Cruz. After talking about the business, I showed him my books, such as they were.

Over dinner and drinks at a seafood restaurant on the Santa Cruz Wharf, we agreed that Stan would be an excellent addition to Turnkey. He would handle all of the finance and administrative parts of the company. We'd open offices, set up lines of credit to float our receivables, and begin hiring personnel instead of using contractors exclusively. Stan explained that Section 1706 of the tax code could cause contractors to be reclassified as employees if they didn't meet certain very arbitrary criteria. Employers could be fined with triple damages on failure to withhold for income tax and benefits, including retirement benefits. Worse, even if the subcontractors paid their taxes, if the government decided you were not compliant with 1706, they could still assess you triple what you should have withheld. My eyes widened in shock as I did some simple math and determined that I could owe the Government nearly a million dollars if they pursued us. We needed to convert most of our subcontractors to employees as soon as possible.

I was almost in awe of Stan's knowledge and realized that if I wanted Turnkey to be a real business, I'd need a lot of help. I agreed to give Stan a salary of one hundred thousand dollars a year, a company car, and twenty percent of the company. Stan also insisted that I buy myself a company car that befitted the image of the CEO of an up and coming technological firm.

The next day, I actually went car shopping. I looked at Mercedes and decided that they gave a message of 'I've made it.' I then looked at BMWs and Jaguars, but the BMW was too yuppie and I remembered Carson's maintenance nightmares with his Jag. Plus, the newer Jags weren't as cool as Carson's.

As I was leaving the Mercedes dealer I saw an unusual car. It was rounded, pearl-white and had an aggressive stance. I asked the salesman what it was and he took me over to see it.

"It's the new Audi 80 Quattro," he explained. "Quite a difference from the old Audi Fox or 5000 series. This is a real sports sedan. Zero to sixty in about six seconds, the best handling car on the road. You do know that Audi has been winning all the races, right? This year they even forced them to go up a class because of huge margins they're winning by in their own classes. Want to take her for a drive?"

I slid into the plush leather of the driver's seat and admired the leather covered steering wheel, burnished woodwork throughout and the rich carpeting. As we pulled out, the five speed transmission was a joy. I got the feel for the smooth ride on the freeway, then followed the salesman's directions as we headed up into the hills above Aptos on small winding roads.

"Don't hold back!" he ordered.

With each curve, I went a little faster. At one point, I felt the centrifugal force was strong enough to make the back end slide out, but it didn't.

"Step on it!" he commanded.

The next time it felt like the rear end was going to break, I stepped on it. Instead of spinning out, the car leveled and gripped the road. This was amazing. I had never driven a car that handled so well.

"That's the beauty of all-wheel drive and a suspension that evenly distributes weight across all four wheels. So, what do you think?"

"I'll take it!" I said impulsively.

To this day, I'm an Audi fanatic. I love to take my Audis out on winding roads. I get the thrill of a rollercoaster with me in control. On the practical side, more than once, the all-wheel drive, low center of gravity, and excellent suspension have helped me stay in control on Highway 17 or in snow and ice in the Sierra when cars around me were spinning out in uncontrollable 360s. I remembered loving my Subaru and realized that with the all-wheel drive, the Audi was just the next step up.

4

The next six months went smoothly. Almost all of our subcontractors became employees after I showed them the economic advantages of having a company pay Social Security taxes, vacation, holidays, and medical insurance, not to mention our profit sharing plan where we split fifty percent of the quarterly profits among them. A few held out, but these really were running their own businesses, so there was little risk from Section 1706.

We moved into small but plush offices in Santa Cruz. We hired a secretary to answer phones and greet visitors, and I frequently took clients to lunch in my new Audi. Its image reflected that of an up and coming entrepreneur. In spite of the offices, secretary, company cars, and Stan's salary, we were still comfortably profitable. We had even paid the employees their first profit sharing bonuses. The work was good, and I was back to my work hard, play hard lifestyle. The only thing missing for me was a woman in my life. I spent a lot of time with Georgette, dated occasionally, but was getting used to not having Shelly around.

In September, Stan's former partner, Robert Manzetti, called. "Jack, you'd better watch out for Stan. He's really screwed me. I still have all these debts with the company and he walked away with over a hundred grand in cash. It's not fair. I'm filing suit to recover it. I strongly suggest you check your books. I think you'll find some problems."

After a long conversation where Robert described the closing audit for the company that showed small sums of money being used to pay a variety of Stan's personal expenses, and the inequity of the final settlement between Robert and Stan, I hung up the phone, shocked. Stan was the most open, friendly guy I knew. Could he really be ripping off the company? Granted, he was a bit aloof with the employees, but he was clearly on my side, encouraging me in business, keeping an eye on contract margins, and managing every penny. Nonetheless, I'd be stupid if I didn't check this out.

I immediately called Dan and asked if he could recommend a discreet local accountant. He suggested his own accountant, Lee Bell. I spoke with Lee briefly and he agreed to meet me at our office on Saturday. I knew Stan would be in Seattle for the weekend visiting his girlfriend.

It was tough waiting for Saturday. Each day Stan came to work normally, arriving a bit late and leaving early as usual. I started scrutinizing his behavior and couldn't believe I hadn't noticed the problems before. He wasn't just aloof, he was a mini-tyrant. He treated Sandy, our secretary, like a slave. She fixed his coffee, brought him lunch, and did personal correspondence for him and he would shout at her if something wasn't done to perfection. He had no time for the programmers. They were just computer nerds who helped pay the bills. As to the rest of it, I guess I'd know more on Saturday.

Lee arrived at the office a few minutes before eight. After offering coffee and bagels, I took him to Stan's office and showed him the books. I also brought up Stan's computer and logged in so that Lee could go through the financial programs there. Lee sent me on my way and said he'd be done in a few hours.

I worked on a customer report and made good progress, managing to temporarily forget about Lee. A few hours later just as my stomach started to growl, Lee knocked on the frame of my open office door. "Lunch?" he asked.

Lee and I walked over to India Joze, a famous Santa Cruz restaurant owned and operated by world-renown chef Jozseph Schultz. The food was an eclectic mix of Middle Eastern, Indian, and Southeast Asian, all authentic. We sat outside on the patio. The surrounding walls were overgrown with bright orange-flowered Passion Vines, Trumpet Vines with their large red dangling tubes, and jasmine. The scents were exotic and it felt as if you'd stepped into Southeast Asia, the brick patio radiating heat, creating a temperate, if not hot oasis on the coolest days of the Northern California coast.

I ordered the Nasi Goreng, a huge very spicy plate of brown rice, calamari, chicken, bok choi and countless other vegetables stir fried. Lee ordered the Persian Wok, chicken braised in and then topped with a pomegranate, ginger, garlic sauce. We both had Joze's strong dark iced tea.

"Okay," he began, "Do you want the good news or the bad news?"

"Why do people ask that question?" I responded jokingly, quite nervous. "Clearly I want both, but I always ask for the bad news first. In this case, I'll be different, give me the good news."

"Well, the good news is that he's not trying to hide anything. Every transaction is properly recorded. His expense reports are detailed and match the payments. About the only irregularity I found is that the shareholder's loan doesn't have a corresponding board resolution. But I do have some questions."

"Shareholder's loan?" I asked cautiously, "What shareholder's loan?"

"Oh! Maybe this is worse than I thought. Still, why would he document it if he were doing anything wrong? Hmm...

"Well, there is a loan of twenty-five thousand dollars to Stan from the company. He has a note, reasonable interest and a payment plan, so it didn't appear irregular. Do you guys do a lot of business in Seattle? I see company credit card charges for roundtrip tickets from San Jose to Seattle almost every other week, and weirdly, roundtrip tickets from Seattle to San Jose almost every other week. I know that some travel agents do this double roundtrip booking to get better fares by making it appear you have a longer stay, but nonetheless, it's a lot of travel. Also, I note that from June 15th to June 30th, there were gas charges on the company credit card bill along with quite a few entertainment charges in bars and clubs in Philadelphia. I know you guys have company cars and I expect to see charges for them, but in Philadelphia? I thought it might be a rental car, but from what I can see, multiple cars were filled up, sometimes in the same day. Also, like most service companies, I can see that you do a lot of entertaining, like this lunch. But it appears Stan is doing this as well. He's charging meals and drinks at least three days a week. Is he doing sales and marketing as well?"

"No. Actually, he really shouldn't be entertaining at all. He doesn't travel on company business, at least not yet, and while we do have a few clients in the Seattle area, Stan has never met them. His girlfriend lives there. So what do you think the total damage is?"

Lee took a deep breath. "I see. Well, knowing what you've told me, I'd need to do a few hours more work to come up with an exact number, but my guess is that you're looking at two thousand or twenty-five hundred dollars a month, not counting the twenty-five thousand dollar loan."

"Lee, I appreciate this. If you have the time this weekend, it would really help me to know exactly what I'm dealing with. I'm probably going to have to confront him on Monday. What do you think I should do? As you say, it's not like he's trying to hide anything, right?"

"Yeah. It's strange. I've been called into situations like this before and I can find embezzlement, but it's usually not so obvious. I have to discover where cash is disappearing and figure out where it's showing up. This is a different situation altogether.

"But before you say anything to him, I suggest you contact a lawyer. You could file criminal charges for embezzlement. You could fire him, but you've got a new business and legal fees could get expensive, especially if he sues you for wrongful dismissal."

"Wrongful dismissal!" I almost shouted, outraged. "The guy steals from the company and if I fire him, I could be sued? How can that be?"

"Jack, you'd probably ultimately win, but the legal costs might kill you in the process. The DA often lets these things go. They have serious crime to prosecute and usually don't want to get involved in what might appear to be squabbles between business partners. I'm sure Stan will say this is just a misunderstanding, that these expenses were like the company cars, perks. If you don't have a criminal conviction, your termination of Stan could be questioned. You need to move carefully."

We finished our meals in silence and I decided to fortify myself with a slice of the Chocolate Spoon Cake, incredibly rich cake and thick dark chocolate ganache in multiple layers, only eight hundred calories a slice.

5

Lee computed the total which came to just under fifteen thousand dollars, plus the loan. I called an attorney who promised me a termination letter by the end of the day. He, too, advised that I keep this simple. After reviewing the letter, I printed and signed it, then called Stan into my office.

"Jack, can this wait until tomorrow? I'm meeting some guys for Monday Night Football."

"No, Stan. I'm afraid it can't. I'm going to have to let you go."

"Let me go? You mean to watch the game?"

Handing him the letter, I said, "No, Stan. I'm asking you to leave the company."

"You've got to be shitting me, Jack. After all I've done for Turnkey? I've put financial systems in place, and I've probably saved you tens of thousands in contractor costs, let alone the potential 1706 penalties. You owe me. I gave up several promising opportunities for this. You can't do it."

"Stan, I went through the books this weekend and saw that you've been charging flights to Seattle on the company credit card. When you were on vacation last summer, you filled up your friend's cars with gas and took them out to clubs, again on the company card. You're spending hundreds each week on yourself for non-company expenses and charging them to the company. Then there's the twenty-five thousand dollar loan.

"Stan, it's not just the company you're ripping off, you're cutting into the profit sharing for the programmers. They work their butts off for us and deserve fairness."

"Hey, I deserve some perks. As executives, we take all the risks. Your employees are a dime a dozen. Lose these and we can replace them in minutes. It's the guys like us, the ones with the brains and guts to put a company together who deserve the compensation.

"Jack, don't fall into this trap. You're better than this. We can go a long way together. You need me in order to become really successful. You're too soft to make it big on your own and you need a real business man to back you up. I'm tough and can do the job. If you want to cut back on the perks, so be it. What's it amount to anyway? Ten, fifteen grand? It's not worth breaking up this team for that."

"What about the loan? That's twenty-five grand you pulled out of our cash flow. What about that?"

"Jack, I saw a personal investment opportunity and had to jump on it. I wrote up a note and am planning to pay it back. Don't do this. At least think about it."

Stan handed me the letter back. "Okay," I replied. I'll sleep on it. Let's talk about it tomorrow."

Stan clapped me on the back and walked confidently out of my office. Our meeting had been short and he would certainly make his Monday Night Football party.

Me, what do I usually do in situations like this? I called Georgette. She had a hot date and didn't have time to meet, so we talked on the phone. After filling her in on the conversation with Stan, Georgette offered her advice, such as it was: "Jack, what is business about for you? You left CIA for a reason: Ethics. While many would disagree with the way you do business, you've chosen your path. Do you really think you could compromise your ideals on a daily basis? That's what it would be with Stan. There'd always be another issue. It would be like having Steve as your constant companion, pushing you to do things you're not comfortable with. I think it would eat you up slowly and inexorably."

"But do you think I'm too soft to run a business?" I asked.

"No, of course not. But you're kind of like a bear in the middle of a hungry group of wolves. They'll kill to eat. You'd rather eat nuts and berries. You certainly won't get as far because you're not willing to cut throats. In fact, I predict that with your egalitarian tendencies, some of your employees will ultimately do better financially than you do. You share equally, but you also take all the risk. This means that sometimes you'll lose and it'll cost you. Your team will always have your protection and failures won't cost them. Still, I suspect you wouldn't want it any other way."

Georgette was right. I was going to build this business my way and if I weren't as successful as Steve, or as Stan probably would be, I'd at least go to sleep with a clear conscience.

The next day I fired Stan. He threatened a wrongful dismissal suit and I threatened to contact the DA. This didn't faze him. He then demanded six months' severance. I called the lawyer who recommended I just get out of the situation intact with no lawsuit. After an hour of wrangling, Stan and I agreed that I'd forget the fifteen thousand in 'perks', and that his loan would be his severance payment. Then I went home and threw up, ashamed at myself for letting Stan get away scot-free.

6

The next day I called a company meeting and let everyone know that Stan was gone. They all cheered. Lee recommended a local bookkeeper who could handle our books and do payroll. Life went on, and Turnkey prospered. The loose knit group of software developers I had hired became a crack team who could quickly develop the most complex networking software. Our clients were as pleased to have found a reliable company as I would have been if I could ever find a building contractor who would actually complete a project on time and within budget.

I wasn't greedy, so when opportunities arose that would have required major expansion, I decided to keep the company stable, banking some monies, sharing the profits, and making sure that if ever bad times befell us, I could keep my team together.

I met Dan every couple of weeks for lunch. We kept each other up to date on the progress of our respective companies. Not surprisingly, our companies had very close to the same revenues, and very similar philosophies in business.

It was over one of these lunches that Dan told me about NewCo.

""Did you hear about NewCo?" he asked.

"No. What happened?"

"They went public! They sold five million shares at thirty dollars each. The stock immediately shot up to over fifty, then slid back to forty where it seems to have stabilized. After fees and commissions, they brought in over a hundred and twenty-five million dollars! How'd you like to have that as working capital. Imagine what you could do with Turnkey if you had that kind of cash!"

"Dan, do you have any regrets about not staying and sharing in this windfall?"

"Hell no! I'm having much more fun now that I ever would have there. And who said anything about not sharing in the windfall? He said grinning like the Cheshire Cat.

"You mean you exercised your options before you left?"

"Jack, my momma didn't raise no fool! Of course I did. While I may not agree with the way that Steve does business, I put in quite a bit of time to help build NewCo. I knew Steve would be successful and didn't see any reason not to profit. Rick and George did all right too."

Companies grant stock options as incentives to employees. The Board of the company sets a price for the options that is supposed to reflect the fair market value of the company. In privately-held companies like most startups, this value is somewhat arbitrary, but is often just pennies a share. The options usually have a vesting schedule that makes them available for exercise over time. Four years is a typical vesting period, so twenty-five percent of the options are available after each year of service.

For a public company, people often exercise their shares at the same time they sell them. This prevents a cash outlay. You call your stock broker and say that you have options to sell. The broker then floats the cash until the transaction is complete, usually in a direct arrangement with the company to issue the real shares.

It's rare for anyone to actually exercise options in a private company. The shares can't be traded on the open market and you have to lay down cash which you may never see again if the company doesn't go public or isn't sold.

I didn't ask Dan how much he made, but I did some quick math in my head. Steve had offered me one percent of the company. Dan probably had the same. Even with only one year's vesting, and it might have been two depending on when the options were issued, Dan was likely sitting on several hundred thousand dollars in NewCo stock. Some guys have all the luck!

7

October of 1989 was like most autumns in Santa Cruz. The beaches are warm and empty as people from Valley have given up their quests for fog free summer days. Somehow the secret of the superb fall and winter beach weather never makes it over Highway 17. With only locals and University students remaining, Santa Cruz slows down. Gone are the frenetic teenagers racing cars, crowding the surf, and fighting on the beach.

On October 17th, at five in the afternoon, I was sitting in my second floor office with Jenny, one of my project leads. I was on the phone with our travel agency booking a flight for the two of us to Binghamton, New York where Jenny and I were planning to present a new product design to IBM the following week. Several of the programmers had left early to see the third game of the Bay Area World Series. The Oakland A's were facing the San Francisco Giants in Candlestick park, just south of San Francisco.

The building started to shake.

Having lived in California for many years, Jenny and I just smiled at each other. Earthquakes were fun and only lasted a few seconds. We'd been through dozens. I loved roller coasters and an earthquake was Nature's version.

But this one was different. The travel agent shouted "Earthquake!" and the phone went dead. The rumble increased from a low growl to the sound of a speeding freight train and the walls twisted back and forth, in and out weirdly, not vertically or horizontally, but at strange angles as the shaking grew stronger and stronger. When I looked out my window, I saw bricks falling from the older buildings across the street. My floor-to-ceiling glass window began to bow. At that moment I realized that what they say is true. Glass is a liquid. There was no way a solid could bend that much without breaking, In fact, I couldn't understand why the window hadn't exploded all over the room.

I grabbed Jenny and pushed her under my desk, then joined her. She held on to me tightly and we kept our heads down as my bookcase crashed down on top of the desk, scattering books and papers all around us. An old disk drive I'd left on the shelf bounced off a wall and skittered under the desk near us. I was glad neither of us had been hit by that flying piece of metal.

And still it didn't stop.

I wondered if this was the 'Big One', the once a century killer earthquake. I'd soon find out that it was. My heavy solid wooden desk rocked above us and my perpetual motion machine toys, which normally rocked, rolled, and gyrated on their own, were brought to a crashing halt as they tumbled to the floor in pieces. Fiberglass ceiling tiles rained down upon everything, many breaking on impact and filling the air with fine, acrid dust.

After what seemed an eternity, it just stopped. Not knowing whether the integrity of the building would hold, we decided to quickly move outside. As we reached the bottom of the stairs, it started again. Ceiling tiles hit us as we moved outside into the parking lot and joined the remaining employees, who appeared to be in a state of shock. The sounds of countless sirens assaulted us and we could see smoke billowing from dozens of places around us. I immediately thought of the great quake of 1906 in San Francisco where it was the fires that destroyed the city, not the quake itself. Were we near the epicenter? This seemed unlikely. If not, what had happened to San Francisco?

My team started moving to their cars when another quake hit. It didn't seem to be quite as strong, but almost knocked us down. We decided to wait. The aftershocks kept coming. At first it was every minute, then every two, then every five. I remembered the birth of Lucas, Shelly's son, and how what appeared to be earth-shaking contractions wracked her with increasing frequency and intensity. These quakes seemed to be doing the opposite. And then, just when it seemed like several small ones had passed at greater intervals, a big one would hit again. All we could do was wait.

I turned to Matt, the programmer we had hired the week before and said, "Matt, you got your wish!"

"I sure did," he replied. "Are they all like this?"

"No. This is the worst one I've been in. And usually there are only one or two minor aftershocks. This isn't good. There could be major damage everywhere, and the seismologists say that in a major quake, it's possible the aftershocks can trigger even bigger quakes."

Ironically, this was Matt's second day working with us. When I'd interviewed him, I asked why he had moved from the Midwest to California. His response was that he'd always wanted to be in an earthquake. I hoped his wife, who worked over the hill, felt the same way.

Several times when it seemed like things had stopped, we tried to go back into the building, only to be assaulted by another aftershock. On one occasion I did make it in and picked up the phone to see if it would work. No dial tone. As I'd learn in coming days, the phone system was only down for a minute or two, but so many people were trying to reach loved ones that there weren't enough dial tones to go around. The phone company uses a statistical model to determine how many lines actually need to be active at any given time. This number represents a fraction of the actual number of telephones. They hadn't planned on such high demand, so the wait for a dial tone was at least fifteen minutes.

I grabbed my car phone and offered it to my employees who had family to check up on. Most of them couldn't reach anyone, but a few got through to other car phones. Electricity was out, so we went to our car radios to see what was happening. The news was dire.

It appeared the epicenter of the quake was in the Santa Cruz Mountains near us. Highways 17 and 9 were blocked by huge landslides and were impassible. To the south, a bridge on Highway 1 had collapsed and Highway 1 to the north was blocked. Santa Cruz was isolated from the world.

The news in the rest of the Bay Area sounded even worse. A roadway on a portion of the Bay Bridge had fallen into the Bay and almost taken several cars with it. Hundreds of vehicles were trapped on the Cypress Section of the Nimitz Freeway near Oakland in the East Bay where the upper deck of the roadway fell onto the lower. The Marina District of San Francisco, which was built on landfill, was devastated. There were reports of fallen buildings in Santa Cruz and Watsonville, and power was out everywhere. Death toll estimates were in the thousands.

After about an hour, people started heading home or off to pick up children from daycare. I locked the office and drove cautiously towards my house, noting that the downtown section of Santa Cruz was cordoned off by police and emergency vehicles. Fire trucks were everywhere and plumes of smoke rose like tornadoes, black and threatening, and much too close for comfort. I worried about my team and hoped their families were safe. With Santa Cruz isolated, those with spouses who worked over the hill would be spending a restless night alone.

I opened the door to my empty house expecting devastation, but inside, I quickly discovered that the only damage was a toppled bookcase I had failed to anchor to the wall. I stood it up and spent a few minutes shelving the books, organizing them by author again. I had basic emergency supplies, water, food, propane lanterns and a camp stove, but I didn't have a battery powered radio. I fixed myself a light dinner and then tried to settle in to read. I say 'tried' because those damn aftershocks just wouldn't let up and you never knew. Was this next one the 'Big One'? Like everyone else in the San Francisco Bay Area, this was the first of many sleepless nights fraught with earthquakes and bad dreams.

They say it's like combat, sitting in a position of powerlessness waiting for the next bomb or shell to fall or the next assault of bullets. You're wary, trying to stay constantly alert, but becoming exhausted. Just when you start to involuntarily relax, the attack begins anew.

Similarly, the aftershocks came at random, some small, some large. Each could have been another killer. You never knew and you couldn't relax. After days upon days of this, everyone I knew was a nervous, paranoid wreck.

Jenny and I postponed our trip to IBM. When we did go, everyone wanted to know about the earthquake. They had seen the pictures of total devastation. We tried to convince them that while four people had died just a few blocks from our office when an unreinforced brick wall fell on students in a popular bookstore coffee shop, the disasters were quite localized. The vast majority of the Bay Area escaped unscathed. After all the twisting and bending, our steel-beamed offices only had a minor crack in the sheetrock on one wall, which the landlord repaired within days.

As we were trying to tell them that instead of thousands as originally predicted, there were sixty-three deaths in an area that housed millions, the room started to vibrate. Jenny and I seized the edge of the table and slid underneath, to the complete bewilderment of our hosts. The shaking stopped and we peered out.

Apparently, the room always vibrated when several people went down the adjacent stairwell together. There was no earthquake. Of course, seeing our reactions to something so insignificant, they believed we were trying to be stoic in our attempts to diminish the ordeal of the Loma Prieta Earthquake. To this day, they remain convinced that we had been to hell and back and returned unwilling to tell about it.

While the earthquake will remain large in my memory for the rest of my life, the buildings, bridges, and roadways weren't the only things that collapsed in 1989. When you say 1989, most of the rest of the world will recall that the Berlin Wall was torn down and this began the succession of fallen communist regimes in Eastern Europe. They may also recall that while a wave of democracy was sweeping the former Soviet Union, it came to a screeching halt in Tiananmen Square in China.

8

The next few years went smoothly. My old girlfriend Susan returned from the East Coast where she had worked for two years as a lecturer after completing her PhD at Boston University. She had been accepted for an Assistant Professor position at the University of California, Berkeley. While our relationship wasn't as intense as it was before, we started going out from time to time, frequently finding ourselves on double dates with Georgette and whoever her current beau happened to be. Often after making love, I found myself thinking of Shelly. But it wasn't Shelly in bed I remembered, it was her green eyes and the way she looked at me when we dazzled the room and each other with our dancing. I missed spinning and spinning, Shelly clutching me, her heart pounding against my chest, and the release, turning her out as I caught her hand and rolled her back in to a deep dip, a spectacular finish.

The world was changing. The Hubble Telescope was launched and immediately had problems. The resolution of its images was worse than those from earth-bound observatories. NASA was in trouble but claimed that a Shuttle mission could repair the problem. Nelson Mandela was released from prison in South Africa and it appeared that international pressure and US boycotts would eventually lead to the end of apartheid there. The Soviet Union officially ceased to exist and formed the Commonwealth of Independent States. Many of us were confused during the 1992 Olympics when athletes would appear with 'CIS' as their country of origin. The USSR was no longer, and some of the athletes actually included their Balkan country names.

Things were changing in the business world too. The loosely knit Internet was being woven together by new software to create the World Wide Web. Microsoft announced Windows 3.0 with graphics and a friendly user interface reminiscent of Apple's. This made the Personal Computer a tool that even non-techies could use. Georgette's company was growing by leaps and bounds as more and more people connected to the Internet from their home and business computers.

During July of 1991, I talked Susan and Craig Stevens, the CEO of one of our customers, into joining me in Cabo San Lucas to see the total eclipse of the sun. I had met Craig several times at his offices near John Wayne airport in Irvine, California, but we had never surfed together. However, whenever we finished discussing business, our conversations always turned to surfing stories and in a recent phone conversation when I mentioned that I was going to see the eclipse and grab some surf, Craig asked if I wanted some company. We agreed it would be fun to spend some time in a 'board' meeting together.

Although Craig lived, worked, and surfed in Southern California, he had never been to Cabo. I had been making annual surf trips there since the early 1980's and enjoyed surfing without a wetsuit in the warm tropical waters, though I was disappointed by the veritable explosion of growth in the area as Californians took advantage of inexpensive beach front property.

We met at the airport two days before the eclipse. Craig looked nothing like the surfers of Northern California. It took stamina and conditioning to surf the big waves and cold water there. Craig was in his mid-forties, potbellied and soft. His wife Jan was blond, tan, and thin. They made a very unlikely couple. We went to baggage claim and Craig picked up a longboard. I'm biased against longboards. They don't have the quickness and maneuverability of short boards, and it seems like more and more people are finding it easy to start surfing because longboards make waves easy to catch and ride. Craig informed me that they were the standard at most of the breaks he surfed in southern California.

We rented a four-wheel drive roofless Jeep and fifteen minutes later, we arrived at the two bedroom condominium we had rented which was just across the highway from Zipper's, the Rock, and Old Man's, three fun surf breaks just outside San Jose del Cabo.

The condo was cavernous. It had high ceilings, white stucco walls and beige tiled floors with just a few small thin rugs on the floor. Our voices echoed off the walls, but I guessed that with all the sand that would be tracked in, this design made it much easier to clean.

After unpacking, Susan and Craig's wife Jan accompanied us to the beach as Craig and I grabbed a few small fast waves at Zipper's. The women were nowhere to be found when we got out of the water so we walked over to the palapas-roofed open walled bar/café, also called Zipper's, where we found them sipping Dos Equis with lime.

That night we drove about a mile towards Cabo San Lucas and dined at La Pamilla. La Pamilla is an exotic hotel perched on a rocky point. Its restaurant features a breezeway that is suspended between two sections of the hotel. In addition to spectacular views, it seems to magically invite a breeze off the ocean, even on the warmest days. The food is all organic, something that was quite unusual in that day: fresh salads and fruits, a huge list of seafood, and oh, the drinks!

After dessert, Craig and I played a game of life-sized chess on the giant board overlooking the crashing surf. Iguanas basked on the rocks soaking up the last rays of the day. The four of us walked on the beach as the sunset slowly faded to darkness.

The next day, we packed a cooler with ice and drinks and began the long trip to the eastern surf breaks. Leaving the pavement just outside of San Jose del Cabo, we spent forty-five minutes on a washboard dirt road. While the ocean was near, the landscape was desert, cactus, sand and rock. We passed volcanic cinder cones and held on as our teeth nearly rattled from our mouths across the non-stop ripples of the washboard road. We all prayed the car wouldn't break down out in the middle of nowhere with no shade and hundred ten degree heat. Periodically, long-legged black and white roadrunners would race the car, usually winning as we tried to slow down to reduce the punishment to our bodies.

Just as we thought we could take it no longer and Susan suggested we just stop and surf whatever was there, we rounded a point and saw nine palm trees. We had arrived at the famous nine-palms!

We helped Susan and Jan set up four large beach umbrellas to create some shade, then after donning reef booties against the coral, lathering up with suntan lotion, putting on long-sleeved T-shirts, visors and sunglasses, Craig and I went out to surf paradise. The water was eighty-eight degrees, which required us to come in periodically to re-wax our boards – wax softened and rubbed off at these water temperatures. The water was the classic azure blue you see in the tropics, though further out it was so dark, it looked like you could dip a bucket and use it as navy-blue paint.

The surf was perfect. From the top of the point, six foot right-breaking waves rolled over a quarter of a mile with fast hollow sections, long slow workable walls and lots of places to use your board to carve your initials into the faces. After a long ride, we'd alternate between the hot paddle back out to the point, or the longer walk along the beach and treacherous climb across the coral at the top of the point. Between the osmosis caused by the intense saltwater, the dry heat, and our working so hard, we had to constantly hydrate ourselves by taking breaks and downing club sodas and bananas. After four hours, we were exhausted and craved only darkness, but we had to endure the forty-five minute bone-jarring drive back to the condo.

We returned for our siestas, and although we tried to be quiet, I'm sure Craig and Jan heard our afternoon lovemaking, just as we heard theirs. We napped, then spent the late afternoon snorkeling below the Pamilla, admiring the brightly-colored angel fish, the green dorados, the eerie four-foot long, two inch thick needlefish, and an occasional sea turtle as we collected bits of coral as souvenirs. We had the world's best margaritas at La Pamilla before heading over to a small garden restaurant in San Jose.

The next morning, Craig and I awoke early and raced down to the Rock to grab a few waves before breakfast and the eclipse. Unfortunately, the surf was small, mostly two to three foot mushy waves with an occasional larger set. Craig was bummed. His plan was to be dropping down a wave as the eclipse went into totality.

We ate pastries from the local bakery for breakfast and talked with people at the pool who had set up exotic telescopes and cameras to capture the eclipse. One guy in scuba gear had his underwater movie camera at the bottom of the pool and was planning to view and record the eclipse from there. To each, his own, I guess. This was to be the only total eclipse viewable in North America for decades and was going to be one of the longest in duration on the planet, seven minutes of totality. I wanted to see it all. I had heard that on the beach, we would see waves of light running up the sand, that the stars would come out and that in addition to the corona around the sun, there was a mountain on the moon that would scatter one large ray of light out to the side. Nocturnal animals were supposed to emerge from their daytime slumbers. This was going to be exciting!

We crossed the highway and stopped in at Zipper's for a cool drink before heading up the beach to the Rock. As we walked in, we were surprised to find that everyone had their eyes glued to spots on the bar and on the floor. The palm fronds of the palapa roof had small spaces that allowed light through. They worked like pin-hole cameras and indeed, we could see that the eclipse had started. There were dozens of tiny suns on the floor and minute by minute, they grew smaller and smaller. When we left, there were half-suns all over the floor.

We hiked up the beach and Craig and I paddled out. The wind turned onshore – from the sea to the land – which made the waves even worse, so I went in. Onshore winds normally occur as the land heats up and the relatively cool air over the ocean moves inland to replace the rising warm air. In the evenings, the land loses its heat and the winds reverse, becoming offshore with the ocean now warmer than the land. For surfers, offshore winds mean great waves as the air rising up the face makes the waves steeper. Onshore winds blow the waves down, creating soft sloppy faces.

Craig was determined to be dropping down a wave during totality. I wanted to spend it with Susan. Jan didn't seem too upset. Maybe this happened after twelve years of marriage.

The light grew dimmer and dimmer, but it was still clearly day time. No stars. We could see that the sun was fading but I didn't sense any major changes. I checked my watch. With only a minute or two to go, it was still awfully bright out. Disappointment started to set in.

And then it went total.

The corona was spectacular, fiery around the blackened disc of the sun, and a single beam of light did, indeed, shoot out at an angle reaching halfway across the sky. After a moment or two, the onshore wind stopped as the land cooled. I looked for stars and could just make out the four corners of Orion. But what was more spectacular was the horizon. We had a three hundred sixty degree sunset. With the clouds in the distance scattering light, we sat in near complete darkness while the horizon in all directions burned a deep crimson. And then the wind turned offshore.

I'm not a terribly religious person. But there was something about these seven minutes. I come up with words like spiritual and transcendent, but they don't capture the hush that ran down the beach or the emotions that came surging forth, not just for me, but for everyone. In science fiction films, you often see spectacular, surreal scenes of other planets with different colored skies and multiple huge moons looming overhead. You know these otherworldly places are simulated. In a total eclipse of the sun, you're in the middle of a special effect, the world has changed from a place that followed certain quotidian rules to one where the rules don't seem apply at all. It's noon and completely dark. All your life, you and your body have learned and believe unquestionably that the sun rises in the morning and sets in the evening; that night and day follow certain rules. Mornings are preceded by sunrises in the east; evenings are preceded by sunsets in the west. And yet, now, you have sunrise in the east, sunset in the west, and both in the north and south. And above you, it is dark, at noon.

The air feels different, it smells different. Your senses are heightened much as they would be in a dangerous situation. The moments become all the more intense. Your breath catches and you can feel your heart and lungs and internal organs, the essence of your life. You understand why people of ancient times were so frightened or awed by these rare events. While logically you know that an eclipse is just the moon passing in between the earth and the sun, you can't help but believe that a greater force is at work and that a message is being sent to you. And you realize that like thousands of others, you could travel around the world chasing the eclipses, hoping to recapture the experience, to again catch a glimpse of one of nature's rarest secrets.

Poor Craig. While there had been numerous small mushy waves before totality, he was now in the midst of a ten minute lull.

Jan was awestruck by this singular event, almost in the throes of a deeply religious experience.

I held Susan in my arms and looked into eyes that were wide with wonder. It's one thing to experience a life altering event alone. It's quite another when two people share a truly transcendental moment, affected simultaneously and identically in visceral ways. You're bound forever, annealed by the event. And this one went on for seven minutes, forging that bond into the strongest steel.

"Jack," Susan said, "This is the most amazing moment of my life. Thank you! Thank you! Thank you!"

Without thinking, and with no previous plans to do so, I said, "Susan, I want someone to share these moments with me for the rest of my life. Will you marry me?"

She kissed me murmuring her assent and we held each other

as the moon continued in its normal orbit around the earth, and daylight slowly intruded into our special moment.

9

Susan and I married that October in a secular ceremony at UC Santa Cruz in a Redwood Grove overlooking the Pacific Ocean. We honeymooned in Big Sur, taking long naked walks on deserted beaches, spending our nights huddled in under deep comforters in a small cabin heated only by a blazing woodstove.

The sole challenge our marriage faced was work. Susan taught at UC Berkeley and my office was in downtown Santa Cruz. Our workplaces were nearly an hour and a half drive apart. Susan decided that she would try to transfer to UC Santa Cruz the following year. She'd move in with me and do the commute most weeknights, staying at her apartment in Berkeley when meetings ran late or she had a very early morning appointment. I tried to talk her into an Audi to help make her commute safer, but she loved her vintage VW bug and refused to drive anything else. We settled into a happy life together.

While it wasn't a grand passion, I loved her. Our lives had a comfortable familiarity that usually requires decades to achieve and we were best friends. We saw movies together, occasionally flew our hang gliders at Waddell Creek up the coast, went skiing, and generally had a good time, saving money, planning for a prosperous retirement. People were envious of our marriage.

Turnkey prospered. My perfect California lifestyle was even better now. Dan's company seemed to be in lock-step with ours and we occasionally employed each other to supplement our in-house expertise. Dan and I continued to meet every few weeks and in addition to discussing our own businesses, Dan kept me up to date on NewCo and Steve's latest efforts at world domination. During the previous year, Steve had acquired three companies using the same technique he applied in his first one: make an offer to the best company in the business; if they refused, acquire and fund their largest competitor and drive the first company out of business. In his latest acquisition, the top company agreed to Steve's terms rather than being put out of business. Steve now had a reputation: either do as Steve asked or suffer the consequences.

Surprisingly, all of the people Steve forced into compliance came to appreciate the financial remuneration. NewCo grew and grew, and its stock soared, split, and soared again. From a business point of view, Steve was certainly doing the right thing.

Too bad his ethics left so much to be desired.

His fame grew as well. He was now a frequent keynote speaker at major industry conferences and conventions. Locally, he was celebrated and toasted and was invited to parties given by the mayors of San Jose and San Francisco, and by California's Senators. There were rumors that he'd met the President.

I saw pictures of Steve and Shelly in the papers and on the news. Shelly appeared to be in her element and became quite outspoken on a number of issues. She was active with most of the community groups and was championing and funding rape crisis centers, homeless shelters, and environmental groups. Her presence on the social scene mirrored Steve's in the business community. She was a force to be reckoned with. While I still remembered and missed our times together, I also realized that these memories were of a person who didn't exist anymore. Perhaps she had never existed in the way I imagined her. As I looked at my life with Susan, I saw a more practical, even, loving relationship and knew that I was over Shelly.

Susan finally got permission to transfer to UC Santa Cruz. Unfortunately, it wouldn't be until Winter Quarter of 1993, right after New Year's, so her commute continued.

On October 19th, 1992, just a few days before our first anniversary, I was sitting at the small table in my office with Ken, one of my software engineers. My phone rang and I ignored it. We were wrapped up in a design review. A few minutes later, Sandy, our receptionist, knocked and entered my office and said there was a call I had to take. When I suggested I call them back, she told me it was the police. I asked Ken if we could pick this up later and then sat at my desk and waited for the call to be transferred.

I picked up the phone on the first ring.

"Sir, this is Officer Brannon of the California Highway Patrol. Does your wife drive a 1969 powder blue Volkswagen Beetle?"

My gut clenched. There must have been an accident. "Yes. Is she okay?"

"No sir, I'm afraid not. A semi jumped the divider on Highway 880 this morning and landed on your wife's car. I'm very sorry.

"We need you to meet us at our San Leandro Office just off Highway 92. Can you get here in the next hour?"

I was too stunned to speak.

"Sir?"

"Ah, yes. I'll be there. Can I get your address and phone number?"

In a daze, I scribbled down the information and then called Mark, my doctor and surfing buddy. He was on his way.

I don't remember much of what happened over the next few days. I know I slept in Mark's spare room that night and he gave me something to help me sleep. I cried a lot. I recall going home for the first time and wondering if the idyllic year of marriage with Susan had just been a dream. Then I found her things. What was I going to do with her things? What about her apartment in Berkeley?

I have vague recollections of the funeral, her casket being lowered into a hole at the foot of a small Magnolia tree. I know people tried to console me. Georgette called often and even came by, but I just didn't have anything to say. I muddled through work for several weeks and people gave me space, or their condolences. I wanted the space.

10

One day Ronn showed up. I hadn't seen him since the funeral and didn't remember much of that visit. He walked into my house and started packing clothes into a bag.

"We're going to Montana for a couple of weeks. No argument from you!" he stated flatly.

I was in no position to put up a fight and found myself on a plane a few hours later. We landed in the early afternoon. I got into his four-wheel drive king cab pickup and rode in silence to Ronn's ranch, about an hour away.

Barb was working a horse in a corral across from the two story white ranch house. I wasn't sure exactly what she was doing but she was on the ground leading a horse in circles around a large barrel. Seeing us pull up, she handed the lead to a ranch hand and jogged over to us, dusting herself off as she approached.

"Jack, it's good to see you!" she said, hugging me fiercely. "Sorry I'm such a mess."

"Thanks for having me," I mumbled.

Barb led us into the house, taking my bag and directing me to a door down a long hall. Inside, I discovered a rustic, wood paneled room, spacious with a sofa and chair, television, a small woodstove, and its own bathroom. Large windows looked out onto a wide fast flowing stream or small river bordered by cottonwood trees. She suggested I unpack and join them in the living room. I felt like falling into the bed and sleeping forever to the sound of rushing water outside. Instead, I put my things into the maple dresser and made my way into their great room, also paneled with rustic wood but with a twenty foot ceiling and a huge stone fireplace. Barb handed me a glass of lemonade and welcomed me to paradise.

We talked about the ranch and ranch life for a while and then Ronn excused himself. When he returned, he was carrying two fly rods, vests, creels, nets, and waders.

"Let's go," he said.

I followed him blindly and he led us down to a shallow spot on the river. Under his direction, I donned waders, the vest and the rest of the equipment. He handed me a dry fly and told me to tie it on.

"You do know how to do that, don't you?" he asked.

"Ronn, I fished for years with my parents and can certainly tie a lure to stay on a fishing line. But, I've never fly fished before. In fact, I pretty much gave up fishing. While it's nice to be out and there's a certain calming effect to it, the bottom line is that it's boring. Some time ago, I discovered that sitting and waiting for a fish to bite just didn't seem to be as much fun as everything else I do."

"Watch and learn. I think you'll find this a bit different."

Ronn waded out into the river and began to cast. He started with a small amount of line, throwing it forward then pulling it back before it ever hit the water. The back part of his cast seemed longer and he waited until the fly extended the length of the line before drawing it forward again. Within a moment or two he had forty or more feet of line moving rhythmically through the air. On his next forward cast, he allowed the line to drop and it unwound across the water like a line of fire racing across a floor. He waited and watched while the fly drifted downstream fifty yards or more, pulling out additional line as it went. Then he pulled in the line by hand and repeated the process.

After four or five casts, he had a hit. A large trout grabbed the fly and jumped from the water as Ronn worked to bring it in. He used his reel to draw in the line and his hand for drag to tire the frantic fish. After nearly five minutes the fish was within a few feet of him. He scooped the fish into a net, submerged in the water. He then gently removed the hook, faced the fish upstream and turned it loose. The fish swam away, apparently unharmed by the experience.

Seeing my surprised expression, he said, "What do you think?"

"That was beautiful," I responded, tears coming to my eyes unbidden. "Do you always turn them loose?"

"Usually. I kept three from my session this morning and we're having them for dinner tonight. It's the fishing not the catching, and certainly not the keeping that is so therapeutic. Let's get you started and see if you can ground yourself a bit with a few days of this."

I burst into tears, consumed by deep sobs. Ronn made his way to shore and began to explain what I needed to do, ignoring my devastation, encouraging me to move on to something new and completely different.

My first attempts were ridiculous. I was clearly incompetent at this. As a child, my mother made me practice casting a weighted line onto targets at varying distances before she ever took me fishing, but this line had no real weight. I tried to muscle it to get distance but it had no effect.

"Eleven o'clock to one o'clock," Ronn chanted, encouraging me to limit the range that the rod moved through on forward and back casts. "Wait on the back casts! No. Stop a second. Let me show you something."

He took the rod from me and brought in the line. "See these?" he asked, showing me small knots in the leader. "These are wind knots. You didn't tie them, but when you force your back casts like that, the fly actually goes through loops in the line and you create them. They'll also ultimately cause your line to break and you'll snap the flies off. Take it easy and be patient on the back casts."

I did as he said and after about half an hour was able to get the fly out about twenty feet. Unfortunately it didn't unwind gracefully like Ronn's casts did. My forecasts reached the end of the line and dropped several feet straight down, the fly snapping back towards me a few feet. Fortunately, the drift of the river caused the line to straighten out and I could let it drift, then would draw it in and start over again.

It required concentration to learn this new thing. And Ronn was right. I didn't care about catching a fish. I just wanted to do a perfect cast like he did. As I was thinking about my next cast, a fish took the fly. Somehow my old reflexes took over and I pulled back on the rod, holding the line which was slack in my hand. I wasn't sure exactly what to do so I kept trying to pull in the line by hand. I stared flailing about and almost dropped the rod. Ronn was laughing almost uncontrollably but managed to suggest I let the fish run a bit. I started letting out the line, trying to keep tension on it and when it was all played out, I switched to the reel, trying to imitate what Ronn did. As the fish approached, I reached behind me for the net, hanging from the back of my vest, not realizing that I'd lowered the rod and introduced more slack. With a quick flip, the fish was gone. I stumbled backwards in response to the fish's release and found myself sitting in two feet of water, my waders filling, laughing for the first time in months, then crying and laughing again.

Ronn dragged me to shore, afraid I'd be swept away and

drowned by the waders. I took them off and after gathering up the gear, we walked back to the house.

"Let's try that again in the morning," Ronn said, "The fishing part, not the swimming."

I spent two weeks with Ronn and Barb, fishing at dawn and sunset, helping around the ranch, even mucking out horse stalls during the day. I slept soundly each night and awoke filled with anticipation for the day and my next fly fishing lessons. Ronn taught me about hatches, about different kinds of flies, dry and wet, and about patience. Fishing became meditative and by the end of the week, the haze had cleared and I was feeling grounded.

Ronn just smiled when I thanked him and Barb before boarding the plane. Upon my return to Santa Cruz, the first thing I did was visit Susan's grave. I hadn't done that since the funeral. I sat down under the magnolia tree and told her about the fly fishing.

Even now, when I have a problem or I'm feeling a bit lost, I visit Susan and talk to her. I don't know if she can hear me, but somehow I leave feeling better and glad I went.

CHAPTER 6

"That's life. That's what all the people say, flying high in April, shot down in May."
- Frank Sinatra

1

With renewed clarity, I looked at my life and decided I needed to work. I'm not sure why, but I wanted to accomplish something significant. Living a semi-prosperous lifestyle with a lot of free leisure time just didn't seem enough anymore, especially now that I was alone. Throughout my adult life, I had never really been outside a relationship with a woman. There was always someone and if there wasn't, I was looking for the next one. Susan was my friend, lover, and ultimately my wife. When I married her, I locked in. I quit looking at other women. Susan was IT. Even though she was now gone, I didn't see that changing. I couldn't even imagine being with anyone else and my fantasies were always about her, about us. If I put aside that aspect of me – needing and being with a partner – I could focus the really important things in life.

Shortly after the New Year, I closed Susan's apartment and packed her belongings in boxes which I placed in my attic. It was 1993, the year of the World Trade Center bombing where six people died when terrorists detonated a bomb in its underground parking garage. It was 1993, when the FBI lost four of its agents as it attacked David Koresh's Branch Davidian compound near Waco, Texas, killing Koresh and seventy-six of his followers, including twenty children.

It was also the year that Mosaic, the first World Wide Web browser appeared. This was the missing piece I had described to Georgette years before. This was the technology that would create the Internet as we know it today. The Internet had grown, and with it Samcom was now a huge company that supplied almost all of the routers in the Internet and the majority of routers that companies used to connect to the Internet.

At Turnkey, I was searching for my own piece, technology that would make a difference. And, after just a few months of meeting with every customer I'd ever had, listening to their problems and trying to find a common thread, I stumbled upon the answer in the place I least expected real technological innovation: IBM.

IBM was going through hard times. It was dramatically reducing the size of its workforce and reorganizing in hopes that it could reposition itself as a major player in the emerging smaller computer world. But once again, Evan Silvers, my former boss and the one who helped get Turnkey started, had the answer. His group had just taken on a project to build a Video Server, a machine that contained video clips, movies, and recorded music and could play it across the Internet with perfect quality. The Server supported a new protocol that did bandwidth reservations. You could actually tell the Internet how much bandwidth you needed and how much delay you could tolerate, and then you could set up a connection that guaranteed the performance from the server to multiple remote computers.

While IBM had built the servers, they didn't have the personnel or the expertise to build the client pieces. They needed software that supported this protocol on IBM PCs, Sun Microsystems' machines, Silicon Graphics' systems, and Apple Macintoshes.

Surprising myself, I negotiated a deal with Evan where not only would they pay us to develop this software on all these systems, but that we, Turnkey, would have ownership of the software, granting IBM a license to sell it only with their Video Server. I could envision countless other applications that needed this.

The Internet uses a protocol called IP, the Internet Protocol. It sends data in packets, but there are no guarantees that a packet will ever arrive, or if it does, how long it will take. In 1993, Videoconferencing over the Internet was in its infancy, telephony over the Internet was unheard of, and distance learning and gaming were only done over dedicated network connections. They couldn't work over the Internet. Turnkey would change all that.

I threw myself into the project. Not only did I get it staffed and underway, I went out to find the roots of the technology. I discovered that the original protocol, called QS-II, was developed by Bolt, Beranek, and Newman, the developers of the ARPANET, which spawned the Internet. Even more interesting was the fact that the protocol was designated IP version 5. The standard Internet Protocol was version 4. It was intended for best-efforts transmissions of things like email and browser traffic, while IP version 5 was intended for real time traffic or anything that absolutely, positively had to be there accurately, on time, and in order. And, I learned about the Internet Engineering Task Force.

The IETF is the group that creates the standards for all things used on the Internet. They meet three times a year and anyone can attend free of charge. Originally staffed by college professors, grad students, and government and BBN personnel, the IETF was growing. In 1993, many people from corporate America were attending, attempting to get visibility into the emerging Internet technologies. I jumped right in. I found it fascinating that even someone from a small company could have major influence on new standards. My previous experience with other standards organizations was that you needed to ante up high five figures in membership fees, and then only had influence if you were from a large company. This was very different and I reveled in the academic atmosphere. Their motto was 'general consensus and working code', meaning if you could get a working group to agree, and could get code actually operating to demonstrate its capabilities, you could create a standard.

I discovered that the QS-II working group was creating a new version and that BBN employees were pushing this forward on behalf of requirements by the government's Defense Simulation Internet group which was part of DARPA, the Defense Advanced Research Project Agency. I also learned that while BBN was the primary supplier of routers for QS-II, the government required a second source for all critical technology and BBN had enlisted Tightship Systems as their second source.

Joy of joys! Turnkey was about to change the world!

I know. You think I'm crazy. But what made this such a unique opportunity is that Tightship was the main competitor of Samcom, the world's largest networking equipment vendor. They had a critical technology that Samcom didn't, and they didn't even know they had it!

With help from the folks at BBN, I set up a meeting in Billerica, Massachusetts, with the Tightship executives and I explained my plan. Turnkey, BBN, and Tightship would introduce technology that would expand the Internet to allow telephony, distance learning, video distribution, videoconferencing, reliable business applications and much more. We had proven technology. Turnkey needed to line up application software companies to use our products, and help them deploy several networks using QS-II. Tightship would bring existing customers to the table and when we had some live networks running, we'd announce this to the world and we'd be on our way.

By early 1994, we had negotiated the maze of government contracts by working through a Systems Integrator headquartered near Washington, D.C., and were now supplying our software to DARPA. Several videoconferencing vendors had incorporated our technology into their products and could demonstrate perfect quality and synchronization of voice and video across the Internet. The average person was about to see an Internet only dreamed of. Free or nearly free long distance communications with the same or better quality than a standard telephone line, and even videophones would be just around the corner. We thought we were ready.

I began presentations to Venture Capitalists. While Turnkey had an excellent cash reserve, I wanted to hire a marketing force that could get this technology into the market on a large scale. Several of the Venture Capitalists were interested and after performing both technical and marketing due diligence by talking to our customers and partners, they were beginning to talk with each other, planning multiple rounds of financing. I was expecting term sheets within days.

2

I had just returned from an IETF meeting and was putting my office in order when the phone rang.

"Hi, Jack, it's Alan Tennel from Hummingbird Ventures." Hummingbird was likely to be our lead Venture Capitalist firm.

"Alan, good to hear from you! To what do I owe the pleasure?"

"Jack, I have a term sheet in front of me. We're prepared to offer you $1.5 million in exchange for thirty percent of Turnkey, post financing. I'd send it over, but there may be a minor problem. As the last stage of our due diligence, we check for legal actions against the company. It appears there's an outstanding lawsuit for wrongful dismissal from a Stan Rathbone. Isn't he one of your shareholders?"

"Alan, this comes as a big surprise to me. I fired Stan several years ago. I would think the statute of limitations would have run out on any claim like this. Plus, we settled this when I terminated him."

"Well, you might be right, the suit was filed quite a while back, but it was never dropped, and from what I've been told, never served on you either. If you've got an agreement with this Stan character, you need to get him to drop the suit. Then we can send over the term sheet."

"Alan, since he still holds shares in the company, I have to believe that he'll want this financing to go through. It could lead to an IPO or major acquisition which would benefit him. I'll track him down and will get this resolved."

I hung up the phone and asked Sandy to find Stan's latest address. Surprisingly, he still lived in Santa Cruz. I called and left a message on his machine, which he returned late in the day.

"Jack, what can I do for you?" he said almost too jovially when I answered the phone.

"Stan, we're looking at taking on some VC money. Can we meet?"

"Sure, Jack. How about the Catalyst at 7?"

When I arrived at the Catalyst, I spotted Stan immediately. He was holding court with what appeared to be several regulars. As I approached, I noticed a wedding band on his left hand. I was hoping that marriage had taken some of the arrogance out of him. I was disappointed.

As I approached, Stan excused himself, nodded and smiled warmly at me, then led me to a table away from the crowd. "So, VC money, huh?"

"Yes. We've stumbled into a really unique technology that could change the face of the Internet and I'm looking primarily for marketing dollars to get us launched. "

"Sounds interesting." Stan said almost gloating. "So why are you talking to me? "

"Well, aside from the fact that you still own a substantial portion of the stock, the lead VCs discovered a lawsuit you filed. They won't invest until you drop the suit. "

"Well, well, well." Stan replied, the smirk on his face growing tighter and crueler. "I always knew you'd do well one day. I wanted to be your partner and help you through the maze of investors and even going public. But you threw me out, just when we were starting to take off. I can't ever forgive you for that.

"So, what are you prepared to offer me to drop the suit? "

"Offer you?" I responded, shocked. "I thought you'd want to see your stock worth something. This investment, with an eye toward an IPO or acquisition, could still make you rich. Why would you want to hold this up?"

"Because you owe me. I was embarrassed. The entire Valley knew what happened. I want to be compensated for the fact that you said I'd be your partner, then threw me out. I'm thinking a million dollars would make me feel better and would allow me to save face."

"Stan, you're fucking nuts. I could have pressed charges and sent you to jail. I gave you a fair severance as settlement. You got to keep the money you stole from the company."

"Jack," he said, getting up, a smug look on his face. "I'll see you in court. My attorney will serve you tomorrow. You're going to pay!"

He walked away and rejoined his friends, speaking a few minutes, then pointing at me and laughing. I left, disappointed in myself for losing my temper.

3

Sure enough, at ten the next morning, a Sheriff arrived and served me with a lawsuit claiming wrongful dismissal against a promise of work for life, and fraud. It asked for direct damages for loss of income for the rest of Stan's life, punitive damages, and triple damages for fraud. The total amounted to over three million dollars! My stomach churned and roiled. I went outside and took a walk along Westcliff Drive to calm down.

Westcliff Drive winds from the Santa Cruz Wharf to Natural Bridges State Park, home of thousands of migrating Monarch Butterflies. In one area of the park, hanging eucalyptus branches become spectacular cascades of orange and black as the butterflies congregate for warmth, seeking shelter and nourishment on their long journey.

A bike and pedestrian path borders the edge of precipitous cliffs that run non-stop for two and a half miles. There are numerous natural bridges along the way where water has carved out tunnels in promontories of sedimentary rock. Seals cavort around Seal Rock and the bulls get into barking matches with each other and with younger up and comers as they try to dominate the rock. Sea otters float restfully on their backs breaking shellfish on their stomachs with small stones, then suddenly roll over and dive for the bottom, often resurfacing with large crabs which they crack and gnaw.

Monterey is visible some twenty-five miles across the open water which is white capped beyond the thick brown kelp beds and glassy smooth closer to shore. It's a peaceful, contemplative place to walk and the nearness of the ocean and the teeming sea life is calming and reassures you that the sea and life go on in spite of our individual crises.

When I returned, I called Alan Tennel and told him the bad news.

"Jack, you need to get this settled ASAP!" he advised avuncularly. "Call David Swan at Kellerbach, Litton, and Swan. He'll negotiate the settlement for you. We can't invest with this hanging over your head, and I can assure you that no one else will either."

Kellerback, Litton, and Swan is one of Silicon Valley's most dynamic law firms. With over three hundred lawyers in multiple offices around the country, they are a favorite of Venture

Capitalists and startups and are involved in most of the IPOs and acquisitions that take place in the Valley. Alan had previously recommended that we retain them as corporate counsel.

"But Alan, it wasn't a wrongful dismissal. The guy was embezzling. I want to pursue this. It's without merit. Besides, when he loses, I can go after him for malicious prosecution. He's just doing this to extort money from us, knowing what a critical time it is for the company."

"Jack, trust me. Right and wrong don't matter in a situation like this. If he's got a decent attorney, he'll have you jumping through hoops in discovery. You'll be turning over your books, correspondence, emails, you name it. Your legal bills will go through the roof and this will drag on for months or even years. I've been there. We recently had one of our companies literally ripped apart by a shareholders' dispute. One of the non-participating founders ended up suing the company for stealing his technology. They burned through our entire investment and more in legal fees alone and we recently closed the company because the dispute was not moving towards resolution. Don't go there too!"

I thanked Alan and put a call in to David Swan. He called back about an hour later and we set up a time to meet the next day.

I gathered all the documentation I could find about Stan, everything from his original offer letter to the evidence of his embezzlement and our short agreement for severance, and drove to the Kellerbach, Litton, and Swan offices in downtown San Jose. I took the elevator to the top floor of the thirty-five story building and was greeted by a friendly receptionist in a tailored dark suit. She offered me coffee or a soft drink which I declined and I took a seat at on a plush sofa in the reception area. I picked up the Wall Street Journal and read the front page until the receptionist approached with David Swan.

Swan was in his mid-fifties, just over six feet tall and a bit portly, with graying hair and smile lines around his intense blue eyes. He greeted me with a deep mellifluous voice and after shaking my hand warmly, he led me to a conference room with floor to ceiling glass windows looking out across the Valley at Mission Peak and the East Bay hills. There was no balcony and I felt a bit of vertigo as I approached the windows and the precipitous drop on the other side.

"Kind of intimidating, isn't it? " David said, chuckling.

"I fly hang gliders, but this is a bit scary. I assume the glass is strong enough to prevent anyone falling through?"

"It's funny. A few years ago, one of our associates was working late in here when the room began filling with smoke. Panicking, he got the brilliant idea to break the window. He picked up one these chairs and threw it at the window with full force. The chair ricocheted and landed on him, breaking his leg. As it turned out, he caused the fire himself. He had been smoking in here, which is not allowed, and had thrown his cigarette into the waste basket. In addition to paper which ignited slowly, there were pizza crusts which smoldered and created all the smoke. Of course he wanted to be compensated for his broken leg.

"In case you're wondering, he's no longer with us, but the settlement was a bit costly to the firm. From what Alan tells me, you're facing something similar."

"I am being sued for wrongful dismissal. It's clearly just an attempt at extortion. The suit is certainly frivolous. I've brought the suit and some documentation."

I presented all of this passionately to David Swan, arrogantly confident that justice would prevail. My voice rose in anger and outrage as I described Stan's actions during his tenure with Turnkey, then I grew even more fervent as I tried to make a case for counter-suing Stan. When I finished, David looked at me for a moment or two, seeming to mull over what he wanted to tell me, then he gave me his opinion.

"Jack, you have a solid case. It's extremely unlikely he can win this in court. I say unlikely because anything can happen once a case goes to trial. But on the surface of the evidence and the complaint, I think it will be pretty straight forward."

"Okay," I said eagerly, almost rubbing my hands in anticipation, ready to begin the battle. "So, how long will it take?"

"Well, the courts are pretty backed up. We've got a litigious society going full bore right now, which is working out well for us lawyers, but it means significant delays. There's a new initiative to try to fast-track cases, but even with that, you'd be looking at a minimum of six months and more likely twelve to eighteen months to get the case heard."

I felt like he'd thrown a bucket of cold water on me. I was

stunned. Sure, I should have expected this. I thought about the fact that we wouldn't see any investment until this was settled and I got angry. Stan stole from the company and now he was holding me up. I really wanted to fight it, but how? I didn't have unlimited cash reserves and while I might recover attorney's fees once we won, in the meantime, I'd be distracted battling with Stan and his attorneys, and we wouldn't be able to take the next step with the venture investments. What could I do?

"David, what do you suggest?"

"First, we have to respond to the complaint. That needs to happen ASAP. Obviously, you're going to have to settle, but we need to position you strongly. If we can intimidate Stan's attorney by showing him that his client's actions were questionable and perhaps even criminal, we'll be in a stronger negotiating position.

"We need to open discovery and get some depositions started. If we get Stan under oath and hit him hard, he may cave.

"I'll assign one of my top associates to the case and we'll get started. His rate is one hundred eighty dollars an hour for non-court time and three hundred an hour for court time. Of course we'll use our legal assistants as much as possible. Their rates range from fifty to seventy-five dollars an hour. We'll need a retainer of ten thousand to start. Let's go meet Mitch Waters. He'll take the lead on this."

I was disappointed that David wasn't handling the negotiations himself, but Turnkey was just a small startup and his thousand dollar per hour and up rates were certainly beyond us. I followed David down the hall to Mitch Waters' office. Mitch rose to greet us as we entered and came around his cherry wood desk to shake my hand. He was small and dark with a wiry body and a fierce intensity about him. His handshake was very strong, and I could sense physical strength behind his grip.

I told Mitch the story of Stan and his dismissal and described Turnkey and our financial situation. I also told him about the technology, which he found intriguing. He read through the complaint, and after about an hour, I left with his promise to have a response faxed to me by noon the next day. I couldn't help feeling like I always did when I entered a whitewater rapid I'd never run before. It's that sudden surge, a rush of excitement, but then there's nothing you can do other than to keep yourself upright. You can't go back. You can't stop in the middle. Even if you can't enjoy it, you need to accept the undeniable fact that you're taking the ride and can't get off until you reach the end.

4

Three months later, our attorney's fees were approaching one hundred thousand dollars. Stan's lawyer was from small two-man office in Santa Cruz, but he knew how to force his adversary into huge expenditures. I'd been to so many depositions that I couldn't count them anymore. So had my staff. Stan and his lawyer deposed everyone, getting their take on the company, past, present and future. He asked about financial procedures in the company and demanded proof that they were followed. He went through every contract we had signed. And though he clearly knew his client was guilty, he really didn't care. His job was to win his client a large settlement and to earn a significant contingency fee.

My team was tired of this. The lawsuit seemed to be more important than our technological and business plans. They felt personally persecuted in the depositions and began to have doubts about our future. I was worried. Forces were at work in the IETF that were trying to suppress our technology. An initiative arose to develop a new protocol called IRES to ensure quality across the Internet. University professors had suddenly found funding for research in pursuit of this new opportunity. The funding appeared to be coming indirectly from Samcom, the networking giant. At that time, I didn't completely understand what had happened, but I could see that our path to success wasn't as clear cut as it had once appeared. The delay in being able to support a major market launch was killing us and giving other larger players a chance to preempt our efforts.

Then finally, it happened. The attorneys reached a settlement agreement. In the course of the negotiations, Stan pushed for more money, then demanded an anti-dilution clause for his stock. This would mean that his percentage of the company couldn't change with new investments from the Venture Capitalists. They could invest tens of millions and Stan would still maintain his percentage. The investors would be diluted by other investors, but Stan wouldn't. The VCs said this was unacceptable.

I think what triggered the settlement was the attitude of me and my staff in some of the final depositions. We were defeated. Our take-the-world-by-storm attitude was fading. We had begun to doubt the chances of our success and the viability of our technology. We made it clear that we might have missed the market window and that the VCs weren't as interested anymore. My guess is that Stan realized he was about to lose it all. And while I can't say that he caved, I can say that both Stan and I were unhappy with the settlement. According to Mitch, this is the goal of a successful negotiation. My philosophy of having both parties happy with the results of a negotiation apparently left something on the table.

So we settled. Stan would get three hundred thousand dollars which would come out of our venture financing. He would retain his stock but would give me a proxy to vote his shares. He could be diluted, but only by outside investment. The hardest thing for me, and what almost broke the deal, was that Stan demanded a written apology from me. It almost killed me to sign it.

While all this kept me occupied during most of 1994, the world outside continued to change. Nelson Mandela was elected President of South Africa and Apartheid was coming to an end. The Internet really took off. Everyone knew what it was and several different browsers were making access easy. A startup company called Netscape seemed to be emerging as a major player in this space though no one could figure out how they would ever make money since they gave their browsers away for free.

Georgette's company, which had been showing steady growth for years, suddenly exploded. With the advent of the average person being able to access the Internet, Modular Communications had taken their dial up modem and added routing features. Now, if you wanted to access the Internet from home or a small business, you purchased one of their boxes. Modular had found a niche in the router market that Samcom either had missed, or didn't care about. Their prices started at a few hundred dollars and consumers began buying them enthusiastically.

With their success, Modular decided to change their name to OptiRoute. They also took what's called a mezzanine round of investment from one of the Valley's largest Venture Capital firms. A mezzanine round is intended to fund the steps necessary to take a company public. The company is restructured to implement corporate procedures specifically required for public companies. Any sloppiness in company books or records is cleaned up. And, the executives of the company begin traveling all over the country to do dog and pony shows for investment bankers who will sell the initial public shares to large investment funds.

Georgette bought an airplane.

5

After the settlement with Stan, we had to wait for the Venture round to close. It looked like it would take another sixty days before we had any money. Tightship was tired of waiting and decided to move ahead. They asked us to demonstrate the IBM video server with our clients running across a heavily loaded simulated Internet at a major show. We set up two five foot movie screens and played Star Wars across the Internet, one with our software, one without. The demo was a huge success. Unfortunately, Tightship made a significant strategic error. To show that they weren't afraid of Samcom, and that they had superior technology, they faced the screens directly at the Samcom booth. Samcom was now aware that we existed. Tightship had fired a shot across their bow.

Suddenly, the trade press was abuzz. Turnkey was voted one of the ten companies to watch by several key publications who said our Quality of Service (QoS) software might just change the world. I was besieged with requests for interviews and demonstrations, and more and more companies began to order our software. It certainly looked like we were on our way.

The VC money came in and with it the VCs 'suggested' that I hire a CEO and that I assume the role of Founder and Chief Technical Officer, remaining Chairman of the Board. Since I really wanted to focus on the technology, I readily agreed, but suspected that large amount of cash going towards the settlement with Stan was part of the reason I wouldn't be CEO. So, I began the search for a CEO. I quickly found a likely candidate in a division of IBM that we were working with.

Alex Nessler had aggressively positioned some of IBM's new, smaller enterprise products, and had business responsibility for an entire product line including research and development, manufacturing, marketing, sales, and group profitability. In a little over two years, he had built his organization from an initial team of ten people to over four hundred. His group was responsible for nearly two hundred million in annual sales. Unfortunately, his almost meteoric rise within the company had come to an abrupt halt. His aggressive, straight-talking style didn't sit well with certain key members of upper management who wanted deference from those below them. He had hit a glass ceiling in IBM. With his options limited there, Alex was ready for a new challenge. In addition to excellent organizational skills, he brought strong contacts with many major enterprises, something Turnkey could leverage.

Physically, Alex was short and very stocky. He was a bodybuilder with remarkable self-discipline, rising at four am after only four or five hours of sleep, and working out for two hours before showing up at the office at seven am. His dark hair was cropped short, reflecting the style he picked up during his years in the Special Forces in Vietnam. One look at his square jaw and formidable frame and you knew he was a force to be reckoned with.

Alex hired Dirk James, an obnoxious, but effective Vice President of Sales. I sat in on Dirk's interview. He was self-centered, a braggart, and argued with you over the most minor points. I didn't like him but it was clear he could open doors and sell. Alex was confident that Dirk would get us in front of some major players.

It took a while to find a good person to head up Finance and Administration. Alex told me he wouldn't bother me until he found a viable candidate, but he informed me when each interview was scheduled so I could be available for follow up. In the course of a week, Alex interviewed seven people and they were all out his office and back in their cars within twenty minutes, some of them clearly fuming as they stomped out.

So, I was surprised when my extension rang and Alex asked me to come in. I quickly grabbed and scanned the resume of Lynne Fein. She had worked as Financial Controller for three different companies. She'd been employed at each for at least four years. She was married and lived in Santa Cruz.

I shook hands with Lynne as I entered Alex's office. She was short and trim with dark hair and almost black eyes, dressed in a gray suit and sensible flat shoes. She didn't seem nervous at all. Alex suggested I take the lead and she answered my questions well. She understood how a small company was run, was willing to handle the entire financial side of the business including bookkeeping, and was prepared to act as head of human resources and do all the administrative work in the company until we were large enough to hire staff for her. She was excited about joining a startup high tech company and had read several of my articles and recent articles about Turnkey in the trade press. She appeared to be a perfect candidate. Then Alex jumped in.

"You told Jack you left your last job because the company was headed in the wrong direction. What did you mean by that?"

Lynne looked uncomfortable. "The CEO decided to change some of the accounting procedures to increase margins."

"That sounds reasonable to me. Why would that cause you to leave? Don't you believe in showing a company in its most favorable light?"

"Well, it was a public company and there are rules for recognizing and reporting revenues and expenses called GAAP – Generally Accepted Accounting Principles."

"Yes," Alex continued, "But doesn't 'generally accepted' mean that there's some flexibility?"

"No. GAAP is the standard. If you don't follow GAAP you're likely breaking the law."

"Wait, wait, wait," Alex said smiling, moving in for the kill. "Not necessarily against the law. After all there's some flexibility in how you recognize revenue and expense. For example, if I have engineers working on Research and Development, I don't have to recognize any of the expense of their salaries or costs, right? I can capitalize the expense and then depreciate it over years if I want to. Even if the product never sells, this is a way for me to reduce expense to make my profit margins look better."

Lynne started to fidget in her chair. She looked like she wanted to be anywhere but in this interview. "You're right, you can capitalize R&D expense and then depreciate it later, but you need to do this carefully. You can't just do it to make the company look good. The R&D needs to be real R&D with a resultant product. You must start depreciating the costs when the product sells and if it's not going to, then you write it all down as soon as you know that."

"Of course it may take years for me to know a product won't sell," Alex said slimily. "Well, what if I want to recognize revenue faster. Say I have a sale to a company and they're going to pay over time or I offer them a money back guarantee and they pay annual maintenance. I can recognize all of this when I want right – all up front, spread across quarters, or at the end."

Lynne started to get angry. "GAAP has very specific rules about how to recognize revenues and which types of contracts require delayed recognition of revenues. You sound just like my old boss.   You'll look at the quarter's results, then adjust the rules so that you can make it look better than it was. You want to move revenue into the quarter and hide or capitalize expense so you can look good."

"So if I asked you to do the books my way, what would you say?"

Lynne stood up, grabbed her briefcase and purse and without offering her hand said, "I'd say goodbye, just like I did to my last boss. I'm sick of working for people who think they can cook their books to look good for their investors. I'm not going to be a part of it. "

With that, she turned and walked out the door.

Alex smiled and picked up his phone. "Sandy, please stop Ms. Fein and send her back in."

"Jack, I know you've had bad experiences with bad financial people. Many don't know what they're doing and some of them are crooks. While the company will have checks and balances, a smart finance person can find ways around them. You need to hire someone you can trust; someone with the highest ethical standards. And once you find this person, never let them go. Build some loyalty and treat them well and they'll take care of you and will keep you from doing stupid things that can get you into big trouble."

Sandy literally led Lynne back into Alex's office by the arm. Alex and I both stood up as she came in. She was clearly angry.

"Ms. Fein," Alex began, "I'd like to offer you a job if you can promise to keep the ethical standards you clearly feel so strongly about. From time to time I may make mistakes and Jack here might as well, and we both want to be confident that you'll speak up and let us know if we're being too aggressive or just plain stupid.

"Plus, if you ever see either of us doing something unethical, we expect you to raise it to both of us. We're a team here. We're not perfect, but we're going to try to be. We want you to help and if we're good and a bit lucky, it will pay off well for all of us.

"Sorry for the test. I just need to know my new head of Finance and Administration has the highest ethical standards."

Lynne took a seat, looking drained but relieved. "When do I start?" she asked.

Over the coming months, Alex and I would realize just how good Lynne was. To this day, I remain good friends with her and her husband Jim.

We were off to the races. We quickly closed deals with major computer vendors and several established and startup software companies. Turnkey was doing extremely well and our both our staff and the investors couldn't have been happier with the positioning of the company. I began to think about retiring to the Basque region of France to begin writing.

Unfortunately, Alex's management style was pretty rough. If you made a mistake, he was screaming in your face. If you were late on a project, he was sitting beside you, looking over your shoulder and demanding that you work evenings and weekends until you caught up. He confronted people when they went to the bathroom 'too many times'. My staff saw the advantages of Alex, but hated him. My management style was much more tolerant. I believed that my engineers were motivated because of the great work. If they were behind, I'd find additional staff to help them. If someone made a mistake, we did a post mortem and made sure we understood the error well enough not to repeat it. Alex and I had almost daily clashes over personnel management, and finally agreed that I would manage the people and he would manage me. If my group didn't deliver as expected, he could yell at me.

At the next IETF meeting, we were working on finalizing the next version of QS-II. It would enable the technology to expand to support the largest networks, perhaps even the Internet itself. As we were about to vote on adoption of a piece of the new specification, the Area Director walked in. This, in itself, is not unusual. ADs often drop by to monitor progress of the working groups. But this time it was different.

"Sorry to interrupt, but I have an announcement to make," the AD stated flatly. He walked to the front of the room and our Working Group Chair took a seat. "Have you seen this?" he asked holding up a recent copy of Network World. "This front page article talks about how QS-II will become the new standard for reliable networking. Jack, I know your company is pushing QS-II based products, but this is unacceptable. QS-II is not the standard for Quality of Service. IRES will be. If you get any more press touting QS-II as a standard, we'll have to shut this working group down."

We tried to reason with him. After all, none of us said that QS-II was a standard. The trade press came to its own conclusions and the market would decide which technologies were the best. But our protestations fell on deaf ears and he walked out, ignoring us. We debated this for quite a while. No one had ever heard of a decision to stop development of a new technology. Politics had arrived at the IETF. No more 'general consensus and working code'. It now appeared that loose and incomplete specifications with no associated working code or deployments could trump real technology.

Several of us were also part of the IRES Working Group. As we walked into the meeting, the Chair and the committee of professors who were leading the group glared at us. If looks could kill, the QS-II group would have been massacred.

I wasn't a fan of IRES. The protocol was being developed largely by academics who had no knowledge of real world networks. It was over-designed, and I didn't believe it was ever going to work or be widely deployed. If I didn't know better, and perhaps I didn't, I would have said that it was an exercise by Samcom, who now had people in key positions in the IETF, to stall the market and to prevent QS-II and Tightship from dominating the QoS space.

When I got back to the office I sat down with Alex and explained what had happened. No stranger to the machinations and politics of large companies, barely taking time to consider, Alex concluded that our future was limited unless we found a partner – read acquirer – who could help position us against such major forces. He called Adam Tennel, our lead investor, and after relaying the story, recommended that we start looking for acquisition candidates. The search for an exit was on.

6

1995 arrived. It was the year of the Oklahoma City terrorist bombing and the trial of O. J. Simpson which captured the attention of the American public to a degree not seen since Watergate over twenty years before. In fact, it was probably bigger than Watergate as everyone in the country speculated on OJ's guilt or innocence.

Netscape, the company that was giving browsers away for free and losing money hand over fist, went public, becoming the first in a series of multimillion dollar dot-com explosions – companies raising millions and making their founders rich without having any real revenue or profits. I didn't understand it. The rule had always been that you needed at least twenty million in sales and three to five years of profitability before you could go public. Why had this changed? How could a company go public with huge losses?

I was working at my desk when Sandy called and told me she had the Santa Cruz police on the line. I asked her to forward the call, remembering the last time the police had called me at work and dreading what I was about to hear.

"Sir, this is Officer Gonzalez of the Santa Cruz PD."

"Yes, officer, what can I do for you?" I replied, trying to maintain my calm.

"I know it's a long shot, but we picked up a vagrant today and he asked us to call you. His name is Carson Ingles. We found him sleeping in the entry way to a bank on Front Street. Bail is one hundred fifty dollars. You don't know him by chance, do you?"

"Officer Gonzalez, I'll be right down."

I'd never been to the Santa Cruz jail. I didn't even know that it was just off Ocean Street, not far from the courthouse, bordering the river. Residing in a large cinderblock building with hurricane fences, it could have been mistaken for an electrical transformer station. That's what I thought it was when I'd biked by on the path along the river in the past.

It took a while, but after an hour and a half of paperwork and waiting, Carson was sitting beside me in my car. He smelled of dirt, sweat and urine and had lost a lot of weight. His once dark, shiny long hair was graying and filled with dreadlocks. His beard had unrecognizable bits of food encrusted throughout. He kept his eyes downcast and said nothing as we drove to my house.

I showed him the shower and pulled out some clean clothes that might fit, then went to the kitchen and prepared a mushroom and cheese omelet with whole wheat toast while he cleaned himself up. He emerged looking a bit more together and smelling much better, then proceeded to wolf down the food and Odwalla orange juice I'd set out for him.

He appeared more relaxed, so I left him with a local barber and returned half an hour later as he was stepping out of the chair.

"You can stay the night at my place if you like," I offered. "What are your plans?"

Carson looked at himself in the mirror, then turned and said, "Plans? I didn't know if I would get through the night. I don't have plans. I've lived from moment to moment for as long as I can remember. Plans?!

"Once again you've come to my aid. I don't know what I did to deserve this kind of loyalty. Nancy is long gone, but you're still here. I now know the extent of my problem. I've lost it all: my houses, cars, artwork, all the money Steve gave me, my lover, my friends, and my career. I'm sure the IRS will be after me soon if they can find me. I think I could start over now that I'm clean, but who's going to hire a cokehead who doesn't even have a high school education? And the IRS will probably put me in jail for the rest of my life."

It's funny. I didn't even think about it. Perhaps I should have just sent him on his way, but my fundamental faith in the inherent goodness of people, or maybe the goodness of Carson, in spite of his mythological fatal flaw, came rushing out.

"Carson, look. I'll bring you into Turnkey. We could use some help in Quality Assurance. We'll take it slowly and I'm going to directly pay any bills you incur. I'm only going to give you enough to live on like Pam did a few years ago, but at an even smaller scale. You're going to have to prove to me that you can work consistently and stay off the drugs.

"I have a friend who is traveling for a few months, and his place is empty. Once you convince me you can handle it, you can house sit. I'll pick you up each morning and will drop you off each evening. It may be like prison, but if you can remain straight and start working a normal schedule, maybe we can get you back on track."

We drove back to my place and I left Carson watching television as I returned to work to tell Alex about our new hire. I'd been through this before. Was I just a masochist? Maybe I was just plain stupid.

I remembered how much work Pam, Nancy and I put into bringing him around. But you know, it almost worked. If it hadn't been for Steve giving him all that cash, I think it would have. I believed it would have. It was worth one more shot.

I expected serious resistance, but there was a bit of a crack in Alex's hard-boiled exterior as I explained who Carson was and how he ended up in his current state. I never asked why. Maybe he had some friends from Nam who ended up like Carson. Perhaps in spite of his tough exterior, he believed in lost causes. But aside from a raised eyebrow, Alex never said a thing against my bringing Carson on board.

The first few weeks were rough. Carson had a hard time focusing. He was forgetful and had to be reminded what he was supposed to do. He became "Jack's project" and the engineers did their best to humor me and to support Carson in his efforts.

After a month, Carson started to show some basic competence. His former genius was clearly gone, but he could now hold his own with our average engineers. He was great at working with customers and we started to let him handle support calls. He seemed to have a knack for understanding people's problems and letting them know that he did. I think this is actually a gift. Too often, when you call for help, it seems that support people either don't really care, or don't know enough to help you. I don't know how he did it, but several customers called and complimented us on Carson. I had hope once again.

7

One day in March, Georgette called and said she had news. She wanted me to meet her at the Livermore airport for a ride in her new plane – something I had avoided.

I met her at the Red Baron, the bar and restaurant shared by the golfers and local pilots. She led me onto the tarmac and pointed at an unusually shaped, almost blindingly white plane.

"It's called a LongEze!" she announced. "The canard makes it more maneuverable and much more stable."

The plane was unlike any I'd ever seen. It had a small wing (the canard) in the front and the propeller was in the back, behind the main wing which had two tail-like fins on it. I thought I'd seen them in the air and they looked like something from the future when flying, but I'd never seen one close up. It was smaller than my hang glider.

"Don't worry, I'm not taking you up in that. It's an experimental kit plane. I love to fly it, but it really isn't intended for two people. I've rented a little Cessna for a few hours."

Taking a seat inside, I was quite nervous as she taxied down the runway. Then we were airborne.

The sky was filled with scattered cumulus clouds, puffballs of cotton casting shadows on the ground four to five thousand feet below us. To the east, we could see the snow-capped peaks of the Sierra Nevada, almost beckoning us to cross the vast Central Valley of California to reach them. To the south, and west, green ridges with narrow canyons led to Mt. Hamilton and we could make out Lick observatory perched on top. We cruised over the twin peaks of Mt. Diablo which stands alone, separate from the coastal mountain ranges. Local Native American tribes believed that Mt. Diablo was a sacred place not to be touched by humans. Today it's a park and recreational area filled with hikers, mountain bikers, equestrians, and even hang glider pilots. We flew around the edges of Livermore Valley over ranches and farms for half an hour, just soaking up the view.

"We've filed our S-1," she declared as we turned back towards the airport.

The S-1 was the official notice that a company would be making a public offering of its stock. It was usually filed with the Security and Exchange Commission a few months before the actual public offer of a company's stock.

"When and how much?" I asked.

"We're looking at the beginning of July and the company is hoping to raise a hundred million, against about ten percent of the stock, but that's not firm yet. I still have more than a third of the company," she said modestly, almost incredulous.

"You're going to be a very rich woman. What are you going to do with all the money?"

"I don't have it yet and really haven't thought about it too much," she lied. "Want to fly this thing?"

My mind was trying to grasp the thought of Georgette being worth over three hundred million dollars. That wasn't well off, it was – I really don't know how to describe it. What would you do with that kind of money? Me, I probably give most of it away after ensuring I had enough to live and retire on. I took the controls of the plane, still shocked at the sheer magnitude of what Georgette had told me.

I don't fly power planes, but have a good understanding of the fundamentals. I doubt I could land one, but the flying was easy. It was fun soaring through the air, and I could almost enjoy the advantage of having an engine to go where you wanted without nature's constraints.

But after a few minutes at the controls, I asked, "How do you cut the engine?"

"Are you nuts?!!"

"Okay. I've done a dead stick landing, but – ah, screw it. Let me."

She idled the engine, disengaging the propeller and suddenly it was silent as the little plane glided downward. I directed us under a cumulus cloud and was rewarded with an upward bump and a nice rise indicated by the variometer. We were climbing at four hundred feet per minute. I waited a moment, then put the plane into a left bank and watched the altimeter climb.

"So this is what hang gliding is all about," Georgette observed, her excitement barely concealed.

"I've always believed that every power pilot should learn to fly without an engine. General Aviation is almost three times as dangerous as hang gliding – per hour of participation. Most of the accidents reported are pilot error and usually involve engine failures, inadvertent spins which pilots haven't been taught to recover from, or bad landings after running out of gas.

"If people realized you don't need an engine and understood

thermals, ridge lift, and rotors, the sky would be a much safer place."

As we climbed silently towards the clouds, I passed the controls to Georgette so that she could experience soaring at its best.

"Georgette, I'm glad all these years of hard work are going to pay off for you."

"Jack, you know, they already have. I've really enjoyed building the company to this point. We've built some great products, and I have the lifestyle I've always wanted. Now maybe I'll have time for other things too."

I didn't think to ask what the 'other things' were, I just nodded and said, "I may be joining you in a financial exit. We've decided that to really get the technology in a position to compete with the big players, we need to find a partner. Alex has begun shopping the company. With luck, we'll be selling it in a few months."

After a few thousand feet of altitude gain, a sailplane decided to join us in the thermal. While I'm used to flying almost wing to wing with other gliders and even sailplanes sharing thermals, power pilots are taught to keep their distance from other aircraft. A midair collision is almost always fatal for all involved.

The sailplane was climbing much faster than we were and Georgette was near panic at the thought of a midair. She started the engine and we left the magic world of silent rising air.

8

It didn't take long. Alex was good. He lined up two potential partners who were interested in acquiring us. One was TLM, a large, established software company that was making an all cash offer. They had products for large corporations and wanted our software to ensure quality for business networks. The example they gave was a large retail chain. These customers needed to run credit authorizations during the day at the highest priority. At night, they needed to download price files to each location and upload the transactions for the day. They needed to conduct video conferences among buyers and had to distribute large catalogs of their products. Their biggest problem was that with the price file distributions, the transaction uploads, and the system backups, they, too, were running out of night – the only time they could send this information. Remembering the project Carson and I did with the May Company, we understood the problem. But now, we had better technology to solve it. We showed them how our software could multicast the price files: do a single transmission and have it arrive at all locations at the same time.

The other acquirer was Core Systems, a small public company that seemed to be growing really fast. Several magazines had named them the fastest growing software company in the world during the previous year. Core made an all-stock offer that was a bit larger than TLM's cash offer, at least at the current stock price. They offered products that complemented Microsoft's Windows. Since Microsoft was introducing new networking software, they wanted our technology to keep them a step ahead of Microsoft.

We had a run rate of about three million dollars a year (we had done two hundred fifty thousand dollars in sales for each of the last few months) and Core's offer was just over eight million in stock, plus additional options and nice guaranteed employment agreements for all the employees. Personally, both Alex and I preferred the TLM offer. It was all cash and they seemed like a much more stable company.

Alex brilliantly played one off against the other to increase the price, and after a week of negotiations, we were at ten million dollars. I owned nearly forty percent of the company, so it was going to work out well for me. Alex had ten percent. He was going to do quite well for a few months' work. Given what he'd accomplished in such a short time, I thought he deserved all of it. Then TLM made a big mistake. Their next offer was not only a bit larger than Core's, they offered Alex and me an additional one hundred thousand dollars each if we'd sway the Board to go with TLM. Of course we couldn't tell the investors or employees about the additional monies.

It was funny. When the official final offer came in on the fax machine after their verbal proposal over the phone, Alex and I only conferred for a minute. In spite of the differences in our management style, we had the same feelings about ethics. I looked at him and after the months of battles over how people were treated and my issues with his 'take no prisoners' style of business, there was this immediate connection. It was as if we knew each other in a past life. We didn't even have to discuss it. Each of us was confident that the other saw the RIGHT thing to do. From that moment forward, we shared mutual admiration.

We agreed that the Board would decide between the two written offers that they saw and that each of us would recuse ourselves from the ultimate decision.

Because of the meteoric rise in Core Systems' stock over the previous year, the Board, actually the Venture Capitalist investors, picked the all-stock deal. They could add the stock to their portfolio and its continued growth would increase the value of their investment fund. With cash, they might have to repay their investors. It looked like we were going to be a part of Core Systems.

There was only one problem. When I brought up the remuneration that Alex and I would receive, Alan Tennel reminded us of the liquidation clause that had been added to the company's bylaws when we signed the Venture Capital deal.

I read the bylaws and looked at the liquidation clause. The intent was that if the company went out of business and the investors needed to liquidate, they would get their investment back before the shareholders were paid. From Alan's point of view, sale of the company represented a liquidation. Therefore, he and the other VCs would take their investment back and then would divide up the remainder among the shareholders, including the VCs themselves. I called this a double dip. They got their money back, then were paid again based on their thirty percent of the company. So, instead of receiving thirty percent of the purchase price, they'd get almost fifty percent. They don't call them Vulture Capitalists for nothing! I was livid.

I sat down with Alex and told him I wasn't prepared to go through with the deal on these terms. He tried to calm me, but I knew that I had enough stock to block the sale of the company. Alex argued that if we didn't have a major partner, we'd be out of business within six months, but still I didn't budge. He called Alan to give him the bad news. Jack was walking from the deal.

Surprisingly, Alan caved. I suspect that Alex did a great job of convincing him that we'd be out of business if this deal fell through. Alan and the investors agreed to not invoke the liquidation clause. After all, it was there in case of business failure, not a successful acquisition. I swore that I'd warn everyone I knew who was looking at Venture Capital to eliminate this type of clause from any agreements.

9

In addition to the SEC approval that required sixty days because Core was a public company, it took some time to work out a transition plan. My team really wanted to continue working in Santa Cruz while Core wanted us to work at their headquarters in San Jose. None of us wanted to do the commute over Highway 17 each day.

I spent a lot of time in meetings with Core's Vice President of Engineering, Richard Dugan. Richard was of Irish descent, dark hair and eyes, balding a bit early for someone in his late thirties. He was obviously an athlete, with the lithe, strong body of someone who did a lot of team sports, baseball, perhaps, or basketball. As I got to know him, I found out it was both.

He was a bit younger than I, and very aggressive. His memory was prodigious. He demanded perfection from his employees and lost his temper easily if someone failed to produce. However, if someone did a great job, he or she got instant recognition in the weekly company meeting. Fortunately, he was consistent, so in spite of angry outbursts, everyone respected him. They always knew where they stood, and if they screwed up, they expected a reaming. But then they worked twice as hard to make up for it and to regain Richard's respect.

Like me, Richard was a technological visionary. Although he had a healthy ego, he respected those that could keep up with him. He was completely enthralled with the potential of our technology and how Core could become one of the most influential companies in networking by employing it in their products and by positioning with companies like Tightship and NTT to challenge the burgeoning dominance of the industry by Microsoft and Samcom. He felt our products could keep Core a step ahead of both, and he was confident that a nimble mid-sized company could move more quickly than the behemoths.

After some heavy negotiation, Richard finally agreed to leave the Turnkey engineering team in Santa Cruz. However, to get this concession, I had to promise to spend two days a week at their offices in San Jose, and the entire team was required to show up on Fridays for the company-wide lunch which was catered each week. The non-engineering people, including Alex, Dirk and Lynne would have to work in the San Jose office. I argued that we needed Lynne to handle our administrative and finance work, but this just got us one day a week of her time (and saved her one day a week of commuting).

While it was an all-stock deal, Core wanted to buy out option and shareholders who didn't have an ongoing stake in the company. So, as part of the deal, Stan would get cash. His twenty percent of the company was diluted to six percent by the Venture Capital and additional options issued to Alex, Dirk and other employees, so he was only going to receive sixty thousand dollars.

Because Dirk was a basically a salesman, Core also decided that they wanted to buy him out as well. His one percent of the company would net him a hundred thousand dollars – like Alex, this was not bad for a few months' work. Of course, he did find TLM, and playing the two companies off against each other netted us another two million dollars, so it seemed fair. He would take a position in the Core sales group, helping train them and continuing sales, but everyone assumed that he would leave after a few months. He loved working for startups.

Alex would become Vice President of Marketing and the deal required him to sign a one-year employment and non-compete agreement (mine was two years). Lynne was moving into the finance department.

My responsibilities were to continue managing our team, to take on one of Richard's groups that would be integrating our technology into theirs, and to assist sales and marketing in understanding, positioning, and selling the new products. It was going to be fun to do all the things I did before without having to worry about making payroll for my team or to have to come up with the money to pay the rest of the bills.

We decided that before the acquisition was complete, we needed to bring Carson up to full salary. For several months, we'd been giving him barely enough to live on, trying to ensure he didn't slip back into his destructive habit. I brought him into my office to give him the news.

"Carson, you really seem to have gotten it back together," I began. "I've been getting excellent reports from our customers about the level of service you've been providing, and the engineers seem to think you have a knack for identifying the problems and helping chase them down."

"Jack, I really owe you. I feel like my brain is coming back. I was in pretty much of a haze when I first started here. My memory was bad and I just couldn't seem to concentrate. Now it's back. It's amazing how resilient the human body and brain can be."

"I hope that doesn't mean you think you could go on another binge and still recover," I said a little hastily, regretting I brought this up at all.

Carson just smiled. "Jack, this was a really close call. Not only did I lose everything and everyone important to me, I almost lost my brain as well. I've now been straight longer than I've ever been since I first tried cocaine. While I can't say it's not a struggle, every day it gets a little easier and at least intellectually, I know I'm off the stuff for good."

"Carson, you know that I've been paying you virtually nothing for fear that if you had money you'd dive back in. You also know that we're being acquired."

"Yes. But in the beginning, you were paying me far more than I was worth. I think it's averaged out, and I hope that I'm finally contributing here."

"Of course you are. In fact, the reason I wanted to talk to you was to tell you that Alex and I have decided to bring you up to full salary. So, you can count on a much larger paycheck from us, and after Core acquires us, you'll be getting a decent salary from them. What do you think?"

"Jack, it constantly amazes me how generous you are. But this does get me thinking. Once I have a decent salary under my belt, I should update my resume and look at leaving the nest you've created for me here. I need to get a real life again. That's not to say I can't do that here, but I really need to be able to do things on my own again. That will actually be the real test as to whether I'm well."

I found it interesting that Carson thought of his cocaine problem as an illness. It was probably a good thing. I just hoped he never got to the point that he thought he was cured. Carson left and although I hate to admit it, I was pretty proud of myself. Maybe I had made a difference in the world.

Contracts were signed, due diligence was completed, and the sixty day clock to closing had started. I called Georgette and told her that I, too, would be a millionaire shortly, though not to the degree that she was. We agreed that after you had enough to retire and live on the rest of your life, it didn't really matter what the exact amount was.

Seeing that there was a great swell running, I decided to take off work a bit early. My surfing buddy Mark decided to join me, and because it was a beautiful day, his wife and kids decided to drive with us up to Four Mile beach, named because it is four miles north of Santa Cruz.

You park on the side of Highway One, then walk down a trail past a saltwater lagoon alive with ducks, cormorants, mud hens, egrets, and herons. A quarter of a mile later you arrive at a gorgeous beach. The north side is protected by cliffs that block the onshore winds. On this particular day, the tide was very low, so even before Mark and I got into our wetsuits, Janet and the kids were exploring the tide pools.

The surf was probably the best I'd ever seen at Four Mile. Six to eight foot westerly swells were breaking outside the point. The rides were long and fast with a nice barrel on the inside. Mark and I competed with fifteen other surfers for waves, but we each got more than our share. The winds were light, the air was warm, the waves were perfect. It was good to be alive.

I took a wave and as I entered the barrel on the inside section, I paused to avoid a surfer paddling out. The wave crushed me, slamming me against the shallow shelf below, holding me under for about thirty seconds. No big deal.

When I surfaced, my board was gone. This was a surprise. I pulled on my surf leash, a strong plastic 'rope' that connected my left foot to the board, and discovered that it wasn't slack. I pulled on it, but my board didn't surface. I pulled harder. Still nothing.

Just then, a wave approached me from behind. My board, which had been stuck under part of the reef responded to the pull of the approaching swell and shot directly at me, hitting me in the face. The tail struck my left eye while the fin hit me just below my mouth.

I didn't feel any pain, but I couldn't see out of my left eye. I've been injured surfing more times than I'll ever admit to Ronn, and painless injuries while surfing are usually the worst. If you can feel the pain, it's usually just a bruise. If you can't, you probably need medical attention. Add in being blind in one eye and a lot of blood on my hands and in the water and this didn't look too good.

I caught a wave in on my stomach and yelled for Janet. She approached and started screaming for Mark. I don't know how he heard her, but he came in.

"I think I lost my eye," I lamented.

I had no idea what I looked like, but Mark approached me clinically. He put his thumb into my left eye socket and lifted my eyelid. I saw light from the left side.

"No," he replied. "You've severed your eyelid and it's fallen over your eye so you can't see. I don't know how much damage there is. Let's get you to a doctor."

"But you're a doctor," I protested.

"Come on. I'm afraid you're going to go into shock."

Janet grabbed my board, called the kids, and we all made the walk back to the car. I held a towel against my face and Mark kept talking to me to ensure I wasn't going into shock.

He drove us to Doc-in-the Box which was the closest medical facility, but after making an assessment of the doctors on duty, he called a plastic surgeon friend and asked him to meet us at Dominican Hospital.

We arrived at Dominican Emergency and they rushed me in. No wait. I guess having a doctor friend had advantages. Nurses started cleaning me up, irrigating the wounds trying to clean out the sand and debris. Sometime later, Frank Lampray introduced himself. Frank was already dressed in surgical scrubs. He looked to be about my age and had a ready smile.

He took a look at my face and told me it would take a while but that they had plenty of anesthetic so other than a few quick sticks of the needles, I wouldn't feel a thing.

"Frank, it's good to meet you," I said extending my hand. "Mark says you're the best."

Frank smiled and shook my hand, surprised, I think, by my formality.

"There is one thing, though," I continued.

"What's that?" he asked.

"Well, I'm allergic to epinephrine. Not allergic exactly, but when I have local anesthetics with epinephrine, I get really sick. I get jittery and nauseous, and sometimes vomit. I really hate nausea. I much prefer pain. Can you use a local without epinephrine?"

"Jack, epinephrine really does two things. It reduces the bleeding and it extends the duration of the anesthetic. I guess I can deal with the extra blood, but this is going to take a while and the anesthetic will wear off before we're done. You'll have to let me know when it starts to hurt and we'll shoot you up again."

Frank was fascinated with technology and since much of the equipment in the operating room was based on fiber optics, we had a nice discussion about fiber optic networks and my work in helping Telefonica deploy a high speed fiber network in Madrid. We discussed how deployment of fiber around our country might ultimately help doctors work together remotely on difficult surgeries.

Three hours and over a hundred very fine stitches later, I was on my way to Mark's house. He had taken Janet and the kids home earlier.

I didn't feel the needles when they injected the anesthetic and didn't ask for more when it wore off.

"You're going to be fine," Mark said compassionately. "But it's going to hurt like hell tomorrow and I expect you'll have double vision once the swelling goes down.

"I spoke with Frank, the plastic surgeon. He reattached your eyelid. He thinks there's some damage to the eye, but don't panic if you can't see well for a while. I have an ophthalmologist ready to see you day after tomorrow. He wants the swelling to go down a bit. You're supposed to keep the eye patch on for thirty-six hours. The bad news is that slice on your chin. Apparently, you severed all the nerves. The fin went entirely through to your teeth. Frank saw one nerve filament and he thinks he saved it, so you may eventually get some feeling there. Until then, you'll probably be dribbling food and drink down the front of yourself. I'm not sure we're going to have you to dinner anytime soon."

I tried to smile, but my lips didn't work.

" Are you in pain? That was a pretty grotesque grimace," he said.

"No, it was just your bad joke," I tried to say, but I don't know if he understood me.

"You're staying with us tonight. I want to keep an eye (sorry about that) on you and help you through tomorrow. We have plenty of pain medication."

11

With the ice, ibuprofen, and pain medication, the swelling decreased quite a bit by the next day. I could see out of my left eye, but everything was doubled. It made me nauseous. I hate nausea. Give me pain any day, but not nausea. I hate vomiting. I also worried that I'd never see straight again. It was terrifying not to be able to see. I couldn't walk around without closing one eye, but Mark counseled me to try to use both after I removed the eye patch. He told me stories about experiments where people were given glasses that made them see things upside down. Within a day, their brains corrected for the glasses and they could see the world normally. Of course when they removed the glasses, the brain required a day to get back to normal.

It actually took two more days of double vision and nausea before my vision began to get better. The transition was strange. I'd be able to see normally if I looked at something sideways, but not if I looked straight on. When I went into a movie theater I'd get flashes of light if I moved my eyes suddenly. I also now had floaters, what looked like small translucent objects in my field of vision. I told all of this to the ophthalmologist, and after he completed his exam (with dilation), he informed me I had torn the sphincter muscle in the pupil and that it wouldn't contract normally in bright light. He strongly recommended I wear hundred percent ultraviolet protection sunglasses. He also wanted me back in three weeks for a follow up to make sure my vision wasn't deteriorating as result of the trauma.

I returned to work after three days and Alex told me he'd seen worse. I didn't probe for details, because I'm sure that in Vietnam, he saw things I certainly didn't want to know about.

Georgette showed up at eleven thirty to take me to lunch.

"Aren't you a pretty sight?!" she said, carefully kissing my right cheek.

It was true. While the swelling of my left eye was almost gone, the area from my hairline to my nose and from my eyebrow to the bottom of my cheek was now green, blue, and black. The stitches above my eye were more than three inches long as were those that led from my lip to below my chin. I couldn't speak perfectly either and certainly couldn't whistle. I used to whistle a lot, even classical pieces. I wondered if I'd get that back.

Georgette drove me to a restaurant at the base of the wharf in Santa Cruz. We sat outside on the deck which extended onto the beach. Volleyball players were playing aggressive games just below us and we both marveled at their remarkable athleticism. The games were two against two on the beach. A ball could go anywhere in a standard sized court. If you've ever tried to run or jump in soft sand, you know how hard it is to move quickly. These men and women moved like lightning and seemed to have no fear of the fast moving ball or of diving into the sand for a save. We saw volleys that went back and forth as many as twenty times before a point was made.

The ocean was glassy and there were no waves. At least I wasn't missing anything. The sound of sea lions barking echoed off the bottom of the wharf where a dozen or more took up residence for most of the year. I had swum around the wharf during a triathlon and saw these huge creatures, fat and slow, jump vertically six feet or more to stretch out on horizontal support beams for the wharf. At night, you could hear their barks for miles.

We ordered iced teas and sat back to enjoy the warmth of the sun and the coolness of the light ocean breeze.

"I take it you haven't told Ronn about this, have you?" Georgette began.

"No, I really haven't felt like talking to anyone. Sorry I haven't called."

"It's okay. Mark let me know what happened. But I'm sure Ronn is going to get a kick out of this. What was it you said? Something about the number of stitches determining which sport is the most dangerous? I guess you lose now. How do you feel about surfing?"

"I'm just upset that I have to stay out of the water for two weeks. I've had surfing injuries before. In college, I had a fin go through my leg, and in another accident, I crushed a disc in my back during a big south swell in southern California. That one had me laid up for almost six months, and it was another six months of yoga before I could touch my toes again. I can't wait to get back in the water. And as far as Ronn is concerned, I suspect the numbers will be close, even with over a hundred new stitches in me. He's had at least ten injuries with more than ten stitches each."

"Well, you certainly seem okay even as bad as you look. As

competitive as always, I see. So how's it feel to almost be a millionaire?"

"While it will be nice not to have to worry about my financial future, I'm really hoping Core can help us change the world with this technology. We can make the Internet predictable. We can move telephony, movies, television, and help businesses run more efficiently. We can get information to places it's never been, and knowledge is power! This technology can really make a difference, but we need a big enough player to help position us against the forces trying to stall the market. It's not about the money for me – well not completely."

"Yeah, I feel the same way. I'm really looking forward to the company having enough money for us to get our products out to the average person. I think we can help make the Internet a part of everyone's life. And as you said, knowledge is power and the Internet has most of the knowledge in the world ready for anyone to take and learn."

We finished lunch and Georgette drove me back to the office. As I got out of the car, she seized my hand and said, "Jack, you know I love you, don't you?"

"I love you too, Georgette," I replied, thinking that Georgette was my best friend in the world.

12

OptiRoute did go public in July of 1995. The stock opened at forty and closed at seventy dollars a share. While it dipped a bit over the next few months, it stabilized at sixty, fifty percent higher than the IPO. Georgette was fifty percent richer than she thought she'd be.

It's important to know how IPOs work for founders. Let's take a simple example. Your company issues a million shares of stock and stock options to its founders. You have thirty percent or three hundred thousand shares. Let's say the company wants to raise one hundred million dollars during the IPO. The monies will be used for expansion of the company, marketing, and as cash reserves against future losses during the expansion.

Investment bankers help set a price that is palatable to large investors. Their primary job is to get agreements from major pension funds, banks and 'significant' private investors to purchase most of the shares in the IPO. The lion's share of any public offering is actually at the set price before the stock is officially listed on a public exchange.

So, to raise a hundred million dollars at an initial offering price of forty dollars a share, you need to provide two and a half million shares of stock. To get this number and to reduce your dilution in the company's ownership, the stock is split before the new shares are issued. In this case, let's assume there's a twenty to one split. You and the other founders now have twenty million shares and you personally now have six million shares. Another two and a half million shares are issued for the IPO. Thus, at IPO, you have six million times forty dollars a share or two hundred forty million dollars in stock. The stock goes up to sixty and you now have three hundred sixty million dollars. Of course you can't touch it. The only shares actually sold on the market are the shares issued for the IPO, including special shares, typically owned by the investors (venture capitalists) that are registered to be traded in the IPO. Your shares are not registered and can't be traded. These unregistered shares are called 144 stock after section 144 of the SEC codes. Depending on your position in the company, you must hold the stock for between twelve and twenty four months before you can trade it. Even then, if you own more than one percent of the company, the amount you can trade in any give quarter is severely restricted so that you can't adversely affect the public's shares by selling a large quantity.

Thus, Georgette's stock was tied up and in spite of the fact that she was worth three hundred sixty million dollars on paper, she couldn't touch a cent!

With our sale of Turnkey to Core Systems, a public company, my stock fell into the same category: 144 stock. In addition, as part of the agreement, I agreed that I would not trade any shares, through any mechanism, for six months after the sale completed. Fortunately, I didn't own one percent of the acquiring company, so when I could trade my shares, I could trade them all if I wanted.

Because this happens all the time and people who sell their companies or go public want some liquidity, there are a number of mechanisms to get around the rules. First, since we can't sell, we should have some protection against a sudden price fall. This can sometimes be done by purchasing special PUT or CALL options against the stock. If the stock falls, you make up the loss in the options. Of course there is an out-of-pocket cost associated with purchasing these options, usually about ten percent.

There are also brokers who will lend you money against your restricted shares. Unfortunately, if the price of your shares falls below what is lent to you, you could end up in big trouble. I decided to pass on both choices. Although my stock was worth more than three million, I didn't have the three hundred thousand dollars to purchase the protection options. I probably should have purchased as many as I could afford.

Georgette, while cautious, decided to borrow against her shares. Unlike me, who had no control over what happened to the acquiring company or how they performed, Georgette was still Chief Technical Officer of OptiRoute and did have a lot of control and visibility into her company's future. Plus, if she wanted a million dollars, it was only a fraction of a percent of her holdings. The stock could drop precipitously and she could still cover it if necessary.

I, on the other hand, was at the mercy of the acquiring company. Although I was given a Director's position, reporting directly to the Vice President of Engineering (who I respected), I had no control over the direction of the company, its products, or its future success. If the stock dropped, I just lost the money.

Worse, with my two year iron-clad non-compete and employment agreement, I would be an indentured servant for two years: unable to leave or work anywhere else, even if the stock became worthless.

Of course that wasn't going to happen. After all, our investors knew what they were doing and they, too, did an all-stock deal, so the only way they made any money was if the Core Systems did well. They had much more experience in this type of transaction, so I trusted them. At least I looked good on paper. I ended up with about three million dollars' worth of stock. Even better, when Core Systems announced our acquisition, their stock went from fourteen to thirty four. Within a month of the acquisition, my stock was worth nearly seven million dollars! Not bad for a military brat whose father qualified for welfare (but didn't take it) in most states we lived in.

Better yet, I found Core's large account salespeople ready to learn and anxious to sell our products. I held weekly classes on the technology and how to position it, and joined the sales folks in customer calls. By the end of the second month, they had closed several large accounts, and Core's Microsoft and Samcom account representatives had opened the doors to get the two companies to look at our technology.

One morning, Ed Smith, the CEO of Core Systems walked into my office.

"Grab your best presentation and let's go!"

"Where are we going?" I asked completely unprepared.

"Samcom! Kaz Sharpe, their CTO called and wants a detailed presentation on QS-II and how we're positioning it in our products."

I got really excited. Our strategy of getting acquired was finally going to pay off. If Samcom adopted our technologies, the entire Internet would change and our dreams of perfect-quality voice, video and data transmissions would finally be realized. On the ride over, I couldn't stop talking about exactly how our products could be integrated with Samcom's.

Once there, Kaz Sharpe, one of the best known technologists in the Silicon Valley, greeted me warmly.

"Jack, I've heard a lot about you and your technology. Show me what you've got."

I went through my standard presentation of the core technology and its history, then talked about the deployments in

DARPA and how successful we'd been in providing perfect quality of service for voice, video, video conferencing, distance learning and war games, all with tens of thousands of users. I then showed him how our current products worked with Core's systems and threw out some ideas about how they could be easily integrated into Samcom's products."

At the end of the meeting, Kaz shook my hand and slapped me on the back amicably.

"This is truly amazing. I guarantee we'll be working together."

I almost missed his wink at Ed before we left, but didn't think anything of it at the time.

I rambled on about possibilities as Ed and I drove back to Core believing more than ever that our technology was going to change the world. Ed reminded me that this meeting was confidential and that I wasn't to disclose the conversation with anyone at Core. Somewhat familiar with SEC rules, I knew that it would take months for any sort of deal between Core and Samcom to be announced, and that I probably wouldn't know anything more until it was finalized, so I went back to work enhancing our products and positioning them for hooks into Samcom's products.

Just before the end of the year, Carson came into my office. He was dressed in casual but expensive clothing.

"Jack, I have news."

Having received a call from a prospective employer a week before, I knew what to expect. I had given Carson an extremely good recommendation, but also spoke honestly about his drug problem and his history. Normally, California employers are told to only state that the person was employed and to give no information other than the dates of employment. There have been countless lawsuits against employers who cost people positions by saying or implying negative things. Unfortunately, I rarely followed these guidelines, or at least, I walked a very fine line. If I had a bad experience with an employee (fortunately this had only happened a few times in my career), even though I wouldn't say anything specific that could be used in court later, I found a way to discourage the potential employer if I thought the fit was bad. I did this by using back-handed compliments like 'He worked incredible hours to resolve the major design flaws in his code.'

For Carson, though, I wanted him to have the best chance of success, but I also didn't want an employer to bet a significant part of his budget on an employee who might flake out. In this case, Carson was being considered for a position as the head of a new Customer Support group for a startup company. This could be a great opportunity for him.

"So," Carson began, almost unable to keep the self-satisfied grin off his face. "With the nice salary you've given me over the last few months, I've renewed my subscription to Ridge Winery. Here's the first bottle."

"Carson, that's great. Congratulations – I think."

Carson's smile grew wider and he broke out into laughter. "Of course, that's not all. Cenitz Systems has offered me a job as head of their Customer Support department, and decent stock options. I start next week. He opened the bottle and poured two glasses. We toasted his success and I remembered the days when we'd share a bottle of a new Ridge release in his office. It always seemed to precede something really good. Perhaps the old Carson was really back.

"I heard about the recommendation you gave me, Jack. Don't worry, I'll do a great job and will validate your confidence in me."

Carson did just that. I was proud of him, which sounds a bit patronizing, but that's what I felt. To some degree he was like an eagle with a broken wing that I had nursed back to health. As corny as it sounds, after months of rehabilitation, he was free to soar again.

13

In early 1996, Ed Smith and Richard had a major falling out. It started when DARPA came back to us and asked to expand their license to our technology so that they could deploy several thousand additional systems. Ed told the salespeople that Core did not work on government contracts and to refuse the deal.

From what I heard, Richard threw a tantrum. However, Ed was apparently used to this and just nodded nicely as Richard presented his arguments after calling Ed a number of unrepeatable names. Nonetheless, Core did tell DARPA to go elsewhere. Of course there was no place to go.

I was livid. My reputation was built on supporting customers and when one walked in the door with a high six-figure check just to expand their license, with no additional work involved, I certainly wouldn't walk away. I was beginning to see the downside of my iron-clad employment agreement.

A few weeks later at the weekly company lunch, Ed did his usual summary of the company's progress from the previous week, recognized key contributors, and asked each of the department heads for a status. He then told everyone he had an announcement to make.

"I've decided to terminate our work with Internet products. Our internet software will no longer be sold or included in our products, and we're going to stop working on the Turnkey technology. I've concluded that there is no money in the Internet and we need to focus our energies elsewhere - on enterprise connectivity. Large Enterprises have money to spend on our networking software products."

Most of us were shocked. Many of us objected and people pointed out that Netscape had recently gone public so there must be money there.

"No," he replied. "Netscape is a big part of my decision. They haven't made a dime and won't for years. The Internet is a red herring. I'll say it again. There is no money in the Internet and we're not going to pursue this business any further!"

I think that most of the employees thought he was kidding or just on a rampage that would burn itself out in a day or two. I knew he wasn't and so did Richard. I went back to my office and was not surprised to see Richard at my door half an hour later. He walked in and closed the door.

"Jack, I'm really sorry. I pushed for the acquisition of your company because I believed in the technology and was sure we could take it forward. Selfishly, I also was convinced that as Microsoft and Samcom put pressure on our products, yours would keep us ahead of them and might even get them worried a bit or at least get them to pay attention to us. Now, all I can do is apologize.

"I've submitted my resignation to Ed. I'm sure he thinks it's just one of my temper tantrums, but it isn't. I've had enough. Ed didn't even consult with me before making his decision. Before lunch, he did send me an email telling me to redirect your team into our system level products. You'll be heading up all of our system software development. Your team will get folded in there. I suspect Ed will want you all in San Jose. I told him you should take my place, but after screwing you over your technology, he doesn't believe you'll do the right thing and doesn't want to trust all of the company's engineering efforts to you.

"I don't think I've ever felt so bad about anything. I've taken your company, forced you into a two-year employment agreement, killed your technology and now I'm walking away. You must think I'm a real asshole."

I really didn't know what to say and just waited for the rest.

"I've been kicking around the idea of starting my own company for years. When you're done with all this, if you want to do something completely different, let's talk. I think we'd be a great team."

He stood up and extended his hand. Stunned speechless, I reached out mine. He grabbed my hand with both of his. I saw tears in his eyes as he turned and left. No notice. He just walked out, never to be seen again at Core Systems. We kept in touch via email and I met him for lunch from time to time. He raised venture money for his new company, but it never really took off.

I was in prison for another year, and my life's work was wasting away.

14

Word of Richard's departure hit the Core System's stock hard. From a high of thirty-four, it dropped below ten within two weeks. Then, the unthinkable happened. In late February, Core Systems announced its financial results for the fourth quarter and showed a loss, the first in five years. This from the fastest growing software company in the world. This from the company that said Netscape wasn't viable because they weren't profitable. The stock dropped below five. Still, I couldn't trade. I also found out that when I could trade, I would be subject to 'blackout' periods from the end of every quarter until a few days after the company announced earnings, usually six to eight weeks after the end of a quarter. The theory is that key people in a company may have inside knowledge and could be exposed (and expose the company) to inside trading accusations. That meant that my windows to trade were only four to six weeks every quarter.

At that week's Friday lunch, Ed told the company that the loss didn't matter.

"We lost five million dollars last quarter," he explained. "We still have eighty million dollars in cash, so don't worry, the future of the company is assured. My new enterprise strategy will take some time to get going, but obviously, even at this loss rate, while it could take a while, it certainly won't take four years for us to be profitable."

I met with Ed that day to discuss his 'enterprise strategy'. I went through the long list of major enterprises I had worked with and what their networking requirements were. I also gave him my IBM resume and told him that IBM 'owned' most of the enterprises and that Microsoft was beginning to make inroads.

"I only need ten percent of the market to get this company really growing," Ed proclaimed.

"Ed, you can't get ten percent of the market. Enterprises are going to stay with IBM and Microsoft. Even if you gave your software away for free, they wouldn't take it. It costs them too much to replace existing software for thousands of employees, and it doesn't matter if you have better functionality. As they say, if it works, don't fix it, and no enterprise is going to take a risk and incur major expense for a few 'nice-to-have' features. "

"Jack, I know you're wrong and I'm sorry you feel this way. It just shows me you're not on board with our mission."

"In that case, Ed, how about letting me and my team leave with the technology we brought in? It can really make a difference in the world and you've decided not to use it. It's just sitting on the shelf. I can give you all my stock back in exchange for the technology."

"Jack, you know we have a critical release of the systems components due out at the end of second quarter. I need you to get that done. When it's ready to ship, let's sit down and see if we can work out a deal for your technology."

I agreed and we tabled the discussion while I got my team fired up to try to accelerate the release. Of course Ed insisted they all work in the San Jose office, so we closed our Santa Cruz office and everyone did the nasty commute over Highway 17.

Just before the one-year anniversary of our acquisition, Ed announced that the company would have to do a reduction in force, colloquially known as a RIF, of fifteen percent. This meant that we had to lay off fifteen percent of our staff. In spite of the fact that my teams were on schedule to hit their release dates, were, in fact, going to beat most of them, I got the wonderful honor of laying off several people, including two from my Turnkey staff. It was then that I made the decision to start another company.

CHAPTER 7

"And you know that when the truth is told that you can get what you want or you can just get old. You're going to kick off before you even get half way through..."
- Billy Joel, Vienna

1

I asked Dan to meet me for lunch. I hadn't spoken with him since the acquisition. I guess I'd just been too busy. For old times' sake, we met at L'Auberge du Soleil. Richard greeted us warmly and remembered me even though I hadn't been there in years.

After seating us, Richard said, "I have just returned from a sejour in the Pays Basque and have learned some new recipes. As an appetizer, I strongly recommend Moules a la Basquaise. These are mussels sautéed in a light but spicy white sauce. For your main course, I recommend Merlu a la Plancha, a filet of haket grilled in the Basque style. I think you will both enjoy this."

Both of us agreed to accept his recommendation and in keeping with the theme I asked for a citron presse, a squeezed lemon with water. Dan ordered iced tea.

"So Jack, how's it feel to have sold out for money?" Dan asked jokingly.

"Actually, it's worse than you'd think. My stock, which was worth several million dollars, is only worth a few hundred thousand after the precipitous stock drop. Now, the CEO has killed off our technology and it's sitting on a shelf while the market goes in another direction, just like the big guys want. And worse, I've got to lay off some very talented members of my team. I didn't sell out for the money. The real objective was to find a partner who could help us position the technology effectively against Microsoft and Samcom. Now that's gone too and I've got to start breaking up my team. I'm pissed."

"You know," Dan said, "I have some new projects waiting in the wings, I could probably take a few people off your hands, give them a place to land."

"Dan, that's a nice thought, but I want to keep them. Core's CEO has said that we can take the technology out after I get the current product set shipped. I'm thinking I want to bootstrap a new company and I was wondering if you could help by taking three or four people and running them as subcontractors. I could keep the rates low so you can maintain your margins."

Just then Richard arrived with a huge pot of mussels. There must have been at least a hundred. He also placed two large bowls beside us for the shells, and brought us towels.

Dan smiled, licked his lips and said, "I don't think I've seen so many mussels in one place. It certainly smells great!"

Richard returned with a basket filled with sliced baguettes. "Bon appetit, gentlemen! Don't forget the sauce at the bottom of the pot."

This was going to be a luxurious but lengthy lunch. Richard was right. The sauce was amazing, light but piquant at the same time. Dan and I quickly filled our shell bowls and Richard was right there with two more bowls as he removed the filled ones.

"This is incredible!" Dan exclaimed. "I can taste the garlic and tarragon. But what's the hot spice?"

"I have no idea. Let's ask Richard on his next pass with the shells."

"Jack, I feel I owe you one after bailing on you when you started Turnkey. So, sure, I can help you get started. Let me look at the upcoming projects. I was planning to hire some subcontractors for them anyway. I'll check, but I know I need three and may need four engineers. There are actually two projects. They'll run at least three months and may extend to six. Will that get you started?"

"Dan, it sure will. That's more than generous. Thanks!"

Richard returned with clean bowls so that we could continue our feast.

"Richard, I can taste garlic and tarragon, but what is the piquant spice?"

"Ah, Jack and Dan, je regrette, but that is a secret. A chef in a little Basque town called Guethary – Jack, you used to surf there – gave me the recipe as long as I promised not to reveal his secret Basque spice. So, you'll have to ask him on your next surfing trip. Visit the Restaurant Kandela in Guethary and see if you can get him to reveal his secret."

He turned and left, smiling, knowing he had us hooked.

Forty-five minutes later, we finished all the mussels. It's funny, there's not a lot of meat in a single mussel, so it's hard to get full even on dozens. Usually, I tire of an appetizer fairly quickly. In general, they're designed to give you a brief taste to whet your appetite for the main course. In this case, though, I could have eaten mussels all day. I think Dan felt the same way.

"So Dan, any interest in selling your company?" I asked.

"My company has remained a service company," he replied. "We really don't want to build and market products. I know that your IBM consulting contract led to your product opportunity, and we've had some projects like that, but I really don't want to get caught up in trying to convince people that my product is better than another. I like the predictability of knowing my margins and controlling my sales. Your product could be hot one day and obsolete the next. It's not for me. So, while I'll probably never make several million dollars all at once, I'm doing okay. It's a smaller, consistent reward with much less risk."

"Dan, you may be right, but as I've watched the value of my stock diminish, I'm finding myself wanting to just build a company for sale so that I can have an assured financial future. It's hard being a millionaire on paper, thinking you'll have plenty for your retirement and could just quit and play for a year if you wanted to, then have it all disappear. Granted, a few hundred thousand dollars isn't bad, but it's not walk away money. I can't retire to the south of France and write full time on that."

The Merlu arrived and while it was quite good, it didn't compare to the mussels. The appetizer was really the main course with the main course almost a dessert.

We agreed to catch up via email and phone over the next few days to get the projects started. Dan filled me in on Sailsoft, and told me that Rick, George and their families were all doing well. Dan was having a great time with his company. Maybe I would again too, someday.

2

The next day, I asked Lynne to lunch in Los Gatos at a small, little-known restaurant called The Peasant Chef, well away from the Core offices in San Jose. I started the conversation in the car on the drive over.

"So, Lynne, how's Core Finance treating you?" I began, somewhat predictably.

"It's boring. I'm working for a bigger company, just one person among over a dozen in Finance, even though I report directly to a pretty savvy Chief Financial Officer. It's not what I signed up for and quite frankly I'm bored. Plus, I don't see a bright future for the company. Part of my job is paying expenses and commissions to the sales people. Their expenses are going up and their commissions are going down. They're also discouraged. They want to sell something new and exciting. The enterprise products that Ed is focused on are old hat. They can't get customers excited about them.

"I suspect you have a reason for asking me to lunch, right?"

"Lynne, I'm a strong believer in keeping a good team together. You know that some of my team have been working with me since my days at Skynet, more than ten years ago. Now, with the RIF, I'm going to be forced to lay off not only some excellent engineers from Core, but two of the team that helped us build some revolutionary products. I'm not prepared to do this."

"So what do you have in mind, Jack? You can't leave for another year."

"No, I can't leave, and I can't compete. I've spoken with Ed about letting us take the technology back and he seems amenable, once the current Core products ship. I'm thinking we need to start a non-competitive company which can be an interim place for my team. I have a feeling there will be more layoffs in the future. Ed really doesn't know what he's doing now. He did a great job of getting his first products to market and capitalizing on a unique niche, but now that he needs to change directions, it's clear that he was lucky to have found his original product set. Granted he was brilliant taking it this far once he stumbled on to it, and that took some serious talent, but in terms of vision, I really don't think he has any left.

"I'd like to set up a new company; I don't have name for it yet. But I'd like to have the new company offer jobs to the two

Turnkey engineers I'm going to have to lay off as well as a couple of the really talented engineers from Core that I'm going to lay off."

"Jack, that's very generous of you, but how are you going to pay these folks? How will you capitalize this new company?"

"I can throw about a hundred grand into this as soon as I can trade my stock, which should be in a few weeks. Also, I've spoken with a friend of mine and his company could use some project help. They're willing to take on a few people at a reasonable contracting rate. I figure this will pay their salaries and let us start banking a little money too."

We arrived at the restaurant and were seated immediately. There was only one other table occupied and it looked like it was just a retired couple having an early lunch together. Whenever I have a business lunch, I look at the people around me to see if there's any possibility that my discussions might be overheard by someone who could use the information. In this case, it looked like the risk was minimal.

Lynne thought for a second, then observed, "Jack, I think you said that 'we' could bank a little money. Does this mean you're asking me to join you in this venture?"

"Of course! I need someone to handle the administrative and financial side of this new company. My plan is to offer all the founders an equal share of the company. I want irrevocable stock proxies from them so I can control the future of the company and an eventual exit, but since we're all in this together, it makes sense to me that we all have equal shares financially. If we do an exit through acquisition, which is my plan, everyone will share equally. My guess is that we'll have two tiers of founders, with about ten to start with. This means that you'd have about ten percent of the company."

"Jack, you know that Alex is leaving Core, don't you?"

"Actually, I haven't talked to him in about a month. We did a sales call together not long ago, but I haven't seen him since. Where's he going?

"Remember Xion Technologies?"

"Yes. They licensed one of our networking toolkits before the acquisition by Core. They're doing something in security, right? A Virtual Private Networking product?"

"Right. Well, they've asked Alex to come in as CEO. They want to raise Venture Capital and really get their product out into the market. Alex has asked me to join him there."

"And?"

"The company is located in Chicago. I don't think I want to live in the windy city. The winters would kill me. Plus, Jim just started a new job and I can't see him leaving. We both want to keep living in Santa Cruz."

"In that case, will you help me incorporate the new company and set up the admin and financial systems so that we can get these new employees started on contracts? I'd like you to work with me on the stock agreements and proxies as well.

"Of course there won't be a salary at first, but you will be earning your ten percent with the hours you put in – classic sweat equity. I expect that all of the former Turnkey personnel will transition out of Core over the next year or so. If Core decides to do more layoffs, this can work well as the employees can use their severance to cover their paychecks for a month or so and simultaneously earn and own their initial stock in the company."

"What about offices?" Lynne asked. "Next to salaries and benefits, office space is the next largest expense for a startup."

"Hey, it's the Internet age. We can all work out of our homes and get together on a regular basis for meetings. We can communicate via email and phone, in fact, email provides a written history so there may be fewer misunderstandings. This will keep our overhead low for some period of time.

"I recognize that at some point this will become impractical. We'll need to build a QA, Support and Administrative departments that will need offices. Plus, there's nothing more productive than several engineers having a spontaneous meeting in a hallway. The best ideas often come during brainstorming sessions, so the virtual office I propose to start with is only temporary until we have a clear mission and revenue stream.

"What do you think?"

"My initial impression is that I'd like to do this. It's kind of nice starting a company part time while being paid full time. Let me talk to Jim and I'll get back to you. It is a bit risky for both of us to be working for startups. Of course, it looks like I'll have a year of security with Core, assuming they don't lay me off in the meantime. I'll get back to you tomorrow if that's okay.

We finished a very nice lunch, each of us having a different kind of salad, and headed back to the office. Lynne was quiet for a while, clearly lost in thought.

"Jack, you should think twice about sharing the company equity equally. Keep in mind that as CEO, you'll be taking a lot of risk. You'll have to offer guarantees to the bank and credit card companies; you'll be doing the initial capitalization; and as a board member and founder, if anything goes wrong, they come after you first. Plus, if the company fails, the creditors will reach through to your personal assets. You should take a larger share."

"Lynne, I understand the risks. I look at a company as a team. We may have different jobs, but no job is really more important than another. Of course pay rates are based on experience and specific position, but that's just because we need to remain competitive in the employment market and keep resumes in good shape for possible future positions.

"I'll take a salary commensurate with my experience and the job description, but in terms of equity, we're all making the same bet with our careers and are going to work doubly hard, so it should be an equal split."

"Jack, that's very altruistic. I suspect someday you'll regret this decision, but I won't argue. After all, if I succeed in making my point, I end up with less stock myself."

Lynne came back to me with a positive answer the next day. We met at her house with her husband Jim listening in and contributing his thoughts. Within a week our lawyer had incorporated Remarkable Systems. A week after that, Tom, Bill, Cynthia, and Sam started working under contract for SailSoft, for eighty dollars an hour. Each worked without pay for two months, earning their shares of stock in the company, and we banked over ninety thousand dollars. After we began paying salaries, they continued to receive benefits under Core's Cobra post-employment benefit program. Remarkable Systems reimbursed them. Even with salaries and benefits, we were still saving over twelve thousand dollars each month. It looked like we could build some cash reserves before we started bringing more people on board, possibly to start working on our own technology - if Ed allowed us to take it back.

3

After we successfully shipped Core's new product release on time and below budget, I asked Ed for a meeting. His secretary, Agnes, put me off for two weeks, canceling meetings an hour before they were supposed to start, then rescheduling. I finally caught up with Ed outside his office and asked if he had a few minutes. He led me safely past his bulldog secretary and closed the door, motioning me to take a seat.

"Congratulations on getting the release out, Jack. The sales team is excited to have the new products in their bag of tricks. I think this will really help us next quarter. So, how's everything else?"

"Ed, as you know, the technology you acquired from us is my life's work. We had major players in the industry looking at us, a few might have been a little scared of it. Now it's sitting on the shelf. Other companies are starting to enter the market and every day we don't ship and continue to develop the products, we lose ground.

"I want to remind you of your promise that once the release of the Core products went out, we could discuss how we'd take the technology out of Core. Frankly, I'd like to spin out a new company. Perhaps Core could own a percentage for contributing the base technology."

"Jack, let me level with you. I'll tell you what's going on but this conversation never took place and if it's raised outside my office, I'll deny ever having said anything. But I think you need to know just so you can move on to something new and focus on Core's needs. Agreed?"

I nodded.

Ed continued, "It was one of those major players who convinced me to shelve your stuff. I did this in exchange for some future considerations that will benefit Core. Unfortunately, I can't let you take the technology out the door. It will never see the light of day. Plus, as I recall, you have almost another year on your employment agreement with us, so it won't do you much good anyway. "

I was almost too stunned to speak. In fact I just sat there and stared. Who was the 'major player'? Was it Samcom, Microsoft, a telephone company who could see us running telephony over the Internet, an IBM or Tightship competitor? Was he really telling me that he had been encouraged to kill our technology in exchange for a favor? Wasn't this bribery? I was angry. Forces beyond my control were preventing technological advancement.

I try to use displays of anger when they will serve me. I didn't think it would here. In my mind, the first person who loses his temper loses the argument as well. I decided I should at least try to reason with him.

"Ed," I said evenly. "You could have had it all with our products. You could have been one of the big players. You still could if you'd just let us develop and sell these new products. You can see that your enterprise efforts haven't had the success you expected. Your sales team needs something sexy to sell, not old technology. Please reconsider."

"Jack, the case is closed. While it's true that things haven't gone as well as I expected, I do have a few surprises up my sleeve. You'll be involved in one of them shortly." Almost on cue, his phone buzzed. He picked up and said, "Okay, I'll be right out." Then he turned to me and told me his eleven o'clock appointment was waiting.

As I left his office, his Agnes beamed an artificial smile at me. "See you later, Jack," she said sarcastically.

I felt manipulated and used. I guess Ed could justify this because he bought the technology and me. Too bad I wasn't going to be paid in full. Perhaps that would have made me feel a little better. I could have just walked away from the industry. But with the current value of the stock and its rate of decline, I'd be working for many years to come.

I stopped by Lynne's cubicle and asked her to lunch.

I recounted my conversation with Ed.

"So, what do we do now?" she asked. "The technology was pretty key to moving ahead, wasn't it?"

"Yes. It was. I suppose we could start over, but there are a lot of players out there now who will be a few steps ahead. Perhaps our experience with real networks, especially DARPA's can help us."

"What about DARPA? Could they fund development of a new version of the technology?"

"Lynne, I think we burned our bridges there when Ed decided not to fulfill the large order they placed. I'm not sure what to do now. This doesn't look too good."

"Say, do you know what these 'surprises up his sleeve' are?"

"Probably, but I can't tell you about them right now. If he said you'd be involved, you'll know in a day or two. In the meantime, the good news is that we're still banking money at Remarkable Systems. You think about what you want to do. I'm sorry I can't help out on the technology side, but I have faith you'll come up with an idea."

4

Front page of almost every trade publication and even the business section of the Wall Street Journal read 'Lucent Acquires OptiRoute in Multi-Billion Dollar Deal'. I called Georgette.

"So, you couldn't tell me?"

"Or course not," she replied. "You know the rules of non-disclosure with public companies. One leak and the whole deal gets cancelled."

"You're working for Ma Bell again. How's it feel to go full circle?"

Lucent was one of the world's largest telephone companies and was the main part of ATT, renamed after divestiture.

"It feels like a black hole. Just when you're sure you've escaped, you're sucked back in. I left ATT to be in a small startup company. Then we find success and go public, so I'm in a medium sized company, which was tolerable enough, though my job as CTO wasn't as hands-on. Now, I'm back in the giant company, or will be once the SEC and FCC approve the deal, which shouldn't be a problem. And I'm stuck for twelve months. I'll soon find out what your indentured servitude is like, but however it works out, I think I'm going to leave at the end of that year."

"How does it affect your stock?"

"Well, it's still 144 stock. But I'll no longer own more than one percent of the company, so I can trade it all if I want. And of course, it's worth quite a bit more now."

"Quite a bit?"

"At today's price, a bit over six hundred million."

"Jesus, Georgette!"

"Jack, I know things are a bit rough with you right now. You're stuck at Core; your technological vision is dead; the acquisition didn't work out financially; and you have no mission for Remarkable Systems yet. I have ultimate faith that you'll come up with the next great idea, but if you really get stuck financially, I can always help."

I don't know why her offer bothered me. Maybe it was jealousy; maybe I felt she pitied me; or maybe I just thought that six hundred million dollars was too much money for anyone. I felt myself pulling back from my best friend. I wondered how many other people were struggling to get closer to her and her money. I guess that bothered me too.

"Oh, I'm sure I'll be fine. Thanks for the offer though. Let's get together after we both get our heads above water.

I knew I wasn't being fair, that Georgette hadn't really changed, but I couldn't help feeling she was someone I didn't want to know anymore.

I put down the phone and it rang almost immediately.

"Jack, my name is Julian Fromer. I'm calling about Stan Rathbone."

"Julian, I don't have much to say about Stan, I haven't spoken to him in over a year and our last conversation wasn't terribly friendly."

"Jack, please bear with me. I'm desperate here. I'm CEO of a small company that builds point of sale software for retail stores. After closing a contract with a major department store, I went out to seek venture capital. After showing them my business plan, and a lot of negotiation, they took nearly fifty percent of the company and insisted I hire a Chief Financial Officer. I hired Stan Rathbone and gave him ten percent of the company. The VCs approved. Things have gone extremely well over the last year, but I've noticed some minor irregularities in the books. I brought them up with Stan and he explained them away, but things have changed. He's now pressing the VCs and the board to remove me. I think there's something he doesn't want me to find, and he's trying to get me out of the way. I know he filed a wrongful dismissal lawsuit against you, but I suspect you had a good reason to fire him. If you can tell me what happened, I may be able to save myself by getting him before he gets me. Can you tell me why you fired him?"

"Julian, I'd like to help, but my settlement agreement with Stan prevents me from saying anything but what was read into the court record which included my 'apology'."

"Jack, I can hear in your voice that you settled under duress. My company is my life. My marriage ended badly because I spent so much time at work. I've given up so much to make this company work and now that I'm about to succeed, I'm going to be forced out. Not only will I lose the business I love, but they'll dilute the hell out of my stock once I'm gone. Please help me!"

"Julian, for reasons I can't go into, I'm in a pretty bad spot myself right now. I know what it means to lose a company and I'd really like to help you, but if I do, my future is ruined. All I can say is that I'll talk to my attorney to see if there's any way I can give you something.

"You do have your work cut out for you. Stan knows how to work the system to his advantage and he seems to make out every time. Some people make it with hard work, some are lucky, some will do anything to be successful, others do all the right things and never make it. Then there are people like Stan who live like leaches, sucking the lifeblood out of people and becoming fat and happy themselves while others do all the real work"

"Jack, I'd appreciate anything you can do. I sense that you do understand, but you should know that if things go south and I lose my job and my company, I'll file a lawsuit, and you'll be the first one I subpoena. Under oath, you'll be compelled to answer and give details. I'm sorry to drag you into this, but I have to protect myself."

I wished him luck and called David Swan. He returned my call late in the afternoon and told me that under no circumstances was I to say anything about what Stan did to Turnkey. However, if I was subpoenaed, I should give whatever information they asked for.

As it turned out, two months later, I did receive a subpoena. It said I could be called to testify in discovery anytime between November first and November thirtieth. December arrived and I was never called. I guess they settled.

5

1996 arrived. This is the year that Princess Diana would die in a car accident that raised more questions than the death of JFK. Steve was appointed to Al Gore's Technical Advisory Committee. The big news for me was that Core acquired its largest competitor. I was involved in the technical evaluation before the deal closed. I really have never understood how Ed pulled this off. He acquired Logical Networks at a price that was lower than the total amount of cash they had. After factoring in all their debts, they still had over one hundred million in cash. Ed paid only fifty million dollars for the company. This just didn't make sense. Was this one of the benefits that 'a major player' offered Ed in exchange for dropping our technology?

Nonetheless, it provided Core with enough cash to keep the business going for the foreseeable future.

Once the acquisition was complete, Core had to consolidate operations. Logical Networks was actually larger than Core, so there was a lot of redundancy in administrative personnel, and, surprisingly in engineering. Core decided to do layoffs and I was asked to cut twenty people from the engineering ranks.

I had met Mitchell French, the VP of Engineering from Logical, and he was quite good. I suggested to him that he might want to take my spot and he readily agreed. The alternative was for him to be laid off.

I asked for a meeting with Ed and Agnes, his secretary, set it up for the next day. Surprisingly, she didn't cancel and at ten a.m., I was in Ed's office.

"Ed, I've been asked to cut twenty people from the combined staff of Logical and Core. You know I'm not happy here, so I'd like to propose that you keep Mitchell French and put him in my place. Since my team really isn't adding anything to Core at this point, I'd suggest that as part of the layoffs, I include them as well. Obviously, my plan is to start a new company. I'd like out of my employment agreement early, but I and my team will go quietly. We won't compete and we won't cause you any trouble. From what I can see, you have a plan and it will work a lot better without us. I think Mitchell is much better qualified to head up Engineering at Core than I am."

"Okay Jack, This makes sense to me. We'll lay off you and your team. I'll hold you to your non-compete and confidentiality agreements, but since we're not doing anything in the QoS space, you can feel free to enter it if you want. I don't consider that competitive. As we discussed before, I can't give you the technology back, but you can try to recreate it if you like. I'm sorry things didn't work out as you hoped, but that's business. It's nothing personal, just business. Good luck, stay in touch!"

He extended his hand and I shook it. I didn't like what he'd done to us and our technology, but he'd played it straight and didn't lie to me. Although I didn't agree with him and the direction he had chosen, I had to respect his business sense. I still believe that he missed a great opportunity, but each of us made our choices and took our chances. Time would tell whether his strategy would succeed.

Ultimately, I pulled a little over half a million dollars out of the acquisition of Turnkey by Core on one of the blips in the Core stock. It wasn't enough to retire on, but it was nothing to sneeze at either. That money, plus the two month's severance paid to each former Turnkey employee enabled us to really launch Remarkable Systems.

6

By spring of 1997, all of my former Turnkey employees plus a few of the best Core people were working for Remarkable Systems. For some reason, Lynne continued her job at Core. I think she just wanted to keep our expenses down and didn't want us to pay her a full salary. I started pressing her to leave, but it always seemed as if there was one more crisis at Core that she had to resolve. Surprisingly, Core acquired another competitor, again for what appeared to be far less than market value, and Lynne became instrumental at merging the financial systems of the acquired companies into Core.

I checked in with Carson regularly and he was doing well in his position as head of Customer Support. Carson had bought a car and a modest home not too far from mine in Santa Cruz. In fact, it looked like his company was about to be acquired. Each time I spoke with him, he seemed more like his old self. Maybe people did get second chances.

At Remarkable, I decided that since there were over forty companies in the QoS space, it would be foolish to compete with them. Instead of fighting the war, I believed it would make more sense to build weapons to enable all of these players to fight it out amongst themselves. Remarkable would provide toolkits that would make it easier to develop security and Quality of Service solutions. We'd be an arms supplier and would benefit no matter who ultimately won the war.

Our business plan was mercenary. We'd bootstrap ourselves with no outside investment, and would sell fundamental technology to those companies who were developing networking products. Within three years, there would be a falling out or consolidation in the market and one of our customers would want to ensure that we couldn't sell the base technology to anyone else. They would acquire us for between twenty and thirty million dollars, making each of the nine founders multimillionaires. In the meantime, our customers would fund our research and development and we'd retain the rights to everything we built. Thanks to Dan and the initial contracts from SailSoft, we were profitable from day one.

With new contracts closing every day, I had need for some application work, and just like we did at Turnkey, I was able to make a deal with Dan to employ some of his people to help us build complete solutions for our customers. This was my way of repaying Dan for his help in getting the company started.

All of us at Remarkable Systems kept our overhead expenses low by working out of our homes in a virtual company as I had proposed to Lynne in our first meeting. We communicated by email and held weekly meetings to resolve any outstanding issues. By May, we had enough money in the bank to consider opening offices. We found a small space in downtown Santa Cruz and I started pressing Lynne even harder to leave Core and join us full time. She really didn't want to add to the company expense and wanted us to have more revenue before she started taking a salary from Remarkable.

The team made this possible. By working ridiculous hours, they build two toolkits that could give potential customers a major boost in their ability to develop QoS and Security products. In June, NAZ, a fast growing, publicly-held security company, licensed both toolkits for over one million dollars. This gave us enough cash for Lynne to join us full time, though she continued to help Core part time, and Remarkable was on its way.

7

Georgette called me in early May and said that she was going to do the Death Ride. She also told me that she was having a home built at Kirkwood and it would be complete in late June. She wanted me to get in cycling shape and join her for the Death Ride and a long weekend at her new mountain home.

With all the sports I do, I keep myself in pretty good shape. I used to compete in swimming and track in High School, getting special permission to do both since they were both spring sports. I've also started doing triathlons. I enjoy what is now called the Olympic distance: a mile swim, a forty kilometer bike ride, and a ten kilometer run. I can finish all three in about two hours and ten minutes. Since I'm a strong swimmer, I am one of the first out of the water. I jump on my bike and begin the ride. Within five miles though, dozens of cyclists pass me like I'm standing still. During the run, I pass many of them. But, since the cycling leg is the longest part of the race, those who are great cyclists do the best. I'm not a great cyclist.

Part of this is because I injured my back in a surfing accident when I was nineteen. I really can't spend a lot of time bent over a bike, peddling for all I'm worth. So, in spite of my very good swimming and running splits in a triathlon, I usually end up near the middle of the pack because of my relatively limited biking skills.

Now Georgette was asking me to do the Death Ride.

The Death Ride is held in the Sierra Nevada each July. When it started, there were only a few dozen riders crazy enough to attempt five mountain passes, over one hundred forty miles, and over fifteen thousand feet of vertical climb, all in one day. The winners do the race in a little over eight hours. Strong cyclists do it in about twelve hours. I couldn't imagine sitting on a bike for more than twelve hours, let alone dealing with the altitude. The race starts in a small picturesque town in the Eastern Sierra called Markleeville at just under six thousand feet of altitude. Most of the five passes are at or above nine thousand feet.

Georgette assured me that I didn't have to finish the race. Most people didn't. Since this would be my first year, I should try for three passes and if I did better, I should be pleased with myself. She planned to complete all five this year. She did four the year before.

At her recommendation, I started taking iron supplements two weeks before the race. I also did this when I went on hang gliding trips in the Owens Valley. The theory was that with increased iron in your system, you'd be better able to fix oxygen in your bloodstream. It seemed to work for hang gliding at altitude. Perhaps it would help me with the Death Ride as well. Of course, maybe the effects were really just psychological.

Over the previous month, I had biked six days a week, at least twenty miles a day up the coast against the strong afternoon northwest winds, and did a fifty mile ride in the hills above San Jose and Santa Cruz on the weekends. I did a lot of climbs in the Santa Cruz Mountains, but I was nervous about the altitude in the Sierra.

I agreed that we'd head up Thursday evening after work and would spend two nights at altitude in Georgette's Kirkwood retreat before the Death Ride on Saturday. We agreed to meet at the Livermore Airport where I could leave my car.

Even on Thursday, traffic headed towards the Central Valley was bad. With home prices rising beyond what even two-income families could afford, many people had begun to commute into the Bay Area from Central Valley bedroom communities like Tracy. What should have been an hour drive from Santa Cruz took me nearly two hours. Georgette was waiting patiently in the bar at the Red Baron, sipping an iced tea and snacking on fried calamari.

"Rough drive?" she asked.

"Yes. It looks like the traffic headed east is even worse. Maybe we should have dinner and head up later."

"Are you hungry?"

"No, not really. I had a big lunch. But with the traffic..."

"I have a better idea."

Georgette paid her tab, then led me out to the runway where a new four-seater Cessna waited.

"Let's rise above those pedestrian traffic problems," she proposed.

"Let's!" I agreed enthusiastically.

Surprisingly, our bikes fit easily into the plane. It was a beautiful evening to fly. As we rose above the Livermore airport, I could see a finger of coastal fog slipping languorously through the Golden Gate. By morning, the entire Bay Area would be enshrouded in a cool white blanket while points east would remain clear and hot.

We turned east and an hour later landed at Lake Tahoe Airport. It was still light.

Georgette tied down her plane in a designated spot and we took our bikes over to a new Toyota Land Cruiser she had waiting in the parking lot. Thirty five minutes later, the sun was setting and we arrived at her new home at Kirkwood. The peaks of the Sierra, some still capped in snow, reflected pink light, the alpine glow that the Sierra is famous for.

Kirkwood recently started substantial development. Once a little-known ski resort, Kirkwood was now trying to become a destination. The base of the resort sits in a beautiful valley created by a creek which has formed an expansive meadow filled with wildflowers. Georgette had built a large log home on the east side of the meadow. It was constructed of huge blond logs and had three stories, each appointed in new, but rustic-looking furniture. The windows were framed in a dark green and all had shutters which we opened before we settled in.

I remembered Alan LaMonte's home in the Eastern Sierra, about half an hour from here where Carson had his first drug experience. Georgette's place was similar in many ways. The floor plan was open with expansive rooms, lots of glass and ceilings that seemed to touch the sky. The views of the meadow and ski slopes were spectacular. It was all that money could buy.

After dropping my stuff in the a large suite with bath, Georgette took us to the Kirkwood Inn, a nineteenth century, wood and log structure with a very low ceiling and a roaring fireplace (even in summer) for dinner.

Since we were in training, and alcohol reduces the body's ability to retain oxygen, we drank only water, beginning to hydrate ourselves for the ordeal ahead. After dinner, only a few locals remained, drinking at the bar. Great blues played on the sound system and we danced to a couple of slow sensuous songs in a small space we cleared between tables.

I was tired and ready for a good night's rest when we returned. Georgette walked me to my room and then gave me a quick kiss goodnight. Did I sense something more? Or, was I just tired?

I fell into a dreamless sleep. I always sleep soundly in the mountains.

The next morning, I awoke early and went for a jog around

the meadow. A light fog radiated from the moist ground along the creek, creating an almost surreal effect as I looked through the mist to the glacier-covered mountains towering above. The three mile loop was just what I needed to loosen up. When I returned to the house, Georgette had bagels and fresh squeezed orange juice on the table.

"I thought we'd do part of the Death Ride today, just enough to show you what you're up against, but not enough to wear you out.

"The ride starts in Markleeville at about fifty five hundred feet. We climb up Monitor Pass and then take a long drop down to Nevada on the east side of the Sierra. At the bottom, you turn around and climb back up. I think this is the hardest part of the ride. It's the longest climb, and most of it is in the sun with no shade. Granted, it's early in the morning when you do this, but depending on the weather, it can be tough.

"Once you get back up Monitor, you drop down it again, but before you get to Markleeville, you turn and go up Ebbet's Pass. Ebbet's is really steep. Parts of it are over twelve percent. The good news is that it's not that long. The bad news is that people have been killed on the way down. The top riders hit nearly seventy miles an hour going downhill and there are cattle catchers and rocks along with tight curves. Occasionally, a cow will wander onto the roadway and both cows and riders have been killed in collisions or attempts to avoid them. If you go off the edge, it's a long way down!

"For those of us who aren't doing it for time, it's not that bad. You just have to watch out for everyone else.

The fourth pass is Luthor. You climb out of Markleeville up Highway 88, then take Highway 89 towards Lake Tahoe. You may remember dropping into the Hope Valley last night. That was Luthor Pass. I think it's the easiest. Keep that in mind if you finish Ebbets'. Luthor is easy. It's not steep and it's not that far.

"Finally, you go up Carson Pass. There's a relatively long, almost flat stretch through the Hope Valley. At this point, I call it the Hope For A Taxi Valley. It's a gentle climb for several miles, then it gets fairly steep for only two miles. But since you're over a hundred and ten miles into the ride, you may be too fatigued to do the relatively short climb. I was too tired last year and quit at the bottom of the steep part, but this year, I'm going to do it.

"Once you make it to the top, it's downhill all the way back to Markleeville. There are rest, water, and food stations all along the way. I'm not going for time, so let's plan on riding together until you've had enough.

"Today, my thought was that we'd start at the top of Monitor and coast down, then ride back up. If you can do that, I think that you'll easily do three passes, maybe four."

We drove to the top of Monitor Pass. I realized that I had flown over this in my hang glider when I'd launched from Slide Mountain about thirty miles to the north. It looked like a great launch itself. The view of Nevada and the snow-capped precipitous Eastern Sierra peaks to the south reminded me of the Alps. While much of Nevada is high desert, verdant fields spread below us. We hopped on our bikes and coasted for miles around curve after curve. There were quite a few other riders doing the same thing, and cars seemed to be pretty tolerant of us, patiently waiting as we took downhill curves in the middle of the road.

We reached the bottom and turned around. The slow climb back up took the better part of two hours, and though I was tired, I wasn't exhausted. My back seemed to be okay. I felt much more confident about my chances not to embarrass myself during the race.

Georgette was obviously pleased. We had lunch at a small café in Markleeville, then soaked in the Grover Hot Springs at the base of Pleasant Valley where we went for a short hike after lunch. I was envious of the fly fishermen along Pleasant Valley Creek, patiently casting and retrieving their lines, almost Zen-like.

As we walked, I was nearly overcome with happiness. I bumped my shoulder into Georgette, then took her in my arms and swung her around, setting her down gently.

"Thanks, Georgette!" I said, grinning wildly.

She smiled and took my hand and we walked along the tree lined creek in a meadow surrounded by huge mountains.

8

The race wasn't what I'd expected. Aside from triathlons where the swim is a mass start and you grab your bike when you've finished, I had never been in a bike race. I certainly didn't have any idea what it was like to start a race with thousands of other riders. For me, this was the most terrifying part. I really didn't trust all these people, and I didn't trust myself to ride a straight line or to pass slower riders safely.

The ride out of Markleeville was insane. Georgette stayed behind me, but the crowd didn't thin until we reached the top of Monitor Pass. Then I became frightened.

Other riders took off down the hill at break-neck speeds. I was passed by people I had overtaken right after the start. I could sense Georgette's impatience with my cautious pace down the hill, but I was terrified.

She pulled beside me and I suggested she just ride on, but seeing my nervousness, her face softened and we rode together at a moderate pace down the hill. We passed a lot of people on the way back up, and the drop down Monitor to the west was pretty easy. I was much more confident with my speed. Then we started up Ebbets'.

I was tired. About half way up, it got really steep. Even in my lowest gear, I was standing up, but it was so steep I thought I'd go over backwards. I'd done steeper climbs on a mountain bike, but it was much different on a road bike. Georgette had no problem with the climb and encouraged me through it. I knew that if I could make this pass, I could do Luthor as well.

Amazingly, I pulled it off. There was a rest stop at the top and we took a break for water and a snack. Then came the downhill. We took it slowly, but people passing us were just plain crazy. I saw one person lose it on a curve and go over the edge. Bystanders quickly went over to help. Later I learned that the woman had suffered both a broken arm and leg with countless contusions.

At Turtle Creek, we stopped for lunch. Georgette cautioned that we shouldn't take too long as inactivity would make it hard to continue. I told her that my male parts were asleep, that I couldn't feel them anymore and needed to take a break. Apparently this is a common problem on long bike rides and has resulted in impotence among male endurance riders.

Georgette was right. My crotch was sore, I felt totally exhausted, and I really didn't think I could do any more. I probably shouldn't have rested so long.

"Come on. Let's do Luthor. I know you can do it. Then you can coast back down while I do Carson."

We headed up Highway 88. The climb was pretty along the Carson River which cascaded along the side of the road. At the turn onto Highway 89, I knew I could do the pass. It was only a few miles and the climb was only a little over a thousand feet.

By the top of Luthor, those tender male organs were asleep again. I needed to stop. Georgette said she'd meet me at Turtle Rock and she took off. I stretched and walked, then sat and stretched some more. I drank lots of Gatorade and ate Power Bars. When feeling returned, I sat gingerly on the bike seat. I was so sore. I coasted back to Turtle Rock standing most of the way, then waited at the finish line for Georgette to return. A little over an hour and half later, she rode in, all smiles. She had completed all one hundred forty miles of the Death Ride.

We joined in the after race feast, then drove back to Kirkwood where we showered. I climbed into bed and Georgette joined me.

There's something special about sex when you're completely exhausted. Your body has given up all tension to the physical effort and lovemaking becomes something very slow and sensual. I was actually surprised Georgette wasn't too sore after sitting on a bike for over twelve hours, but she certainly didn't seem to be in pain when we came together. She got up to pee, then climbed into bed next to me where we slept together until ten the next morning.

We got up and showered together, then fixed bagels, fruit salad, and fresh orange juice for breakfast.

"Jack, I've been thinking. We've been best friends for years. This weekend I've felt closer to you than I ever have."

"Georgette, it's been wonderful, magical. I wish it could go on forever."

"Well, that's what I've been wondering. You'll probably think I'm crazy, but why not?"

"What do you mean?"

"We're such a good fit. Why don't we make it permanent?"

I tried to think quickly. I loved her, but we were at different places in life. She had it made. I was just starting over. She had so much money. If I was going to be successful with Remarkable Systems, I needed to be motivated with a single-mindedness like Steve's. Entrepreneurs who had it too easy usually didn't make it. You needed to be very hungry to put in the effort to be successful. Could I have this level of drive if I were married to Georgette? Was I willing to live off her wealth? Was I done with my career?

A moment or two passed while I tried to think this through. I looked over at Georgette and before I could say anything, I knew that my delayed response had hurt her deeply. She was embarrassed. I tried to reach out to hold her, but she pulled away and apologized.

"It was a stupid idea. I know you have a lot to do. You're not ready are you?"

I tried to explain my thoughts, but I don't think it came out right. I wanted this to work, and I certainly didn't want to lose Georgette. She was my best friend, and sometimes lover. The previous night was incredible. What to do? What should I do?

How can you describe a couple who love each other but can't be together? Can you get past the confusion of feelings to even remain friends? Our lives were headed in different directions, and the hurt and misunderstanding of just those few minutes may have ended our friendship.

9

For nearly all of Bill Clinton's two terms in office, the economy thrived and the world seemed to be moving towards global peace and environmental concern. The Internet was booming and technology was king. Peace was breaking out all over and even the Israelis and Palestinians were living and working together. The world pulled together and put an end to the regime of Slobodan Milosevich.

But, in 1998, Bill Clinton was impeached for lying about his relationship with Monica Lewinsky. Most of the country knew this was a witch hunt by the Republicans who were unable to control one of the most popular Presidents the country had ever seen. In 1999, he was acquitted, but his credibility was destroyed. We knew that powers behind the Republican Party had been successful and that they would find a way to win the 2000 election and turn the country in a different direction. Dark days were looming ahead, and it wasn't just the specter of the world coming to an end with the millennium, something even the most rational of us feared a little. The stock market was at record highs. Many companies' price to earnings ratios were in the hundreds or infinite in the case of Internet companies who had no earnings.

Everyone with an MBA or an idea was raising money to start companies and hundreds of companies went public on nothing but hype. The Internet was the new economy and everyone was jumping on board to cash in. You didn't need profits or a well-run company; you could go public on market projections. Silicon Valley looked like the gold rush of 1849. Everyone was making money, lots of money. And twenty-five year old millionaires cruised the streets in their Ferraris.

It was a big bubble and most of us knew it had to burst. Smart people started taking profits and moving out of the market, but the average person, and most of the pension fund managers, just went along for the ride, seeing wealth build on itself.

Remarkable Systems was on track. We were comfortably profitable, growing steadily and had several large customers who relied on our products. Unlike the Internet Companies, we had real products, real profit, and what we believed was real value. By late 1999, even Microsoft had licensed our toolkits. It was only a matter of time until someone made a move to acquire us. I think people were waiting to see if Y2K was going to be the end of the world as foretold by the prophets.

As the year 2000 approached, the media hype about widespread computer failures had us all concerned about power blackouts, air traffic control problems, and widespread panic. It wasn't just the supermarket tabloids. Y2K was THE topic.

Everyone in the high tech industry was nervous. Could the end of the world be our fault? Almost all computer programs used two digit dates. What was going to happen when the date went to zero? Would anything work?

Virtually everything was run by computer and relied on dates. I mentioned power companies and air traffic control. The latter was scary. These systems calculated position and tracked planes using time calculations. What about our nuclear defense systems? Utilities? Hospitals?

Even our cars had computers to control the ignition, fuel injection and braking systems. Retail stores' transactions were all based on dates and time. All billing systems were computerized. Banks were probably the most exposed as they used outdated software, much of which was written for large mainframe computers in the sixties and seventies. Would the economy come to a complete halt? Would people panic when they couldn't access their money, their credit cards wouldn't work, and the stores were closed?

In the year before Y2K, Venture Capitalists put millions into companies that claimed to have a solution for the Y2K problem. Programmers in data processing departments worldwide scanned millions of lines of software code and worked tremendous hours of overtime to change code to use a new date structure. IBM and Microsoft released new versions of their operating systems which computed dates based on an absolute, consistent format. Everyone in the industry scrambled to make it all work. When Remarkable signed a contract with a new customer, there was always a clause guaranteeing that our code was Y2K compliant. This became the industry standard. We had hope.

Systems were tested and checked. Dates were artificially accelerated on every major computer system in every government agency and company to ensure that the code would handle the millennium transition correctly.

At the same time, those of us in the high tech industry knew software. Software always had bugs and often, no amount of testing would reveal them. Only real world experience created the problem. We were worried.

In the weeks before Y2K, people started stocking up on food, household supplies and emergency water. In California, this was a good thing anyway as we were supposed to have supplies ready in case of a major earthquake. Stores ran short of propane stoves and lanterns. More guns were purchased than ever before as people prepared to fight off their neighbors when the lights went out and the food and fuel supply chains failed. The government warned of terrorist attacks timed to make Y2K worse and to topple the Western economic domination of the world. There were rumors that OPEC would stop supplying oil to further this end.

Even I was concerned. I didn't really think disaster would happen, but many of my friends and acquaintances certainly did. They did buy guns and ammunition. I just restocked my earthquake emergency supplies.

My guess was that there would be some power outages; there would be some problems in a variety of systems, but that if people were patient and no one panicked, within a week or two, things would be back to normal. I remembered and tried to remind everyone I knew how we all pulled together after the Loma Prieta earthquake when we lost roads, power, water, and communication with the outside world for several days. I didn't think Y2K was going to be as bad and if we survived Loma Prieta, Y2K should be a piece of cake.

Santa Cruz holds an alcohol free celebration on New Year's Eve called First Night. They bring in artists, performers, and bands from around the area and there's dancing, food, and lots to see and do.

On December 31st, 1999, First Night Santa Cruz was underway, but there weren't many people. By eight o'clock, the streets were almost deserted. I went home and turned on the television to watch Y2K unfold on the east coast.

So far, in spite of the fact that most of the world was already in the Year 2000, there had been no disasters. Would North America be as lucky?

The news reported terrorists captured trying to cross the border from Canada to the US. When the ball fell in Times Square, we knew that the Y2K disaster had been avoided. Sure, there were problems. My first telephone bill of the new century had January 1999 as the date, but the charges were accurate and my phone service didn't fail.

I met Carson for lunch at L'Auberge Du Soleil to catch up. Richard was delighted to see Carson and told him in French that he thought he had died.

"I almost did," Carson responded.

Richard frowned and a concerned look crossed his face. I quickly changed the subject and asked about lunch. He confirmed that he still had the Moules a la Basquaise, so I ordered those as an 'appetizer' for the two of us.

"How's the new company coming, Jack?" Carson asked.

"It's going really well. We just signed a deal with Compaq to license our software and this is getting a lot of attention. I think it's going to make some of our customers a little nervous. Hopefully, nervous enough to make us an offer."

"You really want to sell out?"

"Well, this was a pure money making play. After my experience with Core and Turnkey, I just wanted to bank enough money to not worry about the future. Then I can decide between building another service company like CIA was, or retiring to the south of France to write full time. I'd really like the luxury of not HAVING to work for a living."

"A lot of people feel that way, Jack. And quite a few are making it with this Internet boom. However, I don't think many will repeat and a lot of them will be bored with a lot of toys and free time, but nothing significant to contribute to the world. "

"Just give me the chance to be bored for a while," I lamented.

"Of course, I just want to take some time off. I have a lot I want to do and if it's another company, I'm confident I can do that again. I've done two and I don't think it's just luck or timing. How are things at Cenitz?"

"Well, I can't tell you who or when, but it looks like we're going to be acquired. This will accelerate my options and if things go well, in about a year, I could walk away with about a hundred grand."

"Walk away?" I queried.

"I've made a lot of contacts leading support for Cenitz. I really feel that I can rebuild a CIA type of company. I'd like to do strategic consulting again, and if you're interested, perhaps you'd like to join me."

"Hmm, I really miss consulting. Maybe once Remarkable

sells, I can consider it. You're thinking a year or so?"

"Yeah, but there is one problem. The IRS has found me. I owe over half a million in taxes; more with penalties and they're threatening to send me to jail."

This wasn't what I had expected.

I suspected the IRS would catch up with him eventually and the amount shouldn't have been a surprise. I could do math in my head pretty well. But somehow, hearing the number and thinking about how hard it would be to pay that off at Carson's salary was a bit frightening. The IRS could be really tough with people. Sometimes people went to jail for stupid mistakes. What would they do with Carson who clearly had just spent all the money?

"After countless written exchanges, my lawyer and I met with them this morning. He's proposed a settlement. They could have sent me to jail, but then they'd see no money. After my lawyer explained my drug problem and that there were no remaining assets to seize, he showed them my track record over the last year and they agreed to consider a settlement of one hundred grand to be paid through wage garnishment over a period of ten years. That's a long time, but at least I'd be free. Of course if I screw up and can't make the payments, they've promised to lock me up and throw away the key."

"My God, Carson. Just when you think you've got a reprieve, the axe falls!"

"It hasn't fallen yet. I hired a good attorney. He's confident that this is the worst case. They're investigating but it looks like they believe him."

"So if this works out, they just garnish your wages?" I asked.

"I hope so, but my attorney may have found something else. At least he feels there's a chance we may turn this situation to my advantage."

"How would that be possible?"

"Well, he decided to look at the original transaction. He needed to find out exactly how much money I was given and what the terms were on the buyout. NewCo provided a little information, but as he dug deeper, they clammed up. He thinks there was something fishy about the deal and he's digging for more information. You know that NewCo is worth billions. When an attorney sees that kind of money, he's got strong motivation to determine why I only ended up with one point five million."

"Come on Carson, if Steve had given you more, it would have gone to coke too. You'd probably be dead now. Plus, you know Steve is dangerous. I don't think you want to mess with him. Given where things are, don't you think you should just settle with the IRS and get on with your life?"

"Jack, I've had a lot of time think since you saved me a couple of years ago. I loved CIA and it was because of me that NewCo got started in the first place. I was back on track. You, Pam and Nancy had done a great job of getting me through rehab and helping me stay straight. Hell, you were doing then what you did after you bailed me out of jail: controlling my money, giving me good work and encouraging me to break the habit by providing a better alternative. If Steve hadn't bought me out, I think I could have stayed clean, just as I've stayed clean these past two years.

"Of course, I was beginning to challenge him, especially his ethics or lack thereof. The more I think about it, the more I think he actually tried to kill me by giving me that much money in one lump sum. I think it was a conscious decision.

"Because of him, I lost my company, my girlfriend, my lifestyle and almost my life itself. It also cost you your share of NewCo and our partnership.

"Steve has walked on a lot of people to get where he is. If there's anything there, I'm going to find it and I'm going to make him pay. If I'm wrong, I settle with the IRS and get on with my life."

"Carson, be careful. Think about this. You've got a future ahead of you again. If you think Steve tried to kill you before, what will he do if you find a way to threaten his multibillion dollar empire?"

"Jack, don't overreact. Steve's too visible to do anything. If it goes anywhere, it'll end up in court, likely with a nice settlement for me."

We finished up a great lunch and agreed to meet again in a couple of weeks. Lunch wasn't sitting well, or maybe it was the conversation. There was something. I couldn't put my finger on it, but there was something about NewCo that none of us knew when Steve bought out Carson. For the life of me, I couldn't remember. Or maybe I didn't want to. It would be a big mistake to open this can of worms or, more likely, deadly snakes.

11

Amazingly, within a week, two of our customers contacted me and asked to acquire us. The first had filed their S-1 intention to go public and couldn't actually start the purchase transaction until after their IPO. The second was about six months away from an IPO. They were a very nice fit, but I was reluctant to do another all-stock deal, especially for privately held stock that might never trade on the market. Even if it did, who knew what the price would be? At least things were starting to move and an exit looked likely. Given the state of the industry and the stock market in early 2000, this certainly looked like a good time to try to cash out.

Then I got lucky. The very aggressive Thunder Networks, a competitor of Kingfisher Telecommunications, one of our largest customers, approached us wanting to use our technology to thwart the gains against them that Kingfisher was making. They wanted to license our toolkits to provide similar capabilities.

I called Bob Morse, the CEO of Kingfisher and told him we were in discussions with Thunder. Within a week, I had a handshake deal and a term sheet was being prepared by the attorneys. Kingfisher would purchase Remarkable Systems for Thirty Five Million Dollars in Stock, half of which would be tradable immediately after the close of the transaction (actually 'as soon as Kingfisher can reasonably register the shares'). The rest of the shares would be tradable in twelve months, and all of the team would have to sign two-year employment and non-compete agreements.

I was a little nervous about an all-stock deal, but when I brought this up to the Remarkable team, they pointed out that as a multibillion dollar Telecommunications Company, the stock was as good as cash. Plus, it had been growing at a prodigious rate over the last several months and was setting all-time highs almost every session. If we could lock in a price and the stock continued to rise, we could do quite well indeed.

12

Pleased with our likely exit, I was taking a shower after a morning of great surf when it hit me. I knew what the issue was with NewCo and Carson. I don't know why it didn't occur to me before; I guess the clue just seemed so minor.

At some point after NewCo had successfully deployed with PacBell, Steve was on the road trying to find another telco to purchase the products. His first efforts were in Europe, and I remember that Steve was supposed be meeting with Telefonica in Spain. But one night, Shelly mentioned that he had called her from Atlanta.

Bell South! Steve wasn't in Spain at all. He closed the deal with Bell South and didn't reveal this to Carson.

The Bell South deal launched NewCo. It was the first major telephone company to purchase NewCo's products and every other one fell into place right afterwards. If Carson had known about the Bell South deal, his share of the company would have been worth much more. And even if the deal were not closed at that time, Steve had a fiduciary obligation to reveal the fact that he was in discussions with them and that a deal was likely. Without Bell South, there was some risk that no one would adopt NewCo's technology. With Bell South following in PacBell's footsteps, the company's success was assured.

Now that I knew, or thought I knew, the real question was whether I should tell Carson.

When I got to the office, I called Georgette. We had never recaptured the weekend of the Death Ride, but we remained the good friends we always were, except for the fact that she was now living in Boston.

She had managed to extricate herself from Lucent, and she and Marty had begun another start up in the 128 corridor. With their track record, they had no problem raising venture money, but from what I could see, neither of them was really hungry enough to make their new company fly. Nonetheless, they were in process of developing some new wireless technology for Bell Atlantic so they decided to locate the company closer to Bell Atlantic's headquarters.

"Jack, I'm glad to hear from you!" Georgette said when she answered the phone. "How's the Kingfisher acquisition going?"

"It's moving along. Everything seems to be on track, but

that's not why I called. I need some advice."

"Sure, just keep in mind that advice is worth what it costs you."

I related my revelation about Steve and NewCo and asked her whether I should tell Carson.

"Of course you should. He's made it clear that he's going to do the ethical thing and try to stop Steve if he can. Or at least make Steve think twice. If he got the information elsewhere, he'd use it. So tell him."

"What if something really bad happens? I'll feel guilty for the rest of my life," I said, a real dark sense of foreboding beginning to weigh down on me.

"Look Jack, you asked for my opinion. Carson is a big boy. He's going to take whatever risks he's decided to take, with or without you. You've always said that knowledge is power. Give Carson the knowledge and he can decide what he wants to do with the power."

I hung up the phone and reluctantly dialed Carson.

"Carson, I think I know what the issue was when Steve bought you out of NewCo."

"Bell South!" he said gleefully.

"You know?" I asked stupidly,

"My attorney looked at what was going on at the time and what really made NewCo. The Bell South deal was announced right after I disappeared. The only thing he could come up with that would scare Steve and NewCo when he inquired about me was that the deal was in progress before Steve bought me out. After checking with some sources at Bell South, he discovered he was right.

"He wants to file a multibillion dollar suit against NewCo, asking for half the company, but I've told him to hold off. I want to meet Steve face to face to tell him what I have and to let him know what I think of him and his sleazy dealings. At the same time, as we've always agreed, I want to give him the opportunity to save face. I'm expecting a decent settlement offer. It doesn't need to be huge, but I know that even a dollar will be painful for Steve. He'll have to admit to me what he's done."

"Carson, don't you think you should just let the lawyers handle this? They'll keep it from getting personal."

"I want it personal. How personal is attempted murder?" Carson asked, completely irate.

I backed off and said, "Good luck. Let me know what happens."

"Jack, before you go, what tipped you off?"

"Oh, I remembered that when he had told everyone in the company that he was going to Spain to meet with Telefonica, I bumped into his wife, Shelly and she just happened to mention that he was working in Atlanta."

"What a strange twist of fate that you'd bump into her and catch him in a lie. I wonder just how far he's gone to get where he is. I suspect there are a lot of these little land mines lying around waiting to explode. He probably pays dearly to keep them from blowing up in his face. Wish me luck!"

"Good luck!" I said to the dial tone.

13

Carson called me back at five o'clock the next day. "Jack, meet me at the Catalyst for happy hour. I met with Steve, and I have a lot to tell you." I agreed to meet him at six thirty. It was a Tuesday night and wasn't too crowded. Although there would be music on the main stage later in the evening, right now, they were playing canned blues in the Garden Room. Since my office was just down Pacific Avenue from the new Catalyst, I got there first. I ordered a Margarita and savored the limey flavor as I waited for Carson to arrive.

The last few years had been interesting. Carson, my hero, had fallen from great heights due to a fatal flaw in his character. In the meantime, I'd watched others like Steve and Stan, do unscrupulous things to get ahead. I guess when I compared the two, I found Steve more worthwhile. While he was ruthless in business, at least he built something positive. NewCo had done a lot of good in the world. It provided jobs, made investors wealthy, and advanced technological innovation. After making it, Steve and Shelly had been very generous to all sorts of charities. Did the ends justify the means?

Stan, on the other hand, was a leach. He lived off the work of others and never produced anything himself. And yet, he had made it too.

As I looked at the people I knew, I was fascinated by the different turns their lives had taken. Some made it, some didn't. Some got lucky, some worked hard to get what they wanted and others stabbed people in the back. I'd made it twice and lost it. The Silicon Valley was certainly an interesting place. Lost in thought, I almost didn't notice when Carson arrived, sat down across from me, and ordered a scotch and soda.

"So?" I said to an obviously excited Carson.

"Jack, I think you're going to be surprised. Steve really isn't the ogre that we thought he was."

I was immediately concerned. I knew that Steve's charm could work wonders. He'd used it on me and even I had succumbed. I wondered what snow job he'd sold Carson. I just looked at him skeptically, grinning like I thought he was crazy.

"Yeah, yeah, I know. You think I've been fooled. But it wasn't that way. I just left him and I think that after you hear what I have to say, you'll think about him differently."

I doubted that. I think I understood Steve quite well.

"Steve has been consistent from the day we formed NewCo," Carson continued, "NewCo was of ultimate importance. He planned to build this multibillion dollar company from the start and he was driven to make it happen. Any weakness, any obstacle that prevented him from reaching this goal had to be removed. He had a vision to create something that was bigger than any single individual, and in his mind, whatever he had to do to accomplish this would be more than made up for by the results: a company that employed thousands, generated millions for its shareholders, advanced technology in the world, and ultimately helped the less fortunate.

"I've quoted you often with your statement that 'knowledge is power'. Steve believes that NewCo increased the availability of knowledge to people all over the world. Information brought down the Berlin wall, and Steve believes that his contributions will free countless others as information becomes disseminated more and more widely. I guess I have to agree.

"Unfortunately, I was one of those weaknesses and obstacles. My drug habit made me a liability to NewCo, and from Steve's point of view, I had to be removed. I'm not as convinced that he meant to kill me, but he certainly wanted to get me out of the way. He believed, and probably still believes that 'once a druggie, always a druggie' and a druggie is the worst thing to have in a growing business. So, he tried to take me out – get me out of the business in the best way possible, by paying me to go away so that he could continue forward with his plan.

"In his mind, he paid me more than I was worth, and as he expected, good money just went up my nose. While it is true that he concealed the real value of NewCo from me given the Bell South deal, from his perspective, it would have just been putting more money up my nose if he'd revealed everything. I guess I can't blame him."

"But Carson –" I began, about to remind him that he was clean and back on track, that he was just trying to introduce more ethics into NewCo's business deals.

Carson held up his hand. "Let me finish the whole story."

"I explained my tax situation, that I had been clean for years, and that I was successful in restarting my career. I told him that I planned to start another CIA.

"He proposed that we not take this public, that we deal with it confidentially. I understand that he's trying to protect himself with this, but he's also protecting the shareholders and pension funds that rely on the NewCo stock price. I agreed.

"He promised me a ten million dollar settlement. Ten Million Dollars!

"I guess I can't complain. I understand what he did and why, and he's certainly giving me more than I ever had. I didn't build NewCo, so I certainly don't deserve more. I'm happy with the deal.

"I told Steve I'd contact my attorney in the morning and we'd get papers drawn up. What do you think?"

"I'm sure your attorney won't be happy. He was probably expecting tens or hundreds of millions from this."

"Yeah, but it would have taken him years to get it. Three million for drawing up a private settlement agreement is nothing to sneeze at, and I suspect he'll be quite happy to take the money and run.

"I'm going to bank the seven mil, pay off my current debt to the IRS, pay them for this windfall, and after the next year at Cenitz, I'm going to restart CIA. I really think you should join me if you can."

"Carson, it looks like I've sold Remarkable, but have a two-year commitment there. Maybe after that…"

We talked for a while and I heard the music start in the main auditorium of the Catalyst. I told Carson I needed to go, that there was a nice south swell running and I'd be at Waddell by first light in the morning. He said he was going to stay a while and savor his victory.

14

The surf at Waddell was classic. I seemed to be in the right place at the right time and got barrel after spitting left barrel. When I got home, I picked up the paper from the driveway and dropped it on the kitchen table while I went to rinse out my wetsuit.

I poured myself a bowl of Cheerios and topped it with a sliced banana, then sat down to read the Sentinel as I sipped my Odwalla orange juice and hungrily wolfed down my Cheerios.

I almost choked.

The front page of the Sentinel read:

LOCAL MAN KILLED IN MUGGING

Carson Ingles, Director of Customer Support for Cenitz Systems in Sunnyvale, was found dead last night in the alley behind the Catalyst. Police say he was mugged. His wallet and jewelry were missing.

Ingles apparently offered some resistance to the mugging and during the ensuing struggle, fell and struck his head on a small concrete abutment bordering the alley. He was pronounced DOA at Dominican Hospital.

Sergeant Michael Brooks of the SCPD says this was an isolated incident, but that people frequenting lower Pacific Avenue late at night should be aware of people around them. "This was most likely the result of a drug addict seeking money for a fix," he told the Sentinel.

While classified a homicide because of the robbery, Brooks believes the death was accidental. Brooks says the SCPD has no leads, but is questioning witnesses.

I called the SCPD and asked for Sergeant Brooks but was told he works the night shift. I asked who was assigned to the Ingles homicide and the dispatcher requested my name and number which I provided enthusiastically. An investigator would call me later. I gave them my office and cell numbers and raced to the office. I called Georgette and told her what had happened.

"Jack, you have to consider the possibility that this is just coincidence."

"Are you crazy? He threatens a multibillion dollar company, is promised a huge settlement, and before he can even talk to his attorney, he ends up dead. Do you really believe this could be a coincidence?"

"Jack, calm down!"

"Georgette, I can't calm down. I know Steve had Carson killed. I need to do something about it."

"Jack, if Steve killed Carson, you're probably in danger too. Did anyone see you talking to Carson last night?"

"Of course! We met at the Catalyst and were together for several hours. But right now I don't care. Carson didn't deserve this and Steve needs to be stopped. I'll be talking to the police today and I'm going to tell them everything. Maybe they can stop Steve."

"Jack, don't do it. I can't lose you and you're stepping into something you need to avoid...

I hung up.

I realized I didn't know the name of Carson's attorney. Perhaps the police could help me track him down.

Just before noon, Inspector Gale Hodges called me. She asked if it would be convenient for her to stop by my office to discuss the death of Carson Ingles. I told her I was anxious to talk with her.

Inspector Hodges was small, dark, and clearly wearing a bullet proof vest. I had expected a plain clothes detective, but she was in the classic SCPD police uniform. Her navy blue slacks and shirt didn't reveal much of what was clearly a very fit body.

I led her into my office and offered her coffee or a soft drink, which she refused. She started questioning me.

"How did you know the deceased?"

I told her how I met him, about CIA, his drug problem, the buyout from NewCo, his disappearance, and his rehabilitation, leading to his current position as Director of Customer support.

"Do you have any information that would relate to his death?"

I told her I met with Carson at the Catalyst and described the content of our conversation. I told her I left about nine.

"The body was found at 11:33 pm by a patron of the Catalyst. The coroner puts the time of death at about 11 pm. Did anyone see you leave?"

I suggested that she check with the bartender and any other patrons. They'd confirm that I left and that Carson stayed. I must admit, under her gaze and questions, I felt like a suspect in his death. I tried to explain the situation with Steve and NewCo, but she looked at me like I was crazy. Still, she said:

"I know that you think you see a connection, but our investigators have concluded that although this was a homicide, it was an accidental death that occurred as part of a mugging. He slipped and hit his head. There was no intentional foul pay. He was just in the wrong place at the wrong time.

"Of course, I'll have to look at the previous drug connections. Perhaps a former dealer decided to take revenge for missed payments. I'll stay in touch."

"But Officer," I almost shouted, "Aren't you going to look into the connection with Steve Caples? There was ten million dollars on the table. Aren't you supposed to 'follow the money'?"

She looked at me like I was a petulant child. "It's 'Inspector', sir. I understand you're upset about this. Of course we'll consider all the evidence and leads on the case. However, there is nothing pointing to anything other than a mugging. If the death had appeared to have been intentionally inflicted, we might look further, but it was almost certainly an accident.

"I'm not going to bother someone like Steve Caples over something where we have no evidence pointing to him. I know you're trying to help, but the 'follow the money' theory really only works in crime fiction and thrillers."

"Officer, er – Inspector Hodges. Please track down Carson's attorney. He was about to file a multibillion – that's BILLION dollar lawsuit against NewCo and Steve Caples. I really believe you should at least take a look at this. Please talk to him."

"Sir, we'll do our best, but you should accept the fact that in spite of the timing, this was most likely just a mugging gone wrong."

As always, I called Georgette.

"Jack, just let the police do their jobs. They're not idiots in spite of what many people think. If there's something there, they'll find it. More and more, it's sounding like bad timing."

"Georgette, you know it's not!"

"Jack, it's not worth it either way."

"Georgette, if you knew for certain that Steve had Carson killed, would you just let him get away with it?"

"Jack, if I knew that the chance of convincing anyone of Steve's guilt was zero, and that in the process of this futile quest I was likely to be killed myself, there's no question that I would just drop it. Sometimes you have to admit when you've lost."

I hated her for saying that, but I knew it was true. I hated myself for being too weak to risk my life over a lost cause, but my life was all I had. I decided I'd do all I could to convince the police, but that I wouldn't get carried away.

In the end, they just kept looking at me like I was nuts. I think they were really considering me as a suspect.

Carson was dead. Steve was in the clear, and life went on. I was supposed to get back to my life's work.

We signed the deal with Kingfisher Telecommunications. Their stock is the highest it has ever been and hopefully, they'll register half the stock very shortly. When they do, I'll have over one and a half million dollars immediately. After another year, assuming their stock continues to climb as it has these past years, I'll have at least another million and a half, plus the stock options they've given me, which could be worth almost as much. Everyone on my staff is receiving exactly the same amount of money, though I have greater financial penalties should I decide to break my employment agreement.

Kingfisher needs our technology and that has kept my team happy. The work will be interesting and for the engineers, the work is more important than the money, particularly now that they don't have to worry about their financial futures. Nonetheless, assuming nothing terrible happens to the Telecommunications market, my team and I will start something new after our employment agreements expire.

I'd certainly hate to see a repeat of the Core Systems fiasco, because it would hit my team, not just me. But with bad things coming for the economy, who knows what will happen? If we can just pull out this first half before it happens, we'll all be fine.

I'm also hoping I can get past this issue with Georgette. I THINK that once I have some basic financial success, I can settle down with her. It's not the final amount of money that counts. I just want to have 'walk-away' money too. At that point, I'll have achieved my goal as she has achieved hers, and we can come together as equals.

EPILOGUE

Several years have passed since I wrote the account of my experiences with Carson Ingles and the Silicon Valley. In looking back at what I thought would happen, it's clear that things didn't go as I expected. I had hoped that the acquisition of Remarkable by Kingfisher would at least bring me to a level of financial independence where I could feel successful enough to ask Georgette to marry me. But as you probably suspected if you remember the state of the industry at the time, there was a telecommunications crash and Kingfisher went down with them. Although I was supposed to be able to trade some stock as soon as they could register it, some irregularities in Kingfisher's officers' stock options prevented them from registering our shares. By time they did register them, their stock, which had a price of one hundred fifty-nine and three-quarters at the time of our acquisition, fell to twenty cents. I still have all of the shares today which I keep as a reminder of my infernal optimism. After their reverse split of twenty to one, their stock hovers around four dollars per share. The value of my shares is about five thousand dollars – a far cry from the more than three million I expected.

Kingfisher the company survived. There were countless shareholder lawsuits filed against them and most of us from Remarkable saw about forty thousand dollars from one of the class actions suits. However, I had more damaging information against them and made a deal that I could buy Remarkable Systems back in exchange for agreeing not to file a lawsuit, and giving them unrestricted licenses to our technology. So, Remarkable was reborn three years later.

Georgette and Marty's company seemed to do reasonably well, but at this point it hasn't become a major success. They employ about one hundred people and remain privately held. Georgette and I saw each other a few times a year, usually if she was on the West Coast or if I was in the East. Of course we stayed in touch via email and phone, but even in our connected society, the distance makes it hard. Plus, though she laughed off her failed proposal, something broke in our relationship. I see now that it was bad enough to make her move to the East. How could I tell her that I was doing my best to fix it? I guess she knew. She knew me better than anyone else and understood my unreasonable pride.

My team and I re-bootstrapped Remarkable and invented a very exciting technology which interested a number of public companies. Right before the 2008 economic disaster, we managed to sell the company for a reasonable amount in a ninety percent cash deal to be paid out over three years with the stock portion vesting over three years as well. Surprisingly, the company's stock, which was at thirty-two at the time of the transaction, is over eighty today. It looked like my luck had finally changed as I was able to fully cash in. I'm actually in a place where I don't HAVE to work anymore. Third time's a charm.

You've probably noticed that I started using the past tense in referring to Georgette. What got me writing again and what will hopefully drive to my long-stated goal of writing full time in the Basque region of France was a call from Marty. Georgette was killed in a plane crash.

"I wanted you to hear it from me before you saw it in the press tomorrow," Marty began. "She took off from Logan in freezing fog. No one knows exactly what happened, but within a few minutes her jet crashed and the plane pretty much disintegrated on impact in the Atlantic. They did recover the bodies."

"Bodies – plural," I asked.

"Jack, if you're not sitting down, please do. Brace yourself. Georgette was killed and so was her son."

"Son?"

"I argued with her for years about this, but she said she'd tell you when you were ready. I'm not exactly sure what 'ready' meant, but I got the impression that she thought things were about to change.

"Anyway, Mark was your son. Jack, I'm really sorry."

I hung up the phone, put on shorts and shoes and started running. I don't know how long I ran, but it was dark when I stumbled back into my empty house. I couldn't stop thinking about how stupid I was; how I'd put my masculine pride and a foolish need for success ahead of love, friendship, compatibility and a singular connection with the most remarkable woman I'd ever know.

I had plans. I thought we had time. But as the Israelis say, 'Man makes plans and God laughs'.

Life in the Silicon Valley these last several years has certainly changed me. Somehow after all that's happened, I remain optimistic. I guess I'm just a little more wary as I realize that the world is filled with both good and bad people. I think I believed that all people were fundamentally good. I don't anymore. There are good people who do bad things to get what they want and good people who refuse to cross the line. Still, they're all just trying to thrive in a world that doesn't often offer second chances. Brilliant people can work hard. Some will make it, others won't. And there are a few just plain evil people out there. The Valley seems to have a place for them all. For some, there just isn't enough time.

As long as I'm writing this epilogue, I might as well tell you what's happened to most of the characters from my story:

Don and Madge Johnson

After the failure of Skynet, Don and Madge divorced. Don started a new Internet-based company out of his home, but it failed to grow. After two years, Don went back to the University of California at Berkeley, where he teaches Computer Science today.

Madge joined another high tech startup which capitalized on the Internet explosion. The company went public, and with only one percent of the company, Madge became a multimillionaire. She wisely put her money into real estate before the Internet market crash, now lives in San Francisco and is very active in raising money for the San Francisco Ballet and various theatre groups in the City.

Ronn and Barb

Ronn and Barb still live on their horse ranch in Montana. They call it God's country and after the visit and intervention or rescue that Ronn and Barb did for me, I can see why. While I can appreciate the solitude, and enjoy periodic visits there, I couldn't see giving up foreign film, theatre, and the fine restaurants the San Francisco Bay Area when I have near-paradise here in Santa Cruz.

Ronn and Barb seem to have no use for the pace of the Valley and although they make some money by running a dude ranch part of the year with Ronn conducting fly fishing classes, they barely tolerate their visitors and cherish the off season where the two of them work their ranch with just a few hands helping out.

Dan, George and Rick

Dan eventually sold Sailsoft to one of the big five accounting firms which was expanding its technology service offerings. The sales price was ten million dollars, and Dan, George, and Rick were equal partners. While they provided options to all of their employees, each of the three walked away with three million before taxes. After serving a year under an employment agreement, Dan retired and helped his family start a chain of pizza restaurants (!). He still runs in competitive races and does strategic consulting in his spare time.

Rick and George continue to work for the acquiring company. They have been able to keep their offices in Santa Cruz and enjoy leading new software development projects.

Without Dan, there is no vision or mission, so their work pays the bills and keeps them occupied, but as Carson predicted, without a mission, they've become a bit bored. I bump into them regularly during my runs on West Cliff Drive.

Alex

Alex, the CEO I brought into Turnkey, did quite well with the Turnkey sale since he was paid out in cash. He joined Xion Systems and helped them raise Venture Capital. They sold the company for five million dollars to a larger player who was then acquired by an even larger Telecom company. Amazingly, that company was acquired by Lucent in a multibillion dollar deal and Alex exited with a cool twenty million dollars after the three acquisitions. He now lives in Plano, Texas and plays golf (!) every day.

Stan

After settling with Julian Fromer for a little over two million dollars, Stan made three million in the sale of Julian's company. Stan has invested his proceeds from that and his other deals very wisely and lives comfortably in the Los Altos Hills. He's married now. Not surprisingly, he moved in on the wife of a friend and she took the kids and left her husband to marry Stan. They've been together for years and it looks like Stan has taken everything he wanted out of life.

The Cool Technology

QS-II died a quiet death not long after our acquisition. Interestingly, as part of their campaign to kill it and replace it with IRES, Samcom convinced Microsoft to make IRES a strategic part of their networking direction and to announce that it would be part of future releases. I frequently encountered and debated Ronen Lior, Microsoft's QoS guru in conferences and seminars on Quality of Service. He was smart and a fervent believer in IRES and convinced hundreds of developers to build products around Microsoft's new interfaces. Unfortunately, as he would later discover, IRES was just Samcom's way of stalling the market until they could invent and standardize a router-based protocol that didn't need Microsoft's QoS software. IRES never really saw the light of day after all of Microsoft's and Ronen's efforts to promote it. Ronen left the Microsoft in disgust, but was able to retire on his Microsoft stock options. He, too, lives on a ranch (in eastern Washington) and has no further use for technology.

Steve and Shelly

Steve is a force to be reckoned with. He's now made the list of the richest people in the world. Every year he climbs a bit higher on the list. It looks like he'll soon be in the top ten. NewCo is huge. They do billions in sales every year and acquire at least a dozen companies. With perseverance and unwavering determination, Steve has achieved his goal. Virtually anything you do with a computer today (and computers touch just about everything), includes NewCo software.

Shelly has ensured that Steve gives generously to charity and together they have made a huge difference in promoting human rights and environmental concerns around the world. They've given hundreds of millions to Aids Research, and are buying up huge plots of Brazilian rainforest and donating them to National Parks.

I often bump into Steve at industry conferences where I give presentations on new networking technologies. Steve is frequently a keynote speaker and he greets me warmly (and artificially). In spite of his broad smile and friendly slap on the back, I can see him looking at me out of the corner of his eye. He knows I know, but I still don't have any proof. I've gone back through this memoir and I think his only potential legal exposure was from Carson, so I've convinced myself I'm safe. I think his arrogance makes him believe that he left no loose ends which might lead back to him. Still, I think he wonders if I'll ever do anything about what I know.

I wonder that myself. Of course, with these passing years, I've begun to question myself and my motives. Was I feeling guilty about Shelly when I blamed Steve for what happened to Carson? Even Carson said that Steve was only trying to protect his company, technology and the employees and their families when he bought Carson out.

Now, I'm not so sure I was right about the murder either. Maybe it was just an unfortunate accident, a bad coincidence. If I was right before and found some proof, what would it accomplish? It wouldn't bring Carson back. Damage to NewCo would hurt the entire industry. The amount of information we're all making available through Internet and computer technologies will save the world.

Whether it's rainforests, global warming, endangered species, or tyrannous political regimes in third world countries, our ability to get information out is helping people come together in unified understanding and educating those who will ultimately solve these problems. So, whether Steve was responsible for what happened to Carson or not, Georgette was right. It's time for me to move on and make a difference in the world with the technologies my team can create. That's real and will have real lasting value.

Other Books by Steve Jackowski

The Shadow of God (2014)

ABOUT THE AUTHOR

Writer, extreme sports enthusiast, serial entrepreneur, technologist.

Born into a military family, Steve traveled extensively throughout the US and overseas, attending fifteen schools before graduating from High School. After studying mathematics, computer science, comparative literature and French at the University of California, Steve began his career with IBM as a software engineer. He later founded three successful high-tech startups.

A former competition hang glider pilot, Steve continues to surf, ski, kayak whitewater, and dance Salsa with his wife Karen whenever possible.

Steve divides his time between Santa Cruz, California and the Basque Region of France.

15771846R00219

Made in the USA
Middletown, DE
21 November 2014